The giant approached, and now Paithan could see why it had seemed the jungle was moving. Its body was covered from head to toe with leaves and vines, its skin was the color and texture of tree bark. Even when the giant was extremely close, Paithan had difficulty separating it from its background. The bulbous head was bare and the crown and forehead, that were a whitish color and bald, stood out against the surroundings.

Glancing around swiftly, the elf saw that there were twenty or thirty of the giants emerging from the jungle, gliding toward them, their movements graceful and perfectly, unnaturally silent.

Paithan shrank back against the tree trunk. It was a hopeless gesture, there was obviously no escape. The heads, with their awful dark and empty holes, stared straight at them. The one nearest put his hands upon the edge of the fungus and jerked on it.

The ledge trembled beneath Paithan's feet. Another giant joined its fellow, large fingers grabbing, gripping. Paithan looked down at the huge hands with a terrible kind of fascination, saw that the fingers were stained red with dried blood.

THE DEATH GATE CYCLE

VOLUME ◆ 2

Elven Star

MARGARET WEIS
AND
TRACY HICKMAN

BANTAM BOOKS
NEW YORK ◆ TORONTO ◆ LONDON ◆ SYDNEY ◆ AUCKLAND

ELVEN STAR

A Bantam Spectra Book

PUBLISHING HISTORY
Bantam hardcover edition / November 1990
Bantam rack edition / August 1991

SPECTRA *and the portrayal of a boxed "s" are trademarks of*
Bantam Books, a division of Random House, Inc.
All rights reserved.
Copyright © 1990 by Margaret Weis and Tracy Hickman.
Cover art copyright © 1991 by Keith Parkinson.

Library of Congress Catalog Card Number: 90-38337.

Maps designed by GDS/Jeffrey L. Ward.

ISBN 0-553-29098-3

Published simultaneously in the United States and Canada

Bantam Books are published by Bantam Books, a division of Random House,
Inc. Its trademark, consisting of the words "Bantam Books" and the portrayal
of a rooster, is Registered in U.S. Patent and Trademark Office and in other
countries. Marca Registrada. Bantam Books, 1540 Broadway, New York, New
York 10036.

His banner over me

was love.

◆

—*Song of Solomon*

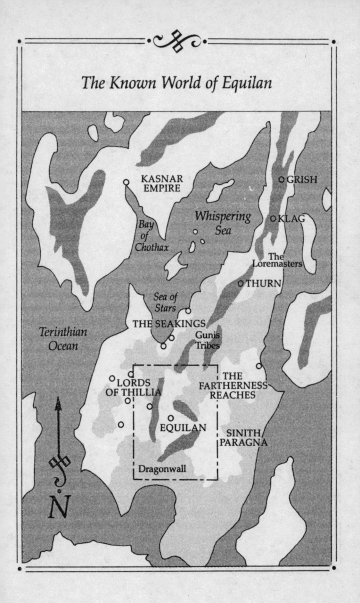

The Known World of Equilan

KASNAR EMPIRE

GRISH

KLAG

Whispering Sea

Bay of Chothax

The Loremasters

THURN

Sea of Stars

THE SEAKINGS

Gunis Tribes

Terinthian Ocean

LORDS OF THILLIA

THE FARTHERNESS REACHES

EQUILAN

SINITH PARAGNA

Dragonwall

N

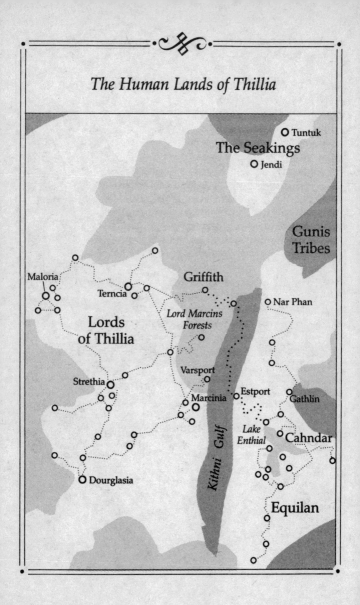

The Human Lands of Thillia

O Tuntuk

The Seakings

O Jendi

Gunis Tribes

O Maloria

Terncia O

Griffith

O Nar Phan

Lords of Thillia

Lord Marcins Forests

Strethia

Varsport

Marcinia

Estport

Gathlin

Kithni Gulf

Lake Enthial

Cahndar

O Dourglasia

Equilan

Dwarven Kingdoms of Equilan

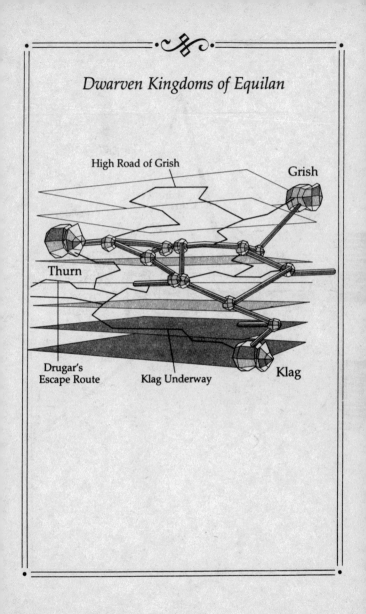

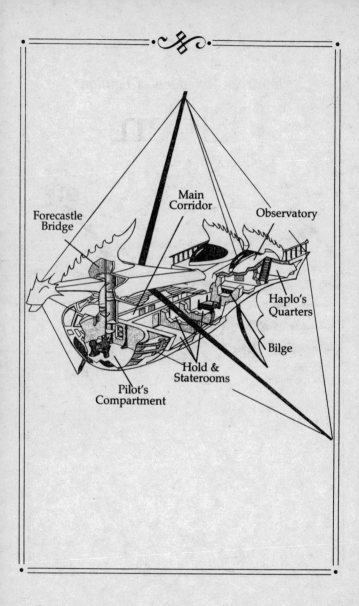

Forecastle
Bridge

Main
Corridor

Observatory

Haplo's
Quarters

Bilge

Hold &
Staterooms

Pilot's
Compartment

Elven
Star

PROLOGUE

". . .WORLD DOMINATION WAS WITHIN OUR GRASP. OUR ANCIENT ENEMY, the Sartan, was powerless to prevent our ascendency. The knowledge that they would be forced to live under our rule was galling to them, bitter as wormwood. The Sartan determined to take drastic measures, committing an act of desperation almost impossible to conceive. Rather than permit us to take over the world, the Sartan destroyed it.

"In its place, the Sartan created four new worlds, formed out of the elements of the old: Air, Fire, Stone, and Water. The peoples of the world who survived the holocaust were transported by the Sartan to live in these new worlds. We, their ancient enemy, were cast into a magical prison known as the Labyrinth.

"According to their records that I discovered in the Nexus, the Sartan hoped that prison life would 'rehabilitate' us, that we would emerge from the Labyrinth chastened, our domineering and, what they term 'cruel,' natures softened. But something went wrong with their scheme. Our Sartan jailers, those who were to control the Labyrinth, disappeared. The Labyrinth itself took over, and turned from prison to executioner.

"Countless numbers of our people have died in that fearsome place. Entire generations have been wiped out, destroyed. But, before it died, each generation sent its children forward, each succeeding generation drew nearer and nearer to freedom. At last, through my extraordinary powers of magic, I was able to defeat the Labyrinth, the first to escape its toils. I passed through the Last Gate and emerged into this world, known as the Nexus. Here, I discovered what had been done to us by the Sartan. More importantly, I discovered the existence of four new worlds and the connections between the worlds. I discovered Death's Gate.

"I returned to the Labyrinth—I return frequently—and used my magic to fight and stabilize parts of it, providing safe havens for the rest of my people still struggling to free themselves from their bonds. Those who have succeeded come to the Nexus and work for me, building up the city, making ready for the day when, once again, we will take our rightful place as rulers of the universe. To this end, I am sending explorers through the Death's Gate into each of the four worlds."[1]

". . . I chose Haplo from the large number of people in my service for several reasons: his coolheadedness, his quick thinking, his ability to speak fluently the various languages, and his skill in magic. Haplo proved himself in his first journey to the Air World of Arianus. Not only did he do what he could to disrupt the world and plunge it into a devastating war, he also provided me with much valuable information, as well as a young disciple—a remarkable child known as Bane.

"I am quite pleased with Haplo and his accomplishments. If I keep a sharp eye on him, it is because he has an unfortunate tendency to be an independent thinker. I say nothing to him; this trait is invaluable to me at the moment. In fact, I do not believe that he himself is even aware of his flaw. He imagines himself to be dedicated to me. He would sacrifice his life for me without hesitation. But it is one thing to offer up one's life, it is another to offer up one's soul.

"Reuniting the four worlds, defeating the Sartan—these will be sweet victories. But how much sweeter will be the sight of Haplo and those like him kneeling before me, acknowledging me, in their hearts *and* in their minds, their absolute lord and master."[2]

Haplo, my dear son.

I hope I may term you thus. You are as dear to me as the children I have fathered. Perhaps that is because I feel that I played a role in your birth—or rebirth. Certainly I plucked you from the jaws of death and gave you back your life. And, after

---

[1] The Lord of the Nexus, *History of the Patryns Following the Destruction of the World.*
[2] Excerpt from the private diaries of the Lord of the Nexus.

all, what does a natural father do to get himself a son except spend a few pleasurable moments with a woman?

I had hoped to be able to speed you on your journey to Pryan, Realm of Fire. Unfortunately, I received word from the watchers that the magical field is crumbling somewhere near the four hundred and sixty-third gate. The Labyrinth has unleashed a swarm of flesh-devouring ants that have killed several hundreds of our people. I must go in and do battle and will, therefore, be absent when you leave. Needless to say, I wish you were at my side as you have been through countless other fights, but your mission is urgent, and I will not take you from your duties.

My instructions to you are similar to those you received setting off for Arianus. You will, of course, keep your magical powers hidden from the populace. As in Arianus, we must keep our return to the world secret. If the Sartan discover me before I am ready to proceed with my plans, they would move heaven and earth (as they did once before) to stop me.

Remember, Haplo, that you are an observer. If possible, take no direct action to alter events in the world, act through indirect means only. When I enter these worlds myself, I do not want to face accusations that my agents committed atrocities in my name. You did an excellent job in Arianus, my son, and I mention this precaution only as a reminder.

About Pryan, the World of Fire, we know little except that its area is purportedly vast. The model left behind by the Sartan pictures a gigantic ball of stone surrounding a core of fire, similar to the ancient world but far, far larger. It is the size that puzzles me. Why did the Sartan feel the need to make this planet so incredibly immense? Something else I do not quite understand and that is—where is its sun? These are among the many questions you will endeavor to answer.

Because of the enormous amount of land space on Pryan, I can only assume that its population must tend to be scattered about in small groups, isolated from each other. I base this on knowledge of the estimated number of people the Sartan transported to Pryan. Even with an unprecedented population explosion, the elves, humans, and dwarves could never have expanded to cover such a large land mass. A disciple to draw the people together, such as you brought me from Arianus, will be of no use to me under such circumstances.

You are being sent to Pryan primarily as investigator. Learn all you can about this world and its inhabitants. And, as in Arianus, search diligently for some sign of the Sartan. Although you did not (with one exception) discover them living in the World of Air, it is possible that they may have fled that world and sought exile on Pryan.

Be careful, Haplo, be circumspect. Do nothing to draw attention to yourself. I embrace you in my heart. I look forward to embracing you in my arms on your safe and successful return. Your lord and father.[3]

---

[3]Haplo, *Pryan, World of Fire,* vol. 2 of *Death Gate Journals.*

CHAPTER ◆ 1

EQUILAN,

TREETOP LEVEL

◆

CALANDRA QUINDINIAR SAT AT THE HUGE POLISHED SCROLL DESK ADDING up the last month's earnings. Her white fingers darted rapidly over the abacus, sliding the beads up and down, muttering the figures aloud to herself as she wrote them in the old leather-bound ledger. Her handwriting was much like herself: thin, upright, precise, and easy to read.

Above her head whirled four plumes made of swans' feathers, keeping the air moving. Despite the suffocating midcycle heat outside, the interior of the house was cool. It stood on the highest elevation in the city and so obtained the breeze that otherwise was often lost in the jungle vegetation.

The house was the largest in the city, next to the royal palace. (Lenthan Quindiniar had the money to build his house larger than the royal palace, but he was a modest elf and knew his place.) The rooms were spacious and airy with high ceilings and numerous windows and the magical system of flutterfans, at least one in every room. The living rooms were on the second floor and were open and beautifully furnished. Drawn shades darkened and cooled them during bright hours of the cycle. During stormtime, the shades were raised to catch the refreshing, rain-drenched breezes.

Calandra's younger brother, Paithan, sat in a rocking chair near the desk. He rocked lazily back and forth, a palm fan in his hand, and watched the rotation of the swans' wings above his sister's head. Several other fans were visible to him from the study—the fan in the living room and beyond that the fan in the dining area. He watched them all waft through the air and between the rhythmic flutter of the wings and the clicking of the beads of the abacus and the gentle creaking of his chair, he fell into an almost hypnotic trance.

A violent explosion that shook the three-level house jolted Paithan upright.

"Damn," he said, looking irritably at a fine sifting of plaster[1] that was falling from the ceiling into his iced drink.

His sister snorted and said nothing. She had paused to blow plaster off the page of the ledger, but did not miss a figure. A wail of terror could be heard, coming from the level down below.

"That'll be the new scullery maid," said Paithan, rising to his feet. "I better go and comfort her, tell her it's only father—"

"You'll do no such thing," snapped Calandra, neither raising her head nor ceasing to write. "You'll sit right there and wait until I'm finished so that we can go over your next trip norinth. It's little enough you do to earn your keep, idling about with your noble friends, doing Orn knows what. Besides, the new girl's a human and an ugly one at that."

Calandra returned to her addition and subtraction. Paithan subsided good-naturedly back into his chair.

I might have known, he reflected, that if Calandra'd hire a human at all the girl'd be some little pig-faced wretch. That's sisterly love for you. Ah, well, I'll be on the road soon and then what dear Cal doesn't know won't hurt her.

Paithan rocked, his sister muttered, the fans whirred contentedly.

The elves revere life and so magically endow it on nearly all their creations. The feathers were under the illusion that they were still attached to the swan. Paithan, watching them, thought that this might be a good analogy for their entire family. They were all under the illusion that they were still attached to something, perhaps even each other.

His peaceful reverie was interrupted by the appearance of a charred, singed, and disheveled man, who bounded into the room, rubbing his hands.

---

[1]Made from a compound of calcium deposits taken from the bones of dead animals and processed with other organic elements to form a pliable paste.

"That was a good one, don't you think?" he said.

The man was short, for an elf, and had obviously once been robustly plump. The flesh had begun to sag lately; the skin had turned sallow and slightly puffy. Though it could not be told beneath the soot, the gray hair standing up around a large bald spot on his head revealed that he was in his middle years. Other than his graying hair, it might have been difficult to guess the elf's age because his face was smooth and unwrinkled—too smooth. His eyes were bright—too bright. He rubbed his hands and looked anxiously from daughter to son.

"That was a good one, wasn't it?" he repeated.

"Sure, Guvnor," said Paithan in good-humored agreement. "Nearly knocked me over backward."

Lenthan Quindiniar smiled jerkily.

"Calandra?" he persisted.

"You've sent the kitchen help into hysterics and put new cracks in the ceiling, if that's what you mean, Father," retorted Calandra, snapping the beads together viciously.

"You've made a mistake!" squeaked the abacus suddenly.

Calandra glared at it, but the abacus held firm. "Fourteen thousand six hundred eighty-five add twenty-seven is not fourteen thousand six hundred twelve. It's fourteen thousand seven hundred twelve. You've neglected to carry the one."

"I'm surprised I can still reckon at all! See what you've done, Father?" Calandra demanded.

Lenthan appeared rather downcast for a moment, but he cheered up almost immediately.

"It won't be long now," he said, rubbing his hands. "That last one lifted the rocket above my head. I think I'm close to discovering the proper mixture. I'll be in the laboratory, my dears, if anyone needs me."

"That's likely!" muttered Calandra.

"Oh, ease up on the guvnor," said Paithan, watching with some amusement as the elf wound his way vaguely around the assortment of fine furnishings to disappear through a door at the back of the dining area. "Would you rather have him the way he was after Mother died?"

"I'd rather have him sane, if that's what you mean, but I suppose that's too much to ask! Between Thea's gallivanting and Papa's idiocy, we're the laughing stock of the city."

"Don't worry, Sister dear. The people may snigger but, with you scooping up the money of the Lords of Thillia, they do so behind their hands. Besides, if the guvnor was sane he'd be back in the business."

"Humpf," snorted Calandra. "And don't use that slang talk. You know I can't abide it. It's what comes of hanging around with that crowd of yours. Idle, time-wasting bunch of—"

"Wrong!" informed the abacus. "It's supposed to be—"

"I'll do it!" Calandra frowned over her latest entry and irritably went back to add up her figures again.

"Let that . . . that thing there do the work," suggested Paithan, motioning to the abacus.

"I don't trust machines. Hush up!" Calandra snarled when her brother would have spoken.

Paithan sat quietly for several moments, fanning himself and wondering if he had the energy to call for the servant to bring him a fresh glass of vindrech—one that didn't have plaster in it. But it was against the young elf's nature to be silent for long.

"Speaking of Thea, where is she?" he asked, peering about as if he expected to see her emerge from under one of the antimacassars.

"In bed, of course. It's not winetime yet," returned his sister, referring to that period late in the cycle[2] known as "storm" when all elves cease their work and relax over a glass of spiced wine.

Paithan rocked. He was getting bored. Lord Durndrun was having a group over for sailing on his treepond and a picnic supper after, and if Paithan was planning to attend it was high time he set about getting dressed and on his way. Although not of noble birth, the young elf was rich enough, handsome enough, and charming enough to make his way into the society of the gently bred. He lacked the education of the nobility but was smart enough to admit it and not try to pretend he was anything other than what he was—the son of a middle-class businessman. The fact that his middle-class businessman father happened to be

[2]Elven society in Equilan regulates time as follows: one hundred minutes to an hour, twenty-one hours in a cycle, fifty cycles to a season, and five seasons to a year. Time measurement varies from place to place on Pryan, according to the local weather conditions. Unlike the planet Arianus, where there is day and night, the sun never sets on Pryan.

the wealthiest man in all of Equilan, wealthier even (so it was rumored) than the queen herself, more than made up for Paithan's occasional lapses into vulgarity.

The young elf was a good-hearted companion who spent his money freely and, as one of the lords said, "He is an interesting devil—can tell the wildest tales . . ."

Paithan's education came from the world, not from books. Since his mother's death, some eight years previous, and his father's subsequent descent into madness and ill-health, Paithan and his elder sister had taken over the family business. Calandra stayed at home and handled the monetary side of the prosperous weapons company. Although the elves hadn't gone to war in more than a hundred years, the humans were still fond of the practice and even fonder of the magical elven weapons created to wage it. It was Paithan's job to go out into the world, negotiate the deals, make certain that shipments were delivered, and keep the customers happy.

Consequently, he had traveled over all the lands of Thillia and had once ventured as far as the realm of the SeaKings to the norinth. Noble elves, on the other hand, rarely left their estates high in the treetops. Many had never been to the lower parts of Equilan, their own queendom. Paithan was, therefore, looked upon as a marvelous oddity and was courted as such.

Paithan knew the lords and ladies kept him around much as they kept their pet monkeys—to amuse them. He was not truly accepted into higher elven society. He and his family were invited to the royal palace once a year—the queen's concession to those who kept her coffers full—but that was all. None of which bothered Paithan in the least.

The knowledge that elves who weren't half as smart or one-fourth as rich looked down on the Quindiniars because they couldn't trace their family back to the Plague rankled like an arrow wound in Calandra's breast. She had no use for the "peerage" and made her disdain plain, at least to her younger brother. And she was extremely put out that Paithan didn't share her feelings.

Paithan, however, found the noble elves nearly as amusing as they found him. He knew that if he proposed marriage to any one of ten dukes' daughters there would be gasps and wailings and tears at the thought of the "dear child" marrying a commoner—

and the wedding would be held as fast as decently possible. Noble houses, after all, are expensive to maintain.

The young elf had no intention of marrying, at least not yet. He came of an exploring, wandering family—the very elven explorers who had discovered ornite. He had been home for nearly a full season now and it was time he was on his way again, which was one reason he was sitting here with his sister when he should be out rowing around some charming young woman in a scull. But Calandra, absorbed in her calculations, appeared to have forgotten his very existence. Paithan decided suddenly that if he heard one more bead click he would go "potty"—a slang expression of "his crowd" that would have set Calandra's teeth on edge.

Paithan had some news for his sister that he'd been saving for just such an occasion. It would cause an explosion akin to the one that had rocked the house previously, but it might shake Calandra loose and then he could escape.

"What do you think of Father's sending for that human priest?" he asked.

For the first time since he entered the room, his sister actually stopped her calculations, lifted her head, and looked at him.

"What?"

"Father's sending for the human priest. I thought you knew." Paithan blinked rapidly, to appear innocent.

Calandra's dark eyes glinted. The thin lips pursed. Wiping the pen with careful deliberation on an ink-stained cloth used expressly for this purpose, she laid it down carefully in its proper place on the top of the ledger and turned to give her full attention to her brother.

Calandra had never been pretty. All the beauty in the family, it was said, had been saved up and given to her younger sister. Cal was thin to the point of boniness. (Paithan, when a child, had once been spanked for asking if his sister's nose had been caught in a winepress.) Now, in her fading youth, it appeared as if her entire face had been caught and pinched. She wore her hair pulled back in a tight knot at the top of her head, held in place by three lethal-looking, sharp-pointed combs. Her skin was dead white, because she rarely went out of doors and then carried a parasol to protect her from the sun. Her severe dresses were made after the same pattern—buttoned to her chin, her skirts trailing the floor. Calandra had never minded that she wasn't pretty. Beauty was given a woman so that she could trap a man, and Cal had never wanted a man.

"What are men, after all," Calandra was fond of saying, "but creatures who spend your money and interfere in your life?"

All except me, thought Paithan. And that's because Calandra's brought me up properly.

"I don't believe you," said his sister.

"Yes, you do." Paithan was enjoying himself. "You know the guv—sorry, slip of the tongue—Father's crazy enough to do just about anything."

"How did you find out?"

"I popped—stopped in at old Rory's last suppertime for a quick one before going to Lord—"

"I'm not interested in where you were going." A line had appeared in Calandra's forehead. "You didn't hear this rumor from old Rory, did you?"

" 'Fraid so, Sister dear. Our batty papa had been in the pub, talkin' about his rockets and comes out with the news that he's sent for a human priest."

"In the pub!" Calandra's eyes widened in horror. "Were there . . . many who heard him?"

"Oh, yes," said Paithan cheerfully. "It was his usual time, you know, right during winetime and the place was packed."

Calandra emitted a low groan, her fingers curled around the frame of the abacus, which protested loudly.

"Maybe he . . . imagined it." Her tone sounded hopeless, however. Their father was sometimes all too sane in his madness.

Paithan shook his head. "Nope. I talked to the birdman. His faultless[3] carried the message to Lord Gregory of Thillia. The note said that Lenthan Quindiniar of Equilan wanted to consult with a human priest about travel to the stars. Food and lodging provided and five hundred stones."[4]

---

[3] A winged fowl of the segrouse family used for long-distance communication. A faultless, once properly trained, will fly unerringly between two points.

[4] The medium of exchange of Equilan. It is a paper equivalent of stones, which themselves are extremely rare, being found generally only at the very bottom of the world.

Calandra groaned again. "We'll be besieged!" She gnawed her lip.

"No, no, I don't think so." Paithan felt somewhat remorseful at being the cause of such agony. He reached out and patted his sister's clenched hand. "We may be lucky this time, Callie. Human priests live in monasteries and take strict vows of poverty and such like. They couldn't accept the money. And they have life pretty good in Thillia, not to mention the fact that they have a strongly organized hierarchy. They're all answerable to some sort of father superior, and one couldn't just pack up and head out for the wilds."

"But the chance to convert an elf—"

"Pooh! They're not like our priests. They haven't time to convert anybody. They're mainly concerned with playing politics and trying to bring back the Lost Lords."

"You're certain?" Calandra had regained some color in the pale cheeks.

"Well, not certain," Paithan admitted. "But I've been around humans a lot and I know them. They don't like coming into our lands, for one thing. They don't like *us*, for another. I don't *think* we have to worry about this priest turning up."

"But why?" Calandra demanded. "Why would Papa do such a thing?"

"Because of the human belief that life came from the stars, which are really and truly cities, and that someday, when our world here below is in chaos, the Lost Lords will return and lead us back."

"That's nonsense!" Calandra said crisply. "All know life came from Peytin Sartan, Matriarch of Heaven, who created this world for her mortal children. The stars are her immortal children, watching over us." She looked shocked, the full implication dawning on her. "You don't mean to say that Father actually believes this? Why that . . . that's heresy!"

"I think he's beginning to," said Paithan, more somberly. "It makes sense for him, Callie, when you think about it. He was experimenting with using rockets to transport goods before Mother died. Then, she leaves and our priests tell him that Mother's gone to heaven to be one of the immortal children. His mind slips one little cog and he lights on the idea of using rockets to go find Mother. Now he misses the next cog and decides that maybe she's not immortal but is living up there, safe and well, in some sort of city.''

"Blessed Orn!" Calandra groaned again. She sat silent for several moments, staring at the abacus, her fingers twitching one of the beads back and forth, back and forth. "I'll go talk to him," she said at last.

Paithan carefully kept his face under control. "Yes, that might be a good idea, Callie. You go talk to him."

Calandra rose to her feet, her skirts rustling stiffly about her. She paused, and looked down at her brother. "We were going to discuss this next shipment—"

"That can wait until tomorrow. This is much more important."

"Humpf. You needn't pretend to look so concerned. I know what you're up to, Paithan. You'll be off on some scatter-brained outing with your fine friends instead of staying home, minding your business as you ought. But you're right, though you probably don't have brains enough to know it. This *is* more important." A muffled explosion came from below, a crash of falling plates, and a scream from the kitchen. Calandra sighed. "I'll go talk with him, though I'm bound to say I doubt if it'll do much good. If I could just get him to keep his mouth shut!"

She slammed down the ledger. Lips compressed, back straight as a bridgepole tree, she marched in the direction of the door at the far end of the dining area. Her hips were straight as her back; no alluring swaying of skirt for Calandra Quindiniar.

Paithan shook his head. "Poor Guvnor," he said with a moment's feeling of true pity. Then, flipping the palm frond fan in the air, he went to his room to get dressed.

CHAPTER 2

EQUILAN,

TREETOP LEVEL

♦

DESCENDING THE STAIRS, CALANDRA PASSED THROUGH THE KITCHEN, located on the first floor of the house. The heat increased noticeably as she moved from the airy upper regions into the more closed and steamy lower part. The scullery maid—eyes red rimmed and a mark on her face from the cook's broad hand—was sullenly sweeping up broken crockery. The maid was an ugly human, as Calandra had said, and the red eyes and swollen lip did nothing to enhance her appearance.

But then Calandra considered all humans ugly and boorish, little more than brutes and savages. The human girl was a slave, who had been purchased along with a sack of flour and a stonewood cooking pot. She would work at the most menial tasks under a stern taskmaster—the cook—for about fifteen of the twenty-one–hour day. She would share a tiny room with the downstairs maid, have no possessions of her own, and earn a pittance by which she might, by the time she was an old woman, buy her way out of slavery. And yet Calandra firmly believed that she had done the human a tremendous favor by bringing her to live among civilized people.

Seeing the girl in her kitchen fanned the coals of Calandra's ire. A human priest! What madness. Her father should have more sense. It was one thing to be insane, quite another to abandon all sense of proper decorum. Calandra marched through the pantry, yanked open the cellar door, and proceeded down the cobwebby steps into the cool darkness below.

The Quindiniar house was built on a moss plain that grew among the upper levels of vegetation of the world of Pryan. The name *Pryan* meant Realm of Fire in a language supposedly used by those first people who came to the world. The nomenclature was appropriate, because Pryan's sun shone constantly. A more apt name for the planet might have been "Realm of Green," for—due to the continual sunshine and frequent rains—Pryan's ground was so thickly covered with vegetation that few people currently living on the planet had ever seen it.

Huge moss plains spanned the branches of gigantic trees, whose trunks at the base were sometimes wide as continents. Level after level of leaves and various plant life extended upward, many levels existing on top of levels beneath them. The moss was incredibly thick and strong; the large city of Equilan was built on a moss bed. Lakes and even oceans floated on top of the thick, brownish green mass. The topmost branches of the trees poked out above it, forming tremendous, junglelike forests. It was here, in the treetops or on the moss plains, that most civilizations on Pryan built their cities.

The moss plains didn't completely cover the world. They came to end in frightful places known as dragonwalls. Few ventured near these chasms. Water from the moss seas leapt over the edge and cascaded down into the darkness with a roar that shook the mighty trees. Any person standing on the edge of the land, staring into that limitless mass of jungle beneath his feet, felt small and puny and fragile as the newest unfurled leaf.

Occasionally, if the observer managed to gather his courage and spend some time staring into the jungle below, he might see ominous movement—a sinuous body humping up among the branches and slithering away, moving among the deep green shadows so swiftly that the brain wondered if the eye was lying. It was these creatures that gave the dragonwalls their name—the dragons of Pryan. Few had ever seen them, for the dragons were as wary of the tiny strange beings inhabiting the tops of the trees as the humans, dwarves, and elves were wary of the dragons. It was believed, however, that the dragons were enormous, wingless beasts of great intelligence who carried on their lives far, far below, perhaps even living on the fabled ground.

Lenthan Quindiniar had never seen a dragon. His father had; he'd seen several. Quintain Quindiniar had been a legendary explorer and inventor. He had helped establish the elven city of Equilan. He had invented numerous weapons and other devices that were immediately coveted by the human settlers in the area. He had used the already considerable family fortune, founded in ornite,[1] to establish a trading company that grew more prosperous every year. Despite his success, Quintain had not been content to stay quietly at home and count his coins. When his only son, Lenthan, was old enough, Quintain turned over the business to his son and went back out into the world. He'd never been heard from again, and all assumed, after a hundred years had passed, that he was dead.

Lenthan had the family's wandering blood in his veins but was never allowed to indulge in it, having been forced to take over the affairs of the business. He also had the family gift for making money, but it didn't seem to Lenthan as if the money he made was *his* money. He was, after all, simply carrying on the trade built up by his father. Lenthan had long sought a way to make his own mark in the world, but, unfortunately, there wasn't much of the world left to explore. The humans held the lands to the norinth, the Terinthian Ocean prohibited expansion to the est and vars and the dragonwall blocked the sorinth. As far as Lenthan was concerned, he had nowhere to go but up.

Calandra entered the cellar laboratory, holding her skirts out of the dirt; the look on her face would have curdled milk. It came near curdling her father. Lenthan, seeing his daughter here in this place he knew she abhorred, blanched and moved nervously nearer another elf who was present in the laboratory. This other elf smiled and bowed officiously. The expression on Calandra's face darkened at the sight.

"How nice—nice to see you down here, m—my dear," stammered poor Lenthan, dropping a crock of some foul-smelling liquid onto a filthy tabletop.

---

[1]Lodestone. An ancestor of Lenthan, Quindiniar was the first to discover and recognize its properties, which—for the first time—made overland travel possible. Before the discovery of ornite, people had no way of telling direction and would become hopelessly lost in the jungle. The location of the motherlode is a closely guarded family secret.

Calandra wrinkled her nose. The moss walls and floor gave off a pungent musky odor that blended ill with the various chemical smells—most notably sulfur—drifting about the laboratory.

"Mistress Quindiniar," said the other elf in greeting. "I trust I find you in health?"

"You do, sir, thank you for asking. And I trust you are the same, Master Astrologer?"

"A slight touch of rheumatism, but that is to be expected at my age."

"I wish your rheumatism would carry you off, you old charlatan!" muttered Calandra beneath her breath.

"Why is this witch down here meddling?" muttered the astrologer into the high, pointed collar that stood up from his shoulders and almost completely surrounded his face.

Lenthan stood between the two, looking forlorn and guilty, though he had no idea, as yet, what he had done.

"Father," said Calandra in a severe voice, "I want to speak to you. Alone."

The astrologer bowed and started to sidle off. Lenthan, seeing his prop being knocked out from beneath him, grabbed hold of the wizard's robes.

"Now, my dear, Elixnoir is part of the family—"

"He certainly eats enough to be part of the family," Calandra snapped, her patience giving way under the crushing blow of the terrible news of the human priest. "He eats enough to be *several* parts."

The astrologer drew himself up tall and stared down his long nose that was nearly as sharply pointed as the tips of the night blue collar through which it was seen.

"Callie, remember, he is our guest!" said Lenthan, shocked enough to rebuke his eldest child. "And a master wizard!"

"Guest, yes, I'll give him that. He never misses a meal or a chance to drink our wine or sleep in our spare bedroom. But master wizard I much doubt. I've yet to see him do anything but mumble a few words over that stinking gunk of yours, Father, and then stand back and watch it fizzle and smoke. You two will likely burn the house down around our ears someday! Wizard! Hah! Egging you on, Papa, with blasphemous stories about ancient people traveling to the stars in ships with sails of fire—"

"That is scientific fact, young woman," struck in the astrologer, the tips of his collar quivering in indignation. "And what your father and I are doing is scientific research and has nothing at all to do with religion—"

"Oh, it doesn't, does it?" cried Calandra, hurling her verbal spear straight for her victim's heart. "Then why is my father importing a human priest?"

The astrologer's eyes widened in shock. The high collar turned from Calandra to the wretched Lenthan, who found himself much disconcerted by it.

"Is this true, Lenthan Quindiniar?" demanded the incensed wizard. "You have sent for a human priest?"

"I—I—I—" was all Lenthan could manage.

"I have been deceived by you, sir," stated the astrologer, his dignity increasing every moment and so, it seemed, the length of his collar. "You led me to believe that you shared our interest in the stars, in their cycles and their places in the heavens."

"I was! I am!" Lenthan wrung his soot-blackened hands.

"You professed to be interested in the scientific study of how these stars rule our lives—"

"Blasphemy!" cried Calandra with a shudder of her bony frame.

"And yet now I find you consorting with—with—"

Words failed the wizard. His pointed collar appeared to close around him so that all that could be seen above it were his glittering, infuriated eyes.

"No! Please let me explain!" gabbled Lenthan. "You see, my son, Paithan, told me about the belief the humans have that there are people living in those stars and I thought—"

"Paithan told you!" gasped Calandra, pouncing on a new culprit.

"People *living* there!" gasped the astrologer, his voice muffled by the collar.

"But it does seem likely . . . and certainly explains why the ancients traveled to the stars and it fits with what our priests teach us that when we die we become one with the stars and I truly do miss Elithenia. . . ."

The last was said in a wretched, pleading tone that moved Lenthan's daughter to pity. In her own way, Calandra loved her father, just as she loved her brother and younger sister. It was a stern and unbending and impatient kind of love, but love it was and she moved over to put thin, cold fingers on her father's arm.

"There, Papa, don't upset yourself. I didn't mean to make you unhappy. It's just that I'd think you would have discussed this with me instead of . . . instead of the crowd at the Golden Mead!" Calandra could not forebear a sob. Pulling out a prim-and-proper lace-edged handkerchief, she clamped it over her nose and mouth.

His daughter's tears had the effect (not unintended) of completely crushing Lenthan Quindiniar into the mossy floor and burying him twelve hands[2] down. Her weeping and the wizard's trembling collar points were too much for the middle-aged elf.

"You're both right," said Lenthan, glancing from one to the other sorrowfully. "I can see that now. I've made a terrible mistake and when the priest comes, I'll tell him to go away immediately."

"When he comes!" Calandra raised dry eyes and stared at her father. "What do you mean 'when he comes'? Paithan said he wouldn't come!"

"How does Paithan know?" Lenthan asked, considerably perplexed. "Did he talk to him after I did?" The elf thrust a waxen hand into a pocket of his silk vest and dragged out a crumpled sheet of foolscap. "Look, my dear." He exhibited the letter.

Calandra snatched it and read it, her eyes might have burned holes in the paper.

" 'When you see me, I'll be there. Signed, Human Priest.' Bah!" Calandra thrust the letter back at her father. "That's the most ridiculous— Paithan's playing a joke. No person in his right mind would send a letter like that, not even a human. 'Human Priest' indeed!"

"Perhaps he's *not* in his right mind," said the Master Astrologer in ominous tones.

---

[2] The thickness of moss used to cover elven dead.

A mad human priest was coming to her house.

"Orn have mercy!" Calandra murmured, gripping the edge of the laboratory table for support.

"There, there, my dear," said Lenthan, putting his arm around his daughter's shoulders. "I'll take care of it. Just leave everything to me. You shan't be bothered in the slightest."

"And if I can be of any help"—the Master Astrologer sniffed the air; the smell of roast targ was wafting down from the kitchen—"I shall be happy to lend my aid. I shall even overlook certain things that were said in the heat of emotional distress."

Calandra paid no attention to the wizard. She had recovered her self-possession and her one thought now was to find her worthless brother and wring a confession out of him. She had no doubt—well, she had little doubt—that this was Paithan's doing, his idea of a practical joke. He was probably laughing heartily at her right now. How long would he laugh when she cut his allowance in half?

Leaving the astrologer and her father to blow themselves to smithereens in the cellar if they liked, Calandra stormed up the stairs. She marched through the kitchen where the scullery maid hid behind a dish towel until the awful specter was gone. Ascending to the third level of the house—the sleeping level—Calandra halted outside her brother's door and banged on it loudly.

"Paithan! Open your door this instant!"

"He's not there," called a sleepy voice from down the hallway.

Calandra glowered at the door, knocked again, and rattled the wooden handle. No sound. Turning, Cal stalked down the hall and entered the room of her younger sister.

Clad in a frilly nightdress that left both white shoulders exposed and just enough of her breasts to make things interesting, Aleatha lounged in a chair before her dressing table, lazily brushing her hair and admiring herself in the mirror. Magically enhanced, the mirror whispered compliments and offered the occasional suggestion as to the correct amount of rouge.

Calandra paused in the doorway, shocked almost beyond words. "What do you mean! Sitting there half-naked in broad daylight with the door wide open! What if one of the servants came by?"

Aleatha raised her eyes. She performed this motion slowly and languorously, knowing and enjoying full well the effect it had. The young elfmaid's eyes were a clear, vibrant blue, but—shadowed over by heavy lids and long, thick lashes—they darkened to purple. Opening them wide, therefore, had the effect of seeming to completely change their color. Numerous elven men had written sonnets to those eyes, and one was rumored to have died for them.

"Oh, one servant has already been past," said Aleatha without the slightest perturbation. "The footman. He's been up and down the hall three times at least in the last half-hour." She turned from her sister and began arranging the ruffles of her nightdress to show off her long, slender neck.

Aleatha's voice was rich, throaty, and sounded perpetually as if she were just about to sink into a deep slumber. This, combined with the heavy-lidded eyes, gave an impression of sweet languor no matter where the young woman went or what she was doing. During the fevered gaiety of a royal ball, Aleatha—ignoring the rhythm of the music—would dance slowly, in an almost dreamlike state, her body completely surrendered to her partner, giving him the delightful impression that without his strong support she would sink to the floor. The languid eyes stared into his, with just a tiny sparkle of fire deep in the purple depths, leading a man to think of what he might do that would cause those sleepy eyes to open wide.

"You are the talk of Equilan, Thea!" snapped Calandra, holding the handkerchief to her nose. Aleatha was spraying perfume over her neck and breast. "Where were you last darktime?"[3]

The purple eyes opened wide, or at least wider. Aleatha would never waste their full effect on a mere sister.

"Since when do you care where I was? What wasp's gotten into your corset this gentle-time, Callie?"

"Gentle-time! It's nearly winetime! You've slept away half the day!"

---

[3] Darktime is not truly dark in terms of night falling. It refers to the time during the cycle when shades are drawn and proper people go to sleep. It is also the time, however, when the lower, "darker" levels of the city come to life, and so has developed a rather sinister connotation.

"If you must know, I was with Lord Kevanish and we went down to the Dark—"

"Kevanish!" Calandra drew a seething breath. "That blackguard! He's being refused admittance to every proper house over that affair of the duel. It was because of him that poor Lucillia hung herself, and he as much as murdered her brother! And you, Aleatha . . . to be seen publicly with him—" Calandra choked.

"Nonsense. Lucillia was a fool for thinking that a man like Kevanish could really be in love with her. Her brother was a bigger fool in demanding satisfaction. Kevanish is the best boltarcher in Equilan."

"There is such a thing as honor, Aleatha!" Calandra stood behind her sister's chair, her hands gripping the back of it, the knuckles white with the strain. It seemed that with very little prompting, she might grip her sister's fragile neck in the same manner. "Or has this family forgotten that?"

"Forgotten?" murmured Thea in her sleepy voice. "No, dear Callie, not forgotten. Simply bought and paid for it long ago."

With a complete lack of modesty, Aleatha rose from her chair and began to untie the silken ribbons that almost held the front of her nightdress closed. Calandra, looking at her sister's reflection in the mirror, could see reddish bruise marks on the white flesh of shoulders and breast—the marks of the lips of an ardent lover. Sickened, Calandra turned her back and walked swiftly across the room to stand staring out the window.

Aleatha smiled lazily at the mirror and allowed the nightdress to slip to the floor. The mirror was rapturous in its comments.

"You were looking for Paithan?" she reminded her sister. "He flew into his room like a bat from the deep, dressed in his lawn suit, and flew out. I think he's gone to Lord Durndrun's. I was invited, but I don't know if I shall go or not. Paithan's friends are such bores."

"This family is falling apart!" Calandra pressed her hands together. "Father sending for a human priest! Paithan a common tramp, caring for nothing except roaming! You! You'll end up pregnant and unwed and likely hang yourself like poor Lucillia."

"Oh, hardly, Callie, dear," said Aleatha, kicking aside the nightdress with her foot. "Hanging oneself takes such a lot of energy." Admiring her slender body in the mirror, which admired it right back, she frowned, reached out and rang a bell made out of the shell of the egg of the carol bird. "Where is that maid of mine? Worry less about your family, Callie, and more about the servants. I never saw a lazier lot."

"It's my fault!" Calandra sighed and clasped her hands together tightly, pressing them against her lips. "I should have made Paithan go to school. I should have supervised you and not let you run wild. I should have stopped Father in this nonsense of his. But who would have run the business? It was sliding when I took it over! We would have been ruined! Ruined! If it had been left up to Father—"

The maid hurried into the room.

"Where have you been?" asked Aleatha sleepily.

"I'm sorry, mistress! I didn't hear you ring."

"Well, I did. But you should know when I want you. Lay out the blue. I'm staying home this darktime. No, don't. Not the blue. The green with the moss roses. I think I'll attend Lord Durndrun's outing, after all. Something amusing *might* occur. If nothing else, I can at least torment the baron, who's simply dying of love for me. Now, Callie, what's this about a human priest? Is he good looking?"

Calandra gave a strangled sob and clenched her teeth over the handkerchief. Aleatha glanced at her. Accepting the flimsy robe the maid draped over her shoulders, Thea crossed the room to stand behind her sister. Aleatha was as tall as Calandra, but her figure was soft and curved where her sister's was bony and angular. Masses of ashen hair framed Aleatha's face and tumbled down her back and around her shoulders. The elfmaid never "dressed" her hair as was the style. Like the rest of Aleatha, her hair was always disheveled, always looked as if she had just risen from her bed. She laid soft hands on her sister's quivering shoulders.

"The hour flower has closed its petals on those times, Callie. Keep longing uselessly for it to open again and you'll soon be insane as Father. If Mother had lived, things might have been different"—Aleatha's voice broke, she drew nearer her sister— "but she didn't. And that's that," she added, with a shrug of her perfumed shoulders. "You did what you had to do, Callie. You couldn't let us starve."

"I suppose you're right," said Calandra briskly, recalling that the maid was in the room and not wanting their affairs discussed in the servant's hall. She straightened her shoulders and smoothed out imaginary wrinkles from her stiff, starched skirts. "So you won't be in to dinner?"

"No, I'll tell the cook, if you like. Why don't you come to Lord Durndrun's, Sister?" Aleatha walked to the bed, where her maid was laying out silken undergarments. "Randolphus will be there. He's never married, you know, Callie. You broke his heart."

"Broke his purse is more like it," said Calandra severely, looking at herself in the mirror, patting her hair where a few wisps had come undone, and stabbing the three lethal combs back into place. "He didn't want me, he wanted the business."

"Perhaps." Aleatha paused in her dressing, the purple eyes going to the mirror and meeting the reflected eyes of her sister. "But he would have been company for you, Callie. You're alone too much."

"And so I'm to let a man step in and take over and ruin what it's cost me years to build just for the sake of seeing his face every morning whether I like it or not? No, thank you. There are worse things than being alone, Pet."

Aleatha's purple eyes darkened almost to wine. "Death, maybe."

Her sister didn't hear her.

The elfmaid shook back her hair, shaking off the gloomy shadow at the same time. "Shall I tell Paithan you're wanting to see him?"

"Don't bother. He must be near to running out of money by now. He'll be around to see me in the toiltime." Calandra marched toward the door. "I have the books to balance. Try to come home at a reasonable hour. Before tomorrow, at least."

Aleatha smiled at her sister's sarcasm and lowered the sleep-heavy eyelids modestly. "If you like, Callie, I won't see Lord Kevanish anymore."

Her sister paused, turned. Calandra's stern face brightened, but she only said, "I should hope not!" Stalking out of the room, she slammed the door shut behind her.

"He's getting to be a bore anyway," remarked Aleatha to herself. She lounged back down at her dressing table and studied her flawless features in the effusive mirror.

CHAPTER ♦ 3

GRIFFITH,

TERNCIA, THILLIA

♦

CALANDRA RETURNED TO HER WORK ON THE ACCOUNT BOOKS AS A soothing antidote to the wild vagaries of her family. The house was quiet. Her father and the astrologer puttered about in the cellar but, knowing that his daughter was more near exploding than his magical powder, Lenthan thought it wise to refrain from any further experiments along those lines.

After dinner, Calandra performed one more act related to the business. She sent a servant with a message for the birdman, addressed to Master Roland of Griffith, Jungleflower Tavern.

> *Shipment will arrive in early Fallow.[1] Payment expected on delivery. Calandra Quindiniar.*

The birdman attached the message to the foot of a fault-less that had been trained to fly to Terncia and cast the brightly colored bird in the air.

The faultless glided effortlessly through the sky, riding the air currents that ebbed and flowed among the towering trees.

---

[1]Seasons on Pryan are named according to the cycle of the crops: Rebirth, Sowing, Younglife, Harvest, Fallow. Rotation of crops is a human concept. The humans, with their skill in elemental magic as opposed to the elven skill in mechanical magic, are much better farmers than the elves.

The bird had her mind strictly on her destination, where her mate, locked in a cage, awaited her. She kept no watch for predators, there was nothing living that wanted her for food. The faultless secretes an oil that keeps its feathers dry during the frequent rainstorms. This oil is deadly poison to all species of life except the faultless.

The faultless winged its way norinth-vars, a route that took it over the grounds and mansions of the elven peerage and across Lake Enthial.

The bird dipped low over the elven farmlands that grew in the upper moss beds, forming a patchwork of unnaturally straight lines. Human slaves toiled in the fields, tending the crops. The faultless wasn't particularly hungry; she'd been fed before starting, but a mouse would top off her dinner nicely. She couldn't see one, however, and continued on, disappointed.

The carefully cultivated elven lands soon disappeared into the jungle wild. Streams, fed by the daily rains, gathered into rivers atop the moss beds. Winding their way through the jungle, the rivers occasionally found a break in the upper layers of the moss and cascaded down into the dark depths below.

Wisps of clouds began to drift before the bird's eyes, and she flew higher, gaining altitude, climbing above the storms of rain's hour. Eventually the thick, black, lightning-shot mass completely blocked her view of the land. She knew where she was, however; instinct guiding her. The Lord Marcins Forests lay below her; they were named by the elves but claimed by neither elves nor human due to the fact that their jungle growth was impenetrable.

The storm came and went, as it had done time out of mind since the creation of the world. The sun shone brightly, and the bird could see settled lands—Thillia, realm of the humans. From her great height, the bird noted three of the sparkling, sunlit towers that marked the five divisions of the Thillian kingdom. The towers, ancient by human standards, were built of crystal bricks, the secret of whose making had been known to human wizards during the reign of King George the Only. The secret, as well as many of the wizards, had been lost in the devastating War for Love that followed the old king's death.

The faultless used the towers to mark her destination, then swooped down, flying low over the humans' lands. Built on a broad moss plain, dotted here and there with trees that had been left standing for their shade, the country was flat, criss-crossed with roads and pockmarked with small towns. The roads were well traveled; humans having a curious need to be constantly on the move, a need the sedentary elves could never understand and one that they considered barbaric.

The hunting was far more favorable in this part of the world, and the faultless took a brief moment to fortify herself on a largish rat. Meal finished, she cleaned her claws on her beak, preened her feathers, and took to the air. When she saw the flat lands begin to give way to thick jungle, the bird felt cheered, for she was nearing the end of her long journey. She was over Terncia, the kingdom farthest norinth. Arriving at the walled city surrounding the crystal brick tower that marked the capital of Terncia, the bird heard the rough call of her mate. She dove from the sky, spiraling down into the city's heart, and landed on the leather-covered arm of a Thillian birdman. He removed the message, noted the designation, and placed the weary faultless into the cage with her mate, who greeted her with tiny nips of his beak.

The birdman handed the message to a circuit rider. Several days later, the rider entered a crude and half-thought-through village standing on the very edges of the jungle and dropped the message off at the village's only inn.

Seated in his favorite booth in the Jungleflower, Master Roland of Griffith studied the fine quin scroll. Grinning, he shoved it across the table to a young woman who sat across from him.

"There! What did I tell you, Rega?"

"Thank Thillia, that's all I can say." Rega's tone was grim, she wasn't smiling. "Now you at least have something to show old Blackbeard and maybe he'll leave us be for a stretch!"

"I wonder where he is?" Roland glanced at the hour flower[2] that stood in a pot on the bar. Almost twenty petals were folded down. "It's past his usual time."

"He'll be here. This is too important to him."

"Yeah, and that makes me nervous."

---

[2]A plant whose perpetually flowering petals curl each cycle in rhythm with the weather cycle. All races use the plant to determine the hours of the day, though each race knows them by a different name. Humans use the actual plant itself, whereas elves have developed magical mechanical devices to mimic its motion.

"Developing a conscience?" Rega drained her mug of kegrot and glanced about for the barmaid.

"No, I just don't like doing business here, in a public place—"

"All the better. Everything's aboveboard and out in the open. No one could have any suspicions of us. Ah, here he is. What did I tell you?"

The inn's door opened and a dwarf stood bathed in the dicing hour's bright sunlight. He was an imposing sight, and nearly everyone in the inn paused in their drinking, gambling, and conversing to stare at him. Slightly above average height for his people, he had ruddy brown skin and a shaggy mane of curly black hair and beard that gave him his nickname among humans. Thick black brows meeting over a hooked nose and flashing black eyes gave him a perpetually fierce expression that served him well in alien lands. Despite the heat, he wore a red-and-white striped silken shirt and over that the heavy leather armor of his people, with bright red pants tucked into tall, thick boots.

Those in the bar sniggered and exchanged grins at the dwarf's garish clothing. If they had known anything at all about dwarven society and what the bright colors of his clothing portended, they wouldn't have laughed.

The dwarf paused in the doorway, blinking his eyes, half-blinded from the bright sun.

"Blackbeard, my friend," Roland called, rising from his seat. "Over here!"

The dwarf clumped into the inn, the black eyes darting here and there, staring down any who seemed too bold. Dwarves were a rarity in Thillia. The dwarven kingdom was far to the norinth-est of the humans' and there was little contact between the two. But this particular dwarf had been in town for five days now and his appearance had ceased to be a novelty. Griffith was a squalid place located on the borders of two kingdoms, neither of which claimed it. The inhabitants did what they liked—an arrangement that suited most of them, because most of them had come from parts of Thillia where doing what they liked generally got them hung. The people of Griffith might wonder what a dwarf was up to in their town, but no one would wonder aloud.

"Barkeep, three more!" called Roland, holding aloft his mug. "We have cause to celebrate, my friend," he said to the dwarf, who slowly took a seat.

"Ya?" grunted the dwarf, regarding the two with dark suspicion.

Roland, grinning, ignored his guest's obvious animosity and handed over the message.

"I cannot read these words," said the dwarf, tossing the quin scroll back across the table.

The arrival of the barmaid with the kegrot interrupted them. Mugs were distributed. The slovenly barmaid gave the table a quick, disinterested swipe with a greasy rag, glanced curiously at the dwarf, and slouched away.

"Sorry, I forgot you can't read elvish. The shipment's on its way, Blackbeard," said Roland in a casual undertone. "It will be here within the Fallow."

"My name is Drugar. And that is what this paper says?" The dwarf tapped it with a thick-fingered hand.

"Sure is, Blackbeard, my friend."

"I am not your friend, human," muttered the dwarf, but the words were in his language and spoken to his beard. His lips parted in what might almost have been a smile. "That is good news." He sounded grudging.

"We'll drink to it." Roland raised his mug, nudging Rega, who had been eyeing the dwarf with a suspicion equal to that with which Blackbeard was eyeing them. "To business."

"I will drink to this," said the dwarf, after appearing to consider the matter. He raised his mug. "To business."

Roland drained his noisily. Rega took a sip. She never drank to excess. One of them had to remain sober. Besides, the dwarf wasn't drinking. He merely moistened his lips. Dwarves don't care for kegrot, which is, admittedly, weak and flat tasting compared to their own rich brew.

"I was just wondering, partner," said Roland, leaning forward, hunching over his drink, "just what you're going to be using these weapons for?"

"Acquiring a conscience, human?"

Roland cast a wry glance at Rega, who—hearing her words repeated—shrugged and looked away, silently asking what other answer he might have expected to such a stupid question.

"You are being paid enough not to ask, but I will tell you anyway because my people are honorable."

"So honorable you have to deal with smugglers, is that it, Blackbeard?" Roland grinned, paying the dwarf back.

The black brows came together alarmingly, the black eyes flared. "I would have dealt openly and legitimately, but the laws of your land prevent it. My people need these weapons. You have heard about the peril coming from the norinth?"

"The SeaKings?"

Roland gestured to the barmaid. Rega laid her hand on his, warning him to go slowly, but he shoved her away.

"Bah! No!" The dwarf gave a contemptuous snort. "I mean norinth of our lands. Far norinth, only not so far anymore."

"No. Haven't heard a thing, Blackbeard, old buddy. What is it?"

"Humans—the size of mountains. They are coming out of the norinth, destroying everything in their path."

Roland choked on his drink and started to laugh. The dwarf appeared to literally swell with rage, and Rega dug her nails into her partner's arm. Roland, with difficulty, stifled his mirth.

"Sorry, friend, sorry. But I heard that story from my dear old dad when he was in his cups. So the tytans are going to attack us. I suppose the Five Lost Lords of Thillia will come back at the same time." Reaching across the table, Roland patted the angry dwarf on the shoulder. "Keep your secret, then, my friend. As long as we get our money, my wife and I don't care what you do or who you kill."

The dwarf glowered, jerked his arm away from the human's touch.

"Don't you have somewhere to go, Husband, dear?" said Rega pointedly.

Roland rose to his feet. He was tall and muscular, blond and handsome. The barmaid, who knew him well, brushed against him when he stood up.

" 'Scuse me. Gotta pay a visit to a tree. Damn kegrot runs right through me." He made his way through the common room that was rapidly growing more crowded and more noisy.

Rega put on her most winning smile and came around the table to seat herself beside the dwarf. The young woman was almost exactly opposite in appearance from Roland. Short and full-figured, she was dressed both for the heat and for conducting business, wearing a linen blouse that revealed more than it covered. Tied in a knot at her breasts, it left her midriff bare. Leather pants, cut off at the knees, fit her legs like a second skin. Her flesh was tanned a deep golden brown and, in the heat of the tavern, glistened with a fine sheen of sweat. Her brown hair was parted in the center of her head and hung straight and shining as rain-soaked tree bark down her back.

Rega knew the dwarf wasn't the slightest bit attracted to her physically. Probably because I don't have a beard, she reflected, grinning to herself, remembering what she'd heard about dwarven women. He did seem eager to discuss this fairy tale his people'd dreamed up. Rega never liked to let a customer go away angry.

"Forgive my husband, sir. He's had a little too much to drink. But I'm interested. Tell me more about the tytans."

"Tytans." The dwarf appeared to taste the strange word. "That is what you call them in your language?"

"I guess so. Our legends tell of gigantic humans, great warriors, formed by the gods of the stars long ago to serve them. But no such beings have been seen in Thillia since before the time of the Lost Lords."

"I do not know if these . . . tytans . . . are the same or not." Blackbeard shook his head. "Our legends do not speak of such creatures. We are not interested in the stars. We who live beneath the ground rarely see them. Our legends tell of the Forgers, the ones who, along with the father of all dwarves, Drakar, first built this world. It is said that someday the Forgers will return and enable us to build cities whose size and magnificence are beyond belief."

"If you think these giants are the—er—Forgers, then why the weapons?"

Blackbeard's face grew shadowed, the lines deepened. "That is what some of my people believe. There are others of us who have talked to the refugees of the norinth lands. They tell of terrible destruction and killings. I think perhaps the legends have got it wrong. That is why the weapons."

Rega had, at first, thought the dwarf was lying. She and Roland had decided that Blackbeard meant to use the weapons to attack a few scattered human colonies. But, seeing the black eyes grow shadowed, hearing the heaviness in the dwarf's voice, Rega changed her mind. Blackbeard, at least, believed in this fantastic enemy and that was truly why he was buying the weapons. The thought was comforting. This was the first time she and Roland had ever smuggled weapons, and—no matter what Roland might say—Rega was relieved to know that she wouldn't be responsible for the deaths of her own people.

"Hey, Blackbeard, what are you doing—getting cosy with my wife, huh?" Roland eased himself back down at the table. Another mug awaited him, and he drank deeply.

Noting the shocked and darkening scowl on Blackbeard's face, Rega gave Roland a swift and painful kick beneath the table. "We were discussing legends, dear. I've heard it said that dwarves are fond of songs. My husband has an excellent voice. Perhaps, sir, you would like to hear the 'Lay of Thillia'? It tells the story of the lords of our land and how the five kingdoms were formed."

Blackbeard's face brightened. "Ya, I would like to hear it."

Rega thanked the stars she had spent time digging up everything she could about dwarven society. Dwarves do not have a fondness for music. They have an absolute passion for it. All dwarves play musical instruments, most of them have excellent singing voices and perfect pitch. They have only to hear a song once to catch the melody and need hear it only a second time to pick up the words.

Roland had an excellent tenor voice, and he sang the hauntingly beautiful lay with exquisite feeling. The people in the bar hushed to hear him, and there were many among the rough crowd who wiped their eyes when the song came to the end. The dwarf listened with rapt attention and Rega, sighing, knew that they had another satisfied customer.

> From thought and love all things once born,
> earth, air, and sky, and knowing sea.
> From darkness old, all light is shorne,
> and rise above, forever free.

In reverent voice, five brothers spoke
of sire's duty and wondered fare.
Their king dying 'neath fortune's yoke,
from each demand their landed care.

Five kingdoms great, born of one land.
To each fair prince his parcel part.
Dictates of will and dead sire's hand,
for each to rule, with just' and heart.

The first the fields, fair flowing flight,
whisp'ring winds the rushes calm move.
Another to sea, ships to right,
and crashing waves, the shorelines soothe.

The third of boles and gentlest sward,
crack of twig and shades darkling eye.
The fourth, the hills and valleys' lord,
where grazing plain and resting lie.

The last, the sun made shining home,
high seething heat, would ever last.
All five in wrote his true heart's tone,
true to all word and great kings past.

Each child did rule with true intent,
Embrac'ng demesne, all ruling fair.
Justice and strength, wisdom full lent,
each mouth to voice a grateful aire.

Yet fates' cruel games their pure hearts waste,
and each to arms this tryst above.
Five men consumed for woman chaste,
and all lives touch'd for strident love.

As gentle as a poem's heart,
was the beauteous woman born.
As subtle as all nature's art,
her wondrous heart all lives did warm.

When five proud men, all brothers born,
beheld this dam, their loves did soar.
For sweet Thillia, five loves sworn,
a handful of kingdoms, to war.

Five armies clashed, their plows to swords,
farmers from fields, passion's commands.
Brothers once fair and loving wards,
sent salt to sea and wounded th' lands.

Thillia stood on bloodied plain,
her arms outstretched, hands open wide.
Her griev'ed heart, cast down from shame,
fled far beneath lake's loving tide.

Perfection mourned her passing soul,
five brothers ceased their hollow fight.
They cried above, their hearts held whole,
and vowed to rise 'neath warrior's night.

In faith they walked with modest stride,
to sleeping Thillia beneath.
The crashing waves their virtue cried,
the kingdoms wept their wat'ry wreath.

From thought and love all things once born,
stone, air, and sky, and knowing sea.
From darkness old, all light is shorne,
and rise above, forever free.

Rega concluded the story. "Thillia's body was recovered and placed in a sacred shrine in the center of the realm in a place that belongs equally to all five kingdoms. The bodies of her lovers were never recovered, and from this sprang the legend that some day, when the nation is in dire peril, the brothers will come back and save their people."

"I liked that!" shouted the dwarf, thumping the table with his hand to express his appreciation. He actually went so far as to tap Roland on the forearm with a stubby finger; the first time in five days the dwarf had ever touched either human. "I like that very much. Have I got the tune?'' Blackbeard hummed the melody in a deep bass.

"Yes, sir! Exactly!'' cried Roland, much amused. "Would you like me to teach you the words?''

"I have them. Up here.'' Blackbeard tapped his forehead. "I am a quick student.''

"I guess so!'' said Roland, winking at the woman.

Rega grinned back.

"I would like to hear it again, but I must be going,'' said Blackbeard with true regret, shoving himself up from the table. "I must tell my people the good news.'' Sobering for a moment, he added, "They will be greatly relieved.'' Putting his hands on a belt around his waist, the dwarf unbuckled it and flung it on the table. "There is half the money, as we agreed. The other half on delivery.''

Roland's hand closed swiftly over the belt and pushed it across to Rega. She opened it, glanced inside, made a swift eye count, and nodded.

"Fine, my friend,'' said Roland, not bothering to stand up. "We'll meet you at the agreed-on place in late Fallow.''

Afraid that the dwarf might be offended, Rega rose to her feet and extended her hand—palm open to show there was no weapon—in the age-old human gesture of friendship. The dwarves have no such custom; there had never been a time when dwarves fought each other. Blackbeard had been around humans long enough to know that this pressing together of palms was significant. He did what was expected of him and hurriedly left the tavern, wiping his hand on his leather jerkin and humming the tune to the "Lay of Thillia" as he walked.

"Not bad for a night's work,'' said Roland, buckling the money belt around his waist, cinching it in, for his waist was trim and the dwarf was robust.

"No thanks to you!'' Rega muttered. The woman drew the raztar[3]

---

[3]Originally a child's toy known as a bandalore, the raztar was made into a weapon by the elves. A round case that fits snugly in the palm holds seven wooden blades attached to a magical spindle. A coiled length of cutvine, wrapped around the spindle, is looped around the middle finger. A quick flick of the wrist sends the spindle lashing out, blades magically extended. Another flick pulls the weapon, blades shut, back into the hand. Those skilled in the art can send the weapon out as far as ten feet, the flashing blades ripping through flesh before the opponent knows what's hit him.

from its round scabbard she wore on her thigh and made a show of sharpening all seven blades, glancing meaningfully at those in the inn who were taking just a bit too much interest in their affairs. "I pulled your fat out of the fire. Blackbeard would've walked out, if it hadn't been for me."

"Ah, I could've cut his beard off and he wouldn't have dared take offense. He can't afford to."

"You know," added Rega in an unusually somber and reflective mood, "he was really, truly frightened."

"So he was frightened? All the better for business, Sis," said Roland briskly.

Rega glanced around sharply, then leaned forward. "Don't call me 'Sis'! Soon we'll be traveling with that elf, and one little slip like that will ruin everything!"

"Sorry, 'Wifey, dear.' " Roland finished off the kegrot, and shook his head regretfully when the barmaid glanced his way. Carrying this much money, he needed to remain relatively alert. "So the dwarves are planning an attack on some human settlement. Probably the SeaKings. I wonder if we couldn't sell our next shipment to them."

"You don't think the dwarves will attack Thillia?"

"*Now* who's getting a conscience? What's it matter to us? If the dwarves don't attack Thillia, the SeaKings will. And if the SeaKings don't attack Thillia, Thillia will attack itself. Whatever happens, as I said, it's good for business."

Depositing a couple of wooden lord's crowns on the table, the two left the tavern. Roland walked in front, his hand on the hilt of his bladewood sword. Rega followed a pace or two behind him to guard his back as was their custom. They were a formidable-looking pair and had lived long enough in Griffith to establish the reputation of being tough, quick, and not much given to mercy. Several people eyed them, but no one troubled them. The two and their money arrived safely at the shack they called home.

Rega pulled shut the heavy wooden door and bolted it carefully from the inside. Peering outdoors, she drew closed the rags that she'd hung over the windows and gave Roland a nod. He lifted a three-legged wooden table and set it against the door. Kicking aside a rag rug lying on the floor, he revealed a trapdoor in the floor and, beneath it, a hole that had been dug in the moss. Roland tossed the money belt into the hole, shut the trapdoor, and arranged the rug and the table over it.

Rega put out a hunk of stale bread and a round of moldy cheese. "Speaking of business, what do you know about this elf, this Paithan Quindiniar?"

Roland tore off a piece of bread with strong teeth, forked a bite of cheese into his mouth. "Nothing," he mumbled, chewing steadily. "He's an elf, which means he'll be a wilting lily, except where it comes to you, my charming sister."

"I'm your charming wife. Don't forget that." Rega playfully poked her brother in the hand with one of the wooden blades of her raztar. She hacked off another slice of cheese. "Do you really think it will work?"

"Sure. The guy who told me about it says the scam never fails. You know elves are mad about human women. We introduce ourselves as husband and wife, but our marriage isn't exactly a passionate one. You're starved for affection. You flirt with the elf and lead him on and when he lays a hand on your quivering breast, you suddenly remember that you're a respectable married lady and you scream like a banshee.

"I come to the rescue, threaten to cut off the elf's pointed . . . um . . . ears. He buys his life by giving us the goods for half price. We sell them to the dwarves at full price, plus a little extra for our 'trouble' and we're set up for the next few seasons."

"But after that, we'll need to deal with the Quindiniar family again—"

"And we will. I've heard that this female elf who runs the business *and* the family is a pickle-faced old prude. Baby brother won't dare tell his sister he tried to break up our 'happy home.' And we can make certain he gets us an extra-good price the next time."

"It sounds easy enough," admitted Rega. Hooking a wineskin with her hand, she tilted the liquid into her mouth, then shoved it across to her brother. "Here's to wedded bliss, my beloved 'Husband.' "

"Here's to infidelity, my dear 'Wife.' "

The two, laughing, drank.

Drugar left the Jungleflower Tavern but the dwarf did not immediately leave Griffith. Slipping into the shadows cast by a gigantic tentpalm plant, he waited and watched until the man and the woman came outside. Drugar would have liked very much to follow them, but he knew his own limitations. The clumsy-footed dwarves are not made for stealthy sneaking. And, in the human city of Griffith, he couldn't simply lose himself in a crowd.

He contented himself with eyeing the two carefully as they walked away. Drugar didn't trust them, but he wouldn't have trusted Saint Thillia had she appeared before him. He hated having to depend on a middle man and would much rather have dealt with the elves directly. That was impossible, however. The current Lords of Thillia had made an agreement with the Quindiniars that they would not sell their magical, intelligent weapons to the dwarves or the barbaric SeaKings. In return, the Thillians agreed to purchase a guaranteed number of weapons per season.

Such an arrangement suited the elves. And if elven weapons found their way into the hands of SeaKings and dwarves, it certainly wasn't the fault of the Quindiniars. After all, as Calandra was wont to state testily, how could she be expected to tell a human raztar runner from a legitimate representative of the Lords of Thillia? All humans looked alike to her. And so did their money.

Just before Roland and Rega vanished from Drugar's sight, the dwarf lifted a black rune-carved stone that hung from a leather thong around his neck. The stone was smooth and rounded, worn down from loving handling, and it was old— older than Drugar's father, who was one of the oldest living inhabitants on Pryan.

Lifting the stone, Drugar held it up in the air so that, from his viewpoint, the stone appeared to cover Roland and Rega. The dwarf moved the rock in a pattern, muttered words accompanied the tracing of the sigil that copied the rune carved into the stone. When he was finished, he slipped the stone reverently back into the folds of his clothing and spoke aloud to the two, who were rounding a corner and would soon be lost to the dwarf's sight.

"I did not sing the rune for you because I have a liking for you—either of you. I put the charm of protection on you so that I may be certain of getting the weapons my people need. When

the deal is done, I will break the rune. And Drakar take you
both."

Spitting on the ground, Drugar plunged into the jungle,
tearing and hacking a path through the thick undergrowth.

CHAPTER ◆ 4

EQUILAN,

LAKE ENTHIAL

◆

CALANDRA QUINDINIAR HAD NO MISCONCEPTIONS CONCERNING THE nature of the two humans with whom she was dealing. She guessed they were smugglers but that was no concern of hers. It was impossible for Calandra to consider any human capable of running a fair and honest business. As far as she was concerned, humans were all smugglers, crooks, and thieves.

It was with some amusement therefore—as much amusement as she ever allowed herself—that Calandra watched Aleatha leave her father's house and walk across the moss yard toward the carriage. Her sister's delicate dress was lifted by the winds rustling among the treetops and billowed around her in airy green waves. Elven fashion at the moment dictated long, cinched-in waists; stiff, high collars; straight skirts. The fashion did not suit Aleatha and, therefore, she ignored fashion. Her dress was cut low to show off her splendid shoulders, the bodice softly gathered to cup and highlight beautiful breasts. Falling in soft folds, the layers of filmy fabric enveloped her like a primrose-stitched cloud, accentuating her graceful movements.

The fashion had been popular in her mother's time. Any other woman—like myself, thought Calandra grimly—wearing that dress would have appeared dowdy and out of current style. Aleatha made current style appear dowdy.

She had arrived at the carriage house. Her back was turned toward Calandra, but the older sister knew what was going on.

Aleatha would be smiling at the human slave who was handing her into the carriage.

Aleatha's smile was perfectly ladylike—eyes cast down as was proper, her face almost hidden by her wide-brimmed, rose-trimmed hat. Her sister could never fault her. But Calandra, watching from the upstairs window, was familiar with Aleatha's tricks. Her eyelids might be lowered, but the purple eyes weren't and flashed beneath the long black lashes. The full lips would be parted slightly, the tongue moving slowly against the upper lip to keep it continually moist. The human slave was tall and well muscled from hard labor. His chest was bare in the midcycle heat. He was clad in the tight-fitting leather pants humans favored. Calandra saw his smile flash in return, saw him take an inordinate amount of time helping her sister into the carriage, saw her sister manage to brush against the man's body as she stepped inside. Aleatha's gloved hand even lingered for a moment on the slave's! Then she had the brazen nerve to lean slightly out of the carriage, her hat brim uptilted, and wave at Calandra!

The slave, following Aleatha's gaze, suddenly remembered his duty and hastened to take up his position. The carriage was made of the leaves of the benthan tree, woven to form a round basket open at the front end. The top of the basket was held in the grip of several drivehands attached to a strong rope running from Aleatha's father's house down into the jungle. Prodded from their drowsy, constant lethargy, the drivehands crawled up the rope, pulling the carriage to the house. Allowed to drift back into slumber, the drivehands would slide down the rope, bringing the carriage to a junction, where Aleatha would transfer to another carriage whose drivehands would carry her to her destination.

The slave, pushing the carriage, started it on its way and Calandra watched her sister—green skirts fluttering in the wind—swoop down into the lush jungle vegetation.

Calandra smiled disdainfully at the slave, who was lounging at his post, gazing admiringly after the carriage. What fools these humans are. They don't even know when they're being teased. Aleatha was wild, but at least her dalliances were with men of her own kind. She flirted with humans because it was enjoyable to watch their brutish reactions. Aleatha, like her older sister, would sooner let the family dog kiss her as she would a human.

Paithan was another story. Settling down to her work, Calandra decided she would send the scullery maid to work in the boltarch shop.

Leaning back in the carriage, enjoying the cool wind blowing against her face as she descended rapidly through the trees, Aleatha foresaw regaling a certain person at Lord Durndrun's with her tale of arousing the human slave's passion. Of course, her story would be told from a slightly different angle.

"I swear to you, My Lord, that his great hand closed over mine until I thought he would crush it, and then the beast had the nerve to press his sweat-covered body up against me!"

"Dreadful!" Lord Someone would say, his pale elven face flushed with indignation . . . or was it with the thought of bodies pressing together. He would lean nearer. "What did you do?"

"I ignored him, of course. That's the best way to handle the brutes, besides the lash, that is. But, of course, I couldn't beat him, could I?"

"No, but I could!" the lord would cry gallantly.

"Oh, Thea, you know you tease the slaves to distraction."

Aleatha gave a slight start. Where had that disturbing voice come from? An imagined Paithan . . . invading her reverie. Catching hold of her hat that was about to be whisked off her head by the breeze, Aleatha made a mental note to make certain her brother was off playing the fool somewhere else before she began relating her enticing little story. Paithan was a good fellow and wouldn't deliberately ruin his sister's fun, but he was simply too guileless to live.

The carriage reached the end of its rope, arriving at the junction. Another human slave—an ugly one, Aleatha didn't bother with him—handed her out.

"Lord Durndrun's," she informed him coolly, and the slave helped her into one of several carriages waiting at the junction, each attached to a rope that headed off into a different part of the jungle. The slave gave the drivehands a prod, they flapped to life, and the carriage sailed off into the gradually darkening shadows, carrying its passenger down deeper into the city of Equilan.

The carriages were for the convenience of the wealthy, who paid a subscription to the city fathers for their use. Those who couldn't afford to subscribe to the carriage system made do with the swinging bridges spanning the jungle. These bridges led from house to house, shop to shop, house to shop, and back again. They had been constructed at the time the early elven settlers founded Equilan, connecting those few houses and businesses that had been built in the trees for defense purposes. As the city grew, so did the bridge system, without any particular order or thought, keeping the houses connected with their neighbors and the heart of the city.

Equilan had flourished and so had its people. Thousands of elves lived in the city and there were nearly as many bridges. Making one's way on foot was extraordinarily confusing, even for those who had lived there all their lives. No one who was any one in elven society walked the bridges, except for possibly a daring foray during darktime. The bridges were, however, an excellent defense against the elves' human neighbors, who had looked—in days long gone by—on the elven treeholdings with covetous eyes.

As time passed, and Equilan grew wealthier and more secure, her human neighbors to the norinth decided it would be wiser to leave the elves alone and fight each other. Thillia was divided into five kingdoms, each one an enemy of the other four, and the elves lived well by supplying weapons to all sides of the conflict. The elven royal families and those of the middle class who had risen to wealth and power moved higher into the trees. Lenthan Quindiniar's home was located on the highest "hill"[1] in Equilan—a mark of status among his fellow middle class but not among the royalty, who built their homes on the shores of Lake Enthial. No matter that Lenthan could buy and sell most of the homes on the lakeshore, he would never be allowed to live there.

To be honest, Lenthan didn't want to. He was quite content

---

[1]Moss beds that grow in the very tops of the gigantic jungle trees.

living where he was, with a fine view of the stars and a clear place amid the jungle's vegetation for the launching of his rockets.

Aleatha, however, had made up her mind to dwell by the lake. Nobility would be purchased with her charm and her body and her share of her father's money when he died. But just which duke or earl or baron or prince Aleatha was going to buy hadn't been decided yet. They were all such bores. The task before Aleatha was to shop around, find one less boring than the rest.

The carriage gently set down Aleatha in Lord Durndrun's ornate receiving house. A human slave started to hand her out, but a young lord, arriving at the same time, beat him to the honor. The young lord was married; Aleatha favored him with a sweet, charming smile anyway. The young lord was fascinated and walked off with Aleatha, leaving his wife to be handed down by the slave.

Running through the annotated list of elven royalty she kept in her head, Aleatha recognized the young lord as a near cousin to the queen, with the fourth finest house on the lake. She permitted him to present her to her host and hostess, asked him to give her a tour of the house (she'd been there many times previous), and was blushingly enthusiastic about a more intimate tour of the lush and shadowy garden.

Lord Durndrun's house, as were all others on Lake Enthial, was constructed on the top edge of a large moss bowl. The houses of the nobility of elven society stood scattered around the "rim" of the bowl. The dwelling of Her Majesty, the queen, was located at the very farthest end, away from the crowded city of her subjects. The other homes were all built facing the palace, as if they were continually paying homage.

In the center of the bowl was the lake, supported on a thick bed of moss, cradled in the arms of gigantic trees. Most lakes in the area were, because of their moss beds, a clear, crystalline green color. Due to a rare species of fish that swam in the lake (a gift to Her Majesty from the father of Lenthan Quindiniar) the water of Lake Enthial was a vibrant, stunning blue and was considered one of the wonders of Equilan.

The view was wasted on Aleatha, who had seen it all before

and whose primary goal was to make it her own. She had been introduced to Lord Daidlus before, but had not noticed until now that he was witty and intelligent and moderately handsome. Seated next to the admiring young man on a teakwood bench, Aleatha was just about to tell him her story of the slave when, as in her reverie, a cheerful voice interrupted her.

"Oh, there you are, Thea. I heard you'd come. Is that you, Daidlus? Did you know your wife's searching for you? She doesn't look pleased, either."

Lord Daidlus did not look pleased himself. He glowered at Paithan, who returned the glare with the innocent and slightly anxious expression of one whose only desire is to help a friend.

Aleatha was tempted to hang on to the lord and get rid of Paithan, but she reflected that there was a certain merit in allowing the pot to simmer before bringing it to a boil. Besides, she needed to talk to her brother.

"I'm ashamed of myself, My Lord," Aleatha said, flushing prettily. "I'm keeping you from your family. It was thoughtless and selfish of me, but I was so enjoying your company. . ."

Paithan, crossing his arms, leaned back against the garden wall and watched with interest. Lord Daidlus protested that he could stay with her forever.

"No, no, My Lord," Aleatha said with an air of noble self-sacrifice. "Go to your wife. I insist."

Aleatha extended her hand to be politely kissed. The young lord did so with rather more ardor than society would have considered proper.

"But I do so want to hear the end of your story," said the besotted Daidlus.

"You shall, My Lord," answered Aleatha, with downcast eyelashes through which glinted sparkles of blue-purple. "You shall."

The young lord tore himself away. Paithan sat down on the bench beside his sister, and Aleatha took off her hat and fanned herself with the brim.

"Sorry, Thea. Did I interrupt something?"

"Yes, but it was all for the best. Things were moving too fast."

"He's quite happily married, you know. Got three little ones."

Aleatha shrugged. The matter didn't interest her.

"Divorce would be a tremendous scandal," Paithan continued, sniffing at a flower he'd stuck in the buttonhole of his long, white linen lawn suit. Loosely made, the coat flowed over white linen pants, gathered at the ankles.

"Father's money would hush it up."

"The queen would have to grant it."

"Father's money would buy it."

"Callie'd be furious."

"No, she wouldn't. She'd be too happy I was finally respectably married. Don't worry about *me*, Brother, dear. You have worries of your own. Callie was looking for you this afternoon."

"Was she?" Paithan asked, trying to appear unconcerned.

"Yes, and the expression on her face could have launched one of Father's infernal devices."

"Worse luck. Been talking to the guvnor, had she?"

"Yes, I think so. I didn't say much. I didn't want to get her started. I'd be there still. Something about a human priest? I— What in Orn's name was that?"

"Thunder." Paithan glanced up into the thick vegetation through which it was impossible to see the sky. "Storm must be coming. Drat. That means they'll cancel the boating."

"Nonsense. It's far too early. Besides, I felt the ground tremble. Didn't you?"

"Maybe it's Callie, stalking me." Paithan removed the flower from his buttonhole and began playfully tearing it up, tossing the petals in his sister's lap.

"I'm so glad you find this amusing, Pait. Wait until she cuts your allowance. What is this about a human priest, anyway?"

Paithan settled himself on the bench, his eyes on the flower he was decapitating, his youthful face unusually serious. "When I came back from that last trip, Thea, I was shocked to see the change in Father. You and Callie don't notice. You're around him all the time. But . . . he looked so . . . I don't know . . . gray, I guess. And woebegone."

Aleatha sighed. "You caught him in one of his more lucid moments."

"Yes, and those damn rockets of his aren't clearing the treetops, let alone coming close to the stars. He was going on and on about Mother . . . and you know how that is!"

"Yes. I know how that is." Aleatha gathered the flower petals in her lap, unconsciously forming them into a miniature grave.

"I wanted to cheer him up, so I said the first jolly thing that popped into my mind. 'Why not send for a human priest?' I said. 'They know an awfully lot about the stars, 'cause that's where they think they come from. Claim that the stars are really cities and all that rot. Well"—Paithan appeared modestly pleased with himself—"it perked the old boy right up. I hadn't seen him so excited since the day his rocket flew into the city and blew up the garbage dump."

"It's all very well for you, Pait!" Aleatha irritably scattered her flowers to the wind. "You get to go off on another one of your trips. But Callie and I will have to live with the brute! That lecherous old astrologer of Father's is bad enough without this."

"I'm sorry, Thea. I really didn't think." Paithan sounded and felt truly ashamed. The one bright spark that burned in all of Quindiniars was their love and affection for each other— an affection that, unfortunately, did not extend to the rest of the world.

Reaching out, Paithan took his sister's hand in his and squeezed it. "Besides, no human priest will ever come. I know them, you see and—"

The moss bed rose up suddenly beneath their feet and then settled back down. The bench on which they were sitting shook and shivered, a pronounced rippling effect marred the smooth and placid surface of the lake. A rumbling sound like thunder, which came from below rather than above, accompanied the ground's shudder.

"That wasn't a storm," said Aleatha, looking about in alarm.

Shouts and screams could be heard in the distance.

Paithan rose to his feet, his expression suddenly grave. "I think, Thea, that we had better move back to the house." He gave his hand to his sister. Aleatha moved with calm alacrity, gathering her flowing skirts around her in unruffled haste.

"What do you think it is?"

"I haven't the vaguest idea," Paithan answered, hurrying through the garden. "Ah, Durndrun! What's this? Some new form of party game?"

"I only wish it were!" The lord appeared considerably harried. "It's sent a big crack through the dining room wall and frightened Mother into hysterics."

The rumbling began again, this time stronger. The ground bucked and quivered. Paithan staggered back against a tree. Aleatha, pale but composed, clung to a hanging vine. Lord Durndrun toppled over, and was almost struck by a falling piece of statuary. The quake lasted for as long as a man might draw three deep breaths, then ceased. A strange smell wafted up from the moss—the smell of chill, dank dampness. The smell of darkness. The smell of something that lives in the darkness.

Paithan moved to help the lord to his feet.

"I think," said Durndrun in an undertone meant for Paithan's ears alone, "that we should arm ourselves."

"Yes," agreed Paithan, glancing askance at his sister and keeping his voice low. "I was about to suggest that myself."

Aleatha heard and understood. Fear tingled through her, a rather pleasant sensation. It was certainly adding interest to what she had expected to be an otherwise boring evening.

"If you gentlemen will excuse me," she said, adjusting the brim of her hat to best advantage, "I will go to the house and see if I may be of assistance to the dowager."

"Thank you, Mistress Quindiniar. I would appreciate it. How brave she is," Lord Durndrun added, watching Aleatha walking fearlessly alone toward the house. "Half the other women are shrieking and flinging themselves about and the other half have dropped over in a dead faint. Your sister is a remarkable woman!"

"Yes, isn't she," said Paithan, who saw that his sister was enjoying herself immensely. "What weapons have you got?"

Hastening toward the house, the lord glanced at the young elf running along beside him. "Quindiniar"—Durndrun edged nearer, took him by the arm—"you don't think this has anything to do with those rumors you told us of the other night. You know, the ones about . . . er . . . giants?"

Paithan appeared slightly shamefaced. "Did I mention giants? By Orn, that was strong wine you were serving that night, Durndrun!"

"Perhaps those rumors aren't rumors, after all," said Durndrun grimly.

Paithan considered the nature of the rumbling sounds, the smell of darkness. He shook his head. "I think we're going to wish we were facing giants, my lord. I'd enjoy a human bedtime story right about now."

The two arrived at the house, where they began going over the catalog of his lordship's armaments. Other male members of the party joined them, shouting and proclaiming and carrying on in an hysterical manner not much better than that of their women, to Paithan's mind. He was regarding them with a mixture of amusement and impatience when he became aware that they were all regarding him and they were extraordinarily serious.

"What do you think we should do?" asked Lord Durndrun.

"I—I—really—" Paithan stammered, looking around at the group of thirty members of the elven nobility in confusion. "I mean, I'm certain you—"

"Come, come, Quindiniar!" snapped Lord Durndrun. "You're the only one of us who's been in the outside world. You're the only one with experience in this sort of thing. We need a leader and you're it."

And if something happens, you'll have me to blame for it, Paithan thought but didn't say, though a wry smile flitted across his lips.

The rumbling began again, strong enough this time to knock many of the elves to their knees. Screams and wails came from the women and children who had been herded into the house for safety. Paithan could hear crashing and breaking tree limbs in the jungle, the raucous cawing of startled birds.

"Look! Look at that! In the lake!" came a hoarse cry from one of the lords standing on the fringes of the crowd.

All turned and stared. The lake's waters were heaving and boiling and, out of the middle, snaking upward, could be seen the shining scales of an enormous green body. A portion of the body surfaced, then slithered under.

"Ah, I thought so," murmured Paithan.

"A dragon!" cried Lord Durndrun. He clutched at the young elf. "My god, Quindiniar! What do we do?"

"I think," said Paithan with a smile, "that we should all go inside and have what will probably be our last drink."

CHAPTER ♦ 5

EQUILAN,

LAKE ENTHIAL

♦

ALEATHA WAS IMMEDIATELY SORRY SHE'D JOINED THE WOMEN. FEAR IS
a contagious disease and the parlor stank of it. The men were
probably every bit as frightened as the women but they were
maintaining a bold front—if not for themselves, at least for each
other. The women were not only able to indulge their terror,
they were expected to. Even fear, however, has socially defined
limits.

The dowager—Lord Durndrun's mother and reigning mistress of the house since her son was not yet married—had the
priority on hysteria. She was the eldest, the highest in status,
and it was her house. No one else present, therefore, had the
right to be as panic-stricken as the dowager. (A mere duke's
wife, who had fainted in a corner, was being ostracized.)

The dowager lay prostrate on a couch, her maid weeping at
her side and applying various restoratives—bathing the dowager's temples in lavender water, dabbing tincture of rose on the
dowager's ample bosom, which was heaving and fluttering as
she sought vainly to catch her breath.

"Oh . . . oh . . . oh!" she gasped, clutching her heart.

The various wives of the guests hovered about her, wringing
their hands, occasionally grasping each other with stifled sobs.
Their fear was inspirational to their children, who had previously
been mildly curious, but who were now wailing in concert and
getting under everyone's feet.

"Oh . . . oh . . . oh!" wheezed the dowager, turning slightly blue.

"Slap her," suggested Aleatha coolly.

The maid seemed tempted, but the wives managed to emerge from their panic long enough to look shocked. Aleatha, shrugging, turned away and walked toward the tall windows that doubled as doors and opened out onto the spacious porch overlooking the lake. Behind her, the dowager's spasms appeared to be easing. Perhaps she had heard Aleatha's suggestion and seen the twitching hand of her maid.

"There's been no sound in the last few minutes," gasped an earl's wife. "Perhaps it's over."

An uneasy silence met the comment. It wasn't over. Aleatha knew it and every woman in the room knew it. For the moment, it was quiet, but it was a heavy, horrible quiet that made Aleatha long for the dowager's wailing. The women shrank together, the children whimpered.

The rumbling struck again. The house shook alarmingly. Chairs skittered across the floor, small ornaments fell off tables and crashed on impact. Those who could, hung onto something; those who couldn't, stumbled and fell. From her vantage point at the window, Aleatha saw the green, scaly body rise up from the lake.

Fortunately, none of the women in the room behind her noticed the creature. Aleatha bit her lips to keep from crying out. Then it was gone—so swiftly that she wondered if she had seen something real or something bred of her fear.

The rumbling ceased. The men were running toward the house, her brother in the lead. Aleatha flung open the doors and dashed down the broad staircase.

"Paithan! What was it?" She caught hold of the sleeve of his coat.

"A dragon, I'm afraid, Thea," answered her brother.

"What will happen to us?"

Paithan considered. "We'll all die, I should imagine."

"It's not fair!" Aleatha raved, stamping her foot.

"No, I suppose not." Paithan considered this a rather odd view of the desperate situation, but he patted his sister's hand soothingly. "Look, Thea, you're not going to go off like those others in there, are you? Hysteria's *not* becoming."

Aleatha put her hands to her cheeks, felt her skin flushed and hot. He's right, she thought. I must look a fright. Drawing a deep breath, she forced herself to relax, smoothed her hair, and rearranged the disheveled folds of her dress. The surging blood drained from her cheeks.

"What should we do?" she asked in a steady voice.

"We're going to arm ourselves. Orn knows it's hopeless, but at least we can hold the monster off for a short time."

"What about the queen's guards?"

Across the lake, the palace regiment could be seen turning out, the men dashing to their posts.

"They're guarding Her Majesty, Thea. They can't leave the palace. Here's an idea, you take the other women and the children down to the cellar—"

"No! I won't die like a rat in a hole!"

Paithan looked at his sister closely, measuring her courage. "Aleatha, there *is* something you can do. Someone has to go into the city and alert the army. We can't spare any of the men, and none of the other women here are fit to travel. It'll be dangerous. The fastest way is the carriage and if this beast gets past us—"

Aleatha envisioned clearly the dragon's huge head rising up, thrashing about, snapping the cables that held the carriage high above the ground. She pictured the plummeting fall. . . .

She pictured herself locked up in a dark, stuffy cellar with the dowager.

"I'll go." Aleatha gathered up her skirts.

"Wait, Thea! Listen. Don't try to go down into the city proper. You'd get lost. Make for the guard post on the var side. The carriages'll take you partway and then you'll have to walk, but you can see it from the first junction. It's a lookout built in the branches of a karabeth tree. Tell them—"

"Paithan!" Lord Durndrun came running out of the house, railbow and quiver in hand. He pointed. "Who the devil is that walking around down there by the lake? Didn't we bring every-one up here with us?"

"I thought so." Paithan stared, squinting. The sunlight off the water was blinding, it was difficult to see. Yet, sure enough, he could make out a figure moving about down by the water's edge. "Hand me that railbow. I'll go. We could have easily lost someone in the confusion."

"Down . . . down there . . . with the dragon?" The lord stared at Paithan in amazement.

Much as he did everything else in his life, Paithan had volunteered without thinking. But before he could announce that he'd suddenly remembered a previous engagement, Lord Durndrun was pressing the bow in the young elf's hands and murmuring something about a medal of valor. Posthumous, no doubt.

"Paithan!" Aleatha caught hold of him.

The elf took his sister's hand in his, squeezed it, then transferred it to Lord Durndrun's. "Aleatha has offered to go and bring the Shadowguard[1] to our rescue."

"Brave heart!" murmured Lord Durndrun, kissing the hand that was cold as ice. "Brave soul." He gazed at Aleatha in fervent admiration.

"Not braver than those of you staying behind, My Lord. I feel like I'm running away." Aleatha drew a deep breath, gave her brother a cool glance. "Take care of yourself, Pait."

"You, too, Thea."

Arming himself, Paithan headed down toward the lake at a run.

Aleatha watched him go, a horrible, smothering feeling in her breast—a feeling she had experienced once before, the night her mother died.

"Mistress Aleatha, let me escort you." Lord Durndrun kept hold of her hand.

"No, My Lord. That's nonsense!" Aleatha answered sharply. Her stomach twisted, bowels clenched. Why had Paithan gone? Why had he left her? She wanted only to escape from this horrid place. "You're needed here."

"Aleatha! You are so brave, so beautiful!" Lord Durndrun clasped her close, his arms around her waist, his lips on her hand. "If, by some miracle, we escape this monster, I want you to marry me!"

---

[1]The eleven army is divided into three branches, the Queen's Guard, the Shadowguard, and the City Guard. The Shadowguard keep to the lower regions of the city and are presumably adept at dealing with the various monsters that dwell beneath the moss plains.

Aleatha started, jolted from her fear. Lord Durndrun was one of the highest ranking elves at court, one of the wealthiest elves in Equilan. He had always been polite to her, but cool and withdrawn. Paithan had been kind enough to inform her that the lord thought her "too wild, her behavior improper." Apparently, he had changed his mind.

"My Lord! Please, I must go!" Aleatha struggled, not very hard, to break the grip of the arm around her waist.

"I know. I will not stop your courageous act! Promise me you'll be mine, if we survive."

Aleatha ceased her struggles, shyly lowered the purple eyes. "These are dreadful circumstances, My Lord. We are not ourselves. Should we survive, I could not hold your lordship to such a promise. But"—she drew nearer him, whispering—"I do promise your lordship that I will listen if you want to ask the question again."

Breaking free, Aleatha sank in a low courtesy, turned and ran swiftly, gracefully across the moss lawn toward the carriage house. She knew he was following her with his eyes.

I have him. I will be Lady Durndrun—supplanting the dowager as first handmaiden to the queen.

Aleatha smiled to herself as she sped across the moss, holding her skirts high to avoid tripping. The dowager'd had hysterics over a dragon. Wait until she heard this news! Her only son, nephew of Her Majesty, joined in marriage with Aleatha Quindiniar, wealthy trollop. It would be the scandal of the year.

Now, pray the blessed Mother, we just live through this!

Paithan made his way down across the sloping lawn toward the lake. The ground began to rumble again, and he paused to glance about hastily, searching for any signs of the dragon. But the rolling ceased almost as soon as it had started, and the young elf took off again.

He wondered at himself, wondered at his courage. He was skilled in the use of the railbow, but the puny weapon would hardly help him against a dragon. Orn's blood! What am I doing down here? After some serious consideration, given while he was skulking behind a bush to get a better view, he decided it wasn't courage at all. Nothing more than curiosity. It had always landed his family in trouble.

Whoever the person was wandering down around the lake's edge, he was beginning to puzzle Paithan immensely. He could see now that it was a man and that he didn't belong to their party. He didn't even belong to their race! It was a human—an elderly one, to judge by appearances: an old man with long white hair straggling down his back and a long white beard straggling down his front. He was dressed in long, bedraggled mouse-colored robes. A conical, shabby hat with a broken point teetered uncertainly on his head. And he seemed—most incredibly—to have just stepped out of the lake! Standing on the shoreline, oblivious to the danger, the old man was wringing water out of his beard, peering into the lake, and muttering to himself.

"Someone's slave, probably," said Paithan. "Got muddled and wandered off. Can't think why anyone would keep a slave as old and decrepit as that, though. Hey, there! Old man!" Paithan threw caution to Orn and careened down the hill.

The old man paid no attention. Picking up a long, wooden walking staff that had clearly seen better days, he began poking around the water!

Paithan could almost see the scaly body writhing up from the depths of the blue lake. His chest constricted, his lungs burned. "No! Old man! Father," he shouted, switching to human, which he spoke fluently, using the standard form of human address to any elderly male. "Father! Come away from there! Father!"

"Eh?" The old man turned, peering at Paithan with vague eyes. "Sonny? Is that you, boy?" He dropped the staff and flung wide his arms, the motion sending him staggering. "Come to my breast, Sonny! Come to your papa!"

Paithan tried to halt his own forward momentum in time to catch hold of the old man, toddling precariously on the shore. But the elf slipped in the wet grass, slid to his knees, and the old man, arms swinging wildly, toppled backward into the lake, landing with a splash.

Slavering jaws, lunging out of the water, snapping them both in two . . . Paithan plunged in after the old man, caught hold of him by something—perhaps his beard, perhaps a mouse-colored sleeve—and dragged him, sputtering and blowing, to the shore.

"Damn fine way for a son to treat his aged parent!" The old man glared at Paithan. "Knocking me into the lake!"

"I'm not your son, Fa— I mean, sir. And it was an accident."
Paithan tugged the old man along, pulling him up the hillside.
"Now, we really should get away from here! There's a dragon—"

The old man came to a dead stop. Paithan, caught off balance, almost fell over. He jerked on the thin arm, to get the old man moving again, but it was like trying to budge a wortle tree.

"Not without my hat," said the old man.

"To Orn with your hat!" Paithan ground his teeth. He looked fearfully back into the lake, expecting at any moment to see the water start to boil. "You doddering idiot! There's a drag—" He turned back to the old man, stared, then said in exasperation, "Your hat's on your head!"

"Don't lie to me, Sonny," said the old man peevishly. He leaned down and picked up his staff, and the hat slipped over his eyes. "Struck blind, by god!" he said in awed tones, stretching out groping hands.

"It's your hat!" Paithan leaped forward, grabbed the old man's hat and yanked it off his head. "Hat! Hat!" he cried, waving it in front of the old man's face.

"That's not mine," said the old man, staring at it suspiciously. "You've switched hats on me. Mine was in much better condition—"

"Come on!" cried Paithan, fighting back a crazed desire to laugh.

"My staff!" shrieked the old man, planting his feet firmly, refusing to move.

Paithan toyed with the idea of leaving the old man to take root in the moss if he wanted, but the elf couldn't watch a dragon devour anyone—even a human. Running back, Paithan retrieved the staff, stuck it in the old man's hand, and began to pull him toward the house.

The elf feared the old human might have difficulty making it back, for the way was long and uphill. Paithan heard the breath begin to whistle in his own lungs and his legs ached with the strain. But the old man appeared to have incredible stamina; he tottered along gamely, his staff thumping holes in the moss.

"I say, I think something's following us!" cried the old man, suddenly.

"There is?" Paithan whirled around.

"Where?" The old man swung his staff, narrowly missing knocking down Paithan. "I'll get him, by the gods—"

"Stop! It's all right!" The elf caught hold of the wildly swinging staff. "There's nothing there. I thought you said . . . something was following us."

"Well, if there isn't why in the name of all that's holy are you making me run up this confounded hill?"

"Because there's a dragon in the la—"

"The lake!" The old man's beard bristled, his bushy eyebrows stuck out in all directions. "So that's where he is! He dunked me in there deliberately!" The old man raised a clenched hand, shook his fist at the air in the direction of the water. "I'll fix you, you overgrown mud worm! Come out! Come out where I can get a look at you!" Dropping his staff, the old man began rolling up the sleeves of his sodden robes. "I'm ready. Yes, sirree-bob, I'm gonna cast a spell this time that'll knock out your eyeballs!"

"Wait a minute!" Paithan felt the sweat begin to chill on his body. "Are you saying, old man, that this dragon's . . . yours?"

"Mine! Of course, you're mine, aren't you, you slithering excuse for a reptile?"

"You mean, the dragon's under your control?" Paithan began to breathe more easily. "You must be a wizard."

"Must I?" The old man appeared highly startled at the news.

"You have to be a wizard and a powerful one at that to control a dragon."

"Well . . . er . . . you see, Sonny." The old man began to stroke his beard in some embarrassment. "That's sort of a question between us—the dragon and me."

"What's a question?" Paithan felt his stomach muscles begin to tighten.

"Er—who's in control. Not that *I* have any doubts, mind you! It's the—uh—dragon who keeps forgetting."

I was right. The old man's insane. I've got a dragon and an insane human on my hands. But what in Mother Peytin's holy name was this old fool doing in the lake?

"Where are you, you elongated toad?" The wizard continued to shout. "Come out! It's no use hiding! I'll find you—"

A shrill scream cut through the tirade.

"Aleatha!" cried Paithan, turning, staring up the hill.

The scream ended in a strangled choke.

"Thea, I'm coming!" The elf broke loose of his momentary paralysis and tore for the house.

"Hey, Sonny!" shouted the old man, glaring after him, arms akimbo. "Where do you think you're going with my hat?"

CHAPTER ♦ 6

EQUILAN,

LAKE ENTHIAL

♦

PAITHAN JOINED A STREAM OF MEN, LED BY LORD DURNDRUN, RUSH-
ing in the direction of the cry. Rounding the norinth wing of the
house, they came to a skidding halt. Aleatha stood immobile on
a small mossy knoll. Before her, its huge body between the
woman and the carriage house, was the dragon.

He was enormous. His head towered above the trees. His
body's full length was lost in the shadowy depths of the jungle.
He was wingless, for he lived all of his life in the dark depths of
the jungle floor, slithering around the boles of Pryan's gigantic
trees. Strong, taloned feet could tear through the thickest vegetation or strike down a man at a blow. His long tail whipped
behind him as he moved, cutting swaths through the jungle,
leaving trails that were well-known (and immensely feared) by
adventurers. His intelligent red eyes were fixed on the woman.

The dragon was not threatening Aleatha; his great jaws had
not parted, though the upper and lower fangs could be seen
protruding from the front of the mouth. A red tongue flicked in
and out between the teeth. The armed men watched, unmoving,
uncertain. Aleatha held very still.

The dragon cocked its head, gazing at her.

Paithan shoved his way to the front of the group. Lord
Durndrun was stealthily releasing the catch on a railbow. The
weapon awoke as Durndrun began raising the stock to his shoulder. The bolt in the rail was screeching, "Target? Target?"

"The dragon," Durndrun ordered.

"Dragon?" The bolt appeared alarmed, and was inclined to argue, a problem with intelligent weapons. "Please refer to owner's manual, section B, paragraph three. I quote, 'Not to be used against any foe larger than—' "

"Just go for the heart!"

"Which one?"

"What the devil do you think you're doing?" Paithan caught hold of the lord's elbow.

"I can get a good shot at the eyes—"

"Are you insane? You miss, and the dragon'll go for Aleatha!"

The lord was pale, his expression troubled, but he continued to make ready his railbow. "I'm an excellent shot, Paithan. Stand aside."

"I won't!"

"It's the only chance we have! Damn it, man, I don't like this any more than you do, but—"

"Excuse me, Sonny," came an irritated voice from behind. "But you're crumpling my hat!"

Paithan swore. He'd forgotten the old man, who was shoving his way through the crowd of tense, glowering men. "No respect for the elderly! Think we're all doddering old fools, don't you? Why I had a spell once that would have fried your socks off. Can't think of the name offhand. Fire bell? No that's not quite it. I have it—tire sale! No, doesn't sound right, either. I'll come up with it. And you, Sonny!" The old man was highly incensed. "Look what you've done to my hat!"

"Take the damn hat and—"

"Hush!" breathed Durndrun.

The dragon had slowly turned its head and was focusing on them. The red eyes narrowed.

"You!" the dragon snarled in a voice that rocked the foundations of the lord's house.

The old man was attempting to beat some sort of shape back into his battered hat. At the sound of the thundering "You!" he peered around bleary-eyed and eventually caught sight of the gigantic green head rearing upward, level with the treetops.

"Ah ha!" cried the old man, staggering backward. He pointed a shaking, accusing finger. "You overgrown frog! You tried to drown me!"

"Frog!"

The dragon's head shot upward, its front feet dug deep into the moss, shaking the ground. Aleatha stumbled and fell with a scream. Paithan and Lord Durndrun took advantage of the dragon's distraction to run to the woman's aid. Paithan crouched by her side, his arms around her. Lord Durndrun stood above her, his weapon raised. From the house came the wails of the women, certain that this was the end.

The dragon's head dove downward, the wind of its passing ripped the leaves from the trees. Most of the elves hurled themselves flat; a few of the bravest held their ground. Lord Durndrun fired a bolt. Shrieking in protest, it struck the green, iridescent scales, bounced off, landed on the moss, and slithered away in the undergrowth. The dragon, seemingly, didn't notice. His head stopped only a few feet from that of the old man.

"You sorry excuse for a wizard! You're damn right I tried to drown you! But now I've changed my mind. Drowning's too good for you, you moth-eaten relic! After I've dined on elf flesh, beginning with that toothsome blond appetizer over there, I'm going to rip the bones out of your skin one by one, starting with your little finger—"

"Oh, yeah?" shouted the old man. He jammed his hat on his head, threw his staff to the ground, and once again began rolling up his sleeves. "We'll see about that!"

"I'll fire now, while he's not looking," whispered Lord Durndrun. "Paithan, you and Aleatha make a run for it—"

"You're a fool, Durndrun! We can't fight that beast! Wait and see what the old man can do. He told me he controls the dragon!"

"Paithan!" Aleatha dug her nails into his arm. "He's a crazy old human. Listen to his lordship!"

"Shhh!"

The old man's voice was rising in a high-pitched quaver. Closing his eyes, he wiggled his fingers in the dragon's general direction and began to chant, swaying back and forth in time to the rhythm of his words.

The dragon's mouth parted, the wickedly sharp teeth glistened in the twilight, the tongue flicked dangerously.

Aleatha closed her eyes and buried her head in Lord Durndrun's shoulder, jostling the railbow, which squeaked in annoyance. The lord juggled the weapon, clumsily clasped his arm around the woman and held her tightly.

"You speak human! What's he saying, Paithan?"

When young I started seeking,
for love and things in dreaming
I set out with clouds a'streaming
and a hat upon my head.
I began with grave intention
hoping for divine intervention;
nothing could prepare me
for the things I learned instead.

At first I looked for battle
seeking mail and sword to rattle
but they herded us like cattle
and we never did see a fight.
I stood in fields for hours,
among the pikes and flowers;
I decided it was time to go
and snuck away at night.

I've been roamin' five and twenty,
seen war and king and shanty,
I've known handsome men aplenty
who've yet to kiss a girl.
Yes, I've roamed the whole world over,
seen men both drunk and sober
but I've never seen a man can
drink as much as Bonnie Earl.

Paithan gasped, gulped. "I'm—I'm not certain. I suppose it must—er—be magic!" He began looking around on the ground for a large tree branch, anything he could use as a weapon. He didn't think this was the time to tell the lord that the old man was attempting to spellbind a dragon by singing one of Thillia's most popular drinking songs.

I moved in royal places
a king took me to 's spaces,
to master courtly graces
and to learn of lordly might.
I took the good king's offer,
but emptied out his coffer,
and with loaded bags a'weigh with gold
I disappeared from sight.

In time I met a lady
in a spot all dark and shady,
with words I was quite handy
and we talked long into night.
That eve she let me bed her,
her fam'ly said to wed her,
so with a price put on my head
I left with morning's light.

I've been roamin' five and twenty,
seen war and king and shanty,
I've known handsome men aplenty
who've yet to kiss a girl.
Yes, I've roamed the whole world over,
seen men both drunk and sober
but I've never seen a man can
drink as much as Bonnie Earl.

"Blessed Orn!" breathed Lord Durndrun. "It's working!"

Paithan lifted his head, looked up in astonishment. The dragon's snout had begun to bob up and down in time to the music.

The old man continued singing, taking Bonnie Earl through innumerable verses. The elves remained frozen, afraid to move, afraid to break the spell. Aleatha and Lord Durndrun held each other a little closer. The dragon's eyelids drooped, the old man's voice softened. The creature seemed almost asleep when suddenly its eyes flew open, its head reared up.

The elves grabbed their weapons. Lord Durndrun pushed Aleatha behind him. Paithan lifted a tree branch.

"My god, sir!" cried the dragon, staring at the old man. "You're soaked through! What *have* you been doing?"

The old man looked sheepish. "Well, I—"

"You must change those wet clothes, sir, or you'll catch your death. A warm fire and a hot bath are requisite."

"I've had enough water—"

"If you please, sir. I know what's best." The dragon glanced about. "Who is the master of this fine house?"

Lord Durndrun shot a swift, questioning look at Paithan.

"Go along with it!" the young elf hissed.

"That—that would be me." The lord seemed considerably at a loss, wondering vaguely if etiquette dictated the proper way to introduce oneself to a large and slavering reptile. He decided to keep it short and to the point. "I—I'm Durndrun. L—lord Durndrun."

The red eyes fixed on the stammering knight. "I beg your pardon, My Lord. I apologize for interrupting your jollifications, but I know my duty and it is imperative that my wizard receive immediate attention. He's a frail old man—"

"Who're you calling frail, you fungus-ridden—"

"I trust my wizard is to be a guest in your house, My Lord?"

"Guest?" Lord Durndrun blinked, dazed. "Guest? Why, uh—"

"Of course, he's a guest!" snapped Paithan in a furious undertone.

"Oh, yes. I see your point," murmured the lord. He bowed. "I will be most honored to entertain—uh— What's his name?" he muttered aside.

"Blessed if I know!"

"Find out!"

Paithan sidled over to the old man. "Thank you for rescuing us—"

"Did you hear what he called me?" demanded the old man. "Frail! I'll frail him! I'll—"

"Sir! Please listen. Lord Durndrun, the gentleman standing over there, would like to invite you to stay with him at his house. If we knew your name—"

"Can't possibly."

Paithan was confused. "Can't possibly what?"

"Can't possibly stay with that fellow. I've made prior commitments."

"What *is* the delay?" demanded the dragon.

"I beg your pardon, sir?" Paithan cast an uneasy glance back at the beast. "I'm afraid I don't understand and, you see, we don't want to upset the—"

"Expected," stated the old man. "I'm expected somewhere else. Chap's house. I promised. And a wizard never breaks his word. Does terrible things to your nose."

"Perhaps you could tell me where. It's your dragon, you see. He seems—"

"Overprotective? A butler in a grade-B movie? Someone's Jewish mother? You got it," said the old man in gloomy tones. "Always happens when he's spellbound. Drives me crazy. I like him better the other way, but he has an irritating habit of eating people if I don't keep a leash on him."

"Sir!" cried Paithan desperately, seeing the dragon's eyes begin to glow red. "Where are you staying?"

"There, there, Sonny. Don't work yourself into a lather. You young people, always in a rush. Why didn't you just ask? Quindiniar. Some fellow calls himself Lenthan Quindiniar. He sent for me," added the old man with a lofty air. "Wanted—a human priest. Actually I'm not a priest. I'm a wizard. Priests were all out fund-raising when the message came through—"

"Orn's ears!" murmured Paithan. He had the strangest feeling that he was wandering about in a dream. If so, it was high time Calandra threw a glass of water in his face. He turned back to Lord Durndrun. "I'm—I'm sorry, My Lord. But the—er—gentleman has already made a prior commitment. He's going to be staying with . . . my father."

Aleatha began to laugh. Lord Durndrun patted her shoulder anxiously, for there was an hysterical edge to her laughter, but she only threw back her head and laughed louder.

The dragon decided apparently that the laughter pertained to him. The red eyes narrowed alarmingly.

"Thea! Stop it!" ordered Paithan. "Pull yourself together! We're not out of danger! I don't trust either of 'em. And I'm not sure who's crazier—the old man or his dragon!"

Aleatha wiped her streaming eyes. "Poor Callie!" She giggled. "Poor Callie!"

"I beg to remind you, gentlemen, that my wizard is standing

around in wet clothing!" thundered the dragon. "He will likely take a chill and he is subject to a weakness in the lungs."

"There's not a thing wrong with my lungs—"

"If you'll provide me with directions," continued the dragon, looking martyred, "I will go on ahead and draw a hot bath."

"No!" Paithan shouted. "That is—" He tried to think, but his brain was having a difficult time adjusting to the situation. Desperately, he turned to the old man. "We live on a hill overlooking the city. The sight of a dragon, coming on our people suddenly like this! . . . I don't mean to be rude, but couldn't you tell him to . . . well . . ."

"Go stick his head in the pantry?" The old man sighed. "It's worth a try. Here, you! Dragon."

"Sir."

"I can draw my own bath. And I never catch cold! Besides, you can't go galumping around the elves' city in that scaly carcass of yours. Scare the bejeebers outta them."

"Bejeebers, sir?" The dragon glared, tilted his head slightly.

"Never mind! Just"—the old man waved a gnarled hand—"take yourself off somewhere until I call for you."

"Very good, sir," the dragon answered in hurt tones. "If that is what you truly want."

"I do. I do. Now, go along."

"I have only your best interests at heart, sir."

"Yes, yes. I know."

"You mean a great deal to me, sir." The dragon began to move ponderously off into the jungle. Pausing, he swung his gigantic head around to face Paithan. "You will see to it, sir, that my wizard puts on his overshoes before going out in the damp?"

Paithan nodded, tongue-tied.

"And that he bundles up well and winds his scarf around his neck and keeps his hat pulled low over his ears? And that he has his warming drink first thing on awakening? My wizard, you see, suffers from irregularity—"

Paithan stiff-armed the old man, who was howling imprecations and making a run for the dragon. "My family and I will take good care of him. He is, after all, our honored guest."

Aleatha had buried her face in a handkerchief. It was difficult to tell if she was laughing or sobbing.

"Thank you, sir," said the dragon gravely. "I leave my wizard in your hands. Mind you take good care of him, or you won't enjoy the consequences."

The dragon's great forefeet dug downward into the moss, sending it rolling, and slowly slithered into the hole it had created. They could hear, from far below, the rending and snapping of huge tree limbs and, finally, a thud. The rumbling continued for several more moments, then all was still and silent. Hesitantly, tentatively, the birds began to chirp.

"Are we safe from him if he's down there?" Paithan asked the old man anxiously. "He isn't likely to break loose from the spell and come looking for trouble, is he?"

"No, no. No need to worry, Sonny. I'm a powerful wizard. Powerful! Why I had a spell once that—"

"Did you? How interesting. If you'll just come along with me, now, sir." Paithan steered the old man to the carriage house. The elf thought it best to leave this place as soon as possible. Besides, it seemed likely that the party was over. But, he had to admit, it'd been one of Durndrun's best. Sure to be talked about the rest of the social season.

The lord himself moved over to Aleatha, who was dabbing her eyes with her handkerchief. He extended his arm.

"May I escort you to the carriage?"

"If you like, My Lord," answered Aleatha, a pretty flush mantling her cheeks, sliding her fingers through the crook of his elbow.

"What would be a convenient time for me to call?" asked Durndrun in an undertone.

"Call, My Lord?"

"On your father," said the lord gravely. "I have something to ask him." He laid his hand over hers, pulled her close. "Something that concerns his daughter."

Aleatha glanced out of the corner of her eye back at the house. The dowager was standing in the window, watching them. The old lady had looked more pleased to see the dragon. Aleatha lowered her eyes, smiled coyly.

"Any time, My Lord. My father is always home and would be very honored to see you."

Paithan was assisting the old man into the carriage.

"I'm afraid I still don't know your name, sir," said the elf, taking a seat next to the wizard.

"You don't?" the old man asked, looking alarmed.

"No, sir. You haven't told me."

"Drat." The wizard stroked his beard. "I was rather hoping you would. You're sure you don't?"

"Yes, sir." Paithan glanced back uneasily, wishing his sister would hurry up. She and Lord Durndrun were, however, taking their time.

"Ah, well. Let's see." The old man muttered to himself. "Fiz—No, I can't use that. Furball. Doesn't seem quite dignified enough. I have it!" he shouted, smiting Paithan on the arm. "Zifnab!"

"Bless you!"

"No, no! My name! Zifnab! What's the matter, Sonny?" The old man glared, eyebrows bristling. "Something wrong with it?"

"Why, er, certainly not! It's . . . uh . . . a nice name. Really . . . nice. Oh, here you are, Thea!"

"Thank you, My Lord," she said, allowing Durndrun to hand her into the carriage. Taking her seat behind Paithan and the old man, she favored the knight with a smile.

"I would escort you to your home, my friends, but I fear I must go and look for the slaves. It seems that the cowardly wretches took off at the sight of the dragon. May dreams light your darktime. My respects to your father and your sister."

Lord Durndrun woke the drivehands, prodding them himself, and—with his own hands—gave the carriage a shove that started it on its way. Aleatha, glancing back, saw him standing, staring after her with a goggle-eyed gaze. She settled herself more comfortably in the carriage, smoothed out the folds of her dress.

"It looks as if you've done well for yourself, Thea," said Paithan, grinning, leaning over the seat to give his sister an affectionate jab in the ribs.

Aleatha reached up to arrange her disheveled hair. "Drat, I've left my hat behind. Ah, well. He can buy me a new one."

"When's the wedding?"

"As soon as possib—"

A snore interrupted her. Pursing her lips, she glanced in

some disgust at the old man, who had fallen fast asleep, his head lolling against Paithan's shoulder.

"Before the dowager has time to change her son's mind, eh?" The elf winked.

Aleatha arched her eyebrows. "She'll try, no doubt, but she won't succeed. My wedding will be—"

"Wedding?" Zifnab woke up with a violent start. "Wedding, did you say? Oh, no, my dear. I'm afraid that won't be possible. No time, you see."

"And why not, old one?" Aleatha asked, teasing, amusing herself. "Why won't there be time for a wedding?"

"Because, children," said the wizard and his tone suddenly changed, darkened, became sadly gentle, "I've come to announce the end of the world."

CHAPTER ♦ 7

TREETOPS,

EQUILAN

♦

"DEATH!" SAID THE OLD MAN, SHAKING HIS HEAD. "DOOM AND—ER—whatever comes after. Can't quite think . . ."

"Destruction?" suggested Paithan.

Zifnab gave him a grateful look. "Yes, destruction. Doom and destruction. Shocking! Shocking!" Reaching out a gnarled hand, the old man gripped Lenthan Quindiniar by the arm. "And you, sir, will be the one who leads his people forth!"

"I—I will?" said Lenthan, with a nervous glance at Calandra, positive she wouldn't let him. "Where shall I lead them?"

"Forth!" said Zifnab, gazing hungrily at a baked chicken. "Do you mind? Just a tad? Dabbling in the arcane, you know. Whets the appetite—"

Calandra sniffed, and said nothing.

"Callie, really." Paithan winked at his irate sister. "This man's our honored guest. Here, sir, allow me to pass it to you. Anything else? Some tohahs?"

"No, thank you—"

"Yes!" came a voice that was like the rumble of thunder stalking the ground.

The others at the table appeared alarmed. Zifnab cringed.

"You must eat your vegetables, sir." The voice seemed to rise up from the floor. "Think of your colon!"

A scream and piteous wailing emanated from the kitchen.

"There's the maid. Hysterics again," said Paithan, tossing aside his lapcloth and rising to his feet. He intended to escape before his sister figured out what was going on. "I'll just go—"

"Who said that?" Calandra grabbed his arm.

"—have a look, if you'd let loose—"

"Don't get so worked up, Callie," said Aleatha languidly. "It's only thunder."

"My colon's none of your damn business!" The old man shouted down at the floor. "I can't abide vegetables—"

"If it was *only* thunder"—Calandra's voice was heavily ironic—"then the wretch is discussing his colon with his shoes. He's a lunatic. Paithan, throw him out."

Lenthan shot a pleading glance at his son. Paithan looked sidelong at Aleatha, who shrugged and shook her head. The young elf picked up his lapcloth and subsided back into his chair.

"He's not crazy, Cal. He's talking to . . . uh . . . his dragon. And we can't throw him out, because the dragon wouldn't take it at all well."

"His dragon." Calandra pursed her lips, her small eyes narrowed. The entire family, as well as the visiting astrologer, who was seated at the far end of the table, knew this expression, known privately to younger brother and sister as "pinch-face." Calandra could be terrible, when she was in this mood.

Paithan kept his gaze on his plate, gathering together a small mound of food with his fork and punching a hole in it. Aleatha stared at her own reflection in the polished surface of the porcelain teapot, tilting her head slightly, admiring the sunlight on her fair hair. Lenthan attempted to disappear by ducking his head behind a vase of flowers. The astrologer comforted himself with a third helping of tohahs.

"That beast that terrorized Lord Durndrun's?" Calandra's gaze swept the table. "Do you mean to tell me you've brought it here? To my house?" Ice from her tone seemed to rime her face with white, much as the magical ice rimed the frosted wineglasses.

Paithan nudged his younger sister beneath the table with his foot, caught her eye. "I'll be leaving this soon, back on the road," he muttered beneath his breath.

"Soon I'll be mistress of my own house," Aleatha returned softly.

"Stop that whispering, you two. We'll all be murdered in our beds," cried Calandra, her fury mounting. The warmer her anger, the colder her tone. "I hope then, Paithan, you'll be pleased with yourself! And you, Thea, I've overheard you talking this nonsense about getting married . . ."

Calandra deliberately left the sentence unfinished.

No one moved, except the astrologer (shoveling buttered tohah into his mouth) and the old man. Apparently having no idea he was a bone of contention, he was calmly dismembering a baked chicken. No one spoke. They could hear, quite clearly, the musical chink of a mechanical petal "unfolding" the hour.

The silence grew uncomfortable. Paithan saw his father, hunched miserably in his chair, and thought again how feeble and gray he looked. Poor old man, he's got nothing else but his wacky delusions. Let him have 'em, after all. What harm is it? He decided to risk his sister's wrath.

"Uh, Zifnab, where did you say father was leading . . . er . . . his people?"

Calandra glared at him, but, as Paithan had hoped, his father perked up. "Yes, where?" Lenthan asked shyly, blushing.

The old man raised a chicken leg toward heaven.

"The roof?" Lenthan was somewhat confused.

The old man raised the chicken leg higher.

"Heaven? The stars?"

Zifnab nodded, momentarily unable to speak. Bits of chicken dribbled down his beard.

"My rockets! I knew it! Did you hear that, Elixnoir?" Lenthan turned to the elven astrologer, who had left off eating and was glowering at the human.

"My dear Lenthan, please consider this rationally. Your rockets are quite marvelous and we're making considerable progress in sending them above treetop level but to talk of them carrying people to the stars! Let me explain. Here is a model of our world according to the legends handed down to us by the ancients and confirmed by our own observations. Hand me that pricklepear. Now, this"—he held up the pricklepear—"is Pryan and this is our sun."

Elixnoir glanced about, momentarily at a loss for a sun.

"One sun," said Paithan, picking up a kumquat.

"Thank you," said the astrologer. "Would you mind—I'm running out of hands."

"Not at all." Paithan was enjoying himself hugely. He didn't dare look at Aleatha, or he knew he'd break out laughing. Acting on Elixnoir's instructions, he gravely positioned the kumquat a short distance from the pricklepear.

"Now this"—the astrologer lifted a sugar cube. Holding it a long distance from the kumquat, he began to rotate it around the pricklepear—"represents one of the stars. Just look at how far it is from our world! You can imagine what an enormous amount of distance you would have to travel . . ."

"At least seven kumquats," murmured Paithan to his sister.

"He was quick enough to believe in Father when it meant a free meal," Aleatha returned coolly.

"Lenthan!" The astrologer looked severe, pointed at Zifnab. "This man is a humbug! I—"

"Who are you calling *humbug*?"

The dragon's voice shook the house. Wine sloshed from glasses, spilling over the lace tablecloth. Small, fragile items slid from end tables and tumbled to the floor. From the study came a thud, a bookcase toppling. Aleatha glanced out a window, saw a girl running, shrieking, from the kitchen.

"I don't believe you'll have to worry about the scullery maid any longer, Cal."

"This is intolerable." Calandra rose to her feet. The frost that rimed her nose had spread across her face, freezing the features and freezing the blood of those who saw her. Her thin, spare body seemed all sharp angles and every angle liable to hurt anyone who got near her. Lenthan cowered visibly. Paithan, lips twitching, concentrated on folding his lapcloth into a cocked hat. Aleatha sighed and drummed her nails on the table.

"Father," spoke Calandra in awful tones, "when dinner is concluded I want that old man and his . . . his . . ."

"Careful, Cal," suggested Paithan, not looking up. "You'll have the house down around our ears."

"I want them out of my house!" Calandra's hands gripped the back of her chair, the knuckles white. Her body shook with the chill wind of her ire, the only chill wind that blew in the tropical land. "Old man!" Her voice rose shrilly. "Do you hear me?"

"Eh?" Zifnab glanced around. Seeing his hostess, he smiled at her benignly and shook his head. "No, thank you, my dear. Couldn't possibly eat another bite. What's for dessert?"

Paithan gave a half-giggle, smothered the other half in his lapcloth.

Calandra turned, and stormed from the room, her skirts crackling about her ankles.

"Now, Cal," Paithan called in conciliatory tones. "I'm sorry. I didn't mean to laugh—"

A door slammed.

"Actually, you know, Lenthan, old fellow," said Zifnab, gesturing with the chicken leg, which he had picked clean, "we won't be using your rockets at all. No, they're not nearly big enough. We'll have a lot of people to transport, you see, and that'll take a large vessel. Very large." He tapped himself thoughtfully on the nose with the bone. "And, as what's-his-name with the collar says, it's a long way to the stars."

"If you will excuse me, Quindiniar," said the elven astrologer, rising to his feet, his eyes flashing fire. "I will be taking my leave, as well."

"—especially since it looks as if dessert's canceled," said Aleatha, her voice pitched so that the astrologer would be certain to hear. He did; his collar tips quivered, his nose achieved a seemingly impossible angle.

"But don't worry," continued Zifnab, placidly ignoring the commotion around him. "We'll have a ship—a big sucker. It'll land right smack-dab in the backyard and it'll have a man to fly it. Young man. Owns a dog. Very quiet—not the dog, the man. Something funny about his hands, though. Always keeps them bandaged. That's the reason why we have to continue firing off the rockets, you see. Most important, your rockets."

"They are?" Lenthan was still confused.

"I'm leaving!" stated the astrologer.

"Promises, promises." Paithan sighed, sipped at his wine.

"Yes, of course, rockets are important. Otherwise how's *he* going to find us?" demanded the old man.

"He who?" inquired Paithan.

"The he who has the ship. Pay attention!" snapped Zifnab testily.

"Oh, *that* he who." Paithan leaned over to his sister. "He owns a dog," he said confidentially.

"You see, Lenthan—may I call you Lenthan?" inquired the old man politely. "You see, Lenthan, we need a big ship because your wife will want to see all the children again. Been a long time, you know. And they've grown so much."

"What?" Lenthan's eyes flared open, his cheeks paled. He clasped a trembling hand over his heart. "What did you say? My wife!"

"Blasphemy!" cried the astrologer.

The soft whir of the fans and the slight rustling of the feathery blades were the room's only sounds. Paithan had set his lapcloth on his plate and was staring down at it, frowning.

"For once I agree with that fool." Aleatha rose to her feet and glided over to stand behind her father's chair, her hands on his shoulders.

"Papa," she said, a tenderness in her voice that no one else in the family ever heard, "it's been a tiring day. Don't you think you should go to bed?"

"No, my dear. I'm not the least bit tired." Lenthan had not taken his eyes from the old man. "Please, sir, what did you say about my wife?"

Zifnab didn't appear to hear him. During the ensuing quiet, the old man's head had slumped forward, his bearded chin rested on his breast, his eyes closed. He gave a muffled snore.

Lenthan reached out his hand. "Zifnab—"

"Papa, please!" Aleatha closed her soft fingers over her father's blacked and burn-scarred hand. "Our guest is exhausted. Paithan, call for the servants to help the wizard to his room."

Brother and sister exchanged glances, both having the same idea. *With any luck we can smuggle him out of the house tonight. Maybe feed him to his own dragon. Then, in the morning, when he's gone, we'll be able to convince Father that he was nothing but an insane old human.*

"Sir . . . " said Lenthan, shaking off his daughter's hand and catching hold of the old man's. "Zifnab!"

The old man jerked awake. "Who?" he demanded, glancing around bleary-eyed. "Where?"

"Papa!"

"Hush, my dear. Go run along and play, there's a good girl.

Papa's busy, right now. Now, sir, you were talking about my wife—"

Aleatha looked pleadingly at Paithan. Her brother could only shrug. Biting her lip, fighting back tears, Aleatha gave her father's shoulder a gentle pat, then fled from the room. Once out of sight in the drawing room, she pressed her hand over her mouth, sobbing. . . .

. . . The child sat outside the door to her mother's bedchamber. The little girl was alone; she'd been alone for the last three days and she was growing more and more frightened. Paithan'd been sent away to stay with relatives.

"The boy is too rambunctious," Aleatha had heard someone say. "The house must be kept quiet." And so Paithan had gone.

Now there was no one for her to talk to, no one to pay any attention to her. She wanted her mother—the beautiful mother, who played with her and sang to her—but they wouldn't let her go inside her mother's room. Strange people filled the house—healers with their baskets of funny-smelling plants, astrologers who stood staring out the windows into the sky.

The house was quiet, so dreadfully quiet. The servants wept while they worked, wiping their eyes on the tips of their aprons. One of them, seeing Aleatha sitting in the hallway, said that someone should really be doing something about the child, but no one ever did.

Whenever the door to her mother's room opened, Aleatha jumped to her feet and tried to go inside, but whoever was coming out—generally a healer or his assistant—would shoo the girl back.

"But I want to see Mama!"

"Your mama is very sick. She must stay quiet. You don't want to worry her, do you?"

"I wouldn't worry her." Aleatha knew she wouldn't. She could be quiet. She'd been quiet for three days. Her mother must miss her terribly. Who was combing out Mama's lovely flaxen hair? That was Aleatha's special task, one she performed every morning. She was careful not to tug on the tangles, but unraveled them gently, using the tortoiseshell comb with the ivory rosebuds that had been Mama's wedding present.

But the door remained shut and always locked. Try as she might, Aleatha couldn't get inside.

And then one darktime the door opened, and it didn't shut again. Aleatha knew, now, she could go inside but now she was afraid.

"Papa?" She questioned the man standing in the door, not recognizing him.

Lenthan didn't look at her. He wasn't looking at anything. His eyes were dull, his cheeks sagged, his step faltered. Suddenly, with a violent sob, he crumpled to the floor, and lay still and unmoving. Healers, hurrying out the door, lifted him in their arms and carried him down the hall to his own bedchamber.

Aleatha pressed back against the wall.

"Mama!" she whimpered. "I want Mama!"

Callie stepped out into the hall. She was the first to notice the child.

"Mama's gone, Thea," Calandra said. She was pale, but composed. Her eyes were dry. "We're alone. . . ."

Alone. Alone. No, not again. Not ever.

Aleatha glanced frantically around the empty room in which she was standing, hurried back into the dining room, but no one was there.

"Paithan!" she cried, running up the stairs. "Calandra!"

Light from her sister's study streamed out beneath the door. Aleatha made a dart for it. The door opened, and Paithan stepped out. His usually cheerful face was grim. Seeing Aleatha, he smiled ruefully.

"I . . . I was looking for you, Pait." Aleatha felt calmer. She put her chilly hands to her burning cheeks to cool them, bring back the becoming pallor. "Bad time?"

"Yeah, pretty bad." Paithan smiled wanly.

"Come take a walk with me. Through the garden."

"Sorry, Thea. I've got to pack. Cal's sending me off tomorrow."

"Tomorrow!" Aleatha frowned, displeased. "But, you can't! Lord Durndrun's coming to talk to Papa and then there'll be the engagement parties and you simply have to be here—"

"Can't be helped, Thea." Paithan leaned down and kissed her cheek. "Business's business, you know." He started off down the hall, heading for his room. "Oh," he added, turning back.

"A word to the wise. Don't go in there now." He nodded his head in the direction of Calandra's study.

Aleatha withdrew her hand slowly from the door handle. Hidden beneath the silky folds of her gown, the fingers clenched.

"Sweet sombertime, Thea," said Paithan. He entered his room and shut the door.

An explosion, coming from the back of the house, set the windows rattling. Aleatha looked out, saw her father and the old man in the garden, gleefully setting off rockets. She could hear, from behind the closed door of her sister's study, the rustle of Cal's skirts, the tap, tap of her high-heeled, tight-laced shoes. Her sister was pacing. A bad sign. No, as Paithan said, it would not do to interrupt Calandra's thoughts.

Moving over to the window, Aleatha saw the human slave, lounging at his post near the carriage house, enjoying the rocket bursts. As she watched, she saw him stretch his arms above his head, yawning. Muscles rippled across his bare back. He began to whistle, a barbaric habit among humans. No one would use the carriage this late into shadow hour. He was due to go off-duty soon, when the storm began.

Aleatha hurried down the hall to her own room. Stepping inside, she glanced into her mirror, smoothing and arranging the luxuriant hair. Catching up a shawl, she draped it over her shoulders and, smiling once again, lightly glided down the stairs.

Paithan started on his journey early the following mistymorne. He was setting off alone, planning to join up with the baggage train on the outskirts of Equilan. Calandra was up to see him away. Arms folded tightly across her chest, she regarded him with a stern, cold, and forbidding air. Her humor had not improved during the night. The two were alone. If Aleatha was ever up at this time of day, it was only because she hadn't yet been to bed.

"Now, mind, Paithan. Keep on eye on the slaves when you cross the border. You know those beasts will run the moment they get a whiff of their own kind. I expect we'll lose a few; can't be helped. But keep our losses to the minimum. Follow the back routes and stay away from civilized lands if possible. They'll be less likely to run if there's no city within easy reach."

"Sure, Callie." Paithan, having made numerous trips to Thillia, knew more about the matter than his sister. She gave him this same speech every time he departed, until it had become a ritual between them. The easygoing elf listened and smiled and nodded, knowing that giving these instructions eased his sister's mind and made her feel that she retained some control over this end of the business.

"Keep sharp watch on this Roland character. I don't trust him."

"You don't trust any humans, Cal."

"At least I *knew* our other dealers were dishonest. I knew *how* they'd try to cheat us. I don't know this Roland and his wife. I'd have preferred doing business with our regular customers but these two came in with the highest bid. Make certain you get the cash before you turn over one single blade, Pait, and check to see that the money's real and not counterfeit."

"Yes, Cal." Paithan relaxed, and leaned on a fence post. This would go on for some time. He could have told his sister that most humans were honest to the point of imbecility, but he knew she'd never believe him.

"Convert the cash into raw materials as soon as you can. You've got the list of what we need, don't lose it. And make certain the bladewood is good quality, not like that stuff Quintin brought in. We had to throw three-fifths of it out."

"Have I ever brought you a bad shipment, Cal?" Paithan smiled at his sister.

"No. Just don't start." Calandra felt imaginary strands of hair coming loose from their tight coil. She smoothed them back into place, giving the hair pins a vicious jab. "Everything's going wrong these days. It's bad enough that I have Father on my hands, now I've got some insane old human, too! To say nothing of Aleatha and this travesty of a wedding—"

Paithan reached out, put his hands on his older sister's bony shoulders. "Let Thea do what she wants, Cal. Durndrun's a nice enough chap. At least he's not after her for her money—"

"Humpf!" Calandra sniffed, twitching away from her brother's touch.

"Let her marry the fellow, Cal—"

"Let her!" Calandra exploded. "I'll have little enough to say about it, you can be sure of that! Oh, it's all very well for you to stand there and grin, Paithan Quindiniar, but you won't be here to face the scandal. This marriage will be the talk of the season. I hear the dowager's taken to her bed over the news. I've no doubt she'll drag in the queen. And I'll be the one to deal with it. Father, of course, is less than useless."

"What's that, my dear?" came a mild voice behind them.

Lenthan Quindiniar stood in the doorway, the old man beside him.

"I said you'll be less than useless in dealing with Aleatha and this insane notion of hers—marrying Lord Durndrun," Calandra snapped, in no mood to humor her parent.

"But why shouldn't they get married? If they love each other—"

"Love! Thea?" Paithan burst out laughing. Noting the confused look on his father's face and the scowl on his sister's, the young elf decided it was high time to hit the bridges. "I've got to run. Quintin'll think I've fallen through the moss or been eaten by a dragon." Leaning over, the elf kissed his sister on her cold and withered cheek. "You will let Thea have her way in this, won't you?"

"I don't see that I've much choice. She's been having her way in everything since Mother died. Remember what I've told you and have a safe trip." Calandra pursed her lips, pecked Paithan's chin. The kiss was nearly as sharp as a bird's beak, and he had to restrain himself from rubbing his skin.

"Father, good-bye." The elf shook hands. "Good luck with the rockets."

Lenthan brightened visibly. "Did you see the ones we set off last night? Brilliant bursts of fire above the treetops. I attained real altitude. I'll bet people could see the blasts all the way to Thillia."

"I'm sure they could, sir," agreed Paithan. He turned to the old man. "Zifnab—"

"Where?" The old man whipped about.

Paithan cleared his throat, kept a straight face. "No, no, sir. I mean you. Your name." The elf held out his hand. "Remember? Zifnab?"

"Ah, pleased to meet you, Zifnab," said the old man, shaking hands. "You know, though, that name sure sounds familiar. Are we related?"

Calandra gave him a shove with her hand. "You better get going, Pait."

"Tell Thea good-bye for me!" Paithan said.

His sister snorted, shook her head, her face grim.

"Have a good trip, Son," said Lenthan in a wistful tone. "You know, sometimes I think maybe I should go out on the road. I think I might enjoy it. . . ."

Seeing Calandra's eyes narrow, Paithan struck in hastily, "You let me handle the travel for you, Father. You've got to stay here and work on your rockets. Leading the people forth, and all that."

"Yes, you're right," said Lenthan with an air of self-importance. "I had better get started working on that, right now. Are you coming, Zifnab?"

"What? Oh, you talking to me? Yes, yes, my dear fellow. Be along in a jiffy. You might want to increase the amount of sinktree ash. I think we'll achieve greater lift."

"Yes, of course! Why didn't I think of that!" Lenthan beamed, waved vaguely at his son, and hurried into the house.

"Probably won't have any eyebrows left," muttered the old man. "But we'll achieve greater lift. Well, you're off, are you?"

"Yes, sir." Paithan grinned, and whispered confidentially, "Mind you don't let any of that death, doom, and destruction start without me."

"I won't." The old man gazed at him with eyes that were suddenly, unnervingly, shrewd and cunning. He jabbed a gnarled finger in Paithan's chest. "Doom will come back with *you*!"

CHAPTER ♦ 8

THE

NEXUS

♦

HAPLO WALKED SLOWLY AROUND THE SHIP, INSPECTING IT CAREFULLY to make certain all was in readiness for his flight. He did not, as had the original builders and masters of the dragonship, inspect the guide ropes and the rigging, the cables that controlled the gigantic wings. He looked intently at the wooden hull, but he wasn't checking the caulking. He ran his hands over the skin on the wings, but he wasn't searching for rips or tears. He studied, instead, strange and elaborate symbols that had been carved, burned, stitched, and painted on the wings and the outside of the ship.

Every conceivable inch was covered with the fantastic designs—whorls and spirals; straight lines and curved; dots and dashes; zigzags, circles, and squares. Passing his hand over the sigla, the Patryn murmured to himself, reciting the runes. The sigla would not only protect his ship, the sigla would fly it.

The elves who had built the vessel—named *Dragon Wing* in honor of Haplo's journey to the world of Arianus—would not have recognized their handiwork. Haplo's own ship had been destroyed on his previous entry through Death's Gate. He had commandeered the elven ship on Arianus. Due to pursuit by an ancient foe, he had been forced to leave Arianus in haste and had inscribed only those runes absolutely necessary to his survival (and that of his young passenger) through Death's Gate. Once safely in the Nexus, however, the Patryn had been able to expend both time and magic on modifying the vessel to his own specifications.

The ship, designed by the elves of the Tribus Empire, had originally utilized elven magic combined with mechanics. Being extraordinarily strong in his own magic, the Patryn did away completely with the mechanics. Haplo cleared the galley of the confused tangle of rigging and the harnesses worn by the slaves who operated the wings. He left the wings themselves outspread, and embroidered and painted runes on the dragonskin to provide lift, stability, speed, and protection. Runes strengthened the wooden hull; no force existed that was strong enough to crush it or stave it in. Sigla etched into the glass windows of the bridge prevented the glass from cracking while, at the same time, permitting an unobstructed view of the world beyond.

Haplo moved inside through the aft hatch, walked the ship's passageways until he came to the bridge. Here, he gazed about in satisfaction, sensing the full power of the runes come to a focus, converge at this point.

He had junked all the elaborate machines devised by the elves to aid in navigation and steering. The bridge, located in the dragon's "breast," was now a large, spacious chamber, empty except for a comfortable chair and a round, obsidian globe resting on the deck.

Haplo walked over to the globe, crouched down to inspect it critically. He was careful not to touch it. The runes carved into the obsidian's surface were so extremely sensitive that even a whisper of breath across them might activate the magic and launch the vessel prematurely.

The Patryn studied the sigla, going over the magic in his mind. The flight, navigation, and protection spells were complex. It took him hours to run through the entire recitation, and he was stiff and sore from lack of movement at the conclusion. But he was satisfied, he had not found a single flaw.

Haplo stood up, grunting, and flexed his aching muscles. Seating himself in the chair, he looked out upon the city he would soon be leaving. A tongue swiped wetly across his hand.

"What is it, boy?" Haplo glanced down at a nondescript, gangly black dog with white markings. "Think I forgot you?"

The dog grinned and wagged its tail. Bored, it had fallen asleep during the inspection of the steering stone and was pleased to have its master pay attention to it again. White eyebrows, slanting above clear brown eyes, gave the animal an unusually intelligent expression. Haplo stroked the dog's silky ears, gazed unseeing out at the world spread before him. . . .

. . . The Lord of the Nexus walked the streets of his world—a world built for him by his enemies, precious to him because of that very fact. Every finely chiseled marble pillar, every towering granite spire, every graceful minaret or sleek temple dome was a monument to the Sartan, a monument to irony. The lord was fond of walking among them and laughing silently to himself.

The lord did not often laugh aloud. It is a noticeable trait among those imprisoned in the Labyrinth that they rarely laugh and when they do, the laughter never brightens their eyes. Even those who have escaped the hellish prison and have entered the wondrous realm of the Nexus do not laugh. Upon their arrival through the Last Gate, they are met by the Lord of the Nexus, who was the first to escape. He says to them only two words.

"Never forget."

The Patryns do not forget. They do not forget those of their race still trapped within the Labyrinth. They do not forget friends and family who died by the violence of magic gone paranoid. They do not forget the wounds they themselves suffered. They, too, laugh silently when they walk the streets of the Nexus. And when they meet their lord, they bow before him in reverence. He is the only one of them who dares go back into the Labyrinth.

And even for him, the return is not easy.

No one knows the lord's background. He never speaks of it, and he is a man not easily approached or questioned. No one knows his age, although it is speculated, from certain things he has said, to be well beyond ninety gates.[1] The lord is a man of keen, cold, sharp intelligence His skills in magic are held in awe

---

[1]Anciently, in the Labyrinth, a person's age was calculated by how many Gates he or she had passed in the attempt to escape. This system was later standardized by the Lord of the Nexus to enable him to keep accurate records regarding the Patryn's population. A person emerging from the Nexus is questioned extensively and, from what details he or she provides, an age is determined and assigned to them by their lord.

by his people, whose own skills would rank them as demigods in the worlds beyond. He has been back to the Labyrinth many, many times since his escape, reentering that hell to carve out safe havens for his people with his magic. And each time, before he enters, this cold and calculating man feels a tremor shake his body. It takes an effort of will for him to go back through that Last Gate. There is always the fear, deep in his mind, that this time the Labyrinth will win. This time it will destroy him. This time, he will never find his way back out.

That day, the lord stood near the Last Gate. Surrounding him were his people, Patryns who had already escaped. Their bodies covered with the tattooed runes that were shield, armor, and weapon, a few had decided that this time they would reenter the Labyrinth in company with their lord.

He said nothing to them, but accepted their presence. Walking to the Gate that was carved of jet, he placed his hands upon a sigil he himself had inscribed. The rune glowed blue at his touch, the sigla tattooed upon the backs of his hands glowed blue in answer and the Gate, that was never meant to open inward but only outward, fell back at the lord's command.

Ahead lay the weird and warped, ever-changing, deadly vistas of the Labyrinth.

The lord glanced around at those who stood near him. All eyes were fixed on the Labyrinth. The lord saw faces lose the color of life, he saw hands clench to fists, sweat trickle down rune-covered skin.

"Who will enter with me?" he asked.

He looked at each one. Each person tried to meet the lord's eyes, each person failed and eventually lowered his gaze. Some sought valiantly to step forward, but muscle and sinew cannot act without the mind's will, and the minds of those men and women were overcome with remembered terror. Shaking their heads, many of them weeping openly, they turned away.

Their lord walked up to them and laid his hands soothingly upon them. "Do not be ashamed of your fear. Use it, for it is strength. Long ago, we sought to conquer the world, to rule over those weak races not capable of ruling themselves. Our strength and our numbers were great and we had nearly succeeded in our goal. The only way the Sartan could defeat us was to sunder the world itself, sundering it into four separate parts. Divided by the chaos, we fell to the Sartan's might, and they locked us away in a prison of their own creation—the Labyrinth. Their 'hope' was that we would come out of it 'rehabilitated.'

"We have come out, but the terrible hardships we endured did not soften and weaken us as our enemies planned. The fire through which we passed forged us into sharp, cold steel. We are a blade to cut through our enemies, we are a blade that will win a crown.

"Go back. Go back to your duties. Keep always before you the thought of what will come when we return to the worlds. Keep always behind you the memory of what was."

The Patryns, comforted, were no longer ashamed. They watched their lord enter the Labyrinth, watched him enter the Gate with firm, unfaltering step, and they honored and worshipped him as a god.

The Gate started to swing shut on him. The lord halted it with a sharp command. He had found, lying near the Gate, stretched prone on the ground, a young man. The muscular, sigil-tattooed body bore the marks of terrible wounds—wounds that the young man had healed by his own magic, apparently, but which had almost drained him of his life. The lord, examining the young Patryn anxiously, could not see any sign that he was breathing.

Stooping, reaching out his hand to the young man's neck to feel for a pulse, the lord was brought up short by a low growling sound. A shaggy head rose up from near the young man's shoulder.

A dog, the lord saw in astonishment.

The animal itself had suffered serious injury. Though its growl was menacing and it was attempting valiantly to protect the young man, it could not hold up its head. The muzzle sank down feebly onto bloodied paws. But the growl continued.

"If you harm him," it seemed to say, "somehow, someway, I'll find the strength to tear you apart."

The lord, smiling slightly—a rare thing for him—reached out gently and stroked the dog's soft fur.

"Be at ease, small brother. I mean your master no harm."

The dog allowed itself to be persuaded and, crawling on its belly, managed to lift its head and nuzzle the young man's neck. The touch of the cold nose roused the Patryn. He glanced up, saw the strange man bending over him and, with the instinct and will that had kept him alive, struggled to stand.

"You need no weapon against me, my son," said the lord. "You stand at the Last Gate. Beyond is a new world, one of peace, one of safety. I am its lord. I welcome you."

The young man had made it to his hands and knees. Swaying weakly, he lifted his head and stared through the Gate. His eyes were glazed, he could see little of the wonders of the world. But a slow smile spread across his face.

"I've made it!" he whispered hoarsely, through blood-caked lips. "I've beaten them!"

"Such were my words when I stood before this Gate. What are you called?"

The young man swallowed, coughed before he could reply. "Haplo."

"A fitting name." The lord put his arms around the young man's shoulders. "Here, let me help you."

To the lord's amazement, Haplo thrust him away. "No. I want to walk . . . through . . . on my own."

The lord said nothing, his smile broadened. He rose to his feet and stood aside. Gritting his teeth against the pain, Haplo struggled to stand upright. He paused a moment, swaying with dizziness. The lord, fearing he would fall, took a step forward, but Haplo warded him off with outstretched hand.

"Dog," he said in a cracked voice. "To me."

The animal rose weakly and limped over to its master. Haplo placed his hand upon the animal's head, steadying himself. The dog stood patiently, its eyes fixed upon Haplo.

"Let's go," said the young man.

Together, step by faltering step, they walked toward the Gate. The Lord of the Nexus, marveling, came behind. The Patryns on the other side, seeing the young man emerge, did not applaud or cheer, but awarded him respectful silence. None offered to help him, though each saw that every movement caused the young man obvious pain. They all knew what it meant to walk through that last gate by oneself, or aided only by a trusted friend.

Haplo stood in the Nexus, blinking under the dazzling sun. Sighing, he keeled over. The dog, whimpering, licked his master's face.

Hastening to the young man's side, the lord knelt down. Haplo was still conscious. The lord took hold of the pale, cold hand.

"Never forget!" whispered the lord, pressing the hand close to his chest.

Haplo looked up at the Lord of the Nexus and grinned. . . .

"Well, dog," said the Patryn, glancing around, giving his ship one last inspection, "I think we're ready. How about it, boy? You ready?"

The animal's ears pricked. It barked once, loudly.

"Good, good. We have My Lord's blessing and his final instructions. Now, let's see how this bird flies."

Reaching out, he held his hands over the steering stone and began to recite the first runes. The stone rose up from the deck, supported by magic, and came to rest beneath Haplo's palms. Blue light welled up through his fingers, matched by red light glowing from the runes on his hands.

Haplo sent his being into the ship, poured his magic into the hull, felt it seep like blood into the dragonskin sails, carrying life and power to guide and control. His mind lifted and it brought the ship with him. Slowly, the vessel began to rise from the ground.

Guiding it with his eyes, his thoughts, his magic, Haplo set sail into the air, granting the ship more speed than its original builders had ever imagined, and flew up and over the Nexus. Crouched at its master's feet, the dog sighed and resigned itself to the journey. Perhaps it remembered its first trip through Death's Gate, a trip that had very nearly proved fatal.

Haplo tested his craft, experimented with it. Flying leisurely over the Nexus, he enjoyed the unusual view of the city from a bird's eye (or dragon's eye) vantage.

The Nexus was a remarkable creation, a marvel of construction. Broad, tree-lined boulevards stretched out like spokes of a wheel from a center point to the dimly seen horizon of the far-off Boundary. Fabulous buildings of crystal and marble, steel and granite, adorned the streets. Parks and gardens, lakes and ponds provided places of quiet beauty in which to walk, to think, to reflect. Far away, near the Boundary, stretched green, rolling hills and fields, ready for the planting.

No farmers plowed that soil, however. No people lingered in the parks. No traffic filled the city streets. The fields, the parks, the avenues, the buildings stood empty, lifeless, waiting.

Haplo steered the ship around the center point of the Nexus, a crystal-spired building—the tallest in the land—which his lord had taken for his palace. Within the crystal spires, the Lord of the Nexus had come across the books left behind by the Sartan, books that told of the Sundering, the forming of the four worlds. Books that spoke of the imprisoning of the Patryns, of the Sartan's hope for their enemies' "salvation." The Lord of the Nexus had taught himself to read the books and so had discovered the Sartan's treachery that had doomed his people to torment. Reading the books, the lord had developed his plan of revenge. Haplo dipped the ship's wings in a gesture of respect to his lord.

The Sartan had intended the Patryns to occupy this wondrous world—after their "rehabilitation," of course. Haplo smiled, settled himself more comfortably in his chair. He let go of the steering stone, allowing the ship to drift with his own thoughts. Soon the Nexus would be populated, but not only by Patryns. Soon the Nexus would be home to elves, humans, and dwarves—the lesser races. Once these people had been transported back through the Death's Gate, the Lord of the Nexus would destroy the four misbegotten worlds created by the Sartan, return everything to the old order. Except, that the Patryns would rule, as was their right.

One of Haplo's tasks on his journeys of investigation was to see if any of the Sartan inhabited the four new worlds. Haplo found himself hoping he discovered more of them—more at least than Alfred, that one pitiful excuse for a demigod he'd confronted on Arianus. He wanted the entire race of Sartan alive, witnesses to their own crushing downfall.

"And after the Sartan have seen all they built fall into ruin, after they have seen the people they hoped to rule come under our sway, then will come the time of retribution. We will send *them* into the Labyrinth."

Haplo's gaze shifted to the red-streaked, black swirl of chaos just visible out the far side of the window. Horror-tinged memories reached out from the clouds to touch him with their skeletal hands. He beat them back, using hatred for his weapon. In place of himself, he watched the Sartan struggle, saw them defeated where he had triumphed, watched them die where he had escaped alive.

The dog's sharp, warning bark shook him from his grim reverie. Haplo saw that, absorbed in his thoughts of revenge, he'd almost flown into the Labyrinth. Hastily, he placed his hands on the steering stone and wrenched the ship around. *Dragon Wing* sailed into the blue sky of the Nexus, free of the grasping tendrils of evil magic that had sought to claim it.

Haplo turned his eyes and thoughts ahead to the starless sky, steering for the place of passage, steering for Death's Gate.

CHAPTER ◆ 9

CAHNDAR TO ESTPORT,

EQUILAN

◆

PAITHAN HAD A GREAT DEAL OF WORK TO DO MAKING HIS CARAvan ready for travel, and the old man's words of doom slipped from his mind. He met Quintin, his foreman, at the city limits of Cahndar—the Queen's City. The two elves inspected the baggage train, making certain the railbows, boltarches, and raztars, packed away in baskets, were attached securely to the tyros.[1] Opening the packs, Paithan inspected the toys that had been spread over the top, taking care to note if he could see any sign of the weapons hidden beneath. Everything appeared satisfactory. The young elf congratulated Quintin on a job well done and promised to recommend the foreman to his sister.

By the time Paithan and his caravan were ready to start, the hour flowers were indicating that toiltime was well advanced and it would soon be midcycle. Taking his place at the head of the line, Paithan told the overseer to begin the march. Quintin mounted the lead tyro, climbing into the saddle between the horns. With much cajoling and flattering, the slaves persuaded the other tyros to crawl into line behind their leader, and the

---

[1] A gigantic spider with a shelled body, the tyro has eight legs. Six are used for tree and web climbing, the two front legs each end in a clawed "hand" that is used for lifting and manipulation. Cargo is mounted on the back of the thorax between the leg joints.

caravan plunged into the jungle lands, soon leaving civilization far behind.

Paithan set a swift pace and the caravan made good traveling time. The trails between the human and elven lands are well tended, if somewhat treacherous. Trade between the realms is lucrative business. Human lands are rich in raw materials—teakwood, bladewood, cutvine, foodstuffs. The elves are adept at turning these resources into useful goods. Caravans between the realms came and went daily.

The greatest dangers to caravans were human thieves, jungle animals, and the occasional sheer drops between moss bed and moss bed. The tyros, however, were particularly effective in navigating difficult terrain—the main reason Paithan chose to use them, despite their shortcomings. (Many handlers, particularly humans, cannot deal with the sensitive tyro, who will curl into a ball and pout if its feelings are hurt.) The tyro can crawl over moss beds, climb trees, and span ravines by spinning its webs across the gap and swinging over. So strong are the tyro webs that some have been turned into permanent bridges, maintained by the elves.

Paithan had been over this route many times previously. He was familiar with the dangers, he was prepared for them. Consequently, he didn't worry about them. He wasn't particularly concerned with thieves. His caravan was large and well armed with elven weapons. Thieving humans tended to prey on lone travelers, particularly their own kind. He knew, though, that if thieves became aware of the true nature of his merchandise, they would risk much to acquire it. Humans have a high regard for elven weaponry—particularly those that are "intelligent."

The railbow, for example, is similar to a human crossbow—being a missile weapon consisting of a bow fixed across a wooden stock, having a mechanism for holding and releasing the string. The "rail" it fires is an arrow magically gifted with intelligence, able to visually sight a target and guide itself toward it. The magical boltarch, a much smaller version of the railbow, can be worn in a scabbard on the hip and is fired with one hand. Neither human nor dwarven magic is capable of producing intelligent weaponry; thieves selling these on the black market could name their price.

But Paithan had taken precautions against being robbed.

Quintin (an elf who had been with the family since Paithan was a baby) had packed the baskets by hand, and only he and Paithan knew what really lay beneath the dolls and sailing ships and jack-in-the-boxes. The human slaves, whose duty it was to guide the tyros, thought they were carrying a load of toys for tots, not the deadlier toys of grown men.

Secretly, Paithan considered it all an unnecessary nuisance. Quindiniar weapons were high quality, a cut above those of ordinary elven manufacture. The owner of a Quindiniar railbow had to be given a special code word before he could activate the magic, and only Paithan had this information, which he would pass on to the buyer. But Calandra was convinced that every human was a spy, a thief, and a murderer just waiting to rob, rape, pillage, and plunder.

Paithan had tried to point out to his sister that she wasn't being rational—she gave the humans credit for a phenomenal and cunning intellect on one hand, while maintaining that they were little better than animals on the other.

"Humans really aren't too different from us, Cal," Paithan had said on one memorable occasion.

He had never tried that logic again. Calandra had been so alarmed by this liberal attitude that she had seriously considered forbidding him to venture again into human lands. The awful threat of having to stay home had been enough to silence the young elf on the subject forever.

The first stage of the journey was easy. Their only obstacle would be the Kithni Gulf, the large body of water that divided the elven and human lands, and that lay far to the vars. Paithan fell into the rhythm of the road, enjoying the exercise and the chance to be his own person once again. The sun lit the trees with jewellike tones of green, the perfume of myriad flowers scented the air, frequent small showers of rain cooled the warmth built up from walking. Sometimes he heard a slink or a slither alongside the path, but he didn't pay much attention to the jungle wildlife. Having faced a dragon, Paithan decided he was equal to just about anything. But it was during this quiet time that the old man's words began buzzing in his head.

Doom will come back with you!

One time, when Paithan had been small, a bee had flown into his ear. The frantic buzzing the creature made had nearly driven him wild until his mother had been able to extricate it. Like that bee, Zifnab's prophecy had become trapped inside Paithan's skull, repeating itself over and over, and there seemed little he could do to rid himself of it.

He tried shrugging it off, laughing. After all, the old man was leaky as a cracked gourd. But just when he had convinced himself, Paithan saw the wizard's eyes—shrewd, knowing, and inexpressibly sad. It was the sadness that bothered Paithan, gave him a chill that his mother would have said came from someone standing on his grave. And that brought memories of his mother; Paithan also remembered that the old man had said that Mother wanted to see her children again.

The young elf felt a pang that was partly sweet, partly remorseful and uneasy. What if his father's beliefs were true? What if Paithan could actually meet his mother after all these years? He gave a low whistle and shook his head.

"Sorry, Mama. Guess you wouldn't be too pleased."

His mother had wanted him to be educated, she'd wanted all her children educated. Elithenia had been a factory wizardess when Lenthan Quindiniar saw her and lost his heart to her. Reputedly one of the most beautiful women in Equilan, Elithenia hadn't been at ease among the high born of the land; a feeling Lenthan had never been able to understand.

"Your dresses are finer, my dear. Your jewels are more costly. What do these lords and ladies have that ranks them higher than the Quindiniars? Tell me, and I'll go out today and buy it!"

"What they have, you can't buy," his wife had told him with wistful sorrow.

"What is it?"

"They *know* things."

And she had been determined that her children would *know* things.

To this end, she hired a governess to give her children schooling such as only the high born received. The children had proved a disappointment. Calandra, even at a young age, knew exactly what she wanted out of life and she took from the governess what she needed—the knowledge necessary to manipulate people and numbers. Paithan didn't know what he wanted but he knew what he didn't want—boring lessons. He escaped the governess when he could, dawdled his time away when he couldn't. Aleatha, learning her powers early, smiled prettily, snuggled in the governess's lap, and was never required to learn to do more than read and write.

After their mother had died, their father kept the governess on. It had been Calandra who let the woman go, to save money, and that was the end of their schooling.

"No, Mother won't be pleased to see us, I'm afraid," Paithan mused, feeling unaccountably guilty. Realizing what he'd been thinking, he laughed—somewhat shamefacedly—and shook his head. "I'll be getting daft as poor Father if I don't cut it out."

To clear his mind and rid it of unwelcome memories, Paithan climbed up on the horns of the lead tyro and began to chat with the overseer—an elf of much sense and worldly experience. It wasn't until sorrowtime that night, the first cycle following torrent's hour, that Paithan would again think of Zifnab and the prophecy—and then only right before he fell asleep.

The journey to Estport, the ferry landing, was peaceful, without incident, and Paithan forgot the prophecy completely. The pleasure of traveling, the heady awareness of his freedom after the stifling atmosphere of home lifted the young elf's spirits. After a few cycles on the road, he could laugh heartily at the old man and his crazy notions, and he regaled Quintin with tales of Zifnab during their rest breaks. When they finally arrived at the Kithni Gulf, Paithan could hardly believe it. The trip had seemed far too short.

The Kithni Gulf is a huge lake that forms the border between Thillia and Equilan, and here Paithan encountered his first delay. One of the ferries had broken down, leaving only one in operation. Caravans were lined up all along the moss shore, waiting to cross.

Upon their arrival, Paithan sent the overseer to find out how long they would have to wait. Quintin returned with a number that marked their place in line and said that they might be able to cross over some time the following cycle.

Paithan shrugged. He wasn't in any particular hurry, and it appeared that people were making the best of a bad situation. The ferry landing had come to resemble a tent city. Caravaners strode about, visiting, trading news, discussing current trends in the marketplace. Paithan saw his slaves settled and fed, his tyros petted and complimented, and the baggage secure. Leaving everything in the capable hands of the overseer, the young elf left to join in the fun.

An enterprising elven farmer, hearing of the plight of the caravanners, had hastened down to the landing with several barrels of homemade vingin packed in a wagon, cooled by ice.[2] Vingin is a strong drink made of crushed grapes, fortified by a liquid derived from fermented tohahs. Its fiery taste is favored by elves and humans alike. Paithan was particularly fond of it and, seeing a crowd gathered around the barrel, he joined them.

Several old friends of Paithan's were among the crowd, and the young elf was welcomed with enthusiasm. Caravanners get to know each other on the trail, sometimes banding together for both safety and companionship. Humans and elves alike made room for Paithan and a cool, frothy mug was thrust into his hand.

"Pundar, Ulaka, Gregor, good to see you again." The elf greeted long-time associates and was introduced to those he didn't know. Seating himself on a crate next to Gregor—a large, redheaded human with a bristling beard—Paithan sipped his vingin and took a brief moment to be thankful Calandra couldn't see him.

Several polite inquiries about his health and that of his family followed, which Paithan answered and returned in kind.

"What are you carrying?" asked Gregor, downing a mug in one long swallow. Belching in satisfaction, he passed his mug to the farmer for a refill.

"Toys," said Paithan, with a grin.

Appreciative laughter and knowing winks.

"You'll be taking them up norinth, then," said a human, who had been introduced as Hamish.

"Why, yes," said Paithan. "How did you know?"

---

[2]Ice does not occur naturally in any of the known lands of Pryan. It came into common use after its discovery through human magical experiments on weather. Ice is one of the few products made by humans that is in demand in elven lands.

"They've a need for 'toys' up that way, so we hear," said Hamish.

The laughter died, and there was gloomy nodding among the humans. The elven traders, looking perplexed, demanded to know what was amiss.

"War with the SeaKings?" guessed Paithan, handing over his empty mug. This news would make Calandra's day. He would have to send a faultless back with it. If anything could put his sister in a good mood, it would be war among the humans. He could almost see her counting the profits now.

"Naw," said Gregor. "The SeaKings has got their own problems, if what we hear be true. Strange humans, coming across the Whispering Sea in crude ships, have been washing up on the SeaKings' shores. At first, the SeaKings took in the refugees, but more and more kept coming and now they are finding it difficult to feed and house so many."

"They can keep 'em," said another human trader. "We've enough problems of our own in Thillia, without taking in strangers."

The elven traders smiled, listening with the smug complacency of those who are completely unaffected, except as it might concern their business. An influx of more humans into the region could only send profits soaring.

"But . . . where are these humans coming from?" asked Paithan.

There was heated discussion among the traders, the argument at last being settled by Gregor stating, "I know. I have talked to them myself. They say they are from a realm known as Kasnar, that is far norinth of us, across the Whispering Sea."

"Why are they fleeing their homeland? Are there great wars being fought there?" Paithan was wondering how difficult it would be to hire a ship to take him and a load of weapons that far.

Gregor shook his head, his red beard brushing against his massive chest. "Not war," he said in grave tones. "Destruction. Total destruction."

Doom, death, and destruction.

Paithan felt footsteps crossing his grave, his blood tingled in his feet and hands. It must be the vingin, he told himself, and set his mug down hastily.

"What is it, then? Dragons? I can't believe that. Since when have dragons attacked a settlement?"

"No, even the dragons flee this menace."

"Then, what?"

Gregor looked around solemnly. "Tytans."

Paithan and the other elves gaped, then burst out laughing.

"Gregor, you old liar! You had me going there for a while!" Paithan wiped tears from his eyes. "I'll buy the next round. Refugees and wrecked ships!"

The humans sat silent, their faces growing dark and shadowed. Paithan saw them exchange grim glances and checked his mirth.

"Come now, Gregor, a joke's a joke. You caught me. I'll admit I was already counting up the coins." He waved his hand toward his compatriots. "We all were. So enough already."

"It is no joke, I am afraid, my friends," said Gregor. "I have talked to these people. I have seen the terror on their faces and heard it in their voices. Gigantic creatures with the bodies and faces of our kind, but who stand taller than the trees came to their land from far norinth. Their voices alone can split rock. They destroy all in their path. They snatch up people in their hands and fling them to their deaths or crush them with their fists. There is no weapon that can stop them. Arrows are to them like gnats to us. Swords will not penetrate their thick hide, nor would blades do any damage, if they did."

The weight of Gregor's words oppressed everyone. All listened in hushed and attentive silence, though there was still some unbelieving shaking of heads. Other caravanners, noting the solemn gathering, came up to see what was going on and added their own dire rumors to those already spreading.

"The Kasnar Empire was great," said Gregor. "Now it is gone. Completely destroyed. All that is left of a once mighty nation are a handful of people who escaped in their boats across the Whispering Sea."

The farmer, noting his sales dropping off, tapped a fresh barrel. Everyone rose to refill their mugs, and began talking at once.

"Tytans? The followers of San? That's only myth."

"Don't speak sacrilege, Paithan. If you believe in the

Mother[3] you must believe in San and his followers, who rule the Dark."

"Yeah, Umbar, we all know how religious you are! If you walked into one of the Mother's temples it'd probably fall down on top of you! Look, Gregor. You're a sensible man. You don't believe in goblins and ghoulies."

"No, but I believe in what I see and hear. And I've seen, in the eyes of those people, terrible things."

Paithan gazed steadily at the man. He'd known Gregor a number of years and had always found the big human reliable, dependable, and fearless. "All right. I'll buy the notion that these people fled *something*. But why are we all in a dither? Whatever it is couldn't possibly cross the Whispering Sea."

"The tytans—"

"Whatever—"

"—could come down through the dwarven kingdoms of Grish and Klag and Thurn," continued Gregor gloomily. "In fact, we have heard rumors that the dwarves are preparing for war."

"Yeah. War against *you*, not giant demons. That's why your lords slapped on that arms embargo."

Gregor shrugged his shoulders, nearly bursting the seams on his tight-fitting shirt, and then grinned, his red-bearded face seeming to split wide apart. "Whatever happens, Paithan, you elves won't have to worry. We humans will stop them. Our legends say that the Horned God constantly tests us, by sending warriors worthy of us to fight. Perhaps, in this battle, the Five Lost Lords will return to help us."

He started to drink, looked disappointed, and upended his mug. It was empty. "More vingin!"

The elven farmer turned the spigot, nothing came out. He

---

[3]Peytin, Matriarch of Heaven. The elves believe that Peytin created a world for her mortal children. She appointed her eldest twin sons, Orn and Obi, to rule over it. Their younger brother, San, become jealous and, gathering together the greedy, warlike humans, waged war against his brothers. This war sundered the ancient world. San was banished below. The humans were cast out of the ancient world and sent to this one. Peytin created a race known as elf and sent them to restore the world's purity.

knocked on the barrels. All gave forth a dismal, hollow sound. Sighing, the caravanners stood and stretched.

"Paithan, my friend," said Gregor. "There's the tavern near the ferry landing. It's packed, just now, but I think I could get us a table." The big human flexed his muscles and laughed.

"Sure," agreed Paithan readily. His overseer was a good man, the slaves were exhausted. He didn't expect any trouble. "You find us a place to sit, and I'll buy the first two rounds."

"Fair enough."

The two, swaying slightly, threw their arms around each other—Gregor's arm nearly engulfing the slender elf—and tottered off toward the Land's End.

"Say, Gregor, you get around a lot," said Paithan. "Ever hear of a human wizard name of Zifnab?"

CHAPTER ◆ 10

VARSPORT,

THILLIA

◆

PAITHAN AND HIS CARAVAN WERE ABLE TO CROSS OVER ON THE FERRY the following cycle. The crossing took an entire cycle, and the elf did not enjoy the trip, due to the fact that he was suffering from the after-effects of vingin.

Elves are notoriously bad drinkers, having no head at all for alcohol, and Paithan knew at the time he shouldn't be attempting to keep pace with Gregor. But he reminded himself that he was celebrating—no Calandra to glare at him sternly for taking a second glass of wine with dinner. The vingin also conveniently fogged up Paithan's remembrance of the daft old wizard, his stupid prophecy, and Gregor's gloomy stories about giants.

The constant clatter of the turning capstan, the snorting and squeals of the five harnessed wild boar who drove it, and the constant urgings of their human driver blasted through the elf's head. The guck-covered, slimy vine cable that drew the ferry over the water slid past him and disappeared, winding around the capstan. Leaning up against a bundle of blankets in the shade of an awning, a wet compress over his aching head, Paithan watched the water slip away beneath the boat and felt extremely sorry for himself.

The ferry had been operating across the Kithni Gulf for about sixty years. Paithan could remember seeing it as a small child, traveling in company with his grandfather—the last journey the two'd made before the old elf vanished into the wilderness. Then Paithan had thought the ferryboat the most wonderful invention in the world and had been extremely upset to find out that humans had been responsible for inventing it.

His grandfather had patiently explained the human thirst for money and power known as ambition—a result of their pitifully short life spans—that led them to all sorts of energetic undertakings. The elves had been quick to take advantage of the ferry service, since it markedly increased trade between the two realms, but they viewed it with suspicion. The elves had no doubt that the ferry—like most other human endeavors—would somehow lead to a bad end. In the meantime, however, the elves magnanimously allowed the humans to serve them.

Soothed by the lapping of the water and the fumes of the vingin lingering in his brain, Paithan grew drowsy in the heat. He had the vague memory of Gregor having becomed embroiled in a brawl and nearly getting him—Paithan—killed. The elf drifted off to sleep. He woke to Quintin, his overseer, shaking him by the shoulder.

"*Auana! Auana*[1] Quindiniar! Wake up. The boat is docking."

Paithan groaned and sat up. He felt somewhat better. Though his head still throbbed, at least he didn't feel like he was about to tumble over in a dead faint when he moved. Staggering to his feet, he lurched across the crowded deck to where his slaves crouched on the wood planking, out in the open, with no shelter from the blazing sun. The slaves didn't appear to mind the heat. They wore nothing but loin cloths. Paithan, who kept every inch of his fair skin covered, looked at the deep brown or black skin of the humans and was reminded of the vast gulf that lay between the two races.

"Callie's right," he muttered to himself. "They're nothing but animals and all the civilizing in the world won't change that. I should have known better than to go off with Gregor last night. Stick to my own kind."

This firm resolve lasted all of, say, an hour, by which time Paithan, feeling much better, was visiting with a bruised, swollen, and grinning Gregor while both stood in line, waiting their turns to present their papers to the port authority. Paithan remained

---

[1]Elven word, meaning "boss."

cheerful during the long wait. When Gregor left for his turn at customs, the elf amused himself by listening to the chatter of his human slaves, who appeared ridiculously excited at seeing their homeland again.

If they're so fond of it, why did they let themselves get sold into slavery? Paithan wondered idly, standing in a line that moved with the speed of a mosslug while human customs officials asked innumerable, inane questions and pawed over the goods of his fellow caravanners. Altercations broke out, generally between humans, who—when caught smuggling—seemed to take the attitude that the law applied to everyone else but them. Elven merchants rarely had any trouble at the borders. They either studiously obeyed the laws or, like Paithan, devised quiet and subtle means to evade them.

At last, one of the officials motioned to him. Paithan and his overseer herded the slaves and the tyros forward.

"What're you haulin'?" The official stared hard at the baskets.

"Magical toys, sir," said Paithan, with a charming smile.

The official's gaze sharpened. "Seems a queer time to be bringing in toys."

"What do you mean, sir?"

"Why, the talk of war! Don't tell me you haven't heard it?"

"Not a word, sir. Who are you fighting this month? Strethia, perhaps, or Dourglasia?"

"Naw, we wouldn't waste our arrows on that scum. There's rumors of giant warriors, coming out of the norinth."

"Oh, that!" Paithan shrugged gracefully. "I did hear of something of the sort, but I discounted it. You humans are well prepared to face such a challenge, aren't you?"

"Of course we are," said the official. Suspecting he was being made the butt of a joke, he stared hard at Paithan.

The elf's face was smooth as silk and so was his tongue.

"The children love our magical toys so much. And Saint Thillia's Day will be coming up soon. We wouldn't want to disappoint the little tykes, now, would we?" Paithan leaned forward confidentially. "I'll bet you're a grandfather, aren't you? How about letting me go on through without the usual rigamorole?"

"I'm a grandfather all right," said the official, scowling darkly. "I got ten grandkids, all of 'em under the age of four and they're all livin' at my house! Open those baskets."

Paithan saw that he had made a tactical error. Heaving the sigh of an innocent wrongfully condemned, he shrugged his shoulders and led the way to the first basket. Quintin—all officious, servile politeness—undid the straps. The slaves, standing nearby, were watching with what Paithan noted were expressions of suppressed glee that made the elf extremely uneasy. What the devil were they grinning about? It was almost as if they knew . . .

The customs official lifted the lid of the basket. An array of brightly colored toys sparkled in the sunlight. Casting a sidelong glance at Paithan, the official thrust his hand deep inside.

He withdrew it immediately with a yelp, waving his fingers. "Something bit me!" he accused.

The slaves roared with laughter. The overseer, shocked, began laying about him with his whip, and soon restored order.

"I'm terribly sorry, sir." Paithan slammed shut the lid of the basket. "It must have been the jack-in-the-boxes. They're notoriously bad about biting. I really do apologize."

"You're giving those fiends to children?" demanded the official, sucking his injured thumb.

"Some parents like a certain amount of aggressive spirit in a toy, sir. Don't want the little tykes to grow up soft, do we? Uh . . . sir . . . I'd be particularly careful with that basket. It's carrying the dollies."

The customs official stretched out his hand, hesitated, and thought better of it. "Go on with you then. Get outta here."

Paithan gave the order to Quintin, who immediately set the slaves to work, hauling at the reins of the tyros. Some of the slaves, despite the fresh lash marks on the skin, were still smirking, and Paithan wondered at the strange human trait that led them to enjoy the sight of another's suffering.

His bill of lading was hastily inspected and passed. Paithan tucked it in the pocket of his belted traveling coat and, bowing politely to the official, was starting to hurry after his baggage train when he felt a hand on his arm. The elf's good humor was rapidly evaporating. He felt a throbbing in his temples.

"Yes, sir?" he said, turning, forcing a smile.

The customs official leaned close. "How much for ten of them jacks?"

◆

The journey through the human lands was uneventful. One of Paithan's slaves escaped, but he'd planned for such an eventuality by bringing along extra hands, and he wasn't overly concerned about many of the others. He'd deliberately chosen men with families left behind in Equilan. Apparently one slave thought more of his freedom than he did of his wife and children.

Under the influence of Gregor's tales, Zifnab's prophecy began to gnaw again at the elf's mind. Paithan tried to discover all he could about the approaching giants and in every tavern, he found someone with something to say on the subject. But he gradually became convinced that it was rumor, nothing more. Outside of Gregor, he couldn't find one other human who had actually talked directly to any of the refugees.

"My mother's uncle ran across three of 'em and they told him and he told my mother that—"

"My second cousin's boy was in Jendi last month when the ships was coming in and he told my cousin to tell his dad who told me that—"

"I heard it from a peddlar who'd been there—"

Paithan decided at length, with some relief, that Gregor'd been feeding him soom candy.[2] The elf put Zifnab's prophecy completely, finally, irrevocably out of his mind.

Paithan crossed the border of Marcinia into Terncia without a border guard so much as glancing into his baskets. They gave his bill of lading—signed by the Varsport official—a bored glance and waved him on. The elf was enjoying his journey, and he took his time. The weather was particularly fine. The humans, for the most part, were friendly and well mannered. Of course, he did encounter the occasional remark about "woman stealers" or "flithy slavers" but Paithan, not one to be hotheaded, either ignored these epithets or passed them off with a laugh and an offer to buy the next round.

Paithan was as fond of human women as the next elf, but—having traveled extensively in human lands—he knew nothing

---

[2]Soom candy, the elven expression for someone passing fiction off as the truth, is a human concoction much loved by elves, who are extremely fond of sweets. The candy tastes quite delicious but eating too much can have dire consequences on elven digestive systems.

could get your ears (and perhaps other portions of one's anatomy) cut off sooner than dallying with human females. He was able to curb his appetite, therefore, contenting himself with admiring stares or snatching a quick kiss in an extremely dark corner. If the innkeeper's daughter came to his door in the dead of night, wanting to test the legendary erotic skill of elven men, Paithan was always careful to bundle her out in the mistymorne, before anyone else was up and stirring.

The elf reached his destination—the small and unsavory town of Griffith—a few weeks past his scheduled arrival. He thought that pretty good, considering how chancey travel was through the constantly warring Thillian states. Arriving at the Jungleflower Tavern, he saw his slaves and the tyros settled in the stable, found a place for his overseer in the loft, and took a room in the inn for himself.

The Jungleflower was apparently not much in the custom of housing elves, for the proprietor looked a long time at Paithan's money and rapped the coin on the table, wanting to make certain that it had the sound of hardwood. Hearing it thump true, he became somewhat more polite.

"What did you say your name was?"

"Paithan Quindiniar."

"Huh." The man grunted. "Got two messages for you. One came by hand, the other by faultless."

"Thanks very much," said Paithan, handing over another coin.

The proprietor's politeness increased markedly.

"You must be thirsty. Seat yourself in the common room, and I'll be bringing you something to wet your throat."

"No vingin," said Paithan and sauntered off, the missives in his hand.

One he recognized as human in origin—a bit of cheap parchment that had been used before. Some attempt had been made to efface the original writing, but that hadn't succeeded well. Untying a frayed and dirty ribbon, Paithan unrolled it and read the message with some difficulty around what apparently had once been a tax notice.

Quindiniar. You're late. This'll . . .   . . . you. We've had to make . . . trip . . . keep customer happy. Back. . . .

Paithan walked over to the window and held the parchment to the light. No, he couldn't make out when they said they were returning. It was signed with a crude scrawl—*Roland Redleaf*. Fishing out the worn bill of lading, Paithan looked for the name of the customer. There it was, in Calandra's precise, up-right hand. *Roland Redleaf*. Shrugging, Paithan tossed the scroll in the slop bucket and carefully wiped his hands after. No telling where it had been.

The proprietor hurried in with a foaming mug of ale. Tasting it, Paithan pronounced the brew excellent and the highly gratified innkeeper was now his slave for life or at least as long as his money held out. Settling down in a booth, propping his feet up on the chair opposite him, Paithan lounged back and opened the other scroll, preparing to enjoy himself.

It was a letter from Aleatha.

CHAPTER ◆ 11

HOUSE OF QUINDINIAR,

EQUILAN

◆

My dear Paithan,

You're probably astonished to hear from me. I'm not one for writing. However, I'm certain you won't be offended if I tell you the truth and that is that I'm writing to you out of sheer boredom. I certainly hope this engagement doesn't last too long or I shall go out of my mind.

Yes, dear brother, I've given up my "wild and wicked ways." At least temporarily. When I'm a "staid old married woman" I intend to pursue a more interesting life; one only needs to be discreet.

As I had foreseen, there is a bit of scandal over the impending marriage. The dowager is a snobbish old bitch who came near to ruining everything. She had the nerve to inform Durndrun that I had been having an affair with Lord K———, that I frequented certain establishments Below and that I even carried on with the human slaves! In short, I was a slut, not worthy of being honored with the Durndrun money, the Durndrun house, and the Durndrun name.

Fortunately, I had foreseen something like this happening and had procured a promise from my "beloved" that he was to inform me of any allegations made by his dear mama and allow me to refute them. He did so, coming to see me in the *mistymorne!* of all times. That's one habit of which I shall *have* to break him! By Orn!

What does one do at such an ungodly hour? There was no help for it. I had to make an appearance. Fortunately, unlike some women, I always look well on arising.

I found Durndrun in the parlor, looking extremely serious and stern, being entertained by Calandra, who was enjoying the whole thing immensely.

She left us alone—quite proper between engaged couples, you know—and, if you will believe this, my dear brother, the man began heaping his mother's accusations upon my head!

I was, of course, prepared.

Once I understood the precise nature of his complaints (and their source), I tumbled down upon the floor in a swoon. (In passing, there is a true art to that. One must fall without doing damage and preferably without any unsightly bruises on the elbows. It is not as easy as it looks.) Anyway, Durndrun was quite alarmed and was obliged—of course—to lift me in his arms and place me on the sofa.

I came to myself just in time to prevent him ringing for help and, seeing him bending over me, called him a "cad" and burst into tears.

He was again obliged to take me in his arms. Sobbing incoherently about my besmirched honor and how I could never love a man who didn't trust me, I attempted to push him away, making certain that in the ensuing struggle my gown tore and the lord discovered that his hand had wandered to a place where it should not have been.

"Ah, so this is what you think of me!" I flung myself on the sofa, taking care that in my frantic attempts to repair the damage, I simply made it worse. My only worry was that he should ring for the servants. I, therefore, did not allow my tears to degenerate into hysterics.

He rose to his feet and I could see, out of the corner of my eye, the struggle ensuing in his breast. I quieted my sobs and turned my head, looking up at him through a veil of golden hair, my eyes shimmering quite prettily.

"I admit that I have been what some might call irresponsible," I said in a choked voice, "but then I never had a mama to guide me! I've been searching so long for someone to love and honor with all my heart, and now that I've found you . . ."

I couldn't go on. Turning my face to the tear-soaked pillow, I stretched out my arm. "Go!" I told him. "Your mama is right! I am not worthy of such love!"

Well, Pait, I'm sure you must have guessed the rest. Before you could say "matrimony," Lord Durndrun was at my feet, begging *my* forgiveness! I allowed him another kiss and a long, lingering glance before I modestly covered the "treasures" he won't acquire until our wedding night.

He was so carried away by his passion he even spoke of turning his mother out of his house! It took a great deal of persuading to convince him that the dowager would be as dear to me as the mother I never knew. I have plans for the old lady. She doesn't know it, but she will cover my little "escapes" when married life becomes too boring.

And so I am well on the way to the altar. Lord Durndrun laid down the law to the dowager, informing her that he would wed me and that if she didn't like it we would live somewhere else. That wouldn't do at all, of course. The house is the main reason I'm marrying him. But I wasn't too afraid. The old woman simply dotes on her son and she gave way, as I knew she must.

The wedding will be in about four months time. I had hoped it would be sooner, but there are certain formalities that must be observed, and Callie is insisting on everything being very proper. In the meantime, I have no choice but to give the appearance that I am a modest, well-bred maiden and stay prudently at home. You will laugh, I'm certain, Paithan, when you read this. But I assure you I have not been with a man this past month. By the time the wedding night comes around, Durndrun himself will look good to me!

(I'm not at all certain I can hold out that long. I don't suppose you've noticed, but one of the human slaves is quite a pretty specimen. He's very interesting to talk to and has even taught me some of that beastly language of theirs. Speaking of beasts, do you suppose it's true what they say about human males?)

. . .

Sorry about the blurred text on that last part. Callie came into my room and I was forced to slip this in among my undergarments before the ink was dry. Can you imagine what she would have done if she'd read that last part?

Fortunately, she needn't worry. Thinking about it, I don't believe I could bring myself to form a liaison with a human. No offense, Pait, but how can you stand to touch them? I suppose it's different for a man.

You're wondering what Callie was doing in here at this hour of stormtime? The rockets were keeping her awake.

Speaking of rockets, home life has gone from bad to worse since you left. Papa and that crazy old wizard spend all toiltime down in the cellar preparing rockets and all darktime out in the backyard, firing them off. We've set a record, I do believe, in the number of servants who've left us. Cal's been forced to pay out large sums to several families in the town below, whose houses caught fire. Papa and the wizard are sending the rockets up, you see, so that this "man with the bandaged hands" will see them and know where to land!

Oh, Paithan, I'm sure you're laughing now, but this is serious. Poor Callie's about to tear the hair off her head in frustration, and I'm afraid I'm not much better. Of course, she's worried about the money and the business and the mayor coming by with a petition to get rid of the dragon.

I'm worried about poor Papa. The crafty old human has Papa completely convinced in this nonsense about a ship and going to see Mama in the stars. It's all Papa talks about. He's so excited he won't eat and he's getting thinner by the day. Callie and I know that old wizard must be up to something—maybe making off with all Papa's fortune. But, if so, he's shown no signs of it.

Cal tried twice to buy Zifnab—or whatever he calls himself—off, offering him more money than most humans would see in a lifetime to go away and leave us alone. The old man took her by the hand and, with a sad look on his face, told her, "But my dear, soon the day will come when money won't matter."

Won't matter! Money won't matter! Callie thought he

was crazy before but now she's convinced he's a raving maniac and should be locked up somewhere. I think she'd do it, too, but she's afraid how Papa might react. And then there was the day the dragon almost got loose.

You remember how the old man keeps the creature under enchantment? (Orn knows how or why.) We were sitting down to breakfast when suddenly there was a terrible commotion outside, the house shook like it would fall apart, tree limbs cracked and thudded into the moss and a fiery red eye appeared, staring into our dining room window.

"Have another muffin, old man!" came this dreadful, hissing voice. "With lots of honey on it. You need fattening, fool. Like the rest of the plump, juicy meat around you!"

Its teeth flashed, saliva dripped from its forked tongue. The old man went pale as a ghost. What few servants we had left ran screaming out the door.

"Ah, ha!" shouted the dragon. "Fast food!"

The eye disappeared. We ran to the front door and saw the dragon's head diving down, its jaws ready to close over the cook!

"No, not her!" shouted the old man. "She does the most wonderful things to a chicken! Try the butler. Never did like him," he said, turning to Father. "Uppity chap."

"But," said poor Papa, "you can't let him eat the staff!"

"Why not?" Cal screamed. "Let him eat all of us! What does it matter to you?"

You should have seen Callie, Brother. It was frightening. She went all stiff and rigid and just stood there on the front porch, her arms crossed over her chest, her face set hard as rock. The dragon seemed to be toying with his victims, driving them like sheep, watching them duck behind trees, lunging at them when they came out in the open.

"What if we let him have the butler," said the old man nervously, "and maybe a footman or two? Take the edge off, so to speak?"

"I—I'm afraid not," answered poor Papa, who was shaking like a leaf.

The old man heaved a sigh. "You're right, I suppose.

Mustn't abuse your hospitality. Seems a pity. Elves are so easily digestible. Slide right down. He always feels hungry right after, though." The old man began rolling up his sleeves. "Dwarves, now. I never let him eat a dwarf. Not since the last time. Up with him all night. Let's see. How did that spell go? Let's see, I need a ball of bat guano and a pinch of sulfur. No, wait. I've got my spells muddled."

The old man strolled out on the lawn, cool as you please, in the midst of the chaos, talking to himself about bat dung! By now, some of the townspeople had arrived, carrying weapons. The dragon was delighted to see them, shouting about "all-you-can-eat buffets." Callie was standing on the porch, screeching, "Eat us all!" Papa was wringing his hands until he collapsed into a chaise lounge.

I hate to admit this, Pait, but I started to laugh. Why is that? It must be some horrible flaw in me that makes me start giggling during disaster. I wished with all my heart you'd been there to help us, but you weren't. Papa was useless, Cal wasn't much better. In desperation, I ran down onto the lawn and caught hold of the old man's arm just as he raised it in the air.

"Aren't you supposed to sing?" I asked. "You know, 'something, something Bonnie Earl'!"

It was all I could understand of the damn song. The old man blinked and his face brightened. Then he whirled around and glared at me, his beard bristling. The dragon, meanwhile, was chasing the townspeople across the lawn.

"What are you trying to do?" the old man demanded angrily. "Take over my job?"

"No, I—"

" 'Don't meddle in the affairs of wizards,' " he said in lofty tones, " 'for they are subtle and quick to anger.' A fellow sorcerer said that. Good at his job, knew a lot about jewelry. Not bad at fireworks, either. Wasn't the snappy dresser Merlin was, though. Let's see, what his name? Raist—no, that was the irritating young chap, kept hacking and spitting up blood all the time. Disgusting. The other's name was Gand-something or other . . ."

I began laughing wildly, Pait! I couldn't help it. I had

no idea what he was yammering about. It was just all so ludicrous! I must be a truly wicked person.

"The dragon!" I grabbed the old man and shook him until his teeth rattled. "Stop him!"

"Ah, yes. It's easy for you to say." Zifnab gave me a hunted look. "You don't have to live with him afterward!"

Heaving another sigh, he began to sing in that high-pitched quavery voice of his that goes right through your head. Just like before, the dragon jerked his head up, and stared at the old man. The creature's eyes glazed over and pretty soon he was swaying in time to the music. Suddenly, the dragon's eyes popped open wide and he stared at the old man in shock.

"Sir!" the creature thundered. "What are you doing out on the front lawn in your nighty? Have you no shame?"

The dragon's head snaked across the lawn and loomed over poor Papa, who was huddled underneath the chaise lounge. The townspeople, seeing the creature distracted, began raising their weapons and creeping up on it.

"Forgive me, Master Quindiniar," said the dragon in a deep, booming voice. "This is my fault entirely. I was not able to catch him before he left this morning." The dragon's head swiveled around to the old man. "Sir, I had laid out the mauve morning coat with the pin-striped pants and the yellow weskit—"

"Mauve morning coat?" screeched the old man. "Did you ever see Merlin strolling around Camelot, casting spells in a mauve morning coat? No, by hoppy toads, you didn't! And you won't catch me in one—"

I missed the rest of the conversation because I had to convince the townsfolk to go home. Not that I would have minded so much getting rid of the dragon, but it was perfectly obvious to me that their puny weapons couldn't do it any serious harm and might only break the spell. It was shortly after this, by the way, around luncheon, that the mayor arrived with the petition.

Something seemed to snap inside Callie after that, Pait. Now she completely ignores the wizard and his dragon. She simply behaves as if they aren't there. She won't look at the old man; she won't speak to him. She spends all her time either at the factory or locked up in her office. She'll barely speak to poor Papa. Not that he notices. He's too busy with his rockets.

Well, Pait, the barrage has ceased for the moment. I must close and go to bed. I'm taking tea with the dowager tomorrow. I believe I'll switch cups with her, just in case she's slipped a little poison in mine.

Oh, I almost forgot. Callie says to tell you that business has really picked up. Something about rumors of trouble coming out of the norinth. Sorry I wasn't paying more attention, but you know how talking about business bores me. I guess it means more money, but, like the old man says, what does that matter?

Hurry home, Pait, and save me from this madhouse!

Your loving sister,
Aleatha

CHAPTER ♦ 12

GRIFFITH, TERNCIA,

THILLIA

♦

INVOLVED IN HIS SISTER'S LETTER, PAITHAN WAS AWARE OF FOOT-steps entering the tavern, but he didn't pay any attention until the chair he was using for a footstool was kicked violently out from underneath his legs.

"About time!" said a voice, speaking human.

Paithan looked up. A human male stood staring down at him. The man was tall, muscular, well built, with long blond hair that he wore tied with a leather thong at the back of his head. His skin was deeply tanned, except where his clothes covered it, and then Paithan could see that it was white and fair as any elf's. The blue eyes were frank and friendly, his lips curved in an ingratiating smile. He was dressed in the fringed leather breeches and sleeveless leather tunic popular among humans.

"Quincejar?" said the human, thrusting out a hand. "I'm Roland. Roland Redleaf. Pleased to meet you."

Paithan glanced at the chair, which had been knocked over and kicked halfway across the common room. Barbarians. Still, it didn't do any good to get angry. Standing up, he stretched out his hand, clasping the human's in the odd custom that both elves and dwarves found so ridiculous.

"The name's Quindiniar. And please join me," said Paithan, retrieving his chair. "What will you have to drink?"

"You speak our language pretty good, without that silly lisp you hear with most elves." Roland yanked over another chair and sat down. "What are you drinking?" Grabbing Paithan's almost full mug, he sniffed at it. "Stuff any good? Usually the ale around here tastes like monkey piss. Hey, bar keep! Bring us another round!

"Here's to the toys," Roland said, lifting his mug.

Paithan took a swallow. The human downed his at one gulp. Blinking, wiping his eyes, he said moistly, "Not bad. You going to finish yours? No? I'll take care of it for you. Can't let it go to waste." He drained the other mugful, slamming it down upon the table when he was finished.

"What were we drinking to? Ah, I remember. The toys. 'Bout time, as I said." Roland leaned across the table, breathing beer fumes into Paithan's face. "The children were getting impatient! It was all I could do to placate the little darlings . . . if you know what I mean?"

"I'm not certain that I do," said Paithan mildly. "Will you have another?"

"Sure. Barkeep! Two more."

"It's on me," said the elf, noting the proprietor's frown.

Roland lowered his voice. "The children—the buyers, the dwarves. They're getting real impatient. Old Blackbeard like to took my head off when I told him the shipment was going to be late."

"You're selling the . . . er . . . toys to dwarves?"

"Yeah, you got a problem with that, Quinpar?"

"Quindiniar. No, it's just that now I understand how you were able to pay top price."

"Between you and me, the bastards would've paid double that to get these. They're all worked up over some kid's fairy tale about giant humans. But you'll see for yourself." Roland took a long pull at the ale.

"Me?" said Paithan, smiling and shaking his head. "You must be mistaken. Once you've paid me the money, the 'toys' are yours. I've got to return home. This is a busy time for us, now."

"And how are we supposed to transport these babies?" Roland brushed his arm across his mouth. "Carry them on our heads? I saw your tyros in the stables. Everything's packed up neat. We'll make the trip and be back in no time."

"I'm sorry, Redleaf, but that wasn't part of the deal. Pay me the money and—"

"But don't you think you'd find the dwarven kingdom fascinating?"

The voice was a woman's, and it came from behind Paithan.

"Quincetart," said Roland, gesturing with his mug. "Meet my wife."

The elf, rising politely to his feet, turned around to face a human female.

"My name's Quindiniar."

"Glad to meet you. I'm Rega."

She was short, dark haired and dark eyed. Her well-muscled body was scantily clad, like Roland's, in fringed leather, leaving little of her figure to the imagination. Her brown eyes, shadowed by long black lashes, seemed filled with mystery. Her full lips kept back untold secrets. She extended her hand. Paithan took it in his. Instead of shaking it, as the woman apparently expected, he carried the hand to his lips and kissed it.

The woman's cheeks flushed. She allowed her hand to linger a moment in Paithan's. "Look here, Husband. You never treat me like this!"

"You're my wife," said Roland, shrugging, as if that settled the matter. "Have a seat, Rega. What'll you have to drink? The usual?"

"A glass of wine for the lady," ordered Paithan. Crossing the common room, he brought a chair back to the table, holding it for Rega to sit down. She slid into it with animallike grace, her movements clean, quick, decisive.

"Wine. Yeah, why not?" Rega smiled at the elf, her head tilting slightly, her dark, shining hair falling over a bare shoulder.

"Talk Quinspar here into coming with us, Rega."

The woman kept her eyes and her smile fixed on the elf. "Don't you have somewhere to go, Roland?"

"You're right. Damn beer runs right through me."

Rising to his feet, Roland sauntered out of the common room, heading for the tavern's backyard.

Rega's smile widened. Paithan could see sharp teeth, white against lips that appeared to have been stained red with some kind of berry juice. Whoever kissed those lips would taste the sweetness . . .

"I wish you would come with us. It's not that far. We know the best route, it cuts through SeaKing lands but on the wilderness side. No border guards the way we go. The path's occasionally treacherous, but you don't look like the type to be bothered by a little danger." She leaned closer, and he was aware of a faint, musky odor that clung to her sweat-sheened skin. Her hand crept over Paithan's. "My husband and I get so bored with each other's company."

Paithan recognized deliberate seduction. He should have; his sister Aleatha could have taught it on a university level and this crude young human could certainly benefit from a few courses. The elf found it all highly amusing and certainly entertaining after long days on the road. He did wonder, though, why Rega was going to all this trouble and he also wondered, somewhere in the back of his mind, if she might be prepared to deliver what she was offering.

I've never been to the dwarven kingdom, Paithan reflected. No elf has. It would be worthwhile going.

A vision of Calandra—mouth pursed, nose bone white, eyes flaring—rose up before Paithan. She'd be furious. He'd lose a season, at least, in getting back home.

But Cal, look, he heard himself saying. I've established trade with the dwarves. Direct trade. No middle men to take a cut . . .

"Say you'll come with us." Rega squeezed his hand. The elf noted that the woman possessed an unladylike strength, the skin of her palm was rough and hardened.

"The three of us couldn't handle all these tyros—" he hedged.

"We don't need all of them." The woman was practical, businesslike. She let her hand linger in the elf's grasp. "You've packed toys for cover, I assume? Get rid of them. Sell them. We'll repack the . . . er . . . more valuable merchandise on three tyros."

Well, it would work. Paithan had to admit it. Plus, the sale of the toys would more than pay for the trip back for his foreman Quintin. The profits might moderate Calandra's fury.

"How can I refuse you anything?" Paithan answered, holding the warm hand a little tighter.

A door from the rear of the tavern slammed. Rega, flushing, snatched her hand away.

"My husband," she murmured. "He's frightfully jealous!"

Roland came strolling back into the common room, lacing up the leather thong on the front of his trousers. Passing by the bar, he appropriated three mugs of ale that had been set out for other customers and carried them over to the table. He slammed them down, sloshing ale over everything and everyone, and grinned.

"Well, Queesinard, my lovely wife talk you into coming with us?"

"Yes," answered Paithan, thinking that Redleaf didn't act like any jealous husband the elf ever'd known. "But I've got to send the overseer and my slaves back. They'll be needed at home. And the name's Quindiniar."

"Good idea. The fewer who know about our route the better. Say, you mind if I call you Quin?"

"My given name's Paithan."

"Sure thing, Quin. A toast to the dwarves, then. To their beards and their money. They keep one and I'll take the other!" Roland laughed. "Here, now, Rega. Quit drinking that grape juice. You know you can't stand it."

Rega flushed again. With a deprecating glance at Paithan, she thrust aside the glass of wine. Lifting a mug of ale to her berry-stained lips, she quaffed it skillfully.

What the hell? thought Paithan, and downed his ale in a gulp.

CHAPTER ♦ 13

SOMEWHERE OVER

PRYAN

♦

THE FLICK OF A WET, ROUGH TONGUE AND AN INSISTENT WHINING nudged Haplo to wakefulness. He sat up immediately, reflexively, his senses attuned to the world around him—though his mind still fought off the effects of whatever it was that had knocked him out.

He was in his ship, he recognized, lying in the captain's berth—a mattress spread over a wooden bed frame built into the ship's hull. The dog crouched on the bed near him, eyes bright, tongue lolling. Apparently, the animal had become bored and had decided that its master had been out long enough.

They had made it, seemingly. They had, once again, passed through Death's Gate.

The Patryn didn't move. He slowed his breathing, listening, feeling. He sensed nothing wrong, unlike the last time he'd come through Death's Gate. The ship was on an even keel. He had no sensation of movement, but assumed it was flying because he had not made the alterations in the magic needed to land the craft. Certain runes on the inside of the hull were glowing, meaning they had activated. He studied them, saw that they were sigla having to do with air, pressure, and maintaining gravity. Odd. He wondered why.

Haplo relaxed, fondled the dog's ears. Brilliant sunshine poured through the hatch above his bed. Turning over lazily, the Patryn stared curiously out a porthole into this new world he had entered.

He saw nothing except sky and, far distant, a circle of bright flame burning through the haze, the sun. At least the world had a sun—it had four, in fact. He remembered his lord's questioning that particular point and wondered, briefly, why the Sartan hadn't thought to include the suns on their charts. Perhaps because, as he had discovered, the Death's Gate was located in the center of the solar cluster.

Haplo climbed out of bed and made his way to the bridge. The runes on the hull and wings would prevent his ship from crashing into anything, but it would be wise to make certain he was not hovering in front of a gigantic granite cliff.

He wasn't. The view from the bridge provided another vast expanse of wide-open sky as far as he could see—up, down, sideways.

Haplo crouched down on his haunches, absently scratching the dog's head to keep the animal quiet. He had not reckoned on this and wasn't certain what to do. In its own way, this slightly green-tinted blue, hazy emptiness was as frightening as the ferocious, perpetually raging storm into which he'd flown entering Arianus. The silence around him now echoed loudly as the booming thunder had then. Admittedly his ship wasn't being tossed about like a toy in the hands of an obstreperous child, rain wasn't lashing the hull—already damaged by his passage through Death's Gate. Here the sky was cloudless, serene . . . and not a single object, except the blazing sun, in sight.

The cloudless sky had a sort of mesmerizing effect on Haplo. He tore his gaze from it, and moved over to the steering stone on the bridge. He placed his hands on it, one on either side, and the action completed the circle—his right hand on the stone, the stone between his hands, his left hand on the stone, his left hand attached to his arm, arm to body, body to arm, and back to his right hand again. Aloud, he spoke the runes. The stone began to gleam blue beneath his hands, light welled up from underneath his fingers; he could see the red veins of his own life. The light grew brighter so that he could barely stand to look at it, and he squinted his eyes. Brighter still and suddenly beams of radiant blue shot out from the stone, extending out in all directions.

Haplo was forced to avert his gaze, half-turning his head against the brilliance. He had to keep looking at the stone, keep watching. When one of the navigational beams encountered solid mass—hopefully land—it would bounce back, return to his ship, and light another rune on the stone, turning it red. Haplo could then steer in that direction.

Confidently, expectantly, he waited.

Nothing.

Patience was one virtue the Patryns had learned in the Labyrinth, learned by having it beaten and twisted and bashed into them. Lose your temper, act impulsively, irrationally and the Labyrinth would claim you. If you were lucky, you died. If not, if you survived, you carried with you a lesson that would haunt the rest of your days. But you learned. Yes, you learned.

Hands on the steering stone, Haplo waited.

The dog sat beside him, ears up, eyes alert, mouth open in an expectant grin. Time passed. The dog eased himself down on the floor, front feet extended, head up, still watching, its plumy tail brushing the floor. More time. The dog yawned. Its head sank beneath its paws; his eyes, on Haplo, became reproachful. Haplo waited, hands on the stone. The blue beams had long since ceased to shoot out. The only object he could see were the suns, gleaming like a superheated coin.

Haplo began to wonder if the ship was still flying. He couldn't tell. Magically controlled, the cables didn't creak, the wings didn't move, the ship made no sound. Haplo had no point of reference, he couldn't see clouds scudding past, he couldn't see land drawing near or receding, there was no horizon.

The dog rolled over on its side and went to sleep.

The runes beneath his hands remained dark and lifeless. Haplo felt fear's small sharp teeth start to gnaw at him. He told himself he was being foolish, there was absolutely nothing to be afraid of.

That's just the point, something inside him answered. There's nothing.

Perhaps the stone was malfunctioning? The thought crossed Haplo's mind, but he immediately banished it. Magic was never fallible. Those using it might be, but Haplo knew he had activated the beams correctly. He envisioned them in his mind, traveling with incredible speed into the void. Traveling, traveling, an immense distance. What did it mean, if the light didn't come back?

Haplo pondered. A beam of light, shining in the darkness of

a cave, lights your way a certain distance, then eventually grows dim and finally fades out completely. The beam is bright, concentrated around its source. But as it travels farther away from the source, it begins to break apart, diffuse. A shiver prickled Haplo's skin, the hair on his arms rose. The dog sat up suddenly, teeth bared, a low growl rumbling in its throat.

The blue beams were incredibly powerful. They would have to travel an immense distance before they weakened to the point where they could not return. Or perhaps they had encountered some sort of obstacle? Haplo slowly withdrew his hands from the stone.

He eased himself down beside the dog, soothing it with his hand. The animal, sensing his master's trouble, gazed at him anxiously, tail thumping against the deck, asking what to do.

"I don't know," Haplo murmured, staring out into the dazzling, empty sky.

For the first time in his life, he felt completely helpless. He'd waged a desperate battle for his life on Arianus and he hadn't experienced the terror he was beginning to feel now. He'd faced countless enemies in the Labyrinth—foes many times his size and strength and sometimes intelligence—and he'd never succumbed to the panic starting to bubble up within him.

"This is nonsense!" he said aloud, leaping to his feet with a suddenness that unnerved the dog and caused it to scramble back, out of his way.

Haplo ran through the ship, staring out every portal, peering through every crack and cranny, hoping desperately to see some sign of something—anything—except endless blue-green sky and those damn, brightly shining suns. He climbed up top, moved out onto the ship's huge wings. The sensation of wind blowing against his face gave him his first impression that they were indeed moving through the air. Grasping onto the rail, he stared out over the ship's hull, stared down, down, down into an endless blue-green void. And he wondered suddenly if he was looking down. Perhaps he was looking up. Perhaps he was flying upside down. He had no way to tell.

The dog stood at the foot of the ladder, gazing up at its master and whining. The animal was afraid to come topside. Haplo had a sudden vision of falling over the hull, falling and falling endlessly, and he didn't blame the dog for not wanting to risk it. The Patryn's hands, gripping the rail, were wet with sweat. With an effort, he pried them loose and hurried back down below.

Once on the bridge, he paced its length, back and forth, and cursed himself for a coward. "Damn!" he swore and slammed his fist hard into the solid wood bulkhead.

The runes tattooed on his skin protected him from damage, the Patryn didn't even have the satisfaction of feeling pain. Furious, he was about to hit the hull again when a sharp, imperative bark halted him. The dog stood on its hind legs, pawing at him frantically, begging him to stop. Haplo saw himself reflected in the animal's liquid eyes, saw a man frantic, on the verge of madness.

The horrors of the Labyrinth had not broken him. Why should this? Just because he had no idea where he was going, just because he couldn't tell up from down, just because he had the horrible feeling he was going to drift endlessly through this empty blue-green sky . . . Stop it!

Haplo drew a deep, shivering breath and patted the dog on the flank.

"It's all right, boy. I'm better now. It's all right."

The dog, eyeing his master uneasily, fell back down on all fours.

"Control," said Haplo. "I've got to get control of myself." The word struck him. "Control. That's what's the matter with me. I've lost control. Even in the Labyrinth, I was in control. I was able to do something to affect my own fate. Fighting the chaodyns, I was outnumbered, defeated before I started, yet I had a chance to act. At the end, I chose to die. Then you came"—he stroked the dog's head—"and I chose to live. But here, I've got no choice, it seems. There's nothing I can do. . . ."

Or was there? Panic subsided, terror was banished. Cool, rational thought poured into the void left behind. Haplo crossed to the steering stone. He put his hands upon it a second time, placing them over a different set of runes. Hand, stone, hand, body, hand. Again the circle was complete. He spoke the runes, and the beams shot out in all directions, this time with a different purpose.

They weren't seeking mass—land or rock. This time he sent them seeking life.

The wait seemed endless, and Haplo began to feel himself sliding into the dark abyss of fear when suddenly the lights returned. Haplo stared, puzzled, confused. The lights were coming from every direction, bombarding him, streaming down onto the stone from above, below, all around him.

That was impossible, it didn't make sense. How could he be surrounded—on all sides—by life? He pictured the world as he had seen it in the Sartan's diagram—a round ball, floating in space. He should be getting readings from only one direction. Haplo concentrated, studied the lights, and decided finally that the beams slanting over his left shoulder were stronger than any of the others. He felt relieved; he would sail in that direction.

Haplo moved his hands to another point on the stone, the ship slowly began to turn, altering course. The cabin that had before been drenched in bright sunlight began to darken, shadows crept across the floor. When the beam was aligned with the proper point on the stone, the rune flashed a bright red. Course was set. Haplo removed his hands.

Smiling, he sat down beside the dog and relaxed. He'd done all he could. They were sailing toward life, of some sort. As for whatever those other confusing signals had been, Haplo could only assume he'd made an error.

Not something he did often. He could forgive himself one, he decided, considering the circumstances.

CHAPTER ◆ 14

SOMEWHERE, GUNIS

◆

"WE KNOW THE BEST TRAILS," REGA HAD TOLD PAITHAN.

As it turned out, there was no best trail. There was one trail. And neither Rega nor Roland had ever seen it. Neither brother nor sister had ever been to the dwarven kingdom, a fact they took care to keep from the elf.

"How tough can it be?" Roland had asked his sister. "It'll be just like all the other trails through the jungle."

But it wasn't, and after a few cycles' travel, Rega was beginning to think they'd made a mistake. Several mistakes, in fact.

The trail, such as it existed and where it existed, was quite new. It had been carved through the jungle by dwarven hands, which meant that it wended its way far beneath the upper levels of the huge trees where humans and elves were more comfortable. It meandered and turned and twisted through dark, shadowy regions. Sunlight, when it could be seen at all, appeared reflected through a roof of green.

The air this far below the upper reaches seemed to have been trapped here for centuries. It was stagnant, hot, and humid. The rains that fell in torrents above trickled below, filtered through innumerable branches and leaves and moss beds. The water was not clear and sparkling, but had a brownish cast to it and tasted strongly of moss. It was a different, dismal world and after a penton's[1]

[1]Human measure of time, equal to a fortnight.

traveling, the humans in the party grew heartily sick of it. The elf, always interested in new places, found it rather exciting and maintained his usual cheerful demeanor.

The trail had not been built to accommodate loaded caravans, however. Often, the vines, trees, and brush were so thick that the tyros could not crawl through with the packs on their hard-shelled backs. This meant that the three had to remove the loaded baskets, lug them through the jungle by hand, all the while cajoling the tyros into following them.

Several times, the path came to a halt at the edge of a bed of shaggy gray moss and plunged downward into even deeper darkness; no bridges had been built connecting the way. Again, the tyros had to be unloaded so that they could spin their webs and float down. The heavy baskets had to be lowered by hand.

Up above, the two men—arms nearly breaking—braced themselves and slowly paid out the rope, lowering the baggage through the air. Most of the heavy work fell to Roland. Paithan's slender body and light musculature were of little help. Eventually he took the job of fixing the rope around a tree limb and holding it fast, while Roland—with a strength that seemed marvelous to the elf—handled the lowering by himself.

They dropped Rega down first, to be on hand to untie the baskets as they were lowered and to keep an eye on the tyros to be certain they didn't crawl off. Standing at the bottom of the cliff in the stagnant gray-green darkness, alone, hearing growls and snufflings and the sudden, hair-raising call of the vampire sloth, Rega gripped her raztar and cursed the day she'd let Roland talk her into this. Not only because of the danger, but because of another reason—something completely unforeseen, unexpected. Rega was falling in love.

"Dwarves really live in places like this?" asked Paithan, looking up, up, up and still not being able to see the sun through the tangled, dark mass of moss and tree limbs overhead.

"Yeah," said Roland shortly, not particularly eager to discuss the issue, afraid that the elf might ask more questions about the dwarves than he—Roland—was prepared to answer.

The three were resting after encountering the steepest drop yet. Their hempen ropes had barely been long enough, and even then Rega'd been forced to climb up a tree and untie the baskets, which were left hovering some three feet off the ground.

"Why, your hands are covered with blood!" Rega exclaimed.

"Oh, it's nothing," said Paithan, looking ruefully at his palms. "I slipped coming down that last length of rope."

"It's this damn wet air," muttered Rega. "I feel like I'm living under the sea. Here, let me treat those for you. Roland, dear, can you bring me some fresh water."

Roland, slumped wearily on the gray moss, glared at his "wife": *Why me?*

Rega shot her "husband" a vicious, sidelong look. *Getting me alone with him was your idea.*

Roland, glowering, rose to his feet and stomped off into the jungle, carrying the waterskin with him.

Now was the perfect time for Rega to continue her seduction of the elf. Paithan obviously admired her, treating her with unfailing courtesy and respect. In fact, she had never met a man who treated her so well. But holding the slim white hands with long graceful fingers in her own short, stubby-fingered brown hands, Rega felt suddenly shy and awkward as a young girl at her first village dance.

"Your touch is very gentle," said Paithan.

Rega blushed hotly and glanced up at him from beneath her long, black eyelashes. Paithan was regarding her with an unusual expression for the carefree elf—his eyes were grave, serious.

I wish you weren't another man's wife.

I'm not! Rega wanted to scream.

Her fingers began to tremble, and she snatched them away, fumbling in her kit. What's wrong with me? He's an elf! His money, that's what we're after. That's all that's important.

"I've got some salve, made of sporn bark. It's going to sting, I'm afraid, but you'll be healed by morning."

"The wound I'm suffering will never heal." Paithan's hand slid over Rega's arm, his touch soft and caressing.

Rega held perfectly still, allowing his hand to glide over her skin, up her arm, lighting fires as it passed. Her skin burned, the flames spread to her chest and constricted her breathing. The elf's hand slid around to the small of her back, he drew her near. Rega, holding onto the bottle of salve tightly, let herself be pulled to him. She didn't look at him, she couldn't. This will work out fine, she told herself.

The elf's arms were slender and smooth skinned, his body

lithe. She tried to ignore the fact that her heart was beating so she thought it might crash through her chest.

Roland will come back and find us . . . kissing . . . and he and I will take this elf . . . for everything . . .

"No!" Rega gasped and broke away from Paithan's embrace. Her skin burned, inexplicably she shook with chills. "Don't . . . do that!"

"I'm sorry," said Paithan, immediately drawing away. His breathing, too, was coming in short, deep gasps. "I don't know what came over me. You're married. I must accept that."

Rega didn't answer. She kept her back to him, wishing more than anything that he'd hold her in his arms, knowing that she'd pull away from him again if he did.

This is insane! she told herself, wiping a tear from her eye with the heel of her hand. I've let men I don't care two stone for put their hands all over me. Yet this one . . . I want him . . . and I can't . . .

"It won't happen again, I promise you," said Paithan.

Rega knew he meant it and cursed her heart for shriveling up and dying at the thought. She'd tell him the truth. The words were on her lips, then she paused.

What would she say? Tell him that she and Roland weren't husband and wife, that they were really brother and sister, that they'd lied in order to trap the elf into an improper liaison, that they were planning to blackmail him? She could see his look of disgust and hatred. Maybe he'd leave!

It would be better if he did, whispered the cold, hard voice of logic. What chance for happiness do you have with an elf? Even if you found a way to tell him you were free to accept his love, how long would it last? He doesn't love you, no elf could truly love a human. He's amusing himself. That's all it would be. A dalliance, lasting a season or two. Then he'll leave, return to his people, and you'll be an outcast among your own kind for having submitted to an elf's caresses.

No, Rega answered stubbornly. He does love me. I've seen it in his eyes. And I've proof of it—he didn't try to force his advances on me.

Very well, then, said that irritating voice, so he loves you. What now? You marry. You're both outcasts. He can't go home, you can't either. Your love is barren, for elves and humans can't reproduce. You wander the world in loneliness, years pass. You grow old and haggard, while he remains young and vital . . .

"Hey, what's going on here?" demanded Roland, leaping unexpectedly out of the brush. He stopped dead in his tracks.

"Nothing," said Rega coldly.

"I can see that," murmured Roland, edging close to his sister. She and the elf were standing at opposite edges of the small clearing in the jungle growth, as far apart as possible. "What's going on, Rega? You two have a fight?"

"Nothing! All right! Just leave me alone!" Rega glanced up into the dark and twisted trees, clasped her arms around her and shivered. "This isn't the most romantic spot, you know," she said in a low voice.

"C'mom, Sis." Roland grinned. "You'd make love to a man in a pigsty if he paid you well enough."

Rega slapped him. The blow was hard, well aimed. Roland, his hand to his aching jaw, stared at her in amazement.

"What'd you do that for? I meant it as a compliment!"

Rega turned on her heel and stalked out of the clearing. At the edge, she half-turned again and tossed something toward the elf. "Here, rub that on the sores."

You're right, she told herself, hurrying into the jungle where she could have her cry out in private. I'll leave things just the way they are. We'll deliver the weapons, he'll leave, and that'll be an end of it. I'll smile and tease him and never let him see he meant anything more to me than just a good time.

Paithan, taken by surprise, just barely caught the thrown bottle before it smashed on the ground. He watched Rega plunge into the brush, he could hear her crashing through the undergrowth.

"Women," said Roland, rubbing his bruised cheek and shaking his head. He took the waterskin over to the elf and dropped it at his feet. "Must be her time of season."

Paithan flushed a deep red and gave Roland a disgusted look.

The human winked. "What's the matter, Quin, I say something to embarrass you?"

"In my land, men don't talk about such things," Paithan rebuked.

"Yeah?" Roland glanced back toward where Rega had disappeared, then looked over at the elf and his grin widened. "I guess in your land men don't do a lot of things."

Paithan's flush of anger deepened to guilt. Did Roland see Rega and me together? Is this his way of letting me know, warning me to keep my hands off?

Paithan was forced, for Rega's sake, to swallow the insult. Sitting down on the ground, he began to spread the salve on his skinned and bloody palms, wincing as the brown-colored gunk bit into raw flesh and exposed nerves. He welcomed the pain. At least it was better than the one biting at his heart.

Paithan had enjoyed Rega's mild flirtations the first cycle or two on their journey until it had suddenly occurred to him that he was enjoying them too much. He found himself watching intently the play of the smooth muscles in her shapely legs, the warm glow of the firelight in her brown eyes, the trick she had of running her tongue across her berry-stained lips when she was deep in thought.

The second night on the trail, when she and Roland had taken their blanket to the other side of the glade and laid down next to each other in the shadowed sunlight of rain's hour, Paithan had thought his insides would twist out of him in jealousy. No matter that he never saw the two kissing or even touching affectionately. Indeed, they treated each other with a casual familiarity he found quite astonishing, even in husband and wife. He had decided, by the fourth cycle on the trail, that Roland—though a good enough fellow as humans go—didn't appreciate the treasure he had for a wife.

Paithan felt comforted by this knowledge, it gave him an excuse to let his feelings for the human woman grow and blossom, when he knew very well he should have ripped them up by the roots. Now the plant was in full bloom, the vine twining around his heart. He realized now, too late, the harm that had been done . . . to them both.

Rega loved him. He knew, he'd felt it in her trembling body, he'd seen it in that one, brief look she'd given him. His heart should have been singing with joy. It was dumb with sick despair. What folly! What mad folly! Oh, sure, he could have his moments of pleasure. He'd done that with countless human women. Love them, then leave them. They expected nothing more, they *wanted* nothing more. And neither had he. Until now.

Yet, what did he want? A relationship that would cut them both adrift from their lives? A relationship looked upon with abhorrence by both worlds? A relationship that would give them nothing, not even children? A relationship he would have to watch come at last and inevitably to a bitter end?

No, nothing good can come of it. I'll leave, he thought. Go back home. I'll give them the tyros. Callie'll be mad at me anyway. I might as well be hung for a sheep as a goat, as the saying goes. I'll leave now. This very moment.

But he continued sitting in the clearing, absently spreading salve on his palms. He thought he could hear, far away, the sound of someone weeping. He tried to ignore it, but eventually he could stand it no longer.

"I think I hear your wife crying," he said to Roland. "Maybe something's wrong."

"Rega?" Roland glanced up from feeding the tyros. He appeared amused. "Crying? Naw, must be a bird you're hearing. Rega never cries, not even the time when she got stabbed in the raztar fight. Did you ever notice the scar? It's on her left thigh, about here . . ."

Paithan rose to his feet and stalked off into the jungle, moving in a direction opposite to that which Rega had taken.

Roland watched the elf leave out of the corner of his eye and hummed a bawdy song currently making the rounds of the taverns.

"He's fallen for her like a rotten tree limb in a storm," he told the tyros. "Rega's playing it cooler than usual, but I guess she knows what she's doing. He's an elf, after all. Still, sex is sex. Little elves come from somewhere and I don't think it's heaven.

"But, ugh! Elven women! Skinny and bony—you might as well take a stick to bed. No wonder poor old Quin's following Rega around with his tongue hanging out. It's only a matter of time. I'll catch him with his pants down in a cycle or two, and then we'll fix him! Too bad, though." Roland reflected. Tossing the waterskin on the ground, he leaned wearily back against a tree and stretched, easing the stiffness from his limbs. "I'm beginning to kind of like the guy."

CHAPTER ♦ 15

THE DWARVEN KINGDOM

THURN

♦

FOND OF DARKNESS AND OF DELVING AND TUNNELING, THE DWARVES of Pryan did not build their cities in the treetops, as did the elves, or on the moss plains, as did the humans. The dwarves carved their way downward through the dark vegetation, seeking the dirt and stone that was their heritage, though that heritage was little more than a dim memory of an ancient past in another world.

The kingdom of Thurn was a vast cavern of vegetation. The dwarves dwelt and worked in homes and shops that had been bored deep and straight into the boles of gigantic chimney trees, so called because the wood did not burn easily and the smoke of dwarven fires was able to rise up through natural shafts in the tree's center. Branches and plant roots formed walkways and streets lit by flickering torchlight. The elves and humans lived in perpetual day. The dwarves lived in endless night—a night they loved and found blessed, but a night that Drugar feared was about to become permanent.

He received the message from his king during the dinner hour. It was a mark of the message's importance that it was delivered to him at mealtime, a time when one's full and complete attention is to be devoted to food and the all-important digestive process afterward. Talking is forbidden during the eating of the food and only pleasant subjects are discussed during the time following, to prevent the stomach's juices from turning rancid and causing gastric upset.

The king's messenger was profuse in his apologies for taking

Drugar from his dinner but added that the matter was quite urgent. Drugar bolted from his chair, scattering crockery, causing his old manservant to grumble and predict dire things occurring in the young dwarf's stomach.

Drugar, who had a dark feeling he knew the purport of the message, almost told the old servant that they'd be fortunate indeed if all the dwarves had to worry about was indigestion. But he kept silent. Among the dwarves, the elderly were treated with respect.

His father's bore-hole house was located next to his and Drugar didn't have far to go. He ran this distance, but then stopped when he reached the door, suddenly reluctant to enter, reluctant to hear what he knew he must. Standing in the darkness, fingering the rune-stone he wore around his neck, he asked for courage of the One Dwarf. Drawing a deep breath, he opened the door and entered the room.

His father's house was exactly the same as Drugar's house, which was exactly the same as every other dwarven house in Thurn. The tree's wood had been smoothed and polished to a warm, yellowish color. The floor was flat, the walls rising to an arched ceiling. It was plainly furnished. Being king gave his father no special privileges, only additional responsibility. The king was the One Dwarf's head and the head, though it thinks for the body, certainly isn't any more important to the body than, say, the heart or (most important to many dwarves) the stomach.

Drugar found his father sitting at his meal, the half-full plates shoved aside. In his hand he held a piece of bark whose smooth side was thickly covered with the strong, angular letters of the dwarven language.

"What is the news, Father?"

"The giants are coming," said the old dwarf. (Drugar was the product of marriage late in life. His mother, though she maintained most cordial relations with Drugar's father, kept her own house, as was the custom of dwarven women when their children had reached maturity.) "The scouts have watched them. The giants wiped out Kasnar—the people, the cities, everything. And they are coming this way."

"Perhaps," said Drugar, "they will be stopped by the sea."

"They will stop at the sea, but not for long," said the old dwarf. "They are not skilled with tools, say the scouts. What tools they use, they use to destroy, not to create. It will not occur to them to build ships. But they will go around, come by land."

"Maybe they will turn back. Maybe all they wanted was to take over Kasnar."

His words were spoken from hope, not belief. And once the words left his lips he knew even his hope was false.

"They did not take over Kasnar," said his father, with a heavy sigh. "They destroyed it—utterly. Their aim is not to conquer, but to kill."

"Then you know what we must do, Father. We must ignore the fools who say that these giants are our brothers! We must fortify our city and arm our people. Listen, Father." Drugar leaned near, lowering his voice, though the two were the only ones present in the old dwarf's dwelling. "I have contacted a human weapons dealer. Elven railbows, boltarches! They will be ours!"

The old dwarf looked at his son, a flame flickered deep in the eyes that had been dark and lackluster. "That is good!" Reaching across, he laid one gnarled hand on his son's strong one. "You are quick thinking and daring, Drugar. You will make a good king." He shook his head, stroked the iron gray beard that flowed almost to his knees. "But I do not believe the weapons will come in time."

"They had better," growled Drugar, "or someone will pay!" The dwarf rose to his feet, began pacing the small, dark room built far below the moss surface, as far from the sun as the dwarves could get. "I will call out the army—"

"No," said the old dwarf.

"Father, you are being stubborn—"

"And you are a khadak!"[1] The old dwarf raised a walking stick, gnarled and twisted as his own limbs, and pointed it at his son. "I said you would make a good king. And so you will. *If!* If you will keep the fire under control! The flame of your thoughts burns clear and rises high, but instead of keeping the fire banked, you let it flare up, blaze out of control!"

Drugar's face darkened, his thick brows came together. The fire of which his father spoke burned within him, heated scorching words. Drugar fought his temper, the words seared his lips but he kept them inside. He loved and honored his father, though he thought the old man was caving in beneath this terrible blow.

---

[1]Firebrand—a length of wood soaked in resin that flames quickly when the proper rune is spoken.

He forced himself to try to speak calmly. "Father, the army—"

"—will turn on itself and fight each other!" the old dwarf said in a quiet voice. "Is that what you want, Drugar?"

The old dwarf drew himself up. His height was no longer impressive: the bowed back would not straighten, the legs could no longer support the body without assistance. But Drugar, towering over his father, saw the dignity in the trembling stance, the wisdom in the dimming eyes, and felt himself a child again.

"Half the army will refuse to bear arms against their 'brothers,' the giants. And what will you do, Drugar? Order them to go to war? And how will you enforce that order, son? Will you command the other half of the army to pick up arms against *their* brothers?

"No!" cried the old king, slamming the walking stick against the floor. The thatched walls quivered at his wrath. "Never will there come a day when the One Dwarf are divided! Never will come a day when the body sheds the blood of itself!"

"Forgive me, Father. I did not think."

The old king sighed, his body shriveled and collapsed in upon itself. Tottering, he grasped his son's hand. With Drugar's aid and that of the walking stick, the old dwarf resumed his chair. "Keep the flames in check, Son. Keep them in check. Or they will destroy all in their path, including you, Drugar. Including you. Now go, return to your meal. I am sorry I had to interrupt it."

Drugar left and returned to his house, but did not finish his meal. Back and forth, back and forth he stumped across his room. He tried hard to bank his inner fire, but it was useless. The flames of fear for his people, once kindled, would not readily die down. He could not and would not disobey his father. The man was not only his father but also his king. However, Drugar decided, he wouldn't let the fire die completely. When the enemy came, they would find scorching flame, not cold, dark ash.

The dwarven army was not mobilized. But Drugar privately (and without his father's knowledge) drew up battle plans and informed those dwarves who believed as he did to keep their weapons close to hand. He kept in close contact with the dwarven scouts, followed through their reports the progress of the giants. Thwarted by the Whispering Sea, the giants turned to the est, traveling overland, moving relentlessly toward their goal—whatever goal that was.

Drugar did not think it was to ally themselves with the dwarves. Dark rumors came to Thurn of massacres of dwarves in the norinth settlements of Grish and Klag, but the giants were difficult to track and the reports of the scouts (those reports that came through) were garbled and made little sense.

"Father," pleaded Drugar, "you must let me call out the army now! How can anyone discount these messages!"

"Humans," said his father, sighing. "The council has decided that it is the human refugees, fleeing the giants, who are committing these crimes! They say that the giants will join us and then we will have our revenge!"

"I've interviewed the scouts personally, Father," said Drugar with rising impatience. "Those who are left. Fewer and fewer come in every day. Those who do are scared out of their wits!"

"Indeed?" said his father, eyeing his son shrewdly. "And what do they tell you they've seen?"

Drugar hesitated, frustrated. "All right, Father! So they've not actually *seen* anything!"

The old dwarf nodded wearily. "I've heard them, Drugar. I've heard the wild tales about 'the jungle moving.' How can I go to the council with such elf-krat?"

It was on Drugar's lips to tell his father what the council could do with its own krat but he knew that such a rude outburst wouldn't help matters any and would only anger his father. It wasn't the king's fault. Drugar knew his father had said much the same to the Council as his son had said to him. The council of the One Dwarf, made up of the elders in the tribe, didn't want to hear.

Clamping his mouth shut so that no hot words might escape him, Drugar stomped out of his father's house and made his way through the vast and complex series of tunnels carved through the vegetation to the top. Emerging, blinking, into the sunlight, he stared into the tangle of leaves.

Something was out there. And it was coming his way. And he didn't believe it was coming in the spirit of brotherly love. He waited, with a sense of increasing desperation, for the arrival of the magical, intelligent, elven weapons.

If those two humans had double-crossed him, he vowed by the body, mind, and soul of the One Dwarf that he would make them pay—with their lives.

CHAPTER ♦ 16

SOMEWHERE ELSE,

GUNIS

♦

"I HATE THIS," SAID REGA.

Two more cycles' traveling took them farther down into the depths of the jungle, down far below the top level, far below bright sunshine and fresh air and cool rain. They had come to the edge of a moss plain. The trail dropped off into a deep ravine that was lost in shadow. Lying flat on top of the moss cliff, peering down into the depths, they couldn't see what was below them. The thick leaves of the tree branches above and ahead of them completely cut off sunlight. Going below, they would be traveling in almost total darkness.

"How far away are we?" asked Paithan.

"From the dwarves? About two cycles' journey, I should think," remarked Roland, peering into the shadows.

"You think? Don't you know?"

The human heaved himself to his feet. "You lose all sense of time down there. No hour flowers, no flowers of any sort."

Paithan didn't comment. He stared over the edge, as if fascinated by the darkness.

"I'm going to go check on the tyros."

Rega stood up, gave the elf a sharp, meaningful glance, and motioned to her brother. Together, silently, the two walked away from the edge, returning to a small glade where the tyros had been tethered.

"This isn't working. You've got to tell him the truth," Rega said, her fingers tugging on the strap of one of the baskets.

"Me?" said Roland.

"Keep your voice down! Well, *we* have to, then."

"And just how much of the truth do you plan to tell him, Wife, dear?"

Rega shot her brother a vicious sidelong glance. Sullenly, she looked away. "Just . . . admit that we've never been on this trail before. Admit we don't know where the hell we are or where the hell we're going."

"He'll leave."

"Good!" Rega gave the strap a violent jerk that made the tyro bleat in protest. "I hope he does!"

"What's got into you?" Roland demanded.

Rega glanced and shivered. "It's this place. I hate it. And" —she turned back, staring at the strap, her fingers absently stroking it—"the elf. He's different. Not like what you told me. He's not smug and overbearing. He isn't afraid to get his hands dirty. He's not a coward. He stands his share of the watch, he's ripped his palms to shreds on those ropes. He's cheerful and funny. He even cooks, which is more than you've ever done, Roland! He's . . . nice, that's all. He doesn't deserve . . . what we were planning."

Roland stared at his sister, saw a faint flush of crimson creep up from her brown throat to her cheeks. She kept her eyes lowered. Reaching out his hand, Roland caught hold of Rega's chin and turned her face toward him. Shaking his head, he let out a low whistle.

"I believe you've fallen for the guy!"

Angrily, Rega struck his hand away.

"No, I haven't! He's an elf, after all."

Frightened by her own feelings, nervous and tense, furious at herself and at her brother, Rega spoke with more force than she intended. Her lips curled at the word "elf," she seemed to spit it out in disgust, like she'd tasted something foul and nasty.

Or at least that's what it sounded like to Paithan.

The elf had risen from his place overlooking the drop and gone back to report to Roland that he thought their ropes were too short, there was no way they could lower the baggage. Moving with elven lightness and grace, he hadn't intentionally planned to sneak up on the two. That was just the way it turned out. Hearing clearly Rega's last statement, he crouched in the shadows of a dangling evir vine, hidden by its broad, heart-shaped leaves, and listened.

"Look, Rega, we've come this far, I say we carry the plan out to the end. He's wild about you! He'll tumble. Just get him alone in some dark patch, maneuver him into a clinch. I'll rush in and save your honor, threaten to tell all. He forks over the cash to keep us quiet and we're set. Between that and this sale, we'll live high for the next season." Roland reached out his hand, affectionately stroked Rega's long, dark hair. "Think about the money, kid. We've gone hungry too many times to pass up this chance. Like you said, he's only an elf."

Paithan's stomach clenched. Hastily, he turned away, moving silently through the trees, not particularly watching or caring where he was going. He missed Rega's response to her husband, but that was just as well. If he had seen her look up at Roland, grinning conspiratorially; if he had heard her pronounce the word *elf* in that tone of loathing one more time, he would have killed her.

Falling against a tree, suddenly dizzy and nauseous, Paithan gasped for breath and wondered at himself. He couldn't believe he was acting like this. What did it matter, after all? So the little slut had been playing with him? He'd noticed her game in the tavern before they ever left on this journey! What had blinded him?

She had. He'd actually been fool enough to think she was falling in love with him! Those conversations they'd had along the trail. He'd told her stories about his homeland, about his sisters, his father, and the crazy old wizard. She'd laughed, she'd seemed interested. Her admiration had shone in her eyes.

And then there had been all those times they'd touched, just by accident, bodies brushing against each other, hands meeting when they reached for the same waterskin. Then there'd been the trembling, quivering eyelids, heaving breasts, flushed skin.

"You're good, Rega!" he whispered through clenched teeth. "Really good. Yes, I'm 'wild about you'! I would have 'tumbled.' But not now! Now that I know you, little whore!" Closing his eyes tightly, squeezing back tears, the elf sagged against the tree. "Blessed Peytin, Holy Mother of us all, why did you do this to me?"

Perhaps it was the prayer—one of the few the elf had ever

bothered to make—but he felt a jab of conscience. He'd known she belonged to another man. The elf had flirted with the woman in Roland's very presence. Paithan had to admit to himself that he'd found it exhilarating, seducing the wife beneath the husband's nose.

"You got what you deserved," Mother Peytin seemed to be saying to him. The goddess's voice bore an unfortunate resemblance to Calandra's, however, and it only made Paithan angrier.

"It was all in fun," he justified himself. "I would never have let it go too far, not really. And I certainly never meant to . . . to fall in love."

That last statement, at least, was true and it made Paithan believe profoundly in all the rest.

"What's wrong? Paithan? What's the matter?"

The elf opened his eyes, turned around. Rega stood before him, her hand reaching for his arm. He drew back, away from her touch.

"Nothing," he said, swallowing.

"But you look terrible! Are you sick?" Rega reached for him again. "Do you have a fever?"

He took another step back. If she touches me, I'll strike her!

"Yeah. No, uh . . . no fever. I've been . . . sick. Maybe the water. Just . . . leave me alone for a bit."

Yes, I'm better now. Practically cured. Little whore. He found it difficult not to let his hatred and disgust show and so he kept his eyes averted, staring fixedly into the jungle.

"I think I should stay with you," said Rega. "You don't look good at all. Roland's gone off scouting around for another way down, maybe a shorter drop. He'll be gone for quite a while, I imagine—"

"Will he?" Paithan looked at her, a look so strange and piercing that it was Rega who now fell back a step before him. "Will he be gone a long, long time?"

"I don't—" Rega faltered.

Paithan lunged at her, grabbed the woman by the shoulders and kissed her, hard, his teeth cutting her soft lips. He tasted berry-juice and blood.

Rega struggled, squirming in his grasp. Of course, she'd have to put up a token resistance.

"Don't fight it!" he whispered. "I love you! I can't live without you!"

He expected her to melt, to moan, to cover him with kisses. And then Roland would come along, shocked, horrified, hurt. Only money would ease the pain of betrayal.

And I'll laugh! I'll laugh at both of them! And I'll tell them where to stick their money . . .

One arm around her back, the elf pressed the woman's half-naked body up against his. His other hand sought soft flesh.

A violent kick to the groin sent a flash of pain through Paithan. The elf doubled over. Strong hands hit him on the collar bone, knocking him backward, sending him crashing into the underbrush.

Face flushed, eyes flaring, Rega stood over him. "Don't you ever touch me again! Don't come near me! Don't even *talk* to me!"

Her dark hair rose, ruffled like the fur of a scared cat. She turned on her heel and stalked off.

Paithan, rolling on the ground in agony, had to admit he was now extremely confused.

Returning from his search for a more suitable way down onto the trail below, Roland crept back stealthily over the moss, hoping—once again—to catch Rega and her "lover" in a compromising position. He reached the place on the trail where he'd left his sister and the elf, drew in a breath to yell the outrage of an offended husband, and peeped out from the cover of a gigantic shadowcove plant. He exhaled in disappointment and exasperation.

Rega was sitting on the edge of the moss bank, huddled up in a ball very much like a bristle-back squirrel, her back hunched, her arms wrapped tightly around her legs. He could see her face from the side and, by her dark and stormy expression, could almost imagine the quills standing up all over her. His sister's "lover" stood as far from her as possible, on the other edge of the bank's lip. The elf was leaning at rather an odd angle, Roland noticed, almost as if favoring some tender part of himself.

"Strangest damn way to conduct a love affair I ever saw!" Roland muttered. "What do I have to do for that elf—draw him a picture? Maybe baby elves *are* slipped under the cracks of the doors at night! Or maybe that's what *he* thinks. We're going to have to have a little man to man talk, looks like.

"Hey," he called aloud, making a great deal of noise plunging out of the jungle, "I found a place, a ways down, where there's what looks like a rock ledge that sticks out of the moss. We can lower the baskets onto that, then drop 'em down the rest of the way. What happened to you?" he added, looking at Paithan, who was walking hunched over and moving gingerly.

"He fell," said Rega.

"He did?" Roland—who had felt much the same way once after an encounter with an unfriendly barmaid—glanced at his sister in some suspicion. Rega hadn't exactly refused to go ahead with the plan to seduce the elf. But, the more Roland thought about it, he recalled that she hadn't exactly said she would, either. He didn't dare say anything more, however. Rega's face might have been frozen by a basilisk, and the look she cast him might have turned her brother to stone, as well.

"I fell," agreed Paithan, voice carefully expressionless. "I—uh—straddled a tree limb coming down."

"Ouch!" Roland winced in sympathy.

"Yeah, ouch," repeated the elf. He didn't look at Rega. Rega wasn't looking at Paithan. Faces set, jaws rigid, both stared straight at Roland. Neither actually saw him.

Roland was completely at a loss. He didn't believe their story and he would have liked very much to question his sister and worm the truth out of her. But he couldn't very well drag Rega off for a chat without making the elf suspicious.

And then, when Rega was like this, Roland wasn't certain he wanted to be alone with her anyway. Rega's father had been the town butcher. Roland's father had been the town baker. (Their mother, for all her faults, had always seen to it that the family was well fed.) There were times when Rega bore an uncanny resemblance to her father. One of those times was now. He could almost see her standing over a freshly butchered carcass, a bloodthirsty gleam in her eye.

Roland stammered and waved his hand vaguely. "The . . . uh . . . spot I found is in that direction, a few hundred feet. Can you make it that far?"

"Yes!" Paithan grit his teeth.

"I'll go see to the tyros," stated Rega.

"Quin, here, can help—"

"I don't need any help!" Rega snapped.

"She doesn't need any help!" Paithan muttered.

Rega went one way, the elf went the opposite, neither looking at the other. Roland stood in the middle of the empty clearing, rubbing his stubbly brownish blond growth of beard.

"You know, I think I was mistaken. She really *doesn't* like him. And I think her hate's beginning to rub off on the elf! Things between them were going so well, too. I wonder what went wrong? It's no good talking to Rega, not when she's in this mood. There must be something I can do." He could hear his sister pleading, flattering, trying to get the reluctant tyros to move. Paithan, hobbling along the edge of the moss bank, cast a disgusted glance in Rega's direction.

"There's only one thing I can think of to do," Roland mused. "Just keep throwing them together. Sooner or later, something's bound to happen."

CHAPTER ♦ 17

IN THE SHADOWS,

GUNIS

♦

"ARE YOU SURE THAT'S ROCK?" PAITHAN ASKED, PEERING DOWN INTO the gloom at a patch of grayish white beneath them, barely visible through a tangle of vines and leaves.

"Sure, I'm sure," answered Roland. "Remember, we've traveled this route before."

"It's just that I've never heard of rock formations this far up in the jungle."

"We're not exactly that far up anymore, remember? We've dropped quite a ways down."

"Well, we're not getting anywhere standing here staring at it!" put in Rega, hands on her hips. "We're cycles late with the delivery as it is. And you mark my words, Blackbeard'll try to shave off the price. I'll go down, if you're afraid, elf!"

"I'll go," countered Paithan. "I don't weigh as much as you do and if the outcrop is unstable, I'll—"

"Weigh as much! Are you saying that I'm fa—"

"You *both* go," interrupted Roland in soothing tones. "I'll lower you and Rega down there, Quin, then you lower Rega on down to the bottom. I'll send the packs to you and you can pass them on down to my sis—er—my wife."

"Look, Roland, I think the elf should lower *you* and I down—"

"Yes, Redleaf, that does, indeed, seem to me to be a much better solution—"

"Nonsense!" Roland interrupted, pleased with his own deviousness, further plots fomenting in his mind. "I'm the strongest and from here down to that outcrop is the longest haul. Any arguments there?"

Paithan glanced at the human male—with his square-jawed handsome face and his rippling biceps—and clamped his mouth shut. Rega didn't look at her brother at all. Biting her lip, she crossed her arms over her chest and glared down into the shadowy gloom of the jungle below.

Paithan fixed a rope around a tree limb, cinched it tight around himself and hopped over the edge of the moss bank almost before Roland was there to steady him. He rappeled himself easily off the steep sides of the bank, Roland holding the line to keep the elf steady.

The line suddenly went slack.

"All right!" came a shout from below. "I'm here!" There was a moment's silence, then the elf's voice echoed upward, filled with disgust. "This isn't rock! It's a damn fungus!"

"A what?" Roland yelled, leaning as far over the edge as he dared.

"A fungus! A giant mushroom!"

Catching his sister's fiery-eyed glance, Roland shrugged. "How was I supposed to know?"

"I think it's stable enough to use for a landing anyway," Paithan returned, after a moment's pause. The two humans caught something additional about being "damn lucky," but the words were lost in the vegetation.

"That's all I needed to know," said Roland cheerfully. "All right, Sis—"

"Stop calling me that! You've done it twice now today! What are you trying to do?"

"Nothing. Sorry. Just a lot on my mind. Over you go."

Rega tied the rope around her waist, but she didn't lower herself over the edge. Looking out into the jungle, she shivered and rubbed her arms. "I hate this."

"You keep saying that, and it's getting boring. I'm not wild about it either. But the sooner finished the sooner ended, as the saying goes. Hop on over."

"No, it's not just . . . the darkness down there. It's something else. Something's wrong. Can't you feel it? It's too . . . too quiet."

Roland paused, looked around and listened. He and his

sister had been together through tough times. The outside world
had been against them since they'd been born, they'd learned to
rely on and trust only each other. Rega had an intuitive, almost
animallike sense about people and nature. The few times Roland—
the elder of the two—had ignored his sister's advice or warnings,
he'd regretted it. He was a skilled woodsman and, now that she
drew his attention to it, he, too, noticed the uncanny silence.

"Maybe it's always quiet down this far," he suggested. "There's
not a breath of air stirring. We're just used to hearing the wind in
the trees and all that."

"It's not just that. There's no sound or sign of animals and
hasn't been for the last cycle or so. Not even at night. And the
birds are silent." Rega shook her head. "It's as if every wild
creature in this jungle is hiding."

"Maybe it's because we're near the dwarven kingdom. That's
got to be it, kid. What else would it be?"

"I don't know," Rega said, staring intently into the shadows.
"I don't know. I hope you're right. Come on!" she added suddenly, "let's end this."

Roland lowered his sister over the edge of the moss bank.
She rappeled skillfully down the side. Paithan, waiting below,
reached up his hands to steady her landing. The look she gave
him from her dark eyes warned him to stand clear. Rega landed
lightly on the wide ledge formed by the fungus, her lips curling
slightly as she eyed the ugly gray and white mass below her feet.
The rope, tossed over the edge by Roland, snaked down and
landed in a coil at her feet. Paithan began attaching his own
length of rope to a branch.

"What's this fungus attached to?" Rega asked, her tone cool
and business-only.

"The bole of a tree," said Paithan, his tone the same.
He pointed out the striations of the bark, wider than both elf and
human standing side by side.

"Is it stable?" she asked, looking over the rim uneasily.
Another moss bank was visible below, not that far if you had a
rope tied securely around your waist, but a long and unpleasant
drop if you didn't.

"I wouldn't jump up and down on it," suggested Paithan.

Rega heard his sarcasm, cast him a angry glance, and then
turned to shout above. "Hurry up, Roland! What are you doing?"

"Just a minute, dear!" he called down. "Having a little trouble with one of the tyros."

Roland, grinning, sat down on the edge of the moss bank, leaned up against a tree limb and relaxed. Occasionally he poked at one of the tyros with a stick, to make it bellow.

Rega scowled, bit her lip, and moved to stand on the edge of the fungus, as far from the elf as she could possibly get. Paithan, whistling to himself, fixed his rope tightly around the tree limb, tested it, then began to fasten Rega's.

He didn't want to look at her, but he couldn't help it. His eyes kept darting glances in her direction, kept pointing out things to his heart that his heart wasn't the least bit interested in hearing.

Look at her. We're out in the middle of this Orn-cursed land, alone, standing on a fungus with a twenty-foot drop beneath us and she's as cool as Lake Enthial. I never met a woman like her!

With luck, whispered a certain vicious part of him, you'll never meet one again!

Her hair is so soft. I wonder what it looks like when she lets it down out of that braid, falling over her bare shoulders, tumbling around her breasts. . . . Her lips, her kiss was just as sweet as I'd imagined . . .

Why don't you just throw yourself off the edge! The nasty voice advised him. Save yourself a lot of agony. She's out to seduce you, blackmail you. She's playing you for a foo—

Rega sucked in her breath and backed up involuntarily, hands clutching at the tree trunk behind her.

"What is it?" Paithan dropped the rope, sprang over to her.

She was staring intently straight ahead, straight out into the jungle. Paithan followed her gaze.

"What?" he demanded.

"Do you see it?"

"What!"

Rega blinked and rubbed her eyes. "I—I don't know." She sounded confused. "It seemed . . . as if the jungle was . . . moving!"

"Wind," said Paithan, almost angrily, not wanting to admit how frightened he'd been, or the fact that the fear hadn't been for himself.

"Do you feel any wind?" she demanded.

No, he didn't. The air was still, hot, oppressive. His thoughts went uneasily to dragons, but the ground wasn't shaking. He didn't hear the rumbling sound the creatures made moving through the undergrowth. Paithan didn't hear anything. It was quiet, too damn quiet.

Suddenly, above them, came a shout. "Hey! Come back here! You blasted tyro—"

"What is it?" Rega yelled, turning, standing back on the ledge as far as she dared, trying hopelessly to see. "Roland!" Her voice cracked with fear. "What's the matter?"

"These stupid tyros! They've all bolted!"

Roland's bellow faded into the distance. Rega and Paithan heard the sound of crashing, tearing leaves and vines, felt the pounding of his feet shiver the tree, and then silence.

"Tyros are tractable beasts. They don't panic," said Paithan, swallowing to moisten his dry throat. "Not unless something really terrifies them."

"Roland!" Rega yelled. "Let them go!"

"Hush, Rega. He can't! They're carrying the weapons—"

"I don't give a damn!" she cried frantically. "The weapons and the dwarves and the money and you can go to the pit for all I care! Roland, come back!" She beat on the tree trunk with clenched fists. "Don't leave us trapped down here! Roland!

"What was that—"

Rega whirled around, panting. Paithan, face ashen, stared out into the jungle.

"Nothing," he said, lips stiff.

"You're lying. You saw it!" she hissed. "You saw the jungle move!"

"It's impossible. It's a trick of our eyes. We're tired, not enough sleep . . ."

A terrifying cry split the air above them.

"Roland!" Rega screamed. Pressing her body against the tree trunk, hands scrabbling at the wood, she tried to crawl up it. Paithan caught hold of her, dragged her down. Furiously, she fought and struggled in his arms.

Another hoarse scream and then there came a cry of "Reg—" The word broke off with a strangled choke.

Rega went suddenly limp, collapsing against Paithan. He held her fast, his hand on her head, pressing her face against his breast. When she was calmer, he backed her up against the tree trunk and moved to stand in front of her, shielding her with his body. Once she realized what he was doing, she tried to shove him aside.

"Rega, don't. Stay where you are."

"I want to see, damn it!" Her raztar flashed in her hand. "I can fight—"

"I don't know what," Paithan whispered. "And I don't know how!"

He stood aside. Rega emerged from behind him, her eyes wide and staring. She shrank against him, her arm stealing around his waist. Paithan put his arm around her and held her tight. Clinging to each other, they watched the jungle move in silently, surrounding them.

They could see no heads, no eyes, no arms, no legs, no body, but they each had the intense impression that they were being watched and listened to and sought out by extremely intelligent, extremely malevolent beings.

And then Paithan saw them. Or rather, he didn't see them. He saw what appeared to be a part of the jungle separate itself from its background and move toward him. Only when it was quite near him, when its head was almost level with his own, did he realize that he was confronting what appeared to be a gigantic human. He could see the outline of two legs and two feet that walked the ground. Its head was even with his. It moved straight up to them, stared straight at them. A simple act, but the creature made this simple action horrible by the fact that it apparently couldn't see what it stalked.

It had no eyes; a large hole surrounded by skin in the center had seemingly been bored into the center of its forehead.

"Don't move!" Rega panted. "Don't talk! Maybe it won't find us."

Paithan held her close, not answering, not wanting to destroy her hope. A moment before, they'd been making so much noise that a blind, deaf, and drunken elflord could have found them.

The giant approached, and now Paithan could see why it had seemed the jungle was moving. Its body was covered from head to toe with leaves and vines, its skin was the color and texture of tree bark. Even when the giant was extremely close, Paithan had difficulty separating it from its background. The bulbous head was bare and the crown and forehead, that were a whitish color and bald, stood out against the surroundings.

Glancing around swiftly, the elf saw that there were twenty or thirty of the giants emerging from the jungle, gliding toward them, their movements graceful and perfectly, unnaturally silent.

Paithan shrank back against the tree trunk, dragging Rega with him. It was a hopeless gesture, there was obviously no escape. The heads, with their awful dark and empty holes, stared straight at them. The one nearest put his hands upon the edge of the fungus and jerked on it.

The ledge trembied beneath Paithan's feet. Another giant joined its fellow, large fingers grabbing, gripping. Paithan looked down at the huge hands with a terrible kind of fascination, saw that the fingers were stained red with dried blood.

The giants pulled, the fungus shivered, and Paithan heard it ripping away from the tree. Almost losing their balance, the elf and human clung to each other.

"Paithan!" Rega cried, her voice breaking, "I'm sorry! I love you. I truly do!"

Paithan wanted to answer, but he couldn't. Fear had closed off his throat, stolen his breath.

"Kiss me!" Rega gasped. "That way, I won't see—"

He caught hold of her head in his hands, blocking her vision. Closing his own eyes, he pressed his lips against hers.

The world dropped out from underneath them.

CHAPTER ♦ 18

SOMEWHERE ABOVE

PRYAN

♦

HAPLO, DOG AT HIS FEET, SAT NEAR THE STEERING STONE ON THE BRIDGE and gazed wearily, hopelessly out the window of the *Dragon Wing*. They had been flying for how long?

"A day," Haplo answered with bitter irony. "One long, stupid, dull, everlasting day."

The Patryns had no timekeeping devices, they did not need them. Their magical sensitivity to the world around them kept them innately aware of the passage of time in the Nexus. But Haplo had learned by previous experience that the passage through the Death's Gate and entering into another world altered the magic. As he became acclimated to this new world, his body would realign itself to it. But for right now, he had no idea how much time had truly passed since he had entered Pryan.

He wasn't accustomed to eternal sunshine, he was used to natural breaks in the rhythm of his life. Even in the Labyrinth there was day and night. Haplo had often had reason to curse the coming of night in the Labyrinth, for with night came darkness and, under the cover of darkness came your enemies. Now he would have fallen on his knees and begged for the blessed respite from the blazing sun, for the blessed shadow that brought rest and sleep—no matter how guarded.

The Patryn had been alarmed to catch himself, after another sleepless sun-lit "night," seriously considering gouging out his own eyes.

He knew, then, that he was going mad.

The hellish terror of the Labyrinth had not been able to defeat him. What another might consider heaven—peace and quiet and eternal light—would be his downfall.

"It figures," he said, and he laughed and felt better. He had staved away insanity for the time being, though he knew it wasn't far off.

Haplo had food and he had water. As long as he had some left of either, he could conjure more. Unfortunately, the food was always the same food, for he could only reproduce what he had, he couldn't alter its structure and come up with something new. He soon grew so sick of dried beef and peas that he had to force himself to eat. He hadn't thought to bring a variety. He hadn't expected to be trapped in heaven.

A man of action, forced to inactivity, he spent much of his time staring fixedly out the windows of his ship. The Patryns do not believe in God. They consider themselves (and grudgingly their enemies, the Sartan) the nearest to divine beings existent. Haplo could not pray for this to end, therefore. He could only wait.

When he first sighted the clouds, he didn't say anything, refusing to admit even to the dog that they might be able to escape their winged prison. It could have been an optical illusion, a trick of the eyes that will see water in a desert. It was, after all, nothing more than a slight darkening of the green-blue sky to a whitish gray.

He took a quick walk around the ship, to compare what he saw ahead of him with what lay behind and all around.

And then it was, staring up into the sky from the ship's top deck, that he saw the star.

"This is the end," he told the dog, blinking at the white light sparkling above him in the hazy, blue-green distance. "My eyes are going." Why hadn't he noticed stars before? If it *was* a star.

"Somewhere on board, there's a device the elves used to see long distances."

The Patryn could have used his magic to enhance his vision, but that would have meant again relying on himself. He had the feeling, however confused, that if he put a purely disinterested object between himself and the star, the object would reveal to him the truth.

Rummaging through the ship, he found the spyglass, tucked away in a chest as a curiosity. He put it to his eye, and focused on the sparkling, twinkling light, half-expecting it to vanish. But it leapt into view, larger, brighter, and pure white.

If it was a star, why hadn't he seen it earlier? And where were the others? According to his lord, the ancient world had been surrounded by countless stars. But during the sundering of the world by the Sartan, the stars had vanished, disappeared. According to his lord, there should be no stars visible on any of the new worlds.

Troubled, thoughtful, Haplo returned to the bridge. I should change course, fly toward the light, investigate it. After all, it *can't* be a star. My Lord has said so.

Haplo put his hands upon the steering stone, but he didn't say the words, he didn't activate the runes. Doubt crept into his mind.

What if My Lord is wrong?

Haplo gripped the stone hard, the sharp edges of the runes bit into the soft, unprotected flesh of his palms. The pain was fitting punishment for doubting his lord, doubting the man who had saved them from the hellish Labyrinth, the man who had established their home in the Nexus, the man who would lead them forth to conquer worlds.

His lord, with his knowledge of astronomy, had said there could be no stars. I will fly toward this light and investigate it. I will have faith. My Lord has never failed me.

But still Haplo didn't speak the runes.

What if he flew toward the light, and his lord was wrong about this world? What if it turned out to be like their ancient world—a planet orbiting a sun set in cold, black and empty space? I could end up flying into a void, flying on and on until death claimed me. At least now, I have sighted what I hope and believe are clouds and where there are clouds there might be land.

My Lord is my master. I will obey him unquestioningly in all things. He is wise, intelligent, all-knowing. I will obey. I will . . .

Haplo lifted his hands from the steering stone. Turning away moodily, he walked over to the window and stared outside.

"There it is, boy," he murmured.

The dog, hearing the troubled tone of his master's voice,

whined in sympathy and brushed his tail against the floor to indicate he was there if Haplo needed him. "Land. At last. We've made it!"

He was certain beyond a doubt. The clouds had parted. He could see dark green beneath them. Flying nearer, he saw the dark green separate into varying shades of green—patches that ranged from a light grayish green to a deep blue-green to a mottled, yellow and emerald green.

"How can I turn back?"

To do so would be illogical, a part of him reasoned. You will land here, make contact with the people as you have been ordered to do, then, upon leaving, you can fly out and investigate the sparkling light.

That made sense, and Haplo was relieved. Never one to waste his time in useless self-recrimination or self-analysis, the Patryn went about his duties calmly, making the ship ready for landing. The dog, sensing his master's growing excitement, jumped about him, nipped at him playfully.

But beneath the excitement and sense of victory and elation ran an undercurrent of darkness. These last few moments had been a dreadful epiphany. Haplo felt unclean, unworthy. He had dared admit to himself that his lord might be fallible.

The ship sailed nearer to the land mass and Haplo realized, for the first time, how fast he'd been traveling. It seemed the ground was hurtling toward him, and he was forced to rechannel the magic in the runes on the wings—a maneuver that reduced the speed and slowed his descent. He could actually make out trees and broad, empty expanses of green that appeared to be suitable for landing. Flying over a sea, he discerned in the distance other bodies of water—lakes and rivers, which he could only barely see for the thick growth of vegetation surrounding them. But he found no signs of civilization.

On and on he flew, skimming over the treetops, and saw no cities, no castles, no walls. At length, weary of watching the endless expanse of green unroll beneath him, Haplo slumped down on the floor in front of the tall windows. The dog had gone to sleep. No ships upon the seas or boats upon the lakes. No roads crisscrossed the open expanses, no bridges spanned the rivers.

According to the records left in the Nexus by the Sartan, this realm should be peopled by elves and humans and dwarfs and perhaps even the Sartan themselves. But if so, where were they? Surely he would have seen some sign of them by now! Or maybe not.

Haplo began, for the first time, to truly envision and understand the enormity of this world. Tens of millions could inhabit it, and he might never find them, though he spent a lifetime in the search. Entire cities might lurk beneath the dense covering of trees and remain invisible to the eye peering down from above. No way to find them, no way to detect their existence except by landing and trying to penetrate that thick green mass.

"This is impossible!" Haplo muttered.

The dog woke up and nuzzled his master's hand with a cold nose. Haplo stroked the soft fur, absently ruffled the silky ears. The dog, sighing, relaxed and closed its eyes.

"It would take an army of us to search this land! And then maybe we wouldn't find anything. Perhaps we shouldn't bother. I— What the— Stop! Wait a minute!"

Haplo jumped to his feet, startling the dog, who leapt up and began to bark. Hands on the steering stone, Haplo sent the ship into a slow turn, staring down below him into a small, light-colored patch of grayish green.

"Yes! There it is!" he cried wildly, pointing out the window, as though exhibiting his discovery to an audience of hundreds instead of one black-and-white dog.

Tiny bursts of light, all different colors, followed by small puffs of black, were plainly visible against the green. He had caught sight of them out of the corner of his eye and turned back to make sure. A moment's pause, and they appeared again. It could be a natural phenomenon, he told himself, forcing himself to calm down, appalled at his own lack of control.

No matter. He would land and check it out. At least he'd get off this blasted ship, breathe fresh air.

Haplo circled, descending, the bursts of light guiding him. Coming down below the level of the very tallest trees, he saw a sight that would have caused him to thank his god for a miracle, if he had believed in any god to thank.

A structure, obviously built by hands guided by a brain, stood next to the open area. The bursts of light were coming from that particular spot. And now he could distinguish people, small forms like bugs standing in the gray-green expanse. The bursts of light began appearing with more frequency now, as if in excitement. It looked as if the lights were shooting forth from out of the midst of the group of people.

Haplo was prepared to meet the inhabitants of this new world. He had his story ready, one similar to that which he'd told the dwarf, Limbeck, on Arianus.

I'm from another part of Pryan, my people (depending on circumstances as he found them) are exactly like you—fighting for their freedom from oppressors. We have won our battle and I have gone forth to help free others.

Of course, there was always the possibility that these people—elves, humans, and dwarves—were living in peace and tranquility with each other, that they had no oppressors, that all was progressing nicely under the rule of the Sartan and they didn't need freeing, thank you. Haplo considered this possibility and, grinning, rejected it. Worlds changed, one factor remained constant. It simply wasn't a mensch's nature to live in harmony with his fellow mensch.[1]

Haplo could see the people on the ground clearly now and he knew that they could see him. People were rushing out of the structure, peering up into the sky. Others were running up the hillside toward the bursts of light. He could begin to make out what appeared to be a large city hidden beneath the overspreading tree branches. Through a break in the jungle growth, he saw a lake surrounded by enormous structures with cultivated gardens and vast expanses of smooth green lawn.

Closer still, and he saw the people staring up at his winged dragonship, its body and head painted so cunningly that it might appear to those below to be a real dragon. He noted that many people were refusing to venture into the open area where it must by now be obvious that Haplo was going to land. They huddled in the shelter of trees, curious, but too prudent to move any closer.

Haplo was, in fact, rather astonished to note that *all* the people weren't fleeing in panic at his approach. But several of

---

[1]A word used by both Sartan and Patryn to designate those of the "lower" races—human, elf, and dwarf. Applies to all equally.

them, two in particular, stood right underneath him, heads tilted upward, hands lifted to shield their eyes from the rays of the blazing sun. He could see one of them—a figure clad in flowing, mouse-colored robes—making gestures with his arms, pointing out a cleared area. If it hadn't been too impossible to even consider, Haplo might have supposed he was expected!

"I've been up here too long," he said to the dog. Feet planted firmly, the animal was staring out the ship's large windows, barking frantically at the people below.

Haplo had no time to continue watching. Hands on the steering stone, he called upon the runes to slow *Dragon Wing*, keep the ship steady, and bring it safely to rest. He could see, out of the corner of his eye, the robed figure hopping up and down, waving a disreputable old hat in the air.

The ship touched ground and, to Haplo's alarm, kept going! It was sinking! He saw then, that he wasn't on firm ground but had landed on a bed of moss that was giving way beneath the ship's weight. He was just about to act to halt the ship's descent when it settled itself with an almost cradling motion, burrowing into the moss like the dog into a thick blanket. At last, after perhaps eons of traveling, Haplo had arrived.

He glanced out the windows, but they were buried beneath the moss. He could see nothing but a gray-green leafy mass pressed up against the glass. He would have to leave by the top deck.

Faint voices were coming from up above, but Haplo figured they would be so awed by his ship that they wouldn't come near. If they did, they would get a shock. Literally. He had activated a magical shield around the ship. Anyone touching it would think, for a split instant, that they'd been struck by lightning.

Now that he had reached his destination, Haplo was himself again. His brain was thinking, guiding, directing. He dressed himself so that every part of his rune-tattooed body was covered by cloth. Soft, supple boots fit over leather trousers. A long-sleeved shirt, gathered tightly at the wrists and at the neck, was covered by a leather doublet. He tied a scarf around his neck, tucking the ends into the shirt.

The sigla did not extend up over the head or onto the face—their magic might interfere with the thought process. Starting from a point on the breast above the heart, the runes traced over the body, running down the trunk to the loins, the thighs, the legs, the tops of the feet but not the soles. Whirls and whorls and intricate designs done in red and blue wrapped around the neck, spread across the shoulder blades, entwined the arms and traveled over the tops and palms of the hands, but left bare the fingers. The brain was left free of magic so that it could guide the magic, the eyes and ears and mouth were left free to sense the world around, the fingers and soles of the feet were left free to touch.

Haplo's last precaution, once his ship was landed and he no longer needed the runes to guide it, was to wrap thick bandages around his hands. He wound the linen around the wrist, covering the palm, lacing it through the bottoms of the fingers; the fingers and thumb he left bare.

A skin disease, he'd told the mensch on Arianus. It is not painful, but the red, puss-filled pustules the disease forms are a sickening sight. Everyone on Arianus, after hearing that story, had taken care to avoid Haplo's bandaged hands.

Well, almost everyone.

One man had guessed he was lying, one man—after casting a spell on Haplo—had looked beneath the bandages and seen the truth. But that man had been Alfred, a Sartan, who had suspected in advance what he might find. Haplo had noticed Alfred paying an unusual amount of attention to his hands, but he'd ignored it—a mistake almost fatal to his plans. Now he knew what to watch for, now he was prepared.

Haplo conjured up an image of himself and inspected himself carefully, walking completely around the illusionary Haplo. At length, he was satisfied. No trace of a rune showed. He banished the illusion. Tugging the bandages over his hands into place, he ascended to the top deck, threw open the hatch, and emerged, blinking, into the bright sun.

The sound of voices hushed at the sight of him. He pulled himself up on the deck and glanced around, pausing a moment to draw a deep breath of fresh, if extremely humid, air. Below, he saw faces, upturned, mouths open, eyes wide.

Elves, he noted, with one exception. The figure in the mouse-colored robes was human—an old man, with long white hair and long white beard. Unlike the others, the old man wasn't gazing at Haplo in awe and wonder. Beaming, stroking his beard, the old man turned this way and that.

"I told you," he was shouting. "Didn't I tell you? By cracky, I guess now you believe me!"

"Here, dog!" Haplo whistled and the animal appeared on deck, trotting along at his heels, to the added astonishment of all observers.

Haplo didn't bother with the ladder; the ship had settled so deeply into the moss—its wings resting on top—that he could jump lightly from the top deck to the ground. The elves gathered around *Dragon Wing* backed up hurriedly, regarding the ship's pilot with suspicious incredulity. Haplo drew in a breath, and was about to launch into his story, his mind working rapidly to provide him with the elven language.

He never got a chance to speak.

The old man rushed up to him, grabbed him by the bandaged hand.

"Our savior! Right on time!" he cried, pumping Haplo's arm vigorously. "Did you have a nice flight?"

CHAPTER ◆ 19

THE BORDER,

THURN

◆

ROLAND SQUIRMED, TRYING TO EASE HIS CRAMPED MUSCLES BY MOVING into another position. The maneuver worked for a few moments, then his arms and buttocks began aching again, only in different places. Grimacing, he tried surreptitiously to twist his wrists out of the vines that bound him. Pain forced him to quit. The vines were tough as leather; he'd rubbed his skin raw.

"Don't waste your strength," came a voice.

Roland looked around, twisting his head to see.

"Where are you?"

"The other side of this tree. They're using pythavine. You can't break it. The more you try, the tighter the pytha'll squeeze you."

Keeping one eye on his captors, Roland managed to worm his way around the large tree trunk. He discovered, on the other side, a dark-skinned human male clad in bright-colored robes. A gold ring dangled from his left ear lobe. He was securely tied, vines wrapped around his chest, arms, and wrists.

"Andor," he said, grinning. One side of his mouth was swollen, dried blood caked half his face.

"Roland Redleaf. You a SeaKing?" he added, with a glance at the earring.

"Yeah. And you're from Thillia. What are you people doing in Thurn territory?"

"Thurn? We're nowhere near Thurn. We're on our way to the Fartherness."

"Don't play dumb with me, Thillian. You know where you are. So you're trading with the dwarves . . ." Andor paused, and licked his lips. "I could sure use a drink about now."

"I'm an explorer," said Roland, casting a wary glance at their captors to see if they were being observed.

"We can talk. They don't give a damn. There's no need to lie, you know. We're not going to live long enough for it to matter."

"What? What do you mean?"

"They kill everyone and everything they come across . . . twenty people in my caravan. All dead, the animals, too. Why the animals? *They* hadn't done anything. It doesn't make any sense, does it?"

Dead? Twenty people dead? Roland stared hard at the man, thinking perhaps he was lying, trying to scare the Thillian away from SeaKing trade routes. Andor leaned back against the tree trunk, his eyes closed. Roland saw sweat trickle down the man's forehead, the dark circles beneath the sunken eyes, the ashen lips. No, he wasn't lying. Fear constricted Roland's heart. He remembered hearing Rega's frantic scream, crying his name. He swallowed a bitter taste in his mouth.

"And . . . you?" he managed.

Andor stirred, opened his eyes, and grinned again. It was lopsided, because of his damaged mouth, and seemed ghastly to Roland.

"I was away from camp, answering nature's call. I heard the fighting . . . I heard the screams. That darktime . . . God of the Waters, I'm thirsty!" He moistened his lips with his tongue again. "I stayed put. Hell, what could I do? That darktime, I circled back. I found them—my business partners, my uncle . . ." He shook his head. "I ran. Kept going. But they caught me, brought me here right before they brought you in. It's weird, the way they can see you without eyes."

"Who . . . what the hell are they?" Roland demanded.

"You don't know? They're tytans."

Roland snorted. "Kids' stories—"

"Yeah! Kids." Andor began to laugh. "My little nephew was seven. I found his body. His head had been split wide open, like someone had stomped on it." His laughter shrilled and broke; he coughed painfully.

"Take it easy," Roland whispered.

Andor drew a shuddering breath. "They're tytans, all right; the ones who destroyed the Kasnar Empire. Wiped it out. Not a building left standing, a person left alive except those who managed to flee ahead of them. And now they're moving south, coming down through the dwarven kingdoms."

"But the dwarves'll stop them, surely . . . ?"

Andor sighed, grimaced, and twisted his body. "Word is that the dwarves are in league with 'em, that they worship these bastards. The dwarves plan to let the tytans march right through and destroy us, then the dwarves'll take over our lands."

Roland recalled vaguely Blackbeard saying something about his people and the tytans, but it was too long ago, swimming in ale.

Movement glimpsed from a corner of his eye caused him to turn. More of the giants appeared, gliding into the large open space where the two humans lay bound, moving more silently than the wind, never fluttering a single leaf.

Roland eyed these new creatures warily, saw that they carried bundles in their arms. He recognized a fall of dark hair. . . .

"Rega!" He sat up, struggling wildly against his bonds.

Andor smiled, his mouth twisting. "More of you, huh? And an elf with you! God of the Waters, if *we* had caught you . . ."

The tytans carried their captives to the base of Roland's tree and laid them down. His heart rose when he saw that they were gentle with their prisoners, taking care to ease them to the ground. Both Paithan and Rega were unconscious, their clothes covered with what looked like pieces of broken fungus. But neither appeared to be injured. Roland could see no blood, no signs of bruising or broken bones. The tytans bound their captives skillfully and efficiently, stared down at them a moment, as if studying them, then left them. Gathering in the center of the clearing, the tytans formed a circle and their heads turned toward the others.

"Spooky bunch," Roland decided. Edging his body as near Rega's as possible, he laid his head down on her chest. Her heart beat was strong and regular. He nudged her with an elbow. "Rega!"

Her eyelids fluttered. She opened them, saw Roland and blinked, startled and confused. Remembered terror flooded her eyes. She tried to move, discovered she was bound, and caught her breath in a fearful gasp.

"Rega! Hush! Lie still. No, don't try! These damn vines tighten if you struggle."

"Roland! What happened? Who are these—" Rega looked at the tytans and shuddered.

"The tyros must have caught wind of these things and bolted. I was chasing after them when the jungle came alive all around me. I had time to scream and that was it. They caught me, knocked me out."

"Paithan and I were standing on the . . . the ledge. They came up and put their hands on it and began to sh—shake it . . ."

"Shhh, there. It's over now. Quin all right?"

"I—I think so." Rega glanced down at her spore-covered clothes. "The fungus must have broken our fall." Leaning near the elf, she spoke softly. "Paithan! Paithan, can you hear me?"

"Ayyyy!" Paithan woke with a cry.

"Shut him up!" growled Andor.

The tytans had ceased observing each other and transferred their sightless gaze to their captives. One by one, moving slowly, gliding gracefully over the jungle floor, the tytans came toward them.

"This is it!" said Andor grimly. "See you in hell, Thillian."

Someone made a whimpering sound. Whether it was Rega or the elf, Roland couldn't tell. He couldn't take his eyes from the giants long enough to find out. He felt Rega's shivering body press against his. Movement in the undergrowth indicated that Paithan, bound like the rest of them, was attempting to wriggle his way over near Rega.

Keeping his eyes on the tytans, Roland saw no reason to be afraid. They were big, but they didn't act particularly menacing or threatening.

"Look, Sis," he whispered out of the corner of his mouth, "if they'd wanted to kill us, they would've done it before this. Just keep calm. They don't look too bright. We can bluff our way outta this."

Andor laughed, a horrible, bone-chilling sound. The tytans—ten of them—had gathered around their captives, forming a semicircle. The eyeless heads faced them. A very soft, very quiet, very gentle voice spoke.

Where is the citadel?

Roland gazed up at them, puzzled. "Did you say something?" He could have sworn that their mouths never moved.

"Yes, I heard them!" Rega answered in awe.

Where is the citadel?

The question was repeated, still spoken quietly, the words whispering through Roland's mind.

Andor laughed again, manically. "I don't know!" he shrieked suddenly, tossing his head back and forth. "I don't know where the goddamn citadel is!"

Where is the citadel? What must we do?

The words were urgent now, no longer a whisper but a cry that was like a scream trapped in the skull.

Where is the citadel? What must we do? Tell us! Command us!

At first annoying, the screaming inside Roland's head became rapidly more painful. He wracked his burning brain, trying desperately to think, but he'd never heard of any "citadel," at least not in Thillia.

"Ask . . . the . . . elf!" he managed, forcing the words out between teeth clenched against the agony.

A terrifying scream behind him indicated that the tytans had taken his advice. Paithan lurched over, rolling on the ground, writhing in pain, shouting something in elven.

"Stop it! Stop it!" Rega begged, and suddenly the voices ceased.

It was quiet inside his head. Roland sagged weakly against his bonds. Paithan lay, sobbing, on the moss. Rega, arms tightly bound, crouched near him. The tytans gazed at their captives and then one of them, without the slightest warning, lifted a tree branch and slammed it into Andor's bound and helpless body.

The SeaKing couldn't cry out; the blow crushed his rib cage, punctured his lungs. The tytan raised the branch and struck again. The blow split the man's skull.

Warm blood splashed on Roland. Andor's eyes stared fixedly at his murderer; the SeaKing had died with that ghastly grin on his face, as if laughing at some terrible joke. The body twitched in its death throes.

The tytan struck again and again, wielding the gore-covered

branch, beating the corpse to a bloody pulp. When the body had been mangled beyond recognition, the tytan turned to Roland.

Numb, horrified, Roland summoned adrenaline-fed strength and plunged backward, knocking Rega to the ground. Wriggling around, he hunched over her, shielding her body with his own. She lay quietly, too quietly, and he wondered if she had fainted. He hoped she had. It would be easier . . . much easier. Paithan lay nearby, staring wide-eyed at what was left of Andor. The elf's face was ashen. He seemed to have quit breathing.

Roland braced himself for the blow, praying that the first killed him swiftly. He heard the scrabbling sound in the moss below him, felt the hand grab onto the buckle of his belt, but the hand wasn't real to him, not as real as the death that loomed above him. The sudden jerk and the plunge down through the moss brought him sharply to his senses. He gasped and spluttered and floundered, as a sleepwalker who stumbles into an icy lake.

His fall ended abruptly and painfully. He opened his eyes. He wasn't in water, but in a dark tunnel that seemed to have been hollowed out of the thick moss. A strong hand shoved him, a sharp blade sliced through his bonds.

"Go! Go! They are thick witted, but they will follow!"

"Rega," Roland mumbled and tried to get back.

"I have her *and* the elf! Now go!"

Rega fell against him, propelled from behind. Her cheekbone struck his shoulder, and her head snapped up.

"Go!" shouted the voice.

Roland caught hold of his sister, dragged her alongside him. Ahead of them stretched a tunnel, leading deeper into the moss. Rega began to crawl down it. Roland followed, fear dictating to his body what it must do to escape because his brain seemed to have shut down.

Dazed, groping through the gray-green darkness, he crawled and lurched and sprawled clumsily headlong in his mad dash. Rega, her body more compact, moved through the tunnel with ease. She paused occasionally, to look back, her gaze going past Roland to the elf behind him.

Paithan's face glimmered an eerie white, he looked more like a ghost than a living man, but he was moving, slithering through the tunnel on hands and knees and belly like a snake. Behind him was the voice, urging them on.

"Go! Go!"

Before long, the strain told on Roland. His muscles ached, his knees were scraped raw, his breath burned in his lungs. We're safe now, he told himself. This place is too narrow for those fiends . . .

A rending and tearing sound, as if the ground were being ripped apart by gigantic hands, impelled Roland forward. Like a mongoose hunting a snake, the tytans were digging for them, widening the tunnel, intending to ferret them out.

Down and down the captives traveled, sometimes falling or rolling where the tunnel turned steep and they couldn't see their way in the darkness. The fear of pursuit and the gruff "Go! Go!" drove them on past the limit of endurance. And then a whoosh of exhaled breath and a crash coming from behind him told Roland that the elf's strength had given out.

"Rega!" Roland called, and his sister halted, turning slowly, peering at him wearily. "Quin's had it. Come help me!"

She nodded, having no breath left to speak, and crawled back. Roland reached out a hand, caught hold of her arm, felt her trembling with fatigue.

"Why have you stopped?" demanded the voice.

"Take a look . . . elf!" Roland gasped for breath. "He's . . . finished . . . All of us. . . . Rest. Must . . . rest."

Rega sagged against him, her muscles twitching, her chest heaving. Blood roared in Roland's ears, he couldn't tell if they were still being pursued. Not, he thought, that it mattered.

"We rest a little," said the gruff voice. "But not long. Deep. We must go deep."

Roland gazed around him, blinking back fiery spots that were bursting before his eyes, obscuring his vision. He couldn't see much anyway. The darkness was thick, intense.

"Surely . . . they won't come . . . this far."

"You don't know them. They are terrible."

The voice—now that he could hear it more clearly—sounded familiar.

"Blackbeard? That you?"

"I told you before. My name is Drugar. Who is the elf?"

"Paithan," said Paithan, easing himself to a crouched position, bracing himself against the sides of the tunnel. "Paithan Quindiniar. I am honored to meet you, sir, and I want to thank you for—"

"Not now!" growled Drugar. "Deep! We must go deep!"

Roland flexed his hands. The palms were torn and bleeding where he'd scraped them against the moss tunnel's rough sides.

"Rega?" he said, concerned.

"Yeah. I can make it." He heard her sigh. Then she left him, and began to crawl again.

Roland drew a breath, wiped the sweat from his eyes, and followed, plunging down into the darkness.

CHAPTER ♦ 20

THE TUNNELS,

THURN

♦

THE ESCAPING CAPTIVES CRAWLED THROUGH THE TUNNEL, DELVING DEEPER and deeper, the voice behind them urging, "Go! Go!" The mind soon lost all awareness of where it was or what it was doing. They became automatons, moving through the darkness like windup toys with no thought of where they were or where they were going, too exhausted, too dazed to care.

Then came an impression of vastness. Reaching out their hands, they could no longer feel the tunnel's sides. The air, though it was still, was surprisingly cool and smelled of dampness and of growth.

"We have reached the bottom," said the dwarf. "Now, you may rest."

They collapsed, rolling over on their backs, gasping for breath, stretching, easing cramped and aching muscles. Drugar said nothing else to them. They might have thought he'd left them, except that they could hear his stentorian breathing. At length, rested, they grew more cognizant of their surroundings. Whatever it was on which they were lying was hard and unresilient, slick and slightly gritty feeling to the touch.

"What is this stuff?" Roland asked, propping himself up. He dug at a handful, ran it through his fingers.

"Who cares?" said Rega. Her voice had a shrill edge, she was panting. "I can't take this! The dark. It's awful. I can't breathe! I'm smothering!"

Drugar spoke words in dwarven, that sounded like rocks

clashing together. A light flared, the brilliance painful to the eyes. The dwarf held a torch in his hand.

"Is that better, human?"

"No, not much," said Rega. Sitting up, she looked around fearfully. "It just makes the darkness darker. I hate it down here! I can't stand it!"

"You want to go back up there?" Drugar pointed.

Rega's face paled, her eyes widened. "No," she whispered, and slid over to be near Paithan.

The elf started to put his arm around her, to comfort her, then he glanced at Roland. His face flushing, Paithan stood up and walked away. Rega stared after him.

"Paithan?"

He didn't look around. Burying her face in her hands, Rega began to sob bitterly.

"What you are sitting on," said Drugar, "is dirt."

Roland was at a loss, uncertain what to do. He knew—as her "husband" he should go comfort Rega, but he had a feeling that his presence would only make matters worse. Besides, he felt in need of comforting himself. Looking down at his clothes, he could see, by the torchlight, splotches of red—blood, Andor's blood.

"Dirt," said Paithan. "Ground. You mean we're actually on ground level?"

"Where are we?" Roland demanded.

"We are in a k'tark, meaning 'crossroad' in your language," answered Drugar. "Several tunnels come together here. We find it is a good meeting place. There is food and water." He pointed to several shadowy shapes barely visible in the flickering torchlight. "Help yourself."

"I'm not all that hungry," mumbled Roland, rubbing frantically at the bloodstains on his shirt. "But I could use some water."

"Yes, water!" Rega lifted her head, the tears on her cheeks sparkled in the firelight.

"I'll get it," offered the elf.

The shadowy shapes turned out to be wooden barrels. The elf removed a lid, peered inside, sniffed. "Water," he reported. He carried a gourd filled with the liquid to Rega.

"Drink this," he said to her gently, his hand touching her shoulder.

Rega cupped the gourd in her hands, drank thirstily. Her eyes were on the elf, his were on her. Roland, watching, felt something dark twist inside him. *I made a mistake. They like each other, like each other a lot. And that's not in the plans. I don't care two sticks if Rega seduces an elf. I'll be damned if she's going to fall in love with one.*

"Hey," he said. "I could use some of that."

Paithan rose to his feet. Rega handed back the empty gourd with a wan smile. The elf headed for the water barrel. Rega flashed Roland a piercing, angry glance. Roland returned it, scowling. Rega flipped her dark hair over her shoulder.

"I want to leave!" she said. "I want out of here!"

"Certainly," said Drugar. "Like I said, crawl back up there. They are waiting for you."

Rega shuddered. Forcing back a cry, she hid her face in her folded arms.

"There's no need to be so rough on her, dwarf. That was a pretty awful experience up there! And if you ask me"—Paithan cast a grim look at their surroundings—"things down here don't look much better!"

"The elf's got a point," struck in Roland. "You saved our lives. Why?"

Drugar fingered a wooden ax that he wore thrust through his wide belt. "Where are the railbows?"

"I thought so." Roland nodded. "Well, if that was why you saved us, you wasted your time. You'll have to ask those creatures for them. But maybe you've already done that! The SeaKing told me you dwarves worship these monsters. He said you and your people are going to join these tytans and take over the human lands. That true, Drugar? Is that why you needed the weapons?"

Rega raised her head, stared at the dwarf. Paithan slowly sipped water from the gourd, his eyes on Drugar. Roland tensed. He didn't like the glitter in the dwarf's dark eyes, the chill smile that touched the bearded lips.

"My people . . ." said Drugar softly, "my people are no more."

"What? Make sense, damn it, Blackbeard!"

"He is," said Rega. "Look at him! Blessed Thillia! He means his people are all dead!"

"Orn's blood," swore Paithan, in elven, with reverence.

"Is that it?" demanded Roland. "Is that the truth? Your people . . . dead?"

"Look at him!" Rega cried, almost hysterically.

Minds confused, blinded by their own fears, they had none of them really seen the dwarf. Eyes open, they saw that Drugar's clothes were torn and stained with blood. His beard, of which he had always taken great care, was matted and tangled; his hair wild and uncombed. A large and ugly gash had opened the skin on his forearm, blood had dried on his forehead. His large hands fingered the ax.

"If we'd had the weapons," said Drugar, his gaze fixed black and unblinking, on the shadows moving in the tunnels, "we could have fought them. My people would still be alive."

"It isn't our fault." Roland raised both hands, palms outward. "We came as fast as we could. The elf"—he pointed at Paithan—"the elf was late."

"I didn't know! How was I supposed to know? It was that damn trail of yours, Redleaf, up and down hundred-foot cliffs that led us right into the bastards—"

"Oh, so now you're going to blame it all on me—"

"Stop arguing!" Rega's voice screeched. "It doesn't matter whose fault it is! The only thing that matters is getting out of here!"

"Yes, you're right," said Paithan, calming down, subdued. "I must return and warn my people."

"Bah! You elves don't have to worry. *My* people will deal with these freaks!" Roland glanced at the dwarf and shrugged. "No offense, Blackbeard, old boy, but warriors—real ones, not a bunch who've been sawed off at the knees—won't have any problem destroying the monsters."

"What about Kasnar?" said Paithan. "What happened to the human warriors in that empire?"

"Peasants! Farmers." Roland dismissed them with a gesture. "We Thillians are fighters! We've had experience."

"In bashing each other, maybe. You didn't look so great up there!"

"I was caught off-guard! What do you expect, elf? They were

on me before I could react. All right, so we won't bring these giants down with one arrow, but I'll guarantee you that when they've got five or six spears through those holes in their heads, they won't be asking any more of their stupid questions about citadels! . . ."

. . . Where are the citadels?

The question reverberated through Drugar's mind, beat and hammered and pounded, each syllable physically painful. From his vantage point in one of the myriad dwarven dwellings, Drugar stared down upon the vast moss plain where his father and most of his people had gone to meet the giant's vanguard.

No, *vanguard* wasn't the correct word. A vanguard implies order, directed movement. To Drugar it appeared that this small group of giants had stumbled over the dwarves, coming across them by accident not design, taking a brief moment away from their larger quest to . . . ask directions?

"Don't go out there, Father!" Drugar had been tempted to plead with the old man. "Let me talk to them if you insist on such folly! Stay behind, where it's safe!"

But he knew that if he had said such words to his father, he might very well feel the lash of that walking stick across his back. And he would have had reason to beat me, Drugar admitted. He is, after all, king. And I should be at his side!

But he wasn't.

"Father, order the people to stay indoors. You and I will treat with these—"

"No, Drugar. We are the One Dwarf. I am king, but I am only the head. The entire body must be present to hear and witness and share in the discussion. That is the way it has been since the time of our creation." The old man's face softened, saddened. "If this is, indeed, our end, let it be said that we fell as we lived—as one."

The One Dwarf was present, streaming up out of their dwellings far beneath the ground, coming to stand on the vast moss plain that formed the roof of their city, blinking and winking and cursing the bright sunlight. In the excitement of welcoming their "brothers" whose huge bodies were almost the size of Drakar, the dwarven god, the dwarves did not notice that many of their number stayed behind, standing near the entrance to their city.

Here Drugar had posted his warriors, hoping to be able to cover a retreat.

The One Dwarf saw the jungle move onto the plain.

Half-blinded by the unaccustomed sunlight, the dwarves saw the shadows between the trees or maybe even the trees themselves glide with silent feet onto the moss. Drugar squinted, staring hard, trying to count the giants' numbers but it was like counting the leaves in the forest. Awed, appalled, he wondered fearfully how you fought something you couldn't see.

With magic weapons, elven weapons, intelligent weapons that sought their prey, the dwarves might have had a chance.

What must we do?

The voice in his head wasn't threatening. It was wistful, sad, frustrated.

Where is the citadel? What must we do?

The voice demanded an answer. It was desperate for an answer. Drugar experienced an odd sensation—for a brief moment, despite his fear, he shared the sadness of these creatures. He truly regretted not being able to help them.

"We have never heard of any citadels, but we will be glad to join you in your search, if you will—"

His father never had a chance to say another word.

Moving silently, acting without apparent anger or malice, two of the giants reached down, grabbed the old dwarf in their large hands, and rent him asunder. They tossed the bloody pieces of the carcass to the ground casually, as one tossed aside garbage. Systematically, again without anger or malice, they started to kill.

Drugar watched, appalled, helpless. His mind numbed by the horror of what he had witnessed and been unable to prevent, the dwarf acted on instinct, his body doing what he'd prepared it to do without conscious thought. Grabbing up a kurth horn, he put his lips to it and blew a loud, wailing blast, calling his people back to their dwellings, back to safety.

He and his warriors, some posted high in the trees, fired their arrows at the giants. The sharp wooden points, that could skewer the biggest human, bounced off the thick hide of the giants. They treated the flights of arrows like flocks of stinging gnats, brushing them away with their hands when they could take time from their butchery to remove them.

The dwarves' retreat was not panicked. The body was one—anything that happened to a single dwarf happened to all dwarves. They stopped to assist those who fell. The older lagged behind, urging the younger forward to safety. The strong carried the weak. Consequently, the dwarves were easy prey.

The giants pursued them, caught them easily, destroyed them without mercy. The moss plain grew soggy with blood. Bodies lay piled on top of each other, some hung from trees into which they'd been hurled. Most had been battered beyond recognition.

Drugar waited until the last moment to seek safety, making certain that those few left alive on that ghastly plain made it back. Even then, he didn't want to leave. Two of his men had to literally drag him down into the tunnels.

Up above, they could hear the rending and breaking of tree limbs. Part of the "roof" of the underground city caved in. When the tunnel behind him collapsed, Drugar and what was left of his army turned to face their foe. There was no longer a need to run to reach safety. No safety existed.

When Drugar came to, he found himself lying in a partially collapsed section of tunnel, the bodies of several of his men lying on top of him. Shoving the corpses aside, he paused to listen, to see if he could hear any sign of life.

There was only silence, dreadful, ominous. For the rest of his life, he would hear that silence and with it the words that whispered in his heart.

"No one . . ."

"I will take you to your people," said Drugar suddenly, the first words he'd spoken in a long, long while.

The humans and the elf ceased their bickering, turned, and looked at him.

"I know the way." He gestured into the deeper darkness. "These tunnels . . . lead to the border of Thillia. We will be safe if we stay down here."

"All that way! Under . . . down here!" Rega blenched.

"You can go back up!" Drugar reminded, gesturing.

Rega looked up, gulped. Shivering, she shook her head.

"Why?" Roland demanded.

"Yes," said Paithan. "Why would you do this for us?"

Drugar stared up at them, the flame of hatred burning, consuming him. He hated them, hated their skinny bodies, their clean-shaven faces; hated their smell, their superiority; hated their tallness.

"Because it is my duty," he said.

Whatever happens to a single dwarf, happens to all.

Drugar's hand, hidden beneath his flowing beard, slipped inside his belt, the fingers closed over a sloth-bone hunting dagger. Terrible joy flared up in the dwarf's heart.

CHAPTER ♦ 21

TREETOPS,

EQUILAN

♦

"AND HOW MANY PEOPLE DO YOU THINK YOUR SHIP WILL CARRY?" inquired Zifnab.

"Carry where?" asked Haplo, cautiously.

"Come fly with me. Up, up, and away in my beautiful baboon. Gone with the wind. Somewhere over the rainbow. I get no kick from champagne. . . . No, wrong verse."

"Look, sir, my ship isn't going anywhere—"

"Well, of course it is, dear boy. You're the savior. Now, let's see." Zifnab began to count on his fingers, muttering to himself. "The Tribus elves had a flight crew of mpfpt and you add the galley slaves and that's mrrk and any passengers would be mpfpt plus mrrk, carry the one—"

"What do you know about Tribus elves?" demanded Haplo.

"—and the answer is . . ." The old wizard blinked. "Tribus elves? Never heard of 'em."

"You brought them up—"

"No, no, dear boy. Your hearing's gone. Such a young man, too. Pity. Perhaps it was the flight. You must have neglected to pressurize the cabin properly. Happens to me all the time. Deaf as a doorknob for days. I distinctly heard myself say 'tribe of' elves. Pass the brandywine, please."

"No more for you, sir," intoned a voice, rumbling through the floor. The dog, lying at Haplo's feet, lifted its head, hackles raised, fur bristling, growling in its throat.

The old man hastily dropped the decanter. "Don't be alarmed," he said, somewhat shamefacedly. "That's just my dragon. He thinks he's Ronald Coleman."

"Dragon," repeated Haplo, looking around the parlor, glancing out the windows. The runes on his skin itched and tingled with danger. Surreptitiously, keeping his hands hidden beneath the white linen tablecloth, he slid aside the bandages, prepared to use his magic to defend himself.

"Yes, dragon," snapped an elven woman peevishly. "The dragon lives beneath the house. Half the time he thinks he's the butler and the other half he's terrorizing the city. Then there's my father. You've met him. Lenthan Quindiniar. He's planning to take us all to the stars to see my mother, who's been dead for years. That's where you come in, you and your winged contraption of evil out there."

Haplo glanced at his hostess. Tall and thin, she was straight up and down, all angles, no curves, and stood and sat and walked stiff as a Volkaran knight in full armor.

"Don't talk like that about Papa, Callie," murmured another elven woman, who was admiring her reflection in a window. "It isn't respectful."

"Respectful!" Calandra rose from her seat. The dog, nervous already, sat up and growled again. Haplo laid a soothing hand on the animal's head. The woman was so furious she never noticed. "When you are 'Lady Durndrun,' miss, you can tell me how to talk, but not before!"

Calandra's flashing-eyed gaze flared around the room, visibly scorching her father and the old man. "It is bad enough that I must put up with entertaining lunatics, but this is the house of my father and you are his 'guests'! Therefore, I will feed you and shelter you but I'll be damned if I have to listen to you or look at you! From now on, Papa, I will take my meals in my room!"

Calandra whirled, skirts and petticoats rustled like the leaves in a wind-tossed tree. She stormed from the parlor and into the dining room, her passing creating a ripple of destruction—overturning a chair, sweeping small fragile objects off a table. She slammed the door to the hall shut with such force the wood nearly splintered. When the whirlwind had blown over, quiet descended.

"I don't believe I have ever been treated to such a scene in my eleven thousand years," intoned the voice beneath the floor in shocked tones. "If you want my advice—"

"We don't," said Zifnab hastily.

"—that young woman should be soundly spanked," stated the dragon.

Haplo unobtrusively replaced the bandages.

"It's my fault." Lenthan hunched miserably into his chair. "She's right. I *am* crazy. Dreaming about going to the stars, finding my beloved again."

"No, sir, no!" Zifnab slammed his hand on the table for emphasis. "We have the ship." He gestured at Haplo. "And the man who knows how to operate it. Our savior! Didn't I tell you he'd come? And isn't he here?"

Lenthan lifted his head, his mild, vague-looking eyes staring at Haplo. "Yes. The man with the bandaged hands. You said that, but—"

"Well, then!" said Zifnab, beard bristling in triumph. "I said I'd be here and I came. I said he'd be here and he came. I say we're going to the stars and we'll go. We haven't much time," he added, his voice lowering. His expression saddened. "Doom is coming. Even as we sit here, it's getting closer."

Aleatha sighed. Turning from the window, she walked over to her father, put her hands gently on his shoulders, and kissed him. "Don't worry about Callie, Papa. She's working too hard, that's all. You know she doesn't mean half what she says."

"Yes, yes, my dear," said Lenthan, patting his daughter's hand absently. He was gazing with renewed eagerness at the old wizard. "So you really, honestly believe we can take this ship and sail to the stars?"

"Not a doubt. Not a doubt." Zifnab glanced nervously about the room. Leaning over to Lenthan, the wizard whispered loudly, "You wouldn't happen to have a pipe and a bit of tobacco about, would—"

"I heard that!" rumbled the dragon.

The old man cringed. "Gandalf enjoyed a good pipe!"

"Why do you think he was called Gandalf the Grey? It wasn't for the color of his robes," the dragon added ominously.

Aleatha walked from the room.

Haplo rose to follow, making a quick gesture to the dog, who rarely took its eyes off his master. The dog obediently stood up, trotted over to Zifnab, and settled down at the wizard's feet. Haplo found Aleatha in the dining room, picking up broken knickknacks.

"Those edges are sharp. You'll cut yourself. I'll do it."

"Ordinarily the servants would clean up the mess," Aleatha said, with a rueful smile. "But we don't have any left. Just the cook, and I think she stays because she wouldn't know what to do with herself if she didn't have us. She's been with us since Mother died."

Haplo studied the smashed figurine he held in his hand. The figure of a woman, it appeared to be a religious icon of some sort, because she was holding her hands up, palm outward, in a ritual expression of blessing. The head had been broken from the body in the fall. Fitting it back into place, Haplo saw the hair was long and white, except for where it turned dark brown at the tips.

"That's the Mother, goddess of the elves. Mother Peytin. Or perhaps you already know that," said Aleatha, sitting back on her heels. Her filmy dress was like a rose cloud around her, her blue-purple eyes, gazing into Haplo's, were alluring, enchanting.

He smiled back, a quiet smile, unassuming. "No, I didn't. I don't know anything about your people."

"Aren't there elves where you come from? Where *do* you come from, by the way. You've been here several cycles now, and I don't recall hearing you say."

Now was the time for the speech. Now was the time for Haplo to tell her the story he'd arranged during his voyage. Behind, in the parlor, the old man's voice was going on and on.

Aleatha, making a pretty grimace, rose and shut the door between the two rooms. Haplo could still hear the wizard's words quite distinctly, coming to his ears through those of his dog.

". . . the heat-resistant tiles kept falling off. Big problem in reentry. Now this ship that's docked out here is made of a material that is more reliable than tiles. *Dragon* scales," he said in a piercing whisper. "But I wouldn't let word of that get around. Might upset . . . you know who."

"Do you want to try to fix this?" Haplo held up the two pieces of the broken icon.

"So you intend to remain a mystery," said Aleatha. Reaching out her hands, she took the pieces from Haplo, letting her fingers brush against his ever so lightly. "It doesn't matter, you know. Papa would believe you if you told him you fell from heaven. Callie wouldn't believe you if you said you walked over from next door. Whatever story you do come up with, try to make it entertaining."

Idly, she fit the pieces of the statue together and held it up to the light. "How do they know what she looked like? I mean, her hair, for example. No one has hair like this—white on top and brown at the tips." The purple eyes gathered Haplo inside, held him fast. "I take that back. It's almost like your hair, except that it's reversed. Yours is brown with white on the edges. Odd, isn't it?"

"Not where I come from. Everyone has hair like mine."

That, at least, was a truthful statement. The Patryns are born with brown hair. When they attain puberty, the tips of the hair begin to turn white. What Haplo did not add was that with the Sartan, it is different. They are born with white hair, the tips eventually turning brown. He looked at the goddess the elven woman held in her hand. Here was proof that the Sartan had been to this world. Were they here now?

His thoughts went to the old man. Zifnab hadn't fooled Haplo. The Patryn's hearing was excellent. The old man had said "Tribus" elves—the elves who lived in Arianus, the elves who lived in another world, far and apart from this one.

". . . solid fuel rocket booster. Blew up on the launch pad. Horrible. Horrible. But they wouldn't believe me, you see. I told them magic was much safer. It was the bat guano they couldn't handle. Need tons of it, you know, to achieve lift-off. . . ."

Not that what the old man was saying now made much sense. Still, there was undoubtedly method in his madness. The Sartan, Alfred, had seemed nothing but a bumbling servant.

Aleatha deposited the two halves of the goddess in a drawer. The remains of a broken cup and saucer ended up in the wastebasket.

"Would you like a drink? The brandy is quite fine."

"No, thank you," said Haplo.

"I thought maybe you might need one, after Callie's little scene. Perhaps we should rejoin the others—"

"I'd rather talk to you alone, if it's allowed."

"You mean can we be alone together without a chaperone? Of course." Aleatha laughed, light, rippling. "My family knows me. You won't damage my reputation with them! I'd invite you out to sit on the front porch, but the crowd's still there, staring at your 'evil contraption.' We can go into the drawing room. It's cool in there."

Aleatha led the way, her body rippling like her laughter. Haplo was protected against feminine charms—not by magic, for not even the most powerful runes ever traced upon a body could guard against love's insidious poison. He was protected by experience. It is dangerous to love, in the Labyrinth. But the Patryn could admire female beauty, as he had often admired the kaleidoscopic sky in the Nexus.

"Please, go in," Aleatha said, extending her hand.

Haplo entered the drawing room. Aleatha came behind him, shut the door, and leaned up against it, studying him.

Located in the center of the house, away from the windows, the room was secluded and private. The fan on the ceiling above rotated with a soft whirring noise—the only sound. Haplo turned to his hostess, who was regarding him with a playful smile.

"If you were an elf, it would be dangerous for you to be alone with me."

"Pardon me, but you don't look dangerous."

"Ah, but I am. I'm bored. I'm engaged. The two are synonymous. You're extremely well built, for a human. Most of the human males I've seen are so big, with hulking bodies. You're slender." Aleatha reached out, laid her hand on his arm, caressing. "Your muscles are firm, like a tree branch. That doesn't hurt you when I touch you, does it?"

"No," said Haplo with his quiet smile. "Why? Should it?"

"The skin disease, you know."

The Patryn remembered his lie. "Oh, that. No, it's only on my hands."

He held them out. Aleatha gave the bandages a look of faint disgust.

"A pity. I am frightfully bored." She leaned up against the door again, studying him languidly. "The man with the bandaged hands. Just like that old looney predicted. I wonder if the rest of what he said will come true." A slight frown marred the smooth, white forehead.

"He really said that?" Haplo asked.

"Said what?"

"About my hands? Predicted . . . my coming?"

Aleatha shrugged. "Yes, he said it. Along with a lot of other nonsense, about my not being married. Doom and destruction coming. Flying a ship to the stars. I'm going to be married." Her lips tightened. "I've worked too hard, gone through too much. And I won't stay in this house any longer than I have to."

"Why would your father want to go to the stars?" Haplo recalled the object he'd seen from his ship, the twinkling light, sparkling brightly in the sun-drenched sky. He'd only seen one. There were more, apparently. "What does he know about them?"

". . . lunar rover! Looked like a bug." The old man's voice rose shrill and querulous. "Crawled around and picked up rocks."

"Know about them!" Aleatha laughed again. Her eyes were warm and soft, dark and mysterious. "He doesn't know anything about them! No one does. Do you want to kiss me?"

Not particularly. Haplo wanted her to keep talking.

"But you must have some legends about the stars. My people do."

"Well, of course." Aleatha moved nearer. "It depends on who is doing the telling. You humans, for example, have the silly notion that they're cities. That's why the old man—"

"Cities!"

"Goodness! Don't bite me! How fierce you look!"

"I'm sorry. I didn't mean to startle you. My people don't believe that."

"Don't they?"

"No. I mean, it's silly," he said, testing. "Cities couldn't rotate around the sky like stars."

"Rotate! Your people must be the ones rotating. *Our* stars never change position. They come and go, but always in the same place."

"Come and go?"

"I've changed my mind." Aleatha leaned closer. "Go ahead. Bite me."

"Maybe later," said Haplo politely. "What do you mean, the stars come and go?"

Aleatha sighed, fell back against the door, and gazed at him from beneath black eyelashes. "You and the old man. You're in this together, aren't you? You're going to swindle my father out of his fortune. I'll tell Callie—"

Haplo stepped forward, reached out his hands.

"No, don't touch me," Aleatha ordered. "Just kiss me."

Smiling, Haplo held his bandaged hands up and out to the side, leaned down, and kissed the soft lips. He took a step back. Aleatha was eyeing him speculatively.

"You weren't much different than an elf."

"Sorry. I'm better when I can use my hands."

"Maybe it's just men in general. Or maybe it's poets, yammering about burning blood, melting heart, skin on fire. Did you ever feel like that when you were with a woman?"

"No," Haplo lied. He could remember a time when the flame had been all he lived for.

"Well, never mind." Aleatha sighed. Turning to go, she placed her hand on the wooden doorknob. "I'm growing rather fatigued. If you'll excuse me—"

"About the stars?" Haplo put his hand on the door, keeping it shut.

Pressed between the door and Haplo's body, Aleatha looked up into the man's face. He smiled into the purple eyes, edged his body nearer, hinting that he was prolonging the conversation for one reason only. Aleatha lowered her eyelashes, but kept close watch from beneath.

"Perhaps I underrated you. Very well, if you want to discuss stars . . ."

Haplo wound a strand of the ashen hair around his finger. "Tell me about the ones that 'come and go.' "

"Just that." Aleatha caught hold of the strand of hair, pulled it, drawing him closer to her, reeling him in like a fish. "They shine for so many years, then they go dark and stay dark for so many years."

"All of them at once?"

"No, silly. Some wink on and others wink off. I really don't know much about it. That lecherous old astrologer friend of father's could tell you more if you're *truly* interested." Aleatha glanced up at him. "Isn't it odd how your hair grows like that, just the opposite of the goddess. Perhaps you *are* a savior—one of Mother Peytin's sons come to rescue me from my sins. I'll give your kiss another try, if you like."

"No, you wounded me deeply. I'll never be the same."

Haplo gave a silent whistle. The woman's aimless throws were hitting their target too near center. He needed to get rid of her, needed to think. There came a scratching sound at the door.

"My dog," said Haplo, removing his hand.

Aleatha made a face. "Ignore it."

"That wouldn't be wise. He probably has to go out."

The scratching sound grew louder, more insistent. The dog began to whine.

"You wouldn't want him to . . . uh . . . well, you know . . . in the house."

"Callie would stew your ears for breakfast. Take the mutt out, then." Aleatha opened the door, and the dog bounded inside. Jumping up on Haplo, it planted its paws on his chest.

"Hi, boy! Did you miss me?" Haplo ruffled the dog's ears, patted its flanks. "Come on, let's go for a walk."

The dog leapt down, yelping gleefully, darting off, then dashing back to make certain Haplo was serious about his offer.

"I enjoyed our conversation," he said to Aleatha.

She had moved aside, standing against the open door, her hands behind her back. "I was less bored than usual."

"Perhaps we could discuss stars again?"

"I don't think so. I've reached a conclusion. Poets are liars. You better get that beast out of here. Callie won't put up with that howling."

Haplo walked past her, turned to add something about poets. She slammed the door shut in his face.

He led the dog outside, sauntered around to the open area where his ship was moored, and stood staring up into the sunlit sky. He could see the stars clearly. They burned bright and steadily, not "twinkling" as the poets were wont to say.

He tried to concentrate, tried to consider the confusing tangle in which he'd found himself—a savior who had come to destroy. But his mind refused to cooperate.

Poets. He had been going to reply to Aleatha's final comment. She was wrong. Poets told the truth.

It was the heart that lied. . . .

. . . Haplo was in his nineteenth year in the Labyrinth when he met the woman. Like him, she was a runner, almost his age. Her goal was the same as his—to escape. They traveled together, finding pleasure in each other's company. Love, if not unknown in the Labyrinth, is not admitted. Lust is acceptable—the need to procreate, to perpetuate the species, to bring children into the world to fight the Labyrinth. By day the two traveled, seeking the next Gate. By night, their rune-tattooed bodies twined together.

And then one day, the two came upon a group of squatters— those in the Labyrinth who travel in packs, who move slowly and represent civilization as far as anything can in that hellish prison. As was customary, Haplo and his companion brought a gift of meat and, as was customary, the squatters invited them to accept the use of their crude lodgings and find a measure of peace and security for a few nights.

Haplo, sitting at ease by the fire, watched the woman play with the children. The woman was lithe and lovely. Her thick chestnut hair fell over firm, round breasts, tattooed with the magical runes that were both shield and weapon. The baby she held in her arms was likewise tattooed—every child was from the day it was born. She looked up at Haplo and something special and secret was shared between them. His pulse quickened.

"Come on," he whispered, kneeling beside her. "Let's go back to the hut."

"No," she said, smiling and looking at him from a veil of thick hair. "It's too early. It would offend our hosts."

"The hell with our hosts!" Haplo wanted her in his arms, wanted to lose himself in the warmth and the sweet darkness.

She ignored him, singing to the baby, teasing him throughout the remainder of the evening until his blood was on fire. When they eventually sought the privacy of their hut, there was no sleep for either of them that night.

"Would you like a baby?" she asked, in one of their quiet moments after the transports of pleasure.

"What does that mean?" He looked at her with a fierce, hungry eagerness.

"Nothing. Just . . . would you want one? You'd have to become a squatter, you know."

"Not necessarily. My parents were runners and they had me."

Haplo saw his parents dead, bodies hacked to pieces. They'd clouted him on the head, knocked him out so that he wouldn't see, so that he wouldn't scream. He said nothing more about babies that night.

The next morning, the squatters had news—a Gate up ahead had supposedly fallen. The way was still dangerous, but if they could get through, it would mean another step nearer to escape, another step nearer reaching the rumored safe haven of the Nexus. Haplo and the woman left the squatters' village.

They made their cautious, wary way through the thick forest. Both were expert fighters—the only reason they had lived this long—and they recognized the signs, the smell, and the prickling of the runes upon their flesh. They were, therefore, almost prepared.

A huge, furry shape, man size, leapt from the leafy darkness. It caught Haplo around the shoulders, trying to sink its teeth in his neck for a quick kill. Haplo grabbed the shaggy arms and jerked it over his head, letting the beast's own momentum carry it forward. The wolfen crashed to the ground, but twisted around and was on its feet before Haplo could drive his spear into its body. Wild yellow eyes fixed on his throat. It jumped again and hauled him to the ground. Grappling for his dagger, he saw—as he fell—the woman's runes on her skin glow bright blue. He saw one of the creatures dive for her, heard the crackle of magic, and then his vision was blocked by a hairy body trying to tear out his life.

The wolfen's fangs slashed at his neck. The runes protected him and he heard the creature snarl in frustration. Lifting his dagger, he stabbed the body on top of his and heard it grunt in pain, saw its yellow eyes blaze in anger. Wolfen have thick hides and are tough to kill. Haplo'd done little more than infuriate it. It was after his face, now—the one place on his body not protected by runes.

He blocked it with his right arm, struggling to push it away, and kept stabbing at it with his left. The wolfen's claw-fingered hands grasped his head. One twist, and it would break his neck.

Claw-fingers dug into his face. Then the creature's body stiffened, it gave a gurgling scream, and slumped over his. Haplo heaved the corpse off of his body, found the woman standing

over him. The blue glow was fading from her runes. Her spear
was in the wolfen's back. She gave Haplo a hand, helped him to
stand. He didn't thank her for saving his life. She didn't expect
it. Today, maybe the next, he'd return the favor. It was that way
. . . in the Labyrinth.

"Two of them," he said, looking down at the corpses.

The woman yanked out her spear, inspected it to make
certain it was still in good condition. The other had died from the
electricity she'd had time to generate with the runes. Its body
still smouldered.

"Scouts," she said. "A hunting party." She shook her chestnut hair out of her face. "They'll be going for the squatters."

"Yeah." Haplo glanced back they way they'd come.

Wolfen hunted in packs of thirty, forty creatures. There were
fifteen squatters, five of them children.

"They don't stand a chance." It was an off-hand remark,
accompanied by a shrug. Haplo wiped the blood and gore from
his dagger.

"We could go back, help fight them," the woman said.

"Two of us wouldn't do that much good. We'd die with
them. You know that."

In the distance, they could hear hoarse shouts—the squatters
calling each other to the defense. Above that, the higher pitched
voices of the women, singing the runes. And above that, higher
still, the scream of a child.

The woman's face darkened, she glanced in that direction,
irresolute.

"C'mom," urged Haplo, sheathing his dagger. "There may
be more of them around here."

"No. They're all in on the kill."

The child's scream rose to a shrill shriek of terror.

"It's the Sartan," said Haplo, his voice harsh. "They put us
in this hell. They're the ones responsible for this evil."

The woman looked at him, her brown eyes flecked with gold.
"I wonder. Maybe it's the evil inside us."

Hefting her weapon, she started to walk. Haplo remained
standing, looking after her. She was moving down a different
path than the one they'd been walking. He could hear, behind
them, the sounds of battle lessening. The child's scream abruptly
ended, mercifully cut short.

"Are you carrying my baby?" Haplo called after her.

If the woman heard him, she didn't answer, but kept walking. The dappled shadows of the leaves closed over her. She was lost to his sight. He strained to listen, to hear her moving through the brush. But she was a runner, she was good. She was silent.

Haplo glanced at the bodies lying at his feet. The wolfen would be occupied with the squatters for a long time, but eventually they'd smell fresh blood and come looking for it.

After all, what did it matter? A kid would only slow him down. He left, heading alone down the path he'd chosen, the path that led to the Gate, to escape.

CHAPTER ♦ 22

THE TUNNELS,

THURN TO THILLIA

♦

THE DWARVES HAD SPENT CENTURIES BUILDING THE TUNNELS. THE passageways branched out in all directions, the major routes extending norinth to the dwarven realms of Klag and Grish—realms now ominously silent—and vars-sorinth, to the land of the SeaKings and beyond to Thillia. The dwarves could have traveled overland; the trade routes to the sorinth, particularly, were well established. But they preferred the darkness and privacy of their tunnels. Dwarves dislike and distrust "light seekers" as they refer disparagingly to humans and elves.

Traveling the tunnels made sense, it was plainly safer; but Drugar took grim delight in the knowledge that his "victims" hated the tunnels, hated the smothering, closed-in feeling, hated—above all—the darkness.

The tunnels were built for people of Drugar's height. The humans and the taller elf had to hunch over when they walked, sometimes even crawl on hands and knees. Muscles rebelled, bodies ached, knees were bruised, palms were raw and bleeding. In satisfaction, Drugar watched them sweat, heard them pant for air and groan in pain. His only regret was that they were moving much too swiftly. The elf, in particular, was extremely anxious to reach his homeland. Rega and Roland were just anxious to get out.

They paused only for short rests, and then only when they were near collapsing from exhaustion. Drugar often stayed awake, watching them sleep, fingering the blade of his knife. He could have murdered them at any time, for the fools trusted him now. But killing them would be a barren gesture. He might as well have let the tytans kill them. No, he hadn't risked his own life to save these wretches just to knife them in their sleep. They must first watch as Drugar had watched, they must first witness the slaughter of their loved ones. They must experience the horror, the helplessness. They must battle without hope, knowing that their entire race was going to be wiped out. Then, and only then, would Drugar permit them to die. Then he could die himself.

But the body cannot live on obsession alone. The dwarf had to sleep himself, and when he could be heard loudly snoring, his victims talked.

"Do you know where we are?" Paithan edged his way painfully over to where Roland was sitting, nursing torn hands.

"No."

"What if he's leading us the wrong way? Up norinth?"

"Why should he? I wish we had some of that ointment stuff of Rega's."

"Maybe she had it with her—"

"Don't wake her. Poor kid, she's about done in." Roland wrung his hands, wincing. "Ouch, damn that stings."

Paithan shook his head. They couldn't see each other, the dwarf had insisted the torch be doused when they weren't moving. The wood used to make it burned long, but they had traveled far, and it was rapidly being consumed.

"I think we should risk going up," said Paithan, after a moment's pause. "I have my etherilite[1] with me. I can tell where we are."

Roland shrugged. "Suit yourself. I don't want to meet those bastards again. I'm considering staying down here permanently. I'm getting kind of used to it."

"What about your people?"

---

[1] A navigational device developed by the Quindiniars. A sliver of ornite is suspended in a tiny globe of magically enhanced glass. Because ornite always points a certain direction (believed by elven astrologers to be a magnetic pole), this direction is labeled *norinth*. The other directions are determined from that point.

"What the hell can I do to help them?"

"You could warn them . . ."

"As fast as those bastards travel, they're probably already there by now. Let the knights fight 'em. That's what they're trained for."

"You're a coward. You're not worthy of—" Paithan realized what he had been about to say, snapped his mouth shut on the words.

Roland kindly finished his sentence for him. "Not worthy of who? My wife? Save-her-skin Rega?"

"Don't talk about her like that!"

"I can talk about her any damn way I feel like, elf. She's my wife, or have you forgotten that little fact? You know, by god, I think you *have* forgotten."

Roland was glib, talked tough. The words were a shell, meant to hold in his quivering guts. He liked to pretend he lived a danger-filled life, but it wasn't true. Once he'd nearly been knifed in a barroom scuffle and another time he'd been mauled by an enraged wildeboar. Then there was the time he and Rega had fought fellow smugglers during a dispute over free trade. Strong and powerful, quick and cunning, Roland had emerged from these adventures with a couple of bruises and a few scratches.

Courage comes easy to a person in a fight. Adrenaline pumps, bloodlust burns. Courage is hard to find, however, when you're tied to a tree and you've been splattered with the blood and brains of the man tied next to you.

Roland was shaken, unnerved. Every time he fell asleep he saw that horrible scene again, played out before his closed eyes. He grew to bless the darkness, it hid his shivering. Time and again he'd caught himself waking with a scream on his lips.

The thought of leaving the security of the tunnels, of facing those monsters was almost more than he could bear. Like a wounded animal who fears to betray its own weakness lest others come and tear it apart, Roland went into hiding behind the one thing that seemed to him to offer shelter, the one thing that promised to help him forget—money.

It'd be a different world up there once the tytans passed through. People dead, cities destroyed. Those who survived would have it all, especially if they had money—elven money.

He'd lost all he'd planned to make on the weapons sale. But there was always the elf. Roland was fairly certain, now, of Paithan's true feelings for Rega. He planned to use the elf's love to squeeze him, wring him dry.

"I've got my eye on you, Quin. You better keep clear of my wife or I'll make you wish the tytans had battered in your head like they did poor Andor." Roland's voice caught, he hadn't meant to bring that up. It was dark, the elf couldn't see. Maybe he'd chalk the quiver up to righteous anger.

"You're a coward and a bully," said Paithan, teeth clenched, his entire body clenched to keep from throttling the human. "Rega is worth ten of you! I—" But he was too furious, he couldn't go on, perhaps he wasn't certain what he'd say. Roland heard the elf move over to the opposite side of the tunnel, heard him throw himself down onto the floor.

If that doesn't force him to make love to her, nothing will, thought Roland. He stared into the darkness and thought desperately about money.

Lying apart from both her brother and the elf, Rega kept very still, pretended to sleep, and swallowed her tears.

"The tunnels end here," announced Drugar.

"Where is 'here'?" demanded Paithan.

"We are at the border of Thillia, near Griffith."

"We've come that far?"

"The way through the tunnels is shorter and easier than the way above. We have traveled in a straight line, instead of being forced to follow the winding trails of the jungle."

"One of us should go up there," said Rega, "see what . . . see what's happening."

"Why don't you go, Rega? You're so all fired hot to get out of here," suggested her brother.

Rega didn't move, didn't look at him. "I . . . I thought I was. I guess I'm not."

"I'll go," offered Paithan. Anything to get away from the woman, to be able to think clearly without the sight of her scattering his thoughts around like the pieces of a broken toy.

"Take this tunnel to the top," instructed the dwarf, holding the torch high and pointing. "It will bring you out in a fernmoss cavern. The town of Griffith is about a mile on your right. The path is plainly marked."

"I'll go with you," offered Rega, ashamed of her fear. "We both will, won't we, Roland?"

"I'll go alone!" Paithan snapped.

The tunnel wound upward through the bole of a huge tree, twisting round and round like a spiral staircase. He stood, looking up it, when he felt a hand touch his arm.

"Be careful," said Rega softly.

The tips of her fingers sent ripples of heat through the elf's body. He dared not turn, dared not look into the brown, fire-lit eyes. Leaving her abruptly, without a word or a glance, Paithan began to crawl up the tunnel.

He was soon beyond the light of the torch and had to feel his way, making the going slow and arduous. He didn't mind. He both longed for and dreaded reaching the world again. Once he emerged into the sun, his questions would be answered, he'd be forced to take decisive action.

Had the tytans reached Thillia? How many of the creatures were there? If no more than they had encountered in the jungle, Paithan could almost believe Roland's boast that the human knights of the five kingdoms could deal with them. He wanted very much to believe in that. Unfortunately, logic kept sticking its sharp point into his rainbow-colored bubbles.

These tytans had destroyed an empire. They had destroyed the dwarven nation. *Doom and destruction,* said the old man. *You will bring it with you.*

No, I won't. I'll reach my people in time. We'll be prepared. Rega and I will warn them.

Elves are, in general, strict observers of the law. They abhor chaos and rely on laws to keep their society in order. The family unit and the sanctity of marriage were held sacred. Paithan was different, however. His entire family was different. Calandra held money and success sacred, Aleatha believed in money and status, Paithan believed in pleasing himself. If at any time society's rules and regulations interfered with a Quindiniar belief, the rules and regulations were conveniently swept into the wastebasket.

Paithan knew he should feel some sort of qualm at asking Rega to run away with him. He was satisfied to discover that he didn't. If Roland couldn't hang onto his own wife, that was his problem, not Paithan's. The elf did remember, now and then, the conversation he'd overheard between Rega and Roland; the one in which it had seemed Rega was plotting to blackmail him. But he remembered, too, Rega's face when the tytans were closing in on them, when they were facing certain death. She'd told him she loved him. She wouldn't have lied to him then. Paithan concluded, therefore, that the scheme had been Roland's, and that Rega had never truly had any part in it. Perhaps he was forcing her, threatening her with physical harm.

Absorbed in his thoughts and the difficult climb, Paithan was startled to find himself at the top sooner than he'd expected. It occurred to him that the dwarven tunnel must have been sloping upward during the last few cycles' travel and that he hadn't noticed. He poked his head cautiously out of the tunnel opening. He was somewhat disappointed to find himself surrounded by darkness, then he remembered that he was in a cavern. Eagerly he gazed around and—some distance from him—he could see sunlight. He drew in a deep breath, tasted fresh air.

The elf's spirits rose. He could almost believe the tytans had been nothing but a bad dream. It was all he could do to contain himself and not leap up out of the tunnel and dash into the blessed sunlight. Paithan pulled himself cautiously up over the lip of the tunnel and, moving quietly, crept through the cavern until he reached the opening.

He peered outside. All seemed perfectly normal. Recalling the terrible silence in the jungle just before the tytans appeared, he was relieved to hear birds squawking and cawing, animals rustling through the trees on their own private business. Several greevils popped up out of the undergrowth, staring at him with their four eyes, their legendary curiosity banishing fear. Paithan grinned at them and, reaching into a pocket, tossed them some crumbs of bread.

Emerging from the cavern, the elf stretched to his full height, bending backward to relieve muscles cramped from traveling stooped and hunched over. He looked carefully in all directions, though he didn't expect to see the jungle moving. The testimony of the animals was clear to him. The tytans were nowhere around.

Perhaps they've been here and moved on. Perhaps when you walk into Griffith, you'll find a dead city.

No, Paithan couldn't believe it. The world was too bright, too sunny and sweet smelling. Maybe it *had* all been just a bad dream.

He decided he would go back and tell the others. There was no reason all of them couldn't travel to Griffith together. He turned around, dreading going back into the tunnels again, when he heard a voice, echoing in the cavern.

"Paithan? Is everything all right?"

"All right?" cried Paithan. "Rega, it's beautiful! Come out and stand in the sunshine! Come on. It's safe. Hear the birds?"

Rega ran through the cavern. Bursting into the sun, she lifted her upturned face to the heavens and breathed deeply.

"It's glorious!" she sighed. Her gaze went to Paithan. Before either quite knew how it happened, they were in each other's arms, holding each other tightly, lips searching, meeting, finding.

"Your husband," said Paithan, when he could catch his breath. "He might come up, might catch us—"

"No!" Rega murmured, clinging to him fiercely. "No, he's down there with the dwarf. He's going to wait . . . to keep an eye on Drugar. Besides"—she drew a deep breath, moved back slightly so that she could look into Paithan's face—"it wouldn't matter if he did catch us. I've made a decision. There's something I have to tell you."

Paithan ran his hand through her dark hair, entangling his fingers in the thick, shining mass. "You've decided to run away with me. I know. It will be for the best. He'll never find us in my country—"

"Please listen to me and don't interrupt!" Rega shook her head, nuzzling it beneath Paithan's hand like a cat wanting to be stroked. "Roland *isn't* my husband." The words came out in a gasp, forced up from the pit of her stomach.

Paithan stared at her, puzzled. "What?"

"He's . . . my brother. My half-brother." Rega had to swallow, to keep her throat moist enough to talk.

Paithan continued to hold her, but his hands were suddenly cold. He recalled the conversation in the glade; it took on a new and more sinister meaning.

"Why did you lie to me?"

Rega felt his hands tremble, felt the chill in his fingers, saw his face pale and grow cold as his hands. She couldn't meet his intense, searching gaze. Her eyes lowered, sought her feet.

"We didn't lie to you," she said, trying to make her voice light. "We lied to everyone. Safety, you see. Men don't . . . bother me if they think . . . I'm married . . ." She felt him stiffen, and looked at him. Her words dried up, cracked. "What's wrong? I thought you'd be pleased! Don't . . . don't you believe me?"

Paithan shoved her away. Tripping over a vine, Rega stumbled and fell. She started to get up, but the elf stood over her, his frightening gaze pinned her to the moss.

"Believe you? No! Why should I? You've lied to me before! And you're lying now. Safety! I overheard you and your brother"—he spit the word—"talking. I heard about your little scheme to seduce me and then blackmail me! You bitch!"

Paithan turned his back on her, stalked over to the path that led into town. He set his foot on it, kept walking, determined to leave the pain and the horror of this trip behind him. He didn't move very fast, however, and his walk slowed further when he heard a rustling in the undergrowth and the sound of light footfalls hurrying after him.

A hand touched his arm. Paithan continued walking, didn't look around.

"I deserved that," said Rega. "I am . . . what you said. I've done terrible things in my life. Oh, I could tell you"—her grip on Paithan tightened—"I could tell you that it wasn't my fault. You might say life has been like a mother to Roland and me: every time we turn around, it smacks us in the face. I could tell you that we live the way we do because that's how we survive. But it wouldn't be true.

"No, Paithan! Don't look at me. I want to say one more thing and then you can go. If you know about the plan we had to blackmail you, then you know that I didn't go through with it. I wasn't being noble. I was being selfish. Whenever you look at me, I feel . . . ugly. I meant what I said. I do love you. And that's why I'm letting you go. Good-bye, Paithan." Her hand slid from his arm.

Paithan turned, captured the hand and kissed it. He smiled ruefully into the brown eyes. "I'm not such a prize, you know.

Look at me. I was ready to seduce a married woman, ready to carry you off from your husband. I love you, Rega. That was my excuse. But the poets say that when you love someone, you want only the best for the other person. That means you come out ahead in our game, because you wanted the best for me." The elf's smile twisted. "And so did I."

"You love me, Paithan? You truly love me?"

"Yes, but—"

"No." Her hand covered his lips. "No, don't say anything else. I love you and if we love each other, nothing else matters. Not then, not now, not whatever comes."

Doom and destruction. The old man's words echoed in Paithan's heart. He ignored the voice. Taking Rega in his arms, he shoved his fear firmly back into the shadows, along with various other nagging doubts such as "where will this relationship lead?" Paithan didn't see why that question needed to be answered. Right now their love was leading to pleasure, and that was all that mattered.

"I warned you, elf!"

Roland had apparently grown tired of waiting. He and the dwarf stood before them. The human yanked his raztar from his belt. "I warned you to keep away from her! Blackbeard, you're a witness—"

Rega, snuggled in Paithan's embrace, smiled at her brother. "It's over, Roland. He knows the truth."

"He knows?" Roland stared, amazed.

"I told him," sighed Rega, looking back up into Paithan's eyes.

"Well, that's great! That's just dandy!" Roland hurled the raztar blades-down into the moss, rage conveniently masking his fear. "First we lose the money from the weapons, now we lose the elf. Just what are we supposed to live on—"

The boom of a huge, snakeskin drum rolled through the jungle, scaring the birds, sending them flapping and shrieking up from the trees. The drum boomed out again and yet again. Roland hushed, listening, his face gone pale. Rega tensed in the elf's arms, her gaze going to the direction of the town.

"What is it?" asked Paithan.

"They're sounding the alarm. Calling out the men to defend the village against an attack!" Rega looked around fearfully. The birds had risen into the air with the sound of the drum, but they had ceased their raucous protest. The jungle was suddenly still, deathly quiet.

"You wanted to know what you were going to live on?" Paithan glanced at Roland. "That might not be much of an issue."

No one was paying any attention to the dwarf, or they would have seen Drugar's lips, beneath the beard, part in a rictus grin.

CHAPTER ♦ 23

GRIFFITH,

THILLIA

♦

THEY RAN DOWN THE TRAIL, HEADING FOR THE SECURITY OF THE VILLAGE. The path was clear, well traveled, and flat. Adrenaline pumped, lending them impetus. They were in sight of the village when Roland came a halt.

"Wait!" he gasped. "Blackbeard."

Rega and Paithan stopped, hands and bodies coming together, leaning on each other for support.

"Why—?"

"The dwarf. He couldn't keep up," said Roland, catching his breath. "They won't let him inside the gates without us to vouch for him."

"Then he'd just go back to the tunnels," said Rega. "Maybe that's what he did anyway. I don't hear him." She crowded closer to Paithan. "Let's keep moving!"

"Go ahead," said Roland harshly. "I'll wait."

"What's got into you?"

"The dwarf saved our lives."

"Your hus—brother's right," said Paithan. "We should wait for him."

Rega shook her head, frowning. "I don't like it. I don't like *him*. I've seen him look at us, sometimes, and I—"

The sound of booted feet and heavy breathing interrupted her. Drugar stumbled along the path, head down, feet and arms pumping. He was watching the path, not where he was going, and would have plowed right into Roland, if the man hadn't reached out a restraining hand.

The dwarf looked up, dizzily, blinking back the sweat that was running into his eyes. "Why . . . stopped?" he demanded when he could spare breath to talk.

"Waiting for you," said Roland.

"All right, he's here. Let's get going!" said Rega, glancing around uneasily. The sound of the drumbeats pounded like their hearts, the only sounds in the jungle.

"Here, Blackbeard, I'll give you a hand," offered Roland.

"Leave me alone!" Drugar snarled, jerking back. "I can keep up."

"Suit yourself." Roland shrugged, and they started off again, pace slightly slower, to accommodate the dwarf.

When they arrived at Griffith, they not only found the gates closed, they discovered the citizens erecting a barricade in front of them. Barrels, pieces of furniture, and other junk were being hastily thrown down from the walls by the panic-stricken populace.

Roland waved and shouted, and finally someone looked over the edge.

"Who goes there?"

"It's Roland! Harald, you jackass. If you don't recognize me, you must recognize Rega! Let us in!"

"Who's that with you?"

"An elf, name's Quin. He's from Equilan and a dwarf, name of Blackbeard, from Thurn . . . or what's left of it. Now are you going to let us in or stand here and jaw all day?"

"You and Rega can come in." The crown of a balding head appeared over the top of an overturned barrel. "But not the other two."

"Harald, you bastard, once I get in there I'm gonna break—"

"Harald!" Rega's clear voice rang over her brother's. "This elf is a weapons dealer! Elven weapons! Magical! And the dwarf has information about the . . . the . . ."

"Enemy," said Paithan quickly.

"Enemy." Rega swallowed, her throat gone dry.

"Wait here," said Harald. The head disappeared. Other heads replaced it, staring out at the four standing in the path.

"Where the hell else does he think I'm gonna go?" muttered

Roland. He kept glancing back, over his shoulder. "What was that? Over there?"

All of them turned fearfully, stared.

"Nothing! Just the wind," said Paithan, after a moment.

"Don't do that, Roland!" Rega snapped. "You nearly scared me to death."

Paithan was eyeing the barricade. "That won't keep them out, you know . . ."

"Yes, it will!" whispered Rega, twining her fingers with the elf's. "It has to!"

A head and shoulders appeared, looking at them over the barricade. The head was encased in brown, highly polished, tyro-shell armor, matching armor gleamed on the shoulders.

"You say these people are from the village?" the armored head asked the balding one next to it.

"Yes. Two of them. Not the dwarf and the elf—"

"But the elf is a weapons dealer. Very well. Let them inside. Bring them to headquarters."

The armored head left. There was a momentary delay, barrels and crates had to come down, carts had to be pushed aside. Finally the wooden gates swung open only far enough to permit the four to squeeze their bodies through. The stocky dwarf, encased in his heavy leather armor, got stuck in the middle and Roland was forced to push him through from behind, while Paithan pulled from the front.

The gate was swiftly shut behind them.

"You're to go see Sir Lathan," instructed Harald, jerking a thumb at the inn. Several armored knights could be seen pacing about, testing their weapons, or clustered in groups, talking, keeping themselves aloof from the crowd of worried townspeople.

"Lathan?" said Rega, lifting her eyebrows. "Reginald's younger brother? I don't believe it!"

"Yeah, I didn't think we were worth that much to him," added Roland.

"Reginald who?" asked Paithan. The three moved toward the inn, the dwarf following, staring around him with his dark, shadowed gaze.

"Reginald of Terncia. Our liege lord. Apparently he's sent a regiment of knights down here under his little brother's command. I guess they figure on stopping the tytans here, before they reach the capital."

"It may not be those . . . those creatures that brought them," said Rega, shivering in the bright sunlight. "It could be anything. A raid by the SeaKings. You don't know, so just shut up about it!"

She stopped walking, stared at the inn, the people milling about, frightening themselves and each other. "I'm not going in there. I'm going home to . . . to . . . wash my hair." Rega flung her arms around Paithan's neck, stood on her tiptoes, and kissed him on the lips. "I'll see you tonight," she said breathlessly.

He tried to stop her, but she left too quickly, practically running, shoving her way through the milling crowd.

"Perhaps I should go with her—"

Roland put his hand on the elf's arm. "Just leave her alone. She's scared, scared as hell. She wants time to get a grip on herself."

"But I could help her—"

"No, she wouldn't like that. Rega's got a lot of pride. When we were kids, and Ma'd beat her till the blood ran, Rega never let anyone see her cry. Besides, I don't think you've got a choice."

Roland gestured to the knights. Paithan saw that they had ceased their discussions and were staring straight at him. The human was right, if the elf left now, they would think he was up to no good.

He and Roland continued their walk toward the inn, Drugar tromping noisily behind them. The town was in chaos, some hurrying toward the barricade, weapons in their hands, others hurrying away from it, families moving out, abandoning their homes. Suddenly Roland stepped in front of him, halting him with outstretched arm. Paithan was forced to either back up or run the man down.

"See here, Quindiniar, after we talk to this knight and we convince him that you aren't in league with the enemy, why don't you just head out for home . . . alone."

"I won't leave without Rega," said Paithan quietly.

Roland squinted up at him, smiled. "Oh? You going to marry her?"

The question caught Paithan by surprise. He firmly intended

to answer yes but a vision of his older sister rose up before him.
"I . . . I—"

"Look, I'm not trying to protect Rega's 'honor.' We never
had any, either of us; couldn't afford it. Our ma was the town
whore. Rega's done her share of bed hopping, but you're the
first man she's ever cared about. I won't let her get hurt. You
understand?"

"You love her very much, don't you?"

Roland shrugged, turned abruptly, and resumed walking.
"Our ma ran off when I was fifteen. Rega was twelve. All we
had left was each other. We've made our own way in this world,
never asking help from anybody. So you just clear off and leave
us alone. I'll tell Rega you had to go on ahead to see about your
family. She'll be hurt some, but not as much as if you . . . well
. . . you know."

"Yes, I know," said Paithan. Roland's right. I should leave,
leave immediately, go on by myself. This relationship can come
to nothing but heartache. I know that, I've known it from the
beginning. But I never felt about any woman the way I feel about
Rega!

Paithan's desire ached and burned inside him. When she'd
said that about seeing him tonight, when he'd looked into her
eyes and seen the promise there, he hadn't thought he could
bear it. He could hold her tonight, sleep with her tonight.

And leave tomorrow?

So I'll take her with me tomorrow. Take her home, take her
to . . . Calandra. He could picture his sister's fury, hear her
scathing, flesh-stripping remarks. No, it wouldn't be fair, wouldn't
be fair to Rega.

"Hey." Roland punched him in the side with his elbow.

Paithan glanced up, saw that they'd reached the inn. A
knight stood guarding the door. His gaze flicked over Roland,
fixed earnestly on Paithan, then on Drugar, standing behind
them.

"Go on in," said the knight, throwing open the door.

Paithan walked inside, stared. He wouldn't have recognized
the inn. The common room had been transformed into an arse-
nal. Shields decorated with each knight's device stood against
the walls, each knight's weapons stacked neatly in front. Additional arms had been piled in the center of the floor, presumably

to be distributed to the general populace in time of need. Paithan noted some magical elven weapons among the knights' retinue, but not many.

The room was empty, except for a knight, seated at a table, eating and drinking.

"That's him," said Roland, out of the corner of his mouth.

Lathan was young, no more than twenty-eight years old. He was handsome, with the black hair and black mustache of the Thillian lords. A jagged battle scar cut into his upper lip, giving him a slight, perpetual sneer.

"Excuse me if I am so unmannerly as to dine in front of you," said Sir Lathan. "I've had nothing to eat or drink the last cycle."

"We haven't had much to eat ourselves," said Paithan.

"Or drink," Roland added, eyeing the knight's full mug.

"There are other taverns in this town," said Sir Lathan. "Taverns that serve your kind." He looked up from his plate long enough to fix his eyes on the elf and the dwarf, then returned his attention to his food. He forked meat into his mouth, and washed it down with a drink. "More ale," he shouted, looking around for the innkeeper. He banged his mug on the table and the innkeeper appeared, a sullen look on his face.

"This time," said Sir Lathan, flinging the mug at the man's head, "draw it from the good barrel. I won't drink slop."

The innkeeper scowled.

"Don't worry. It will be paid for out of the royal treasury," said the knight.

The innkeeper's scowl deepened. Sir Lathan stared coldly at the man. Retrieving the mug, which had clattered to the floor, the innkeeper vanished.

"So, you've come from the norinth, have you, elf. What were you doing there, with *that*." The knight gestured with his fork in the direction of the dwarf.

"I'm an explorer," said Paithan. "This man, Roland Redleaf, is my guide. This is Blackbeard. We met—"

"Drugar," growled the dwarf. "My name is Drugar."

"Uh, huh." Sir Lathan took a bit, chewed, then spit the meat back into his plate. "Pah! Gristle. So what's an elf doing with the dwarves? Forging alliances, perhaps?"

"If I was, it's my business."

"The lords of Thillia could make it their business. We've let you elves live in peace a long time. Some are thinking it's been too long, My Lord among them."

Paithan said nothing, merely cast a significant glance at the elven weapons standing among the knights' own. Sir Lathan saw the glance, understood, and grinned. "Think we can't get along without you? Well, we've come up with some devices that'll make you elves sit up and take notice." He pointed. "See that? It's called a crossbow. Drive an arrow through any type of armor you name. Even send it through a wall."

"It will do you no good against the giants," said Drugar. "It will be like throwing sticks at them."

"How would you know? You met up with them?"

"They wiped out my people. Slaughtered them."

Sir Lathan paused in the act of lifting a piece of bread to his mouth. He looked at the dwarf intently, then tore off a bit of bread with his teeth.

"Dwarves," he muttered disparagingly, his mouth full.

Paithan glanced swiftly at Drugar, interested in the dwarf's reaction. Drugar was eyeing the knight with a strange expression; the elf could have sworn it was glee. Startled, Paithan began to wonder if the dwarf was insane. Considering this, he lost the thread of the conversation and only picked it up again when he heard the word *SeaKings*.

"What about the SeaKings?" he asked.

Sir Lathan grunted. "Keep awake, elf. I said that the tytans have attacked them. They've been routed, seemingly. The bastards actually had the nerve to beg us for help."

The innkeeper returned with the ale, set the mug down in front of the knight.

"Back off," Lathan commanded, waving a greasy hand.

"And did you send aid?" Paithan inquired.

"They're the enemy. It could have been a trick."

"But it wasn't, was it?"

"No," the knight admitted. "I guess not. They were soundly trounced, according to some of the refugees we talked to before we turned them away from the walls—"

"Turned them away!"

Sir Lathan lifted the mug, drank long and deep, wiped the back of his hand across his mouth. "What would happen if we sent sorinth for aid, elf. What would happen if we asked *your* people for help?"

Paithan felt a hot flush spread from his neck to his cheeks. "But you and the SeaKings are both human." It was lame, but all he could think of to say.

"Meaning you'd help us if we were your kind? Well, you can make good on that one, elf, because we've heard rumors that your people in the Fartherness Reaches have been attacked, as well."

"That means," said Roland, quickly calculating, "that the tytans are spreading out, moving est and vars, surrounding us, surrounding *Equilan*," he said with emphasis.

"I've got to go! Got to warn them," murmured Paithan. "When do you expect them to reach Griffith?"

"Any day now," said Lathan. Wiping his hands on the table-cloth, he rose to his feet, the tyro armor making a clattering sound. "The flood of refugees has stopped, which means they're all probably dead. And we've heard nothing from our scouts, which means they're probably dead, too."

"You're being awfully cool about this."

"We'll stop them," said Sir Lathan, buckling on his sword belt.

Roland stared at the sword, with its honed, wooden blade and suddenly began to laugh, a high-pitched, shrill cackle that made Paithan shudder. By Orn, maybe the dwarf wasn't the only one going crazy.

"I've seen them!" cried Roland, in a low, hollow voice. "I saw them beat a man. . . . He was tied up. They hit him and hit him"—his voice rose, fists clenched—"and hit him and—"

"Roland!"

The human was curling up, body hunching over, fingers twitching spasmodically. He seemed to be falling apart.

"Roland!" Paithan flung his arms around the man, gripped the shoulders hard, fingers digging into the flesh.

"Get him out of here," said Sir Lathan, in disgust. "I've no use for cowards." He paused a moment, considering his words, rolling them in his mouth as if they tasted bad. "*Could* you get weapons to us, elf?" He asked the question grudgingly.

No, Paithan was on the verge of saying. But he stopped the words, nearly biting off his tongue to keep them from blurting out. I need to reach Equilan. Fast. And I can't if I'm going to be stopped and questioned at every border between here and Varsport.

"Yes, I'll get you weapons. But I'm a long way from home—"

Roland lifted a ravaged face. "You're going to die! We're all going to die!"

Other knights, hearing the commotion, peered in the window. The innkeeper's face had gone livid. He began to babble, his wife started to wail. Sir Lathan put his hand on his sword, loosened the blade in its scabbard. "Shut him up before I run him through!"

Roland shoved the elf aside, bolted for the door. Chairs toppled, he overturned a table, and nearly knocked down two knights trying to stop him. At Lathan's gesture, they let him pass. Glancing through a window, Paithan saw Roland staggering down the street, weaving on unsteady feet like a drunken man.

"I'll give you a permit," said Lathan.

"Cargans,[1] as well." The elf pictured the puny barricades, imagined the tytans smashing through them, walking over them as if they were nothing but piles of leaves thrown in their path. This town was dead.

Paithan made up his mind. I'll take Rega to Equilan with me. She won't go without Roland, so I'll take him back, too. He's not a bad fellow. Not really.

"Cargans enough to carry me and my friends."

Sir Lathan was scowling, obviously not pleased.

"That's the deal," Paithan said.

"What about the dwarf? He one of your friends, too?"

Paithan had forgotten about Drugar, standing silently beside him the entire time. He looked down, to see the dwarf looking up, the black eyes flickering with that queer, gleeful gleam.

"You're welcome to come with us, Drugar," said Paithan, trying to sound as if he meant it. "But you don't have to—"

"I'll come," said the dwarf.

---

[1] An extremely large, squirrellike animal that can bound swiftly over flat plains on all fours or can glide from treetop to treetop, utilizing a winglike flap of skin, connecting its front and hind legs.

Paithan lowered his voice. "You could go back to the tunnels. You'd be safe there."

"And what would I go back to, elf?"

Drugar spoke quietly, one hand toyed with his long, flowing beard. The other hand was hidden, thrust into his belt.

"If he wants to come with us, he can," said Paithan. "We owe him. He saved our lives."

"Pack your gear then and make ready. The cargans will be saddled and waiting in the yard out there. I'll give the orders." Lathan picked up his helm, and prepared to walk out the door.

Paithan hesitated, conflicting emotions tugging at him. He caught hold of the knight's arm as Lathan passed him.

"My friend isn't a coward," said the elf. "He's right. Those giants are deadly. I—"

Sir Lathan leaned near, his voice low and quiet, for the elf alone. "The SeaKings are fierce warriors. I know. I've fought them. From what we heard, they never had a chance. Like the dwarves, they were destroyed. One word of advice, elf." The knight's eyes gazed steadily into Paithan's. "Once you're gone, keep going."

"But . . . the weapons?" Paithan stared, confused.

"Just talk. To keep up appearances. For my men and the people around here. You couldn't get back here fast enough. And I don't think weapons—magical or not—will make any difference anyway. Do you?"

Slowly, Paithan shook his head. The knight paused, his face grave and thoughtful. He seemed, when he spoke, to be talking to himself.

"If ever there was a time for the Lost Lords to return, that time is now. But they won't come. They're asleep beneath the waters of the Kithni Gulf. I don't blame them for leaving us to fight this alone. Theirs was an easy death. Ours won't be."

Lathan straightened, glowering at the elf. "Enough haggling!" the knight said loudly, rudely shoved his way past. "You'll get your blood money." He tossed the words over his shoulder. "That's all you blasted elves care about, isn't it? You there, boy! Saddle three—"

"Four," corrected Paithan, following Sir Lathan out the door.

The knight frowned, appeared displeased. "Saddle *four*

cargans. They'll be ready in half a petal's fold, elf. Be here on time."

Paithan, confused, didn't know what to say and so he said nothing. He and Drugar started off down the street, following after Roland, who could be seen in the distance, leaning weakly against a building.

The elf halted then, half-turned. "Thanks," he called back to the knight.

Lathan brought his hand to the vizor of his helm in a solemn, grim salute.

"Humans," muttered Paithan to himself, heading after Roland. "Try to figure them."

CHAPTER ♦ 24

SORINTH,

ACROSS THILLIA

♦

"THE KNIGHT AS MUCH AS ADMITTED TO ME THAT HE AND HIS MEN can't hold out against these monsters. We've got to head sorinth, to the elven lands. And we've got to leave now!" Paithan stared out the window, eyes on the eerily silent jungle. "I don't know about you, but the air feels or smells strange, like that time the tytans caught us. We can't stay here!"

"What makes you think it'll make any difference where we go?" Roland demanded in a dull voice. He sat in a chair, his head in his hands, elbows leaning on the crude table. By the time Drugar and Paithan had managed to get the human to his home, he was in a sorry state. His terror, so long held inside, had exploded, piercing his spirit with its deadly fragments. "We might as well stay, die with the rest."

Paithan's lips tightened. He was embarrassed by the man, probably because he knew the wreck huddled at the table could very well be him. Every time the elf thought about facing those terrible, eyeless beings, fear shriveled his stomach. Home. The thought was a knife's prod to his back, keeping him moving.

"I'm going. I have to go, back to my people—"

The sound of the snakeskin drums began again, the beating louder, more urgent. Drugar, watching out the window, turned.

"What does that mean, human?"

"They're coming," Rega said, lips stiff. "That's the alarm that means the enemy's in sight."

Paithan stood, irresolute, divided between his loyalty to his

family and his love for the human woman. "I've got to go," he
said finally, abruptly. The cargans, tethered outside the door,
were nervous, tugging against their reins, growling in fright.
"Hurry! I'm afraid we'll lose the animals!"

"Roland! Come on!" Rega's grip tightened on her brother.

"Why bother!" He shoved her away.

Drugar clomped across the room, leaned over the table where
Roland sat, shivering. "We must not separate! We go together.
Come! Come! It is our only hope." Pulling a flask from out of his
wide belt, the dwarf thrust it at Roland. "Here, drink this. You
will find courage in the bottom."

Roland reached out his hand, snatched the flask, and put it
to his lips. He drank deeply, choked, coughed. Tears glistened in
his eyes, rolled down his cheeks, but a faint flush of blood
stained the pallid skin.

"All right," said Roland, breathing heavily. "I'll come." He
picked up the flask, took another swallow, and cradled it close.

"Roland—"

"Let's go, Sis. Can't you see your elf lover waiting? He wants
to take you home, to the bosom of his family. If we ever make it
that far. Drugar, old buddy, old pal. Got any more of this stuff?"

Roland flung his arm around the dwarf, the two of them
headed for the door. Rega was left standing alone in the center of
the small house. She gazed around, shook her head, and followed, nearly running into Paithan, who had come back, searching for her.

"Rega! What's wrong?"

"I never thought it would hurt me to leave this hovel, but it
does. I guess it's because it was all I ever had."

"I can buy you whatever you want! You'll have a house a
hundred times this big!"

"Oh, Paithan! Don't lie to me! You don't have any hope. We
can run"—she looked up into the elf's eyes—"but where will we
go?"

The sound of the drums grew more urgent, the rhythm
thumping through the body.

Doom and destruction. You'll bring it with you.

And you, sir, shall be the one who leads his people forth!

Heaven. The stars!

"Home," said Paithan, holding Rega close. "We're going home."

They left the sound of the drumbeats behind, riding through the jungle, urging the cargans as fast as they dared. Riding cargans takes skill and practice, however. When the creature spreads its batlike wings to take off, to glide through the trees, it is necessary to cling with the hands, grip with the knees, and almost bury one's head in the animal's furry neck—or risk being brushed off by hanging vines and branches.

Paithan was a skilled cargan rider. The two humans, though not as easy in their saddles as the elf, had ridden before, and knew the technique. Even Roland, dead drunk, managed to hang on to his cargan for dear life. But they nearly lost the dwarf.

Never having seen such an animal, Drugar had no idea that the cargan was capable of nor had any inclination toward flight. The first time the cargan leapt from a tree branch, it sailed gracefully outward, the dwarf fell like a rock.

By some miracle—Drugar's boot becoming entangled in the stirrup—the cargan and the dwarf managed to land in the next tree almost together. But it took precious time assisting the shaken Drugar back into the saddle, more time convincing the cargan it still wanted to carry the dwarf as a passenger.

"We've got to go back to the main highway. We'll make better time," said Paithan.

They reached the main highway, only to discover it was almost a solid mass of people—refugees, fleeing sorinth. Paithan reined in, staring. Roland, having drained the flask, began to laugh.

"Damn fools!"

The humans flowed sluggishly down the road that had become a river of fear. Bent beneath bundles, carrying children too young to walk, they pulled those too old along in carts. Their path was strewn with flotsam, washed up along the shore—household goods that had become too heavy, valuables that had lost their value when life was at stake, vehicles that had broken down.

Here and there, fallen by the wayside, human jetsam—people

too exhausted to walk farther. Some held out their hands, pleading to those with wagons to take them up. Others, knowing what the answer would be, sat, staring about them with dull, fear-glazed eyes, waiting for their strength to return.

"Back to the woods," said Rega, riding up beside Paithan. "It's the only way. We know the paths. This time, we really do," she added, flushing slightly.

"Smuggler's Road," slurred Roland, weaving in his saddle. "Yes, we know them."

Paithan couldn't move. He sat, staring. "All these humans, heading for Equilan. What will we do?"

"Paithan?"

"Yes, I'm coming."

They left the broad trails of the moss plains, taking to the jungle trails. "Smuggler's Road" was thin and twisting, difficult to traverse, but far less crowded. Paithan forced them to ride hard, driving their animals, driving themselves—cycle after cycle—until they dropped from exhaustion. Then they slept, often too tired to eat. The elf allowed them only a few hours before he had them up and traveling again. They met other people on the trails—people like themselves, living on society's fringes, who were well acquainted with these dark and hidden paths. They, too, were fleeing sorinth. One of these, a human, stumbled into their camp, three cycles into their journey.

"Water," he said, and collapsed.

Paithan fetched water. Rega lifted the man's head, and held the drinking gourd to his lips. He was middle-aged, his face gray with fatigue.

"That's better. Thanks."

Some color returned to the sagging cheeks. He was able to sit up on his own, and let his head sink between his knees, drawing deep breaths.

"You're welcome to rest here with us," offered Rega. "Share our food."

"Rest!" The man lifted his head, gazed at them in astonishment. Then he glanced around the jungle, shivering, and staggered to his feet. "No rest!" he muttered. "They're behind me! Right behind me!"

His fear was palpable. Paithan jumped up, regarding the man in alarm.

"How far behind you?"

The man was fleeing the campsite, taking to the trail on legs that could barely support him. Paithan ran after him, caught hold of his arm.

"How far?"

The man shook his head. "A cycle. Not more."

"A cycle!" Rega sucked her breath through her teeth.

"The man's crazed," muttered Roland. "You can't believe him."

"Griffith destroyed! Terncia burning! Lord Reginald, dead! I know." The man ran a trembling hand through grizzled hair. "I was one of his knights!"

Looking at the man more closely, they could see he was dressed in the quilted cotton undergarments worn beneath the tyro shell armor. It was no wonder they had not recognized it earlier. The fabric was ripped and stained with blood, hanging from the man's body in tattered, filthy fragments.

"I got rid of it," he said, his hands plucking at the cloth covering his chest. "The armor. It was too heavy and it didn't do any good. They died in it. The fiends caught them and crushed them . . . arms wrapping around them. The armor cracked, blood . . . came out from between. Bones stuck through . . . and the screams . . ."

"Blessed Thillia!" Roland was white, shuddering.

"Shut him up!" Rega snapped at Paithan.

No one noticed Drugar, sitting alone as he always did, the slight, strange smile hidden by his beard.

"Do you know how I escaped?" The man clutched Paithan by the front of his tunic. The elf, glancing down, saw the man's hand was dappled with splotches of reddish brown. "The others ran. I was . . . too scared! I was scared stiff!" The knight began to giggle. "Scared stiff! Couldn't move. And the giants went right by me! Isn't that funny! Scared stiff!" His laughter was shrill, unnerving. It ended in a choked cough. Roughly, he shoved Paithan backward, away from him.

"But now I can run. I've been running . . . three cycles. Not stop. Can't stop." He took a step forward, paused, turned and glared at them with red-rimmed, wild eyes. "They were supposed to come back!" he said angrily. "Have you seen them?"

"Who?"

"Supposed to come back and help us! Cowards. Bunch of damn, good-for-nothing cowards. Like me!" The knight laughed again. Shaking his head, he lurched off into the jungle.

"Who the hell's he talking about?" Roland asked.

"I don't know." Rega began packing their equipment, throwing food into leather pouches. "And I don't care. Crazed or not, he's right about one thing. We've got to keep moving."

> In faith they walked with modest stride,
> to sleeping Thillia beneath.
> The crashing waves their virtue cried,
> the kingdoms wept their wat'ry wreath.

The dwarf's rich bass voice rose in song. "You see," said Drugar, when the verse ended, "I have learned it."

"You're right," said Roland, making no move to help pack. He sat on the ground, arms dangling listlessly between his knees. "That's who the knight meant. And they *didn't* come back. Why not?" He looked up, angry. "Why didn't they? Everything they worked for—destroyed! Our world! Gone! Why? What's the sense?"

Rega's lips tightened, she was flinging packs onto the cargan. "It was only a legend. No one really believed it."

"Yeah," muttered Roland. "Nobody believed in the tytans either."

Rega's hands, tugging at the straps, started to shake. She lowered her head onto the cargan's flank, gripping the leather hard, until it hurt, willing herself not to cry, not to give way.

Paithan's hand closed over hers.

"Don't!" she said in a fierce tone, elbowing him aside. She lifted her head, shook her hair around her face, and gave the strap a vicious tug. "Go on. Leave me alone." Surreptitiously, when the elf wasn't looking, she wiped her hand across wet cheeks.

They started on their way, disheartened, dispirited, fear driving them on. They had traversed only a few miles when they came upon the knight, lying face down across the trail.

Paithan slid from the cargan, knelt beside the man, his hand on the knight's neck.

"Dead."

They traveled two more cycles, pressing the weary cargans to their limit. Now, when they halted, they didn't unpack, but slept on the ground, the reins of the cargans wrapped around their wrists. They were giddy with exhaustion and lack of food. Their meager supplies had run out and they dared not take time to hunt. They talked little, saving their breath, riding with slumped shoulders, bent heads. The only thing that could rouse them was a strange sound behind them.

The breaking of a tree limb would cause them to jerk up, swinging around fearfully in the saddle, peering into the shadows. Often the humans and the elf fell asleep while riding, swaying in the saddle until they slumped sideways and came to themselves with a start. The dwarf, riding last, bringing up the rear, watched all with a smile.

Paithan marveled at the dwarf, even as the elf's uneasiness over Drugar grew. He never appeared fatigued; he often volunteered to keep watch while the others slept.

Paithan woke from terrifying dreams in which he imagined Drugar, dagger in hand, slipping up on him as he slept. Starting awake, the elf always found Drugar sitting patiently beneath a tree, hands folded across the beard that fell in long curls over his stomach. Paithan might have laughed at his fear. After all, the dwarf had saved their lives. Looking back at Drugar, riding behind them, or glancing at him during the few times they stopped to rest, the elf saw the gleam in the watchful black eyes, eyes that seemed to be always waiting, and Paithan's laughter died on his lips.

Paithan was thinking about the dwarf, wondering what drove him, what terrible fuel kept such a fire burning, when Rega's shout roused him from his bleak reverie.

"The ferry!" She pointed at a crude sign, tacked up onto a tree trunk. "The trail ends here. We have to go back to the—"

Her voice was cut off by a horrible sound, a wail that rose from hundreds of throats, a collective scream.

"The main highway!" Paithan clutched his reins with sweating, trembling hands. "The tytans have reached the main highway."

The elf saw in his mind the stream of humanity, saw the giant, eyeless creatures come upon it. He saw the people scatter, try to flee, but there was nowhere to go on the wide-open plains, no escape. The stream would turn to a river of blood.

Rega pressed her hands against her ears. "Shut up!" she was screaming over and over, tears streaming down her cheeks. "Shut up! Shut up! Shut up!"

As if in answer, a sudden, eerie silence fell over the jungle, silence broken only by the not-too-distant cries of the dying.

"They're here," said Roland, a half-smile playing on his lips.

"The ferry!" Paithan gasped. "The creatures may be giants, but they're not tall enough to wade the Kithni Gulf! That will stop them, for a time at least." He spurred his cargan on. The startled animal, terrified itself, leapt forward in panic.

The others followed, flying through the jungle, ducking overhanging limbs, vines slapping them in the face. Breaking out into the open, they saw ahead of them the sparkling, placid surface of the Kithni Gulf, a startling contrast to the chaos erupting on the water's edge.

Humans were running madly down the main highway that led to the ferry, fear stripping them of any consciousness they might have had for their fellows. Those who fell were trampled beneath pounding feet. Children were swept from their parents' arms by the crush of the mob, small bodies hurled to the ground. Those who stopped to try to help the fallen never rose again. Looking far back, on the horizon, Paithan saw the jungle moving.

"Paithan! Look!" Rega clutched at him, pointing.

The elf shifted his gaze back to the ferry. The pier was mobbed, people pushing and shoving. Out in the water, the boat, overloaded, was riding too low and sinking deeper by the minute. It would never make it across. And it wouldn't matter if it did.

The other ferry boat had put out from the opposite shore. It was lined with elven archers, railbows ready, arrows pointing toward Thillia. Paithan assumed at first that the elves were coming to the aid of the humans, and his heart swelled with pride. Sir Lathan had been wrong. The elves would drive the tytans back!

A human, attempting to swim the gulf, came near the boat, stretched out with his hand for help.

The elves shot him. His body slid down beneath the water

and vanished. Sickened, disbelieving, Paithan saw his people turn their weapons not on the coming tytans, but on the humans trying to flee the enemy.

"You bastard!"

Paithan turned to see a wild-eyed man attempting to drag Roland from his saddle. People on the highway, seeing the cargans, realized that the animals offered escape. A frenzied mob started toward them. Roland beat the man off, clouting him to the moss with his strong hand. Another came at Rega, a branch in his hand. She kicked him in the face with her boot, sending him reeling backward. The cargans, already panicked, began to leap and buck, striking out with their sharp claws. Drugar, cursing in dwarven, was using his reins as a lash to keep the mob at bay.

"Back to the trees!" Paithan cried, wheeling his animal.

Rega galloped beside him, but Roland was caught, unable to extricate himself from grasping hands. He was nearly pulled from the saddle. Drugar, seeing the human in trouble, forced his cargan between Roland and the mob. The dwarf grabbed hold of Roland's reins and yanked the cargan forward, joining up with Paithan and Rega. The four galloped back into the shelter of the jungle.

Once safe, they paused to catch their breath. They avoided looking at each other, none of them wanting to see the inevitable in his companion's face.

"There must be a trail that leads to the gulf!" said Paithan. "The cargan can swim."

"And get shot by elves!" Roland wiped blood from a cut lip.

"They won't shoot me."

"A lot of good that does us!"

"They won't harm you if you're with me." Paithan wished he was certain of that fact, but right now he supposed it didn't matter.

"If there is a trail . . . I don't know it," said Rega. A tremor shook her body, she gripped the saddle to keep from falling.

Paithan plunged off the path, heading in the direction of the gulf. Within moments, he and the cargan became hopelessly entangled in the thick undergrowth. The elf fought on, refusing to admit defeat, but he saw that even if they did manage to hack their way through, it would take hours. And they did not have hours. Wearily, he rode back.

The sounds of death from the highway grew louder. They could hear splashes, people hurling themselves into the Kithni.

Roland slid from his saddle. Landing on the ground, he gazed around. "This looks as good a place to die as any."

Slowly, Paithan climbed from his cargan and walked over to Rega. He held out his arms. She slipped into them, and he clasped her tightly.

"I can't watch, Paithan," she said. "Promise me I won't have to see them!"

"You won't," he whispered, smoothing the dark hair. "Keep your eyes on me."

Roland stood squarely on the path, facing the direction in which the tytans must come. His fear was gone, or perhaps he was just too tired to care anymore.

Drugar, a ghastly grin on his bearded face, put his hand to his belt and drew the bone-handle knife.

One stroke for each of them, and a final for himself.

CHAPTER ◆ 25

TREETOPS,

EQUILAN

◆

HAPLO LAY FLAT ON HIS BACK ON THE MOSS, SHIELDING HIS EYES FROM the sun, counting stars.

He had come up with twenty-five bright lights that he could see clearly from this vantage point. Lenthan Quindiniar had assured him that—all told—the elves had counted ninety-seven. Not all of these were visible all the time, of course. Some of them winked out and stayed out for a number of seasons before returning. Elven astronomers had also calculated that there were stars near the horizon that could not be seen due to the atmosphere. They had estimated, therefore, that there might be anywhere from 150 to 200 stars total in the heavens.

Which was certainly different from any stars Haplo'd ever heard about. He considered the possibility of moons. There had been a moon in the ancient world, according to his lord's research. But there had been no moon in the Sartan rendering of this world and Haplo hadn't seen any moonlike objects during his flight. Again, he thought it likely that moons would revolve around the world and these lights were, apparently, stationary. But then the sun was stationary. Or rather the planet of Pryan was stationary. It didn't revolve. There was no day or night. And then there was the strange cycle of the stars—burning brightly for long periods of time, then going dark, then reappearing.

Haplo sat up, glanced about for the dog, discovered it wandering about the yard, sniffing at the strange smells of people and other animals it didn't recognize. The Patryn, alone in the yard, everyone else asleep, scratched at his bandaged hands. The binding always irritated his skin the first few days he wore it.

Maybe the lights are nothing more than a natural phenomenon peculiar to this planet. Which means I'm wasting my time, speculating about them and the sun. After all, I wasn't sent here to study astronomy. I've got more important problems. Like what to do about this world.

Last evening, Lenthan Quindiniar had drawn Haplo a picture of the world as the elves viewed it. The drawing was similar to the drawing Haplo'd seen in the Nexus—a round globe with a ball of fire in the center. Above the world, the elf added the "stars" and the sun. He pointed out their own location on this world—or what the elven astrologers had plotted was their location—and told him how the elves had, centuries ago, crossed the Paragna Sea to the est and arrived at the Fartherness Reaches.

"It was the plague," Lenthan had explained. "They were fleeing it. Otherwise they never would have left their homes."

Once they reached the Fartherness, the elves burned their ships, severing all contact with their former life. They turned their backs on the sea and looked inland. Lenthan's great-great grandfather had been one of the few willing to explore the new territory to the vars and, in doing so, came across ornite, the navigational stone that was to make his fortune.[1] Using the stone, he was able to return to the Fartherness. He informed the elves of his discovery, and offered jobs to those willing to venture into the wilderness.

Equilan had started out as a small mining community. It might have remained no more than that, but for the development of the human realms to the vars. The humans of what was now known as Thillia traveled there, by their own account, through a passage that led beneath the Terinthian Ocean. King George the Only—the father of the five brothers of legendary fame—led his people to this new land, supposedly running from a terror, whose name and face had been lost in the past.

Elves are not a race who must constantly expand. They feel

---

[1] Without any means to navigate, exploration was extremely hazardous because the odds were slim that a person leaving one place would ever find his way back to it.

no driving urge to conquer other people, to gobble up land. Having established a hold on Equilan, the elves had all the land they wanted. What they needed was trade.

The elves welcomed the humans who, in turn, were extremely pleased to acquire elven weapons and other goods. As time went by and the human population grew, they were less happy about the elves taking up so much valuable land on their sorinth border. The Thillians tried to expand norinth, but ran into the SeaKings—a fierce warrior people who had crossed the Sea of Stars during a time of war in the Kasnar Empire. Farther norinth and est were the dark and gloomy strongholds of the dwarves. By this time, the elven nation had grown strong and powerful. The humans were weak, divided, and dependent on the elves. The Thillians could do nothing but grumble and regard their neighbor's land with envy.

As for the dwarves, Lenthan knew little, except that it was said that they had been well established in their kingdoms, long before his grandfather's time.

"But where did you all come from originally?" Haplo had asked. He knew the answer, but was curious to see what, if anything, these people knew about the Sundering, hoping such information might give him a clue to the whereabouts and doings of the Sartan. "I mean, way, way, way back in time."

Lenthan had launched into a long and involved explanation and Haplo soon became lost in the complex myths. It depended on who you asked, apparently. Among the elves and humans, creation had something to do with being cast out of paradise. Orn-only-knew-what the dwarves believed in.

"What's the political situation in the human realm?"

Lenthan had looked downcast. "I'm afraid I really can't tell you. My son is the explorer in the family. Father never thought I was quite suited—"

"Your son? Is he here?" Haplo had glanced about, wondering if the elf might be hiding in a closet—which, considering this wacky household, might not be at all unusual. "Can I talk to him?"

"Paithan. No, he's not here. Traveling in the human realm. He won't be back for some time, I'm afraid."

All of this had been little help to Haplo. The Patryn was beginning to feel that his mission here was a lost cause. He was supposed to foment chaos, make it easy for his lord to step in and take over. But on Pryan, the dwarves asked nothing more than to be let alone, the humans fought each other, and the elves supplied them. Haplo didn't stand much chance of urging the humans to war against the elves—it's difficult to attack someone who's providing you with the only means you have of attacking. No one wanted to fight the dwarves—no one wanted anything the dwarves had. The elves couldn't be stirred to conquest, apparently because the word simply wasn't in their vocabulary.

"*Status quo*," Lenthan Quindiniar had said. "It's an ancient word meaning . . . well . . . 'status quo.' "

Haplo recognized the word and knew what it meant. Unchanging. Far different from the chaos he'd discovered (and helped along) in Arianus.

Watching the bright lights shining in the sky, the Patryn grew more annoyed, more perplexed. Even if I manage to stir up trouble in this realm, how many more realms am I going to have to visit to do the same thing? There could be as many realms as . . . as there are shining lights in the sky. And who knows how many more beyond that? It might take me a lifetime just to find all of them! I don't have a lifetime. And neither does My Lord.

It didn't make sense. The Sartan were organized, systematic, and logical. They would never have scattered civilizations around at random like this and then left them to survive on their own. There had to be some unifying something. Haplo didn't have a clue, at this moment, how he was going to find it.

Except possibly the old man. He was crazy, obviously. But was he crazy as a gatecrasher[2] or crazy as a wolfen? The first meant he was harmless to everyone except perhaps himself, the second meant he needed to be watched. Haplo remembered his mistake in Arianus, when he'd thought a man a fool who had turned out to be anything but. He wouldn't make the same mistake again. He had a lot of questions about the old man.

And as if thinking of him had conjured him (as occasionally

---

[2]The Labyrinth takes its toll on those imprisoned there. Those Patryns who are driven insane by the hardships are known as "gatecrashers" due to the peculiar form the madness took, leading all its victims to run blindly into the wilderness, imagining that they have reached the Last Gate.

happened in the Labyrinth), Haplo looked up to discover Zifnab looking down.

"Is that you?" came the old man's quavering voice.

Haplo rose to his feet, brushing off bits of moss.

"Oh, no, it isn't," said Zifnab in disappointment, shaking his head. "Still"—he peered closely at Haplo—"I seem to remember looking for you, too. Come, come." He took hold of Haplo's arm. "We've got to take off— Go to the rescue! Oh, dear! Nice Doggie. N—nice doggie."

Seeing a stranger accost its master, the dog left off its pursuit of nonexistent game and dashed over to confront live quarry. The animal stood in front of the wizard, bared its teeth, and growled menacingly.

"I suggest you let go of my arm, old man," advised Haplo.

"Uh, yes." Zifnab removed his hand hastily. "Fine . . . fine animal." The dog's growls ceased, but it continued to regard the old man with deep suspicion.

Zifnab felt in a pocket. "I had a milk bone in here a few weeks ago. Left over from lunch. I say, have you met my dragon?"

"Is that a threat?" Haplo demanded.

"Threat?" The old wizard seemed staggered, so completely taken aback that his hat fell off. "No, of . . . of course not! It's just that . . . we were comparing pets . . . " Zifnab lowered his voice, glanced around nervously. "Actually, my dragon's quite harmless. I've got him under this spell—"

"Come on, dog," said Haplo in disgust, and headed for his ship.

"Great Gandalf's ghost!" shouted Zifnab. "If he had a ghost. I doubt it. He was such a snob . . . Where was I? Yes, rescue! Almost forgot." The old man gathered up his robes and began running along at Haplo's side. "Come on! Come on! No time to waste. Hurry!"

His white hair stood up all over his head, his beard stuck out in all directions. Zifnab dashed past Haplo. Looking back, he put his finger to his lips. "And keep it quiet. Don't want *him*"—he pointed downward, grimacing—"along."

Haplo came to a halt. Crossing his arms over his chest, he waited with some amusement to see the old man come crashing up against the magical barrier the Patryn had established around his vessel.

Zifnab reached the hull, laid a hand on it.

Nothing happened.

"Hey, stay away from there!" Haplo broke into a run. "Dog, stop him!"

The dog sped ahead, flying over the mossy ground on silent paws, and caught hold of the old man's robes just as Zifnab was attempting to climb up over the ship's rail.

"Get back! Get back!" Zifnab flapped his hat at the dog's head. "I'll turn you into a piglet! *Ast a bula*— No, wait. That turns *me* into a piglet. Unhand me, you beast!"

"Dog, down," ordered Haplo, and the dog obediently dropped to a sitting position, releasing the old man, keeping a watchful eye on him. "Look you, old man. I don't know how you managed to break through my magic, but I'm giving you fair warning. Stay off my ship—"

"We're going off on a trip? Well, of course we are." Zifnab reached out, gingerly patted Haplo's arm. "That's why we're here. Nice young man you've got," he added, speaking to the dog, "but addled."

The wizard hopped over the rail and proceeded across the top deck, moving toward the bridge with surprising speed and agility for one of "advanced years."

"Damn!" swore Haplo, bounding after him. "Dog!"

The animal leapt ahead, sped across the deck. Zifnab had already disappeared down the ladder leading to the bridge. The dog jumped after him.

Haplo followed. Sliding down the ladder, he ran after and onto the bridge. Zifnab was staring curiously at the rune-covered steering stone. The dog stood beside him, watching. The old man stretched out a hand to touch. The dog growled, and Zifnab quickly snatched his hand back.

Haplo paused in the hatchway, considering. He was a passive observer, not supposed to directly interfere with life in this world. But now he had no choice. The old man had seen the runes. Not only that, he had unraveled them. He knew, therefore, who the Patryn was. He couldn't be allowed to spread that knowledge further. Besides, he was—he must be—a Sartan.

Circumstances on Arianus prevented me from avenging myself on our ancient enemy. Now, I've got another Sartan, and this time it won't matter. No one will miss crazy Zifnab. Hell, that Quindiniar woman will probably give me a medal!

Haplo stood in the hatchway, his body blocking the bridge's only exit. "I warned you. You shouldn't have come down here, old man. Now you've seen what you shouldn't have seen." He began to unwind the bandages. "Now you're going to have to die. I know you're a Sartan. They're the only ones who have the power to unravel my magic. Tell me one thing. Where are the rest of your people?"

"I was afraid of this," said Zifnab, gazing at Haplo sadly. "This is no way for a savior to behave, you know that."

"I'm no savior. In a way, you might say I'm the opposite. I'm supposed to bring trouble, chaos, to prepare for the day when My Lord will enter this world and claim it for his own. We will rule who, by rights, should have ruled long ago. You must know who I am, now. Take a look around you, Sartan. Recognize the runes? Or maybe you've known who I was all along. After all, you predicted my coming. I'd like to know how you did that."

Unwinding the bandages, revealing the sigla tattooed on his hands, Haplo advanced on the old man.

Zifnab did not back up, did not retreat before him. The old man stood his ground, facing the Patryn with an air of quiet dignity. "You've made a mistake," he said, his voice quiet, his eyes suddenly sharp and shrewd. "I'm not a Sartan."

"Uh, huh." Haplo tossed the bandages onto the deck, rubbing the runes on his skin. "Just the fact that you're denying it proves my point. Except the Sartan were never known to lie. But then, they were never known to go senile either."

Haplo grabbed hold of the old man's arm, feeling the bones fragile and brittle in his grasp. "Talk, Zifnab, or whatever your real name is. I have the power to rupture the bones, one by one, inside your flesh. It's an extremely painful way to die. I'll start on the hands, work my way down your body. By the time I reach your spine, you'll be begging me for release."

At his feet, the dog whined and rubbed against the Patryn's knee. Haplo ignored the animal, his grip tightened around Zifnab's wrist. He placed his other hand, palm down, directly over the old man's heart. "Tell me the truth, and I'll end it quickly. What I do to bones, I can do to organs. The heart bursts. It's painful, but fast."

Haplo had to give the old man credit. Stronger men than Zifnab had trembled in the Patryn's grasp. The old man was calm. If he was afraid, he controlled his fear well.

"I am telling you the truth. I'm not a Sartan."

Haplo's grip tightened. He made ready to speak the first rune, the rune that would send a jolt of agony through the frail body. Zifnab held perfectly still.

"As for how I undid your magic, there are forces in this universe of which you have no knowledge." The eyes, never leaving Haplo's face, narrowed. "Forces that have remained hidden because you have never searched for them."

"Then why don't you use these forces to save your life, old man?"

"I am."

Haplo shook his head in disgust and spoke the first rune. The sigla on his hand glowed blue. The power flowed from his body into the old man's. Haplo could feel wrist bones burst and turn to mush in his grip. Zifnab gave a suppressed groan.

Haplo barely saw, out of the corner of his eye, the dog hurtling through the air toward him. He had time to raise his arm to block the attack. The force of the blow knocked him to the deck, slammed the air from his body. He lay gasping, trying to catch his breath. The dog stood over him, licking his face.

"Dear, dear. Are you hurt, my boy?" Zifnab leaned over him solicitously, offering a hand to help him up—the same hand Haplo had crushed.

Haplo stared at it, saw the wrist bones standing out clearly beneath the stretched, aged skin. They appeared whole and intact. The old man had not spoken any runes, traced any in the air. Haplo, studying the field of magic around him, could detect no sign that it had been disturbed. But he had felt the bone break!

Shoving the old man's hand aside, Haplo regained his feet. "You're good," he acknowledged. "But how long can you keep it up? An old geezer like you." He took a step toward the old man and halted.

The dog stood between them.

"Dog! Get!" ordered Haplo.

The animal held its ground, gazed up at its master with unhappy, pleading eyes.

Zifnab, smiling gently, patted the black-furred head. "Good boy. I thought so." He nodded wisely, solemnly. "I know all about the dog, you see."

"Whatever the devil that means!"

"Precisely, dear boy," said the old man, beaming at him. "And now that we're all nicely acquainted, we'd best be on our way." Zifnab turned around, hovered over the steering stone, rubbing his hands eagerly. "I'm really curious to see how this works." Reaching into a pocket of his mouse-colored robes, he pulled out a chain to which nothing was attached, and stared at it. "My ears and whiskers! We're late."

Haplo glared at the dog. "Get!"

The dog slunk down on its belly, crawled across the deck and took refuge in a corner. Head lying on its paws, the animal whimpered. Haplo took a step toward the old man.

"Let's get this show on the road!" Zifnab stated emphatically, snapping shut nothing and slipping the chain back in his pocket. "Paithan's in danger—"

"Paithan." Haplo paused.

"Quindiniar's son. Fine lad. You can ask him those questions you've been wanting to ask: all about the political situation among the humans, what it would take to make the elves go to war, how to stir up the dwarves. Paithan knows all the answers. Not that it will make much difference now." Zifnab sighed, shook his head. "Politics don't matter to the dead. But we'll save some of them. The best and the brightest. And, now, we really must be going." The old man gazed around with interest. "How do you fly this contraption anyway?"

Irritably scratching the tattoos on the back of his hand, Haplo stared at the old wizard.

A Sartan—he has to be! That's the only way he could heal himself. Unless he didn't heal himself. Maybe I made a mistake in the rune-twining, maybe I only thought I crushed his wrist. And the dog, protecting him. That doesn't mean much.

The animal takes strange likings. There was that time on Arianus when the mutt saved the life of that dwarven woman I was going to have to kill.

Destroyer, savior . . .

"All right, old man. I'll go along with whatever game you're playing." Haplo knelt down, scratched the dog's silky ears. The animal's tail brushed the floor, pleased that all was forgiven. "But just until I figure out the rules. When I do, it's winner take all. And I intend to win."

Straightening, he placed his hands upon the steering stone. "Where are we headed?"

Zifnab blinked, confused. "I'm afraid I haven't the slightest idea," he admitted. "But, by god!" he added solemnly. "I'll know when I get there!"

CHAPTER 26

VARSPORT,

THILLIA

◆

THE DRAGONSHIP SKIMMED OVER THE TOPS OF THE TREES. HAPLO FLEW in the direction according to what he'd been told were the human landholdings. Zifnab peered out the window, anxiously watching the landscape slide away beneath them.

"The gulf!" the old man cried out suddenly. "We're close. Ah, dear, dear."

"What's going on?"

Haplo could make out a line of elves drawn up in military formation along the shore. He sailed out farther over the water. Smoke from distant fires obscured his view momentarily. A gust of wind blew the smoke apart, and Haplo could see a burning city, masses of people swarming onto the beach. A few hundred feet from shore, a boat was sinking, to judge by the number of black dots visible in the water.

"Terrible, terrible," Zifnab ran a trembling hand through his sparse white hair. "You'll have to fly lower. I can't see."

Haplo was interested in having a closer look himself. Maybe he'd been wrong about the peaceful situation in this realm. The dragonship swooped low. Many on the shore, feeling the dark shadow pass over them, looked up, pointed. The crowd wavered, some starting to run from what might be a new threat, others milling about aimlessly, realizing that there was no place to go.

Wheeling *Dragon Wing* around, Haplo made another pass. Elven archers on a boat in the middle of the gulf lifted their bows, turned their arrows on the ship. The Patryn ignored them, soared low to get a better view. The runes protecting his ship would protect them against the puny weapons of this world.

"There! There! Turn! Turn!" The old man clutched at Haplo, almost dragging him off his feet. Zifnab pointed into a densely wooded area, not far from the shoreline where the crowds of people were massed. The Patryn steered the ship in the direction indicated.

"I can't see a thing, old man."

"Yes! Yes!" Zifnab was hopping up and down in anxiety. The dog, sensing the excitement, leapt about the deck, barking frantically.

"The grove, down there! Not much room to land, but you can make it."

Not much room. Haplo bit back the words he would have liked to use to describe his opinion of their landing site—a small clearing, barely visible beneath a tangle of trees and vines. He was about to tell the wizard that it would be impossible to set his ship down, when a closer, grudging look revealed that—if he altered the magic and pulled the wings in tight—there might be a chance.

"What do we do once we get down there, old man?"

"Pick up Paithan, the two humans, and the dwarf."

"You still haven't told me what's going on."

Zifnab turned his head, regarded Haplo with a shrewd look. "You must see for yourself, my boy. Otherwise, you wouldn't believe."

At least that's what Haplo thought he said. He couldn't be sure, over the dog's barking. Undoubtedly I'm about to put my ship down in the middle of a raging battle. Coming in low, he could see the small group in the clearing, see their faces staring up at him.

"Hold on!" he shouted to the dog . . . and the old man, if he was listening. "It's going to be rough!"

The ship smashed through the tops of the trees. Limbs dragged at them, snapped and broke apart. The view out the window was obscured by a mass of green, the ship lurched and pitched. Zifnab fell forward, ended up spraddled-legged against the glass. Haplo hung on to the steering stone. The dog spread its legs, fighting for purchase on the canting deck.

A grinding crash, and they broke through, swooping into the clearing. Wrestling with the ship, Haplo caught a glimpse of the mensch he was going to rescue, huddled together at one edge of the jungle, apparently uncertain if this was salvation or more trouble.

"Go get them, old man!" Haplo told the wizard. "Dog, stay."

The animal had been about to bound gleefully after Zifnab, who had unpeeled himself from the window and was tottering toward the ladder leading to the upper deck.

The dog obediently sank back down, gazing upward with intense eagerness, tail wagging. Haplo silently cursed himself and this crazy situation. He would have to keep his hands bare to fly and was wondering how he would explain the sigla tattooed on his skin when a sudden blow against the hull sent a shudder through the ship.

Haplo almost lost his footing. "No," he muttered to himself. "It couldn't be."

Holding his breath, every sense alert, the Patryn held perfectly still and waited.

The blow came again, stronger, more powerful. The hull shivered, the vibrations tore into the magic, tore into the wood, tore into Haplo.

The rune structure was unraveling.

Haplo turned in upon himself, centered himself, body reacting instinctively to a danger his mind told him was impossible. On the deck above, he could hear feet pounding, the old man's shrill voice, screeching, yelling something.

Another blow shook the ship. Haplo heard the old man cry out for help, but ignored his pleas. The Patryn was tasting, smelling, listening, stretching out with all his senses. The rune's magic was being unraveled, slowly, surely. The blows hadn't hurt his ship, not yet. But they had weakened his magic. The next strike or the one after would break through, deal damage, destroy.

The only magic strong enough, powerful enough to oppose his own was the rune-magic of the Sartan.

A trap! The old man baited me! I was fool enough to fly right into the net!

Another blow rocked the ship; Haplo thought he heard wood splinter. The dog's teeth bared, the fur rose on its neck.

"Stay, boy," said Haplo, stroking the head, bidding it stay with the pressure of his hand. "This is my fight."

He had long wanted to meet, to battle, to kill a Sartan.

Haplo vaulted up to the top deck. The old man was scrambling to his feet. Leaping for him, Haplo was brought to a halt by the look of sheer terror on Zifnab's face. The old man was yelling frantically, pointing up, over Haplo's head.

"Behind you!"

"Oh, no, I'm not falling for that—"

Another blow threw Haplo to his knees. The blow had come from behind. He steadied himself, glanced around.

A creature, standing some thirty feet tall, was bashing what appeared to be a small tree trunk into the hull of the dragonship. Several creatures, standing near it, were watching. Others were completely ignoring the attack, advancing with single-minded purpose on the small group crouched at the edge of the glade.

Several planks on the hull had already been staved in, protecting sigla smashed, useless, broken.

Haplo traced the runes in the air, watched them multiply with lightning speed, and zip away from him toward their target. A ball of blue flame exploded on the tree branch, jarring it from the creature's hands. The Patryn wouldn't kill, not yet. Not until he found out what these beings were.

He knew what they weren't. They weren't Sartan. But they were using Sartan magic.

"Nice shot!" yelled the old man. "Wait here. I'll get our friends."

Haplo couldn't turn to look, but he heard feet clattering off behind him. Presumably the wizard was going to try to bring the elf and his trapped companions on board. Seeing in his mind's eye more of these beings descending on them, Haplo wished the old man luck. The Patryn couldn't help. He had his own problems.

The creature stared dazedly at its empty hands, as if trying to comprehend what had happened. Slowly it turned its head toward its assailant. It had no eyes, but Haplo knew it could see him, perhaps see him better than he himself could see the creature. The Patryn felt waves of sensing streak out from the being, felt them touch him, sniff at him, analyze him. The creature wasn't using magic now. It was relying on its own senses, odd as those might be.

Haplo tensed, waiting for an attack, his mind devising the rune structure that would entrap the creature, paralyze it, leave it subject to the Patryn's interrogation.

Where is the citadel? What must we do?

The voice startled Haplo, speaking to his mind, not his ears. It wasn't threatening. The voice sounded frustrated, desperate, almost wistfully eager. Other creatures in the grove, hearing the silent question of their companion, had ceased their murderous pursuit to turn to watch.

"Tell me about the citadel," said Haplo cautiously, spreading his hands in a gesture of appeasement. "Perhaps I can—"

Light blinded him, concussive thunder blasted him from his feet. Lying face down on the deck, dazed and stunned, Haplo fought to retain consciousness, fought to analyze and understand.

The magical spell had been crude—a simple elemental configuration calling upon forces present in nature. A child of seven could have constructed it, a child of seven should have been able to protect himself against it. Haplo hadn't even seen it coming. It was as if the child of seven had cast the spell using the strength of seven hundred. His own magic had shielded him from death, but the shield had been cracked. He was hurt, vulnerable.

Haplo enhanced his defenses. The sigla on his skin began to glow blue and red, creating an eerie light that shone through his clothing. He was vaguely aware that the being had retrieved its tree trunk and lifted it high, preparing to smash it down on him. Rolling to a standing position, he cast his spell. Runes surrounded the wood, caused the trunk to disintegrate in the creature's hand.

Behind him came shouts and the thudding of feet, panting breath. His diversion of the creature's attention must have given the old man time to rescue the elf and his friends. Haplo felt, more than saw or heard, one of them come creeping up to him.

"I'll help—" offered a voice, speaking in elven.

"Get below!" the Patryn snarled, enraged, the interruption unweaving an entire fabric of runes. He didn't see whether the elf obeyed him or not. Haplo didn't care.

He was intent upon the creature, analyzing it. It had ceased using its potent magic, turned again to brute force. Dull-witted, stupid, Haplo decided. Its reactions had been instinctive, animal-like, unthinking.

Perhaps it couldn't consciously control the magic— He started to stand up.

The blast of wind hit him with hurricane force. Haplo struggled against the spell, creating dense and complex rune constructs to surround him, protect him.

He might have built a wall of feathers. The raw power of the crude magic seeped through minuscule cracks in the sigla and blew them to tatters. The wind battered him to the deck. Branches and leaves hurtled past him, something struck him in the face, nearly knocking him senseless. He fought against the pain, clinging to the wooden rails with his hands, the gusts pummeling, hammering. He was helpless against the magic, he couldn't reason with it, speak to it. His strength was seeping from him rapidly, the wind increasing in force.

A grim joke among the Patryns purports that there are only two kinds of people in the Labyrinth: the quick and the dead, and advises, "When the odds are against you, run like hell."

It was definitely time to get out of here.

Every move taking a supreme effort against the force of the wind, Haplo managed to turn his head and look behind him. He spotted the open hatch, saw the elf crouched, waiting there, his head poking up. Not a hair on the elf's head was ruffled. The full force of the magic was being expended against Haplo alone.

That might end soon.

Haplo released his hold on the rail. The wind blew him across the deck, toward the hatch. Making a desperate lunge, he grabbed the rim of the hatch as he slithered past, and held on. The elf grasped him by the wrists and fought to drag him below. The wind fought them. Blinding, stinging, it howled and pounded at them like a live thing who sees its prey about to escape.

The elf's grip loosened, suddenly broke. The elf disappeared.

Haplo felt his hold on the rim weakening. Inwardly cursing, he concentrated all his strength, all his magic into just hanging on. Down below, he heard the dog barking frantically, and then hands had hold of him again—not slender elf hands, but strong human hands. Haplo saw a human face—grim, determined, flushed red with the effort the man was expending. Haplo, with his failing energy, wove his magic around the man. Red and blue sigla from the runes on his own arms and hands twisted and twined around the human's arms, lending him Haplo's strength.

Muscles bunched, jerked, heaved, and Haplo was flying head first down the hatch.

He landed heavily on top of the human, heard the breath leave the man's body in a whoosh and a grunt of pain.

Haplo was on his feet, moving, reacting, ignoring the part of his mind that was trying to draw his attention to his own injuries. He didn't glance at the human who had saved his life. He rudely shoved aside the old man who was yammering something in his ear. The ship shuddered; he heard timber cracking. The creatures were venting their rage against it or perhaps endeavoring to crack open the shell protecting the fragile life inside.

The steering stone was the only object in Haplo's line of sight. All else disappeared, was swallowed up in the black fog that was slowly gathering about him. He shook his head, fought the darkness back. Sinking to his knees before the stone, he placed his hands upon it, summoning from the deep well within him the strength to activate it.

He felt the ship shudder beneath him, but it was a different type of shudder than the one the creatures were inflicting. *Dragon Wing* rose slowly off the ground.

Haplo's eyes were gummed almost completely shut with something, probably his own blood. He peered through them, struggled to see out the window. The creatures were behaving as he had anticipated. Amazed, startled by the ship's sudden lift into the air, they had fallen back away from it.

But they weren't frightened. They weren't fleeing from it in panic. Haplo felt their senses reaching out, smelling, listening, seeing without eyes. The Patryn fought back the black haze and concentrated his energy on keeping the ship floating up higher and higher.

He saw one of the creatures lift its arm. A giant hand reached out, grabbed hold of one of the wings. The ship lurched, throwing everyone to the deck.

Haplo held onto the stone, concentrated his magic. The runes flared blue, the creature snatched its hand back as if in pain. The ship soared into the air. Looking out from beneath his gummed eyelashes, Haplo saw green treetops and the hazy blue-green sky and then everything was covered by a dense black, pain-tinged fog.

CHAPTER ◆ 27

SOMEWHERE ABOVE

EQUILAN

◆

"WHAT . . . WHAT IS HE?" ASKED REGA, STARING AT THE UNCONSCIOUS man lying on the deck. The man was obviously seriously injured—his skin was burned and blackened, blood oozed from a wound on his head. But the woman held back, afraid to venture too close. "He . . . he glowed! I saw him!"

"I know it's been a difficult time for you, my dear—" Zifnab gazed at her in deep concern.

"I did!" Rega faltered. "His skin glowed! Red and blue!"

"You've had a hard day," said Zifnab, patting her solicitously on the arm.

"I saw it, too," added Roland, rubbing his solar plexus and grimacing. "And what's more, I was about to lose my hold on him, my arms were getting weak, and those . . . those markings on his hand lit up like a torch. Then *my* hands lit up, and suddenly I had enough strength to drag him down through the hatch."

"Stress," said the old man. "Does queer things to the mind. Proper breathing, that's the key. All together, with me. Good air in. Bad air out. Good air in."

"I saw him standing out there on the deck, fighting those creatures," murmured Paithan, awed. "His entire body radiated light! He *is* our savior! He is Orn! Mother Peytin's son, come to lead us to safety!"

"That's it!" said Zifnab, mopping his brow with his beard. "Orn, favors his mother—"

"No, he doesn't," argued Roland, gesturing. "Look! He's human. Wouldn't Mother what's-her-name's kid be an elf— Wait! I know! He's one of the Lords of Thillia! Come back to us, like the legend foretold!"

"That, too!" said the old wizard hastily. "I don't know why I didn't recognize him. The spitting image of his father."

Rega appeared skeptical. "Whoever he is, he's in pretty bad shape." Cautiously approaching him, she reached out a hand to his forehead. "I think he's dying—Oh!"

The dog glided between her and its master, its glance encompassing all of them, saying plainly, *We appreciate the sympathy. Just keep your distance.*

"There, there, good boy," said Rega, moving a little nearer. The dog growled, bared its sharp teeth. The plumed tail began to slowly brush from side to side.

"Let him alone, Sis."

"I think you're right." Rega edged back, came to stand beside her brother.

Crouched in the shadows, forgotten, Drugar said nothing, might not have even heard the conversation. He was staring intently at the markings on the back of Haplo's hands and arms. Slowly, making certain no one was looking at him, Drugar reached within his tunic and drew forth a medallion that he wore around his neck. Holding it up to the light, he compared the rune carved into the obsidian with the sigla on the man's skin. The dwarf's brow furrowed in puzzlement, his eyes narrowed, his lips tightened.

Rega turned slightly. The dwarf thrust the medallion beneath his beard and shirt.

"What do you think, Blackbeard?" the woman asked.

"My name is Drugar. And I think I do not like being up here in the air in this winged monster," stated the dwarf. He gestured toward the window. The vars shore of the gulf was sliding beneath them. The tytans had attacked the humans on the bank. Around the shore's edge, crowded with helpless people, the gulf water was beginning to darken.

Roland looked out, said grimly, "I'd rather be up here than down there, dwarf."

The slaughter was progressing swiftly. A few of the tytans

left it to their fellows and were attempting to wade into the deep gulf water, their eyeless heads staring in the direction of the opposite shore.

"I've got to get back to Equilan," said Paithan, drawing out his etherilite and studying it intently. "There isn't much time. And I think we're too far north."

"Don't worry." Zifnab rolled up his sleeves, rubbed his hands together eagerly. "I'll take over. Highly competent. Frequent flyer. Over forty hours in the air. DC-three. First class, of course. I had a superb view of the control panel every time the stewardess opened the curtain. Let's see." The wizard took a step toward the steering stone, hands outstretched. "Flaps up. Nose down. I just—"

"Don't touch it, old man!"

Zifnab started, snatched his hands back, and attempted to look innocent. "I was just—"

"Not even the tip of your little finger. Unless you think you'd enjoy watching your flesh melt and drop off your bones."

The old man glowered at the stone fiercely, eyebrows bristling. "You shouldn't leave a thing that dangerous lying around! Someone could get hurt!"

"Someone nearly did. Don't try that again, old man. The stone's magically protected. I'm the only one who can use it."

Groggy, Haplo sat up, stifling a groan. The dog licked his face, and he put his arm around the animal's body for support, hiding his weakness. The urgency had subsided, his injuries needed healing—not a difficult task for his magic, but one that he preferred undertaking without an audience.

Fighting dizziness and pain, he buried his face in the dog's flank, the animal's body warm beneath his hands. What did it matter if they saw? He'd already revealed himself to them, revealed to them the use of rune magic, of *Patryn* rune magic, that had been absent from their world for countless generations. These people might not recognize it, but a Sartan would. A Sartan . . . like the old man. . . .

"Come, come. We're most grateful that you rescued us and we're all extremely sorry for your suffering but we don't have time to watch you wallow in it. Heal yourself, and let's get this ship back on the right heading," stated Zifnab.

Haplo looked up, fixed the old man with a narrow-eyed stare.

"After all, you *are* a god!" Zifnab winked several times.

A god? Hell, why not. Haplo was too tired, too drained to worry about where deification might lead him.

"Good boy." He patted the dog, eased the animal away from him. The dog looked around worriedly, and whined. "It'll be all right." Haplo lifted his left hand, placed it—runes down—over his right hand. He closed his eyes, relaxed, let his mind flow into the channels of renewal, revival, rest.

The circle was formed. He felt the sigla on the back of his hands grow warm to the touch. The runes would glow as they did their work, smoothing, healing. The glow would spread over his entire body, replacing damaged skin with whole. A murmur of voices told him that this sight was not lost on the audience.

"Blessed Thillia, look at that!"

Haplo couldn't think about the mensch, couldn't deal with them now. He didn't dare break the concentration.

"Quite well done," crowed Zifnab, beaming at Haplo as if the Patryn were a work of art he, the wizard, had conjured. "The nose could use a little touching up."

Lifting his hands to his face, Haplo examined himself with his fingers. His nose was broken, a cut on his forehead dripped blood into his eye. One cheekbone appeared to be fractured. He would have to perform superficial repair for the moment. Anything more would send him into a healing sleep.

"If he *is* a god," questioned Drugar suddenly, only the second time the dwarf had spoken since the rescue, "then why couldn't he stop the tytans? Why did he run away?"

"Because those creatures are spawns of evil," answered Paithan. "All know that Mother Peytin and her sons have spent eternity battling evil."

Which puts me on the side of good, thought Haplo, with weary amusement.

"He fought them single-handedly, didn't he?" the elf was continuing. "He held them off so that we could escape, and now he's using the power of the wind to fly us to safety. He has come to save my people—"

"Why not my people?" demanded Drugar, angrily. "Why didn't he save them?"

"And ours," Rega said, lips trembling. "He let our people all die—"

"Everyone knows elves are the blessed race," snapped Roland, casting Paithan a bitter glance.

Paithan flushed, faint red staining the delicate cheek bones. "I didn't mean that! It's just—"

"Look, be quiet a minute! All of you!" Haplo ordered. Now that his pain had eased and he was able to think clearly, he decided he was going to have to be honest with these mensch, not because he was any great believer in honesty, but because lying looked as if it was going to be a damn nuisance. "The old man's got it wrong. I'm not a god."

The elf and the humans began babbling at once, the dwarf's scowl grew darker. Haplo raised a tattooed hand for silence. "What I am, who I am, doesn't matter. Those tricks you saw me do were magic. Different from your own wizards', but magic just the same."

He shrugged, wincing. His head throbbed. He didn't think the mensch would use this information to figure out he was the enemy—the ancient enemy. If this world was in any way similar to Arianus, the people had forgotten all about the dark demigods who had once sought to rule them. But if they figured it out and came to realize who he was, that was their hard luck. Haplo was too hurt and too tired to care. It would be easy to get rid of them before they did his cause any harm. And right now, he needed answers to his questions.

"Which way?" he demanded, not the most pressing question, but one that should keep everyone occupied.

The elf lifted some sort of device, fiddled with it, and pointed. Haplo steered the ship in the direction indicated. They left the Kithni Gulf and the slaughter on its banks far behind. The dragonship cast its shadow over the trees beneath them, sailing through the variegated shades of green—a dark reflection of the real ship.

The humans and the elf remained standing, huddled together in the same spot, staring with rapt fascination out the window. Every once in a while, one of them would cast Haplo a sharp, darting glance. But he noted that they would occasionally look at each other with the same suspicion. The three had not moved since coming aboard, not even when arguing, but held themselves tense, rigid. They were probably afraid that any sort of movement might send the ship spinning out of control, crashing to the trees below. Haplo could have reassured them, but he didn't. He was content to let them stay where they were, frozen to the deck, where he could keep an eye on them.

The dwarf remained crouched in his corner. He, too, had not moved. But Drugar kept his dark-eyed gaze fixed on Haplo, never once looking out the window. Knowing that dwarves always preferred being underground when they could, the Patryn understood that flying through the air like this must be a traumatic experience for the dwarf. Haplo didn't notice fear or uneasiness in Drugar's expression, however. What he saw, oddly enough, was confusion and bitter, smoldering anger. The anger was directed, seemingly, at Haplo.

Reaching out his hand, ostensibly to stroke the dog's silky ears, the Patryn turned the animal's head, aiming the intelligent eyes at the dwarf. "Watch him," Haplo instructed softly. The dog's ears pricked, the tail brushed slowly side to side. Settling down at Haplo's feet, the animal laid its head on its paws, gaze fixed, focused.

That left the old man. A snore told Haplo he didn't have to worry about Zifnab for the moment. The wizard, his battered hat stuck over his face, lay flat on his back on the deck, hands crossed over his chest, sound asleep. Even if he was shamming, he wasn't up to anything. Haplo shook his aching head.

"Those . . . creatures. What did you call them? Tytans? What are they? Where did they come from?"

"I wish to Orn we knew," said Paithan.

"You don't?" Haplo stared suspiciously at the elf, certain he was lying. He switched his gaze to the humans. "Either of you?"

Both shook their heads. The Patryn looked to Drugar, but the dwarf apparently wasn't talking.

"All we know," said Roland, elected to speak by his sister's poke in the ribs, "is that they came down from the norinth. We heard they destroyed the Kasner Empire there, and now I believe it."

"They wiped out the dwarves," added Paithan, "and . . . well . . . you saw what they did to the Thillian realm. And now they're moving into Equilan."

"I can't believe they came out of nowhere!" Haplo persisted. "You must have heard of them before this?"

Rega and Roland looked at each other, the woman shrugged helplessly. "There were legends. Old wives' tales—the kind you tell when it's darktime and you're sitting around, trying to see who can come up with the scariest story. There was one about a nursemaid—"

"Tell me," urged Haplo.

Rega, pale, shook her head and turned her face away.

"Why don't you drop it, all right?" Roland said harshly.

Haplo glanced at Paithan. "How deep's the gulf, elf? How long will it take them to cross it?"

Paithan licked dry lips, drew a shivering breath. "The gulf is very deep, but they could go around it. And we've heard they're coming from other directions, from the est as well."

"I think you had better tell me all you know. Old wives have been known to hold onto the wisdom of generations."

"All right," said Roland, in resigned tones. "There was an old woman who came to stay with the king's children while the king and queen were off doing whatever it is kings and queens do. The children were spoiled brats, of course. They tied the nursemaid up in a chair, and proceeded to wreck the castle.

"After a while, though, the children got hungry. The old woman promised that, if they let her loose, she'd bake them some cookies. The children untied the nursemaid. The old woman went to the kitchen and baked cookies that she made in the shape of men. The old woman was, in reality, a powerful wizardess. She took one of the man-shaped cookies and breathed life into it. The cookie grew and grew until it was larger than the castle itself. The nursemaid set the giant to watch the children while she took a nap. She called the giant a tytan—"

"That word, *tytan*," Paithan interrupted. "It's not an elven word, it's not human. Is it dwarven?" He glanced at Drugar.

The dwarf shook his head.

"Then where does that word come from? Maybe knowing its original meaning and source would tell us something?"

It was an arrow shot at random, but it might land too close to the bull's eye. Haplo knew the word, knew its source. It was a word from his language and that of the Sartan. It came from the ancient world, referring originally to that world's ancient shapers. Over time, its meaning had broadened, eventually becoming synonymous with *giant*. But it was an unsettling notion. The only people who could have called these monsters tytans were the Sartan . . . and that opened up entire realms of possibility.

"It's just a word," Haplo said. "Go on with the story."

"The children were afraid of the tytan, at first. But they soon found out it was gentle and kind and loving. They began to tease it. Snatching up the man-shaped cookies, the children would bite the heads off and threaten to do the same to the giant. The tytan grew so upset that it ran away from the castle and . . . " Roland paused, frowning thoughtfully. "That's odd. I didn't think of it before now. The tytan in the story loses his way and goes around asking people—"

" 'Where is the castle'!" Paithan murmured.

" 'Where is the citadel,' " Haplo echoed.

Paithan nodded, excited. " 'Where is the citadel? What must we do?' "

"Yes, I heard it. What's the answer? Where *is* the citadel?"

"*What* is a citadel?" Paithan asked, gesturing wildly. "Nobody even knows for certain what the word means!"

"Anyone who knows the answer to their questions would truly be a savior," said Rega, her voice low. Her fist clenched. "If only we knew what they wanted!"

"Rumor has it that the wisest men and women in Thillia were spending day and night studying the ancient books, searching desperately for a clue."

"Maybe they should have asked the old wives," said Paithan.

Haplo rubbed his hands absently over the rune-covered steering stone. *Citadel*, meaning "little city." Another word in his language, and that of the Sartan. The path before him stretched smooth and clear, leading one direction. Tytans—a Sartan word. Tytans—using Sartan magic. Tytans—asking about Sartan citadels. And here the path led him slam up against a stone wall.

The Sartan would never, never have created such evil, brutal beings. The Sartan would never have endowed such beings with magic . . . unless, perhaps, they knew for certain that they could control them. The tytans, running amok, running out of control— was it a clear indication that the Sartan had vanished from this world as they had vanished (with one exception) from Arianus?

Haplo glanced at the old man. Zifnab's mouth gaped wide open, his hat was slowly slipping down past his nose. A particularly violent snore caused the old man to inhale the battered brim, nearly strangling himself. He sat up, coughing and spluttering and glaring about suspiciously.

"Who did that?"

Haplo glanced away. He was beginning to reconsider. The Patryn had met only one Sartan before—the bumbling man of Arianus who called himself Alfred Montbank. And though Haplo hadn't recognized it at the time, he came to realize that he felt an affinity for Alfred. Deadly enemies, they were strangers to the rest of the world—but they were not strangers to each other.

This old man was a stranger. To put it more precisely, he was strange. He was probably nothing more than a crackpot, another crazy, bug-eating prophet. He had unraveled Haplo's magic, but the insane had been known to do a lot of bizarre, inexplicable things.

"What happened at the end of the story," he thought to ask, guiding the ship in for a landing.

"The tytan found the castle, came back, and bit off the children's heads," answered Roland.

"You know," said Rega, softly, "when I was little and I heard that story, I always felt sorry for the tytan. I always thought the children deserved such a horrible fate. But now—" She shook her head, tears slid down her cheeks.

"We're nearing Equilan," said Paithan, leaning forward gingerly to look out the window. "I can see Lake Enthial. At least I think that's it, shining in the distance? The water looks odd, seen from above."

"That's it," said Haplo without interest, his thoughts on something else.

"I didn't catch your name," said the elf. "What is it?"

"Haplo."

"What does it mean?"

The Patryn ignored him.

"Single," said the old man.

Haplo frowned, cast him an irritated glance. How the devil did he know that?

"I'm sorry," said Paithan, ever courteous. "I didn't mean to pry." He paused a moment, then continued hesitantly. "I . . . uh, that is Zifnab said . . . you were a savior. He said you could take . . . people to the . . . uh . . . stars. I didn't believe it. I didn't think it would be possible. Doom and destruction. He said I'd bring it back with me. Orn help me, I am!" He gazed a moment out the window, to the land below. "What I want to know is . . . can you do it? *Will* you do it? Can you save us from . . . those monsters?"

"He can't save all of you," said Zifnab sadly, twisting his battered hat in his hands, finishing it off totally. "He can only save some. The best and the brightest."

Haplo glanced around, saw eyes—slanted elf eyes, the human woman's wide dark eyes, the human male's bright blue eyes, even the dwarf's black, shadowed eyes, Zifnab's crazed, shrewd eyes. All of them staring at him, waiting, hoping.

"Yeah, sure," he answered.

Why not? Anything to keep peace, keep people happy. Happy and ignorant.

In point of fact, Haplo had no intention of saving anyone except himself. But there was one thing he had to do first. He had to talk to a tytan.

And these people were going to be his bait. After all, the children had asked for exactly what they got.

CHAPTER ♦ 28

TREETOPS,

EQUILAN

♦

"So," said Calandra, looking from Paithan to Rega, standing before her on the porch, "I might have known."

The elf woman started to slam the front door. Paithan interposed his body, preventing the door from shutting, and forced his way inside the house. Calandra backed up a pace, holding herself tall and straight, her hands clasped, level with her cinched-in waist. She regarded her brother with cold disdain.

"I see you have adopted their ways already. Barbarian! Forcing your way into *my* home!"[1]

"Excuse me," began Zifnab, thrusting in his head, "but it's very important that I—"

"Calandra!" Paithan reached out to his sister, grasped hold of her chill hands. "Don't you understand? It doesn't matter anymore? Doom is coming, like the old man said! I've seen it, Callie!" The woman attempted to pull away. Paithan held onto her, his grip tightening with the intensity of his fear. "The dwarven realm is destroyed! The human realm dying, perhaps dead, right now! These three"—he cast a wild-eyed glance at the

---

[1]The elves are a matriarchal society; by elven law, land holdings, residence, and household goods pass from mother to eldest daughter. Businesses remain in the hands of the elven males. The house, therefore, belongs to Calandra. All the Quindiniars—including Lenthan, her father—live there by her sufferance. Elves have great respect for their elders, however, and therefore Calandra would politely term the house "her father's."

dwarf and the two humans standing, ill-at-ease and uncomfortable, in the doorway—"are perhaps the only ones left of their races! Thousands have been slaughtered! And it's coming down on us next, Callie! It's coming on us!"

"If I could add to that—" Zifnab raised a forefinger.

Calandra snatched her hands away and smoothed the front of her skirt. "You're certainly dirty enough," she remarked, sniffing. "You've gone and tracked filth all over the carpet. Go to the kitchen and wash up. Leave your clothes down there. I'll have them burned. I'll have clean ones sent to your room. Then sit down and have your dinner. Your friends"—sneering, she cast a scathing glance at the group in the doorway—"can sleep in the slave quarters. That goes for the old man. I moved his things out last night."

Zifnab beamed at her, bowed his head modestly. "Thank you for going to the trouble, my dear, but that really wasn't neces—"

"Humpf!" Turning on her heel, the elf woman headed for the stairway.

"Calandra, damn it!" Paithan grabbed his sister's elbow and spun her around. "Didn't you hear me?"

"How dare you speak to me in that tone!" Calandra's eyes were colder and darker than the depths of the dwarven underground. "You will behave in a civilized manner in this house, Paithan Quindiniar, or you can join your barbaric companions and bed with the slaves." Her lip curled, her gaze went to Rega. "Something you must be used to! As for your threats, the queen received news of the invasion some time ago. If it is true—which I doubt, since the news came from humans—then we are prepared. The royal guard is on alert, the shadowguard is standing by if they are needed. We've supplied them with the latest in weaponry. I must say," she added grudgingly, "that all this nonsense has, at least, been good for business."

"The market opened bullish," offered Zifnab to no one in particular. "Since then, the Dow's been steadily dropping—"

Paithan opened his mouth, but couldn't think of anything to say. Homecoming was like a dream to him, like falling asleep after grappling with terrible reality. Not longer than the turning of a few petals, he had been facing a gruesome death at the rending hands of the tytans. He had experienced unnameable horrors, had seen dreadful sights that would haunt him for the rest of his life. He had changed, sloughed off the carefree, indolent skin that had covered him. What had emerged was not as pretty, but it was tougher, resilient, and—he hoped—more wise. It was a reverse metamorphosis, a butterfly transformed into a grub.

But nothing here had changed. The royal guard on alert! The shadowguard standing by, *if they are needed!* He couldn't believe it, couldn't comprehend it. He had expected to find his people in turmoil, sounding alarms, rushing hither and thither. Instead, all was peaceful, calm, serene. Unchanged. Status quo.

The peace, the serenity, the silence was awful. A scream welled up inside him. He wanted to shriek and ring the wooden bells, he wanted to grab people and shake them and shout, "Don't you know! Don't you know what's coming! Death! Death is coming!" But the wall of calm was too thick to penetrate, too high to climb. He could only stare, stammering in tongue-tied confusion that his sister mistook for shame.

Slowly, he fell silent, slowly loosened his grip on Calandra's arm.

His elder sister, without a glance at any of them, marched stiffly out of the room.

Somehow I've got to warn them, he thought confusedly, somehow make them understand.

"Paithan . . ."

"Aleatha!" Paithan turned, relieved to find someone who would listen to reason. He held out his hand—

Aleatha slapped him across the face.

"Thea!" He put his hand over his stinging cheek.

His sister's face was livid, her eyes feverish, the pupils dilated. "How dare you? How dare you repeat these wicked human lies!" She pointed at Roland. "Take this vermin and get out! Get out!"

"Ah! Charmed to see you again, my—" began Zifnab.

Roland couldn't hear what was being said but the hatred in the blue eyes staring at him spoke for her. He raised his hands in apology. "Listen, lady, I don't know what you're saying, but—"

"I said get out!"

Fingers curled to claws, Aleatha flew at Roland. Before he could stop her, sharp nails dug into his cheek, leaving four long bleeding tracks. The startled man tried to fend the elf woman off without hurting her, tried to grasp the flailing arms.

"Paithan! Get her off me!"

Caught flat-footed by his sister's sudden fury, the elf jumped belatedly after her. He grasped Aleatha around the waist, Rega tugged at her arms and, together, they managed to drag the spitting, clawing woman away from Roland.

"Don't touch me!" Aleatha shrieked, striking out impotently at Rega.

"Better let me handle her," gasped Paithan, in human.

Rega backed off, moved to her brother's side. The human dabbed at his injured cheek with his hand, glared at the elf woman sullenly.

"Damn bitch!" he muttered in human, seeing blood on his fingers.

Not understanding his words, but fully comprehending their tone, Aleatha lunged at him again. Paithan held her, wrestling her back, until suddenly her anger was spent. She went limp in her brother's grip, breathing heavily.

"Tell me it's all a lie, Paithan!" she said in a low, passionate voice, resting her head on his chest. "Tell me you've lied!"

"I wish to Orn I could, Thea," Paithan answered, holding her, stroking her hair. "But I can't. I've seen . . . oh, blessed Mother, Aleatha! What I've seen!" He sobbed, clasped his sister convulsively.

Aleatha put both hands on his face, lifted his head, stared into his eyes. Her lips parted in a slight smile, her eyebrows lifted. "I am going to be married. I am going to have a house on the lake. No one, nothing can stop me." She squirmed out of his embrace. Smoothing back her hair, she arranged the curls prettily over her shoulders. "Welcome home, Paithan, dear. Now that you're back, take the trash out, will you?"

Aleatha smiled at Roland and Rega. She had spoken the last words in crude human.

Roland put his hand on his sister's arm.

"Trash, uh? Come on, Sis. Let's get out of here!"

Rega cast a pleading glance at Paithan, who stared at her helplessly. He felt like a sleeper who, on first awakening, can't move his limbs.

"You see how it is!" Roland snarled. "I warned you!" He let loose of her, took a step off the porch. "Are you coming?"

"Pardon me," said Zifnab, "but I might point out that you haven't really any place to go—"

"Paithan! Please!" Rega begged.

Roland stomped down the stairs onto the mossy lawn. "Stay here!" he shouted back over his shoulder. "Warm the elf's bed! Maybe he'll give you a job in the kitchen!"

Paithan flushed in anger, took a step after Roland. "I love your sister! I—"

The sound of horns trumpeted through the still, morning air. The elf's gaze turned in the direction of Lake Enthial, his lips tightened. Reaching out, he caught hold of Rega, drew her close. The moss began to rumble and quake beneath their feet. Drugar, who had said no word, made no movement the entire time, slid his hand into his belt.

"Now!" cried Zifnab testily, clinging to the porch railing for support. "If I may be allowed to finish a sentence, I'd like to say that—"

"Sir," intoned the dragon, its voice rising from beneath the moss, "they're here."

"That's it," muttered Haplo, hearing the horn calls. He looked up from his hiding place in the wilderness, made a gesture to the dog. "All right. You know what to do. Remember, I just want one!"

The dog bounded off into the jungle, disappearing from sight in the thick foliage. Haplo, tense with anticipation, glanced around the coppice where he lay hidden. All was ready. He had only to wait.

The Patryn had not gone to the elven house with the rest of his shipboard companions. Making some excuse about performing repairs on his vessel, he had stayed behind. When he had seen them cross the large backyard, its moss blackened and charred from Lenthan's rocketry experiments, Haplo had climbed over the ship's hull to walk along the wooden "bones" of the dragon wing.

To walk the dragon wing. To risk everything, life included, to gain your goal. Where had he heard that saying? He seemed to recall Hugh the Hand mentioning it. Or had it been the elf captain whose ship the Patryn had "acquired"? Not that it mattered. The saying didn't count for much with the ship parked securely on the ground, the drop beneath only about three feet instead of three thousand. Still, Haplo had thought, jumping down lightly to the ground, the sense of the saying was, at this moment, appropriate.

To walk the dragon wing.

He crouched in his hiding place, waiting, running over the runes he would use in his mind, fingering each like an elven jeweler searching for flaws in a string of pearls. The construct was perfect. The first spell cast would trap the creature. The second hold it, the third bore into its mind—what mind there was.

In the distance, the horn bleats grew louder and more chaotic, sometimes one would end in a horrible, gurgling cry. The elves must be battling their enemy, and the fighting was drawing near his position from the sounds of it. Haplo ignored it. If the tytans handled the elves the way they had handled the humans—and Haplo didn't have any reason to suppose the elves would do any better—the fight wouldn't last long.

He listened, straining, for another sound. There it came—the dog's barking. It, too, was moving in his direction. The Patryn heard nothing else, and at first he was worried. Then he remembered how silently the tytans moved through the jungle. He wouldn't hear the creature, he realized, until it was on him. He licked his dry lips, moistened his throat.

The dog bounded into the coppice. Flanks heaved, tongue lolled from its mouth, its eyes were wide with terror. Wheeling, it turned in the middle of the grove and barked frantically.

The tytan came close behind. As Haplo had hoped, the creature had been lured away from its fellows by the pesky animal. Entering the grove, it stopped, sniffed. The eyeless head revolved slowly. It smelled or heard or "saw" man.

The tytan's giant body towered over Haplo, the eyeless head stared directly at the Patryn. When the tytan ceased movement, its camouflaged body blended almost perfectly into the background of the jungle. Haplo blinked, almost losing sight of it. For a moment, he panicked, but he calmed himself. No matter. No matter. If my plan works, the creature'll be moving, all right. No doubt about that!

Haplo began to speak the runes. He raised his tattooed hands, the sigla seemed to glide off his skin and dance into the air. Flashing fiery blue and flaming red, the runes built upon themselves, multiplying with extraordinary speed.

The tytan gazed at the runes without interest, as if the creature had seen all this before and found it intensely boring. The tytan moved toward Haplo, the incessant question rattled in his head.

"Citadel, right. Where is the citadel? Sorry, I can't take time to answer you right now. We'll talk in just a few moments," Haplo promised, backing up.

The rune construct was complete, and he could only hope it was working. He eyed the tytan closely. The creature continued coming toward him, its wistful pleading changing instantly to violent frustration. Haplo felt a qualm, his stomach clenched. Beside him, the dog whined in terror.

The tytan paused, turned its head, slavering mouth gaped open in confusion. Haplo began to breathe again.

Sigla, glowing red and blue, had twined together, draping themselves like huge curtains over the jungle trees. The spell wrapped completely around the coppice, surrounding the tytan. The creature turned this way and that. The runes were reflecting its own image back to it, flooding its brain with pictures and sensations of itself.

"You're all right. I'm not going to hurt you," said Haplo soothingly, speaking in his own language—the language of the Patryns, similar to that of the Sartan. "I'll let you go, but first we're going to talk about the citadel. Tell me what it is."

The tytan lunged in the direction of Haplo's voice. The Patryn moved, darting aside. The tytan grabbed wildly at air.

Haplo, having expected this attack, repeated his question patiently.

"Tell me about the citadel. Did the Sartan—"

Sartan!

The tytan's fury struck, astonishing in its raw power, a stunning blow to Haplo's magic. The runes wavered, crumbled. The creature—freed from the illusion—turned its head toward Haplo.

The Patryn fought to regain his control, and the runes strengthened. The tytan lost him, groped blindly for its prey.

You are Sartan!

"No," replied Haplo. Praying his strength held, he wiped

sweat from his face. "I am not a Sartan. I am their enemy, like yourself!"

You lie! You are Sartan! You trick us! Build the citadel, then steal our eyes! Blind us to the bright and shining light!

The tytan's rage hammered at Haplo, he grew weaker with every blow. His spell wouldn't hold much longer. He had to escape now, while the creature was, for the moment, still confused. But it had been worth it. He had gained something. *Blind us to the bright and shining light.* He thought he might be starting to understand. Bright and shining . . . before him . . . above him. . . .

"Dog!" Haplo turned to run, stopped dead. The trees had vanished. Standing before him, all around him, everywhere he looked, he saw himself.

The tytan had turned the Patryn's own magical spell against him.

Haplo fought to quell his fear. He was trapped, no escape. He could shatter the spell surrounding him, but that would shatter the spell surrounding the tytan at the same time. Drained, exhausted, he didn't have the strength to weave another rune fabric, not one that would stop the creature. The Patryn turned to his right, saw himself. He turned left, faced himself—wide-eyed, pale. The dog, at his feet, dashed about in frantic circles, barking wildly.

Haplo sensed the tytan, blundering about, searching for him. Sooner or later, the creature would stumble into him. Something brushed against him, something warm and living, perhaps a gigantic hand . . .

Blindly, Haplo hurled himself to one side, away from the creature, and slammed into a tree. The impact bruised him, drove the breath from his body. He gasped for air, and realized suddenly that he could see! Trees, vines! The illusion was ending. Relief flooded him, banished instantly by fear.

That meant the rune spell was unwinding. If he could see where he was, then so could his enemy.

The tytan loomed over him. Haplo lunged, diving into the moss, scrabbling to escape. He heard the dog behind him, valiantly trying to defend its master, heard a sharp, pain-filled whine. A dark, furry body crashed to the ground beside him.

Grabbing a tree branch, Haplo staggered to his feet.

The tytan plucked the weapon from his grip, reached down, grabbed his arm. The tytan's hand was enormous, the palm engulfed the bone and muscle, fingers squeezed. The tytan pulled, wrenched Haplo's arm from the socket. He sagged to the ground.

The tytan jerked him back up, tightened its grip. Haplo fought the pain, fought gathering darkness. The next tug would rip the limb from his body.

"Pardon me, sir, but may I be of any service?"

Fiery red eyes poked up out of the moss, almost on a level with Haplo.

The tytan pulled; Haplo heard cracking and snapping, the pain nearly made him lose consciousness.

The red eyes flared, a scaly green head, festooned with vines, thrust up from the moss. A red-rimmed mouth parted, shining white teeth glistened, the black tongue flickered.

Haplo felt himself released, hurled to the ground. He clasped his shoulder. The arm was dislocated, but it was still attached. Gritting his teeth against the pain, afraid to draw attention to himself, he lay on the moss, too weak to move, and watched.

The dragon spoke. Haplo couldn't understand what it said, but he sensed the tytan's rage seeping away, replaced by awe and fear. The dragon spoke again, tone imperative, and the tytan fled back into the jungle, its green, dappled body moving swiftly and silently, making it seem to the Patryn's dazed eyes as if the trees themselves were running away.

Haplo rolled over, and blacked out.

CHAPTER ♦ 29

TREETOPS,

EQUILAN

♦

"ZIFNAB, YOU'RE BACK!" CRIED LENTHAN QUINDINIAR.

"I am?" said the old man, looking extremely startled.

Running out onto the porch, Lenthan grabbed Zifnab's hand and shook it heartily. "And Paithan!" he said, catching sight of his son. "Blessed Orn! No one told me. Do your sisters know?"

"Yes, Guvnor. They know." The elf gazed at his father in concern. "Have you been well, sir?"

"And you brought guests?" Lenthan switched his vague, shy smile to Roland and Rega. The one, nursing his injured cheek, nodded sullenly. The other, moving to stand near Paithan, clasped hold of his hand. The elf put his arm around her and the two stood together, staring at Lenthan defiantly.

"Oh, my," murmured Lenthan, and began to pluck at the tails of his topcoat. "Oh, my."

"Father, listen to the trumpet calls." Paithan placed a hand on his father's thin shoulder. "Terrible things are happening. Did you hear? Did Callie tell you?"

Lenthan glanced around, as if he would be very glad to change the subject, but Zifnab was staring off into the wilderness with a pensive frown. And there was a dwarf, crouched in a corner, chewing on bread and cheese that Paithan had gone into the kitchen to acquire. (It had become fairly obvious that no one intended inviting them in for luncheon.)

"I . . . believe your sister mentioned something—but the army has everything under control."

"They don't, Father. It's impossible. I've seen these fiends! They destroyed the dwarven nation. Thillia is gone, Father! Gone! We're not going to stop them. It's like the old man said—doom and destruction."

Lenthan squirmed, twisting his coattails into knots. He lowered his eyes to the wooden slats of the porch. Those, at least, were safe, weren't going to spring any surprises on him.

"Father, are you listening?" Paithan gave his father a slight shake.

"What?" Lenthan blinked up at him, smiled anxiously. "Oh, yes. A fine adventure you've had. That's very nice, dear boy. Very nice, indeed. But now why don't you come in and talk to your sister. Tell Callie you're home."

"She's knows I'm home!" Paithan exclaimed, frustrated. "She forbid me the house, Father. She insulted me and the woman who is going to be my wife! I will not enter that house again!"

"Oh, dear." Lenthan looked from his son to the humans to the dwarf to the old man. "Oh, dear."

"Look, Paithan," said Roland, coming to stand beside the elf, "you've been home, you've seen your family. You did your best to warn them. What happens now isn't any of your concern. We've got to hit the trail, if we're going to clear out of here ahead of the tytans."

"And where will you go?" demanded Zifnab, head snapping up, chin jutting forward.

"I don't know!" Roland shrugged, glanced at the old man, irritated. "I'm not that familiar with this part of the world. Maybe the Fartherness Reaches. That's to the est, isn't it? Or Sinith Paragna—"

"The Fartherness Reaches have been destroyed, its people massacred," stated Zifnab, eyes glittering beneath his white bushy brows. "You *might* elude the tytans for a time in the jungles of Sinith Paragna but eventually they would find you. And then what would you do, boy? Keep running? Run until you're backed up against the Terinthian Ocean? Will you have time to build yourself a ship to cross the water? And even then it would be only a matter of time. Even then they will follow you."

"Shut up, old man! Just shut up! Either that, or tell us how we're going to get out of here!"

"I will," snapped Zifnab. "There's only one way out." He lifted a finger. "Up."

"To the stars!" At last it seemed to Lenthan that he understood. He clasped his hands together. "It's like you said? I lead my people—"

"—forth!" Zifnab carried on enthusiastically. "Out of Egypt! Out of bondage! Across the desert! Pillar of fire—"

"Desert?" Lenthan looked anxious again. "Fire? I thought we were going to the stars?"

"Sorry." Zifnab appeared distraught. "Wrong script. It's all these last-minute changes they make in the text. Gets me quite muddled."

"Of course!" Roland exclaimed. "The ship! To hell with the stars! It will fly us across the Terinthian Ocean. . . ."

"But not away from the tytans!" struck in the old man testily. "Haven't you learned anything, child? Wherever you go on land in this world, you will find them. Or rather they will find you. The stars. That is the only place of safety."

Lenthan stared up into the sun-drenched sky. The bright lights shone steadfastly, serenely, far above blood and terror and death. "I won't be long, my dear," he whispered.

Roland plucked Paithan by the sleeve, drew him aside, over to the house, near an open window.

"Look," he said. "Humor the crazy old geezer. Stars! Pah! Once we get inside that ship, we'll take it wherever we want to go!"

"You mean we'll take it wherever that Haplo wants to go." Paithan shook his head. "He's strange. I don't know what to make of him."

Absorbed in their worries, neither man noticed a delicate white hand lay hold of the window curtain, draw it slightly to one side.

"Yeah, well, neither do I," Roland admitted. "But—"

"And I don't want to tangle with him! I saw him knock that tree trunk out of that tytan's hand like it was nothing but a piece of straw! And I'm worried about my father. The guvnor's not well. I'm not sure he can make this crazy trip."

"We don't have to tangle with Haplo! All right, then we'll just go wherever he takes us! My bet is *he's* not going to be all-fired hot to chase off to the stars."

"I don't know. Look, maybe we won't have to go anywhere. Maybe our army *can* stop them!"

"Yeah, and maybe I'll sprout wings and fly up to the stars myself!"

Paithan cast the human a bitter, angry glance and stalked off, moving down to the end of the porch. Standing by himself, he pulled a flower from a hibiscus bush and began ripping the petals apart, moodily tossing them into the yard. Roland, intent on his argument, started to go after him. Rega caught hold of her brother's arm.

"Let him alone for a little while."

"Bah, he's talking nonsense—"

"Roland, don't you understand? He has to leave all this behind! That's what's bothering him."

"Leave what? A house?"

"His life."

"You and I didn't have much trouble doing that."

"That's because we've always made up our lives as we went along," said Rega, her face darkening. "But I can remember when we left home, the house where we'd been born."

"What a dump!" Roland muttered.

"Not to us. We didn't know any better. I remember that time, the time Mother didn't come home." Rega drew near her brother, rested her cheek on his arm. "We waited . . . how long?"

"A cycle or two." Roland shrugged.

"And there was no food and no money. And you kept making me laugh, so I wouldn't be frightened." Rega twined her hand in her brother's, held it fast. "Then you said, 'Well, Sis, it's a big world out there and we're not seeing any of it cooped up inside this hovel.' We left then and there. Walked out of the house and into the road and followed it where it led us. But I remember one thing, Roland. I remember you stopping there, on the path, and turning around to look back at the house. And I remember that, when you came back to me, there were tears—"

"I was a kid, then. Paithan's an adult. Or passes for one. Yeah, all right. I won't bother him. But I'm getting on board that ship whether he does or not. And what are *you* going to do if he decides to stay behind?"

Roland walked away. Rega remained standing near the window, her troubled gaze on Paithan. Behind her, inside the house, the hand slipped from the curtain, letting the lacy fabric fall gently, softly back in place.

◆

"When do we go?" Lenthan asked the old man eagerly. "Now? I just have to get a few things to pack . . ."

"Now?" Zifnab looked alarmed. "Oh, no, not now. Not time yet. Got to get everyone rounded up. We've got time, you see. Not much, but some."

"Look, old man," said Roland, breaking in on the discussion. "Are you sure this Haplo's going to go along with your plan?"

"Why, yes, of course!" stated Zifnab confidently.

Eyes narrowing, Roland gazed at him.

"Well," the old man faltered, "maybe not right at first."

"Uh, huh." Roland nodded, lips tightening.

"In fact," Zifnab appeared more uncomfortable, "he doesn't really want us along at all. We may . . . er . . . sort of have to sneak on board."

"Sneak on board."

"But leave that to me!" the old man said, nodding his head wisely. "I'll give you the signal. Let's see." He mulled it over in his mind. "When the dog barks! That's the signal. Did you hear that everyone!" Zifnab raised his voice querulously. "When the dog barks! That's when we board the ship!"

A dog barked.

"Now?" said Lenthan, nearly leaping out of his shoes.

"Not now!" Zifnab appeared highly put out. "What's the meaning of this? It's not time!"

The dog came dashing around the side of the house. Running up to Zifnab, it caught hold of the old man's robes in its teeth, and began to tug.

"Stop that! You're tearing out the hem. Let go!"

The animal growled and pulled harder, its eyes fixed on the old man.

"Great Nebuchadnezzar! Why didn't you say so in the first place? We've got to go! Haplo's in trouble. Needs our help!"

The dog let loose of the old man's robes, raced away, heading in the direction of the jungle. Gathering his skirts, hiking them up above his bare, bony ankles, the old wizard ran off after the animal.

The rest stood, staring, ill-at-ease, suddenly remembering what it was like to face the tytans.

"Hell, he's the only one knows how to fly that ship!" said Roland, and started off after the old man.

Rega raced after her brother. Paithan was about to follow when he heard a door slam. Turning, he saw Aleatha.

"I'm coming, too."

The elf stared. His sister was clad in his old clothes—leather pants, white linen tunic, and leather vest. The clothes didn't fit her, they were too tight. The pants strained to cover the rounded thighs, the seams seeming likely to split apart. The fabric of the shirt stretched taut over the firm, high breasts. So closely did everything fit, she might well have been naked. Paithan felt hot blood seep into his cheeks.

"Aleatha, get back in the house! This is serious—"

"I'm going. I'm going to see for myself." She cast him a lofty glance. "I'm going to make you eat those lies!"

His sister walked past him, striding purposefully after the others. She had bundled the beautiful hair up in a crude bun at the back of her neck. In her hand she carried a wooden walking stick, holding it awkwardly like a club, perhaps with some idea of using it for a weapon.

Paithan heaved a frustrated sigh. There would be no arguing with her, no reasoning. All her life she had done exactly as she pleased; she wasn't going to stop now. Catching up with her, he noticed, somewhat to his consternation, that Aleatha's gaze was fixed on the man running ahead of her, on the strong back and rippling muscles of Roland.

Left alone, Lenthan Quindiniar rubbed his hands, shook his head, and muttered, "Oh, dear. Oh, dear."

High above, standing in her office, Calandra glanced out her window, saw the procession straggling across the smooth lawn, hastening for the trees. In the distance, the trumpets were blowing wildly. Snorting, she turned to the figures in her books, noting, with a tight-lipped smile, that they were likely to beat last year's profit by a considerable margin.

CHAPTER ◆ 30

TREETOPS,

EQUILAN

◆

HAPLO REGAINED CONSCIOUSNESS TO FIND HIMSELF SURROUNDED—NOT by tytans—but by everyone he'd met in this world, plus what appeared to be half the elven army. Groaning, he glanced at the dog.

"This is all your doing."

The dog wagged its tail, tongue lolling, grinning, relishing the praise, not realizing it wasn't. Haplo stared at those hovering above him. They stared back—their gazes suspicious, dubious, expectant. The old man, alone, regarded him with intense anxiety.

"Are . . . are you all right?" asked the human woman—he couldn't remember her name. Her gaze went to his shoulder. Timidly, she reached out a hand. "Can we do . . . anything!"

"Don't touch!" Haplo said, through clenched teeth.

The woman's hand darted back. Of course, that was an open invitation for the elf female to kneel down beside him. Sitting up painfully, he thrust her aside with his good hand.

"You!" he said, looking at Roland. "You've got to help me . . . put this back!" Haplo indicated his dislocated shoulder, hanging at an odd angle from the rest of his body.

Roland nodded, crouched down on his knees. His hands moved to take off Haplo's shirt, the leather vest he wore over it. The Patryn caught hold of the human's hand in his own.

"Just set the shoulder."

"But the shirt's in the way—"

"Just the shoulder."

Roland looked into the man's eyes, looked hurriedly away. The human began to gently probe the injured area. More elves moved closer to watch; Paithan among them. He had been standing on the fringes of the group surrounding Haplo, conversing with another elf dressed in the torn and bloody remnants of what must have been an elegant dress uniform. Hearing Haplo's voice, the two elves broke off their conversation.

"Whatever's underneath that shirt of yours must be something special," said the elf woman. Aleatha. "Is it?"

Roland cast her a dark glance. "Don't you have somewhere else to go?"

"Sorry," she answered coolly, "I didn't understand what you said. I don't speak human."

Roland scowled. He'd been speaking elven. He tried to ignore her. It wasn't easy. She was leaning over Haplo, exposing the full curve of her round breasts.

For whose benefit, the Patryn wondered. He would have been amused if he hadn't been so angry at himself. Looking at Roland, Haplo thought that this time Aleatha might have met her match. The human was strictly business. The human's strong hands grasped Haplo's arm firmly.

"This is going to hurt."

"Yeah." Haplo's jaw ached from gritting his teeth. It didn't need to hurt. He could use the magic, activate the runes. But he was damn sick and tired of revealing his power to one-fourth the known universe! "Get on with it!"

"I think you should hurry," said the elf standing near Paithan. "We've beaten them back, but it's only for the time being, I'm afraid."

Roland glanced around. "I need one of you men to hold him—"

"I can do it," answered Aleatha.

"This is important," Roland snapped. "I don't need some female who's going to pass out—"

"I never faint . . . without a good reason." Aleatha favored him with a sweet smile. "How's your cheek? Does it hurt?"

Roland grunted, keeping his eyes on his patient. "Hold

him fast, brace him back against this tree so that he doesn't twist when I pop the bone in place."

Aleatha grasped hold of him, ignoring Haplo's protests.

"I don't need anyone to hold me!" He brushed aside the woman's hands. "Wait a minute, Roland. Not yet. Let me ask . . ." He twisted his head, trying to see the elf in the elegant uniform, interested in what he had said. "Beat them! What— How? . . ."

Pain flashed through his arm, shoulder, down his back, up his head. Haplo sucked in a breath that caught and rattled in his throat.

"Can you move it now?" Roland sat back on his haunches, wiped sweat from his face.

The dog, whimpering, crept to Haplo's side and licked his wrist. Gingerly, biting his teeth against the agony, Haplo moved his arm in the shoulder socket.

"I should bandage it," protested Roland, seeing Haplo struggling to stand. "It could go back out again, real easy. Everything's all stretched inside."

"I'll be all right," Haplo said, holding his injured shoulder, fighting back the temptation to use the runes, complete the healing. When he was alone . . . and that would be soon, if all went well! Alone and away from this place! He leaned back against the tree trunk, closed his eyes, hoping the man and the elf woman would take the hint and leave him to himself. He heard footsteps walking away, he didn't care where. Paithan and the elflord had resumed their conversation.

" . . . scouts reported that conventional weapons had no effect on them. The humans' defeat in Thillia made that obvious. Humans using our magical weapons proved somewhat more effective, but were eventually beaten. That's to be expected. They can use the magic that is in the weapon, but they can't enhance it, as we can. Not that enhancing helped us much. Our own wizards were completely at a loss. We threw everything we had at them and only one proved successful."

"The dracos, my lord?" said Paithan.

"Yes, the dracos."

What the devil was a draco? Haplo opened his eyes, peered through half-closed lids. The elflord held one in his hands, apparently. Both he and Paithan were studying it intently. So did Haplo.

The draco was similar in appearance to a railbow, except that it was considerably larger. The projectiles it fired were carved out of wood, fashioned to resemble small dragons.

"It's effectiveness doesn't appear to be in the wounds the draco inflicts. Most didn't get close enough to the tytans to inflict any," the lord added ruefully. "It's the look of the draco itself that frightens them. Whenever we loose the dracos, the monsters don't try to fight. They simply turn and run!" The elflord glared at the weapon in frustration, shaking it slightly. "I wish I knew what it was about this particular weapon that frightens them off! Maybe we could defeat them!"

Haplo stared at the draco, eyes narrowed. He knew why! He presumed that when it was fired at the enemy, it came to life— elven weapons sometimes operated that way. It would appear to the tytans' senses as if they were being attacked by a small dragon. He recalled the sensation of overwhelming terror emanating from the tytan when the dragon had appeared in the glade. So, the dragons could conceivably be used to control the monsters.

My lord will find that most interesting, thought Haplo, smiling quietly and rubbing his shoulder.

A nudge at his belt drew his attention. Looking down, he saw the dwarf, Blackbeard or Drugar or whatever he was called. How long has he been standing there? Haplo hadn't noticed, and he cursed himself for not noticing. One tended to forget the dwarf and, from the look in the dark eyes, that tendency could be fatal.

"You speak my language." It wasn't a question. Drugar already knew the answer. Haplo wondered briefly, how?

"Yes." The Patryn didn't think it necessary to lie.

"What are they saying?" Drugar nodded a shaggy head at Paithan and the elflord. "I speak human, but not elven."

"They're talking about that weapon the elf's holding in his hand. It apparently has some effect on the tytans. It makes them run away."

The dwarf's brows beetled, his eyes seemed to sink back into his head, practically invisible except for the sparkling hate in their black depths. The Patryn knew and appreciated hatred— hatred kept those trapped in the Labyrinth alive. He had been wondering why Drugar was traveling with people the dwarf made no secret of despising. Haplo thought suddenly that he understood.

"Elven weapons"—Drugar spoke into his thick beard—"drive them away! Elven weapons could have saved my people!"

As if in response, Paithan's grim voice rose, "But it didn't drive them far, Durndrun."

The lord shook his head. "No, not far. They came back, attacked us from behind, using that deadly elemental magic of theirs—hurling fire, rocks dragged from the Mother-knows-where. They took care not to come within sight of us and, when we fled, they didn't follow."

"What do they say?" Drugar asked. His hand was beneath his beard; Haplo could see the fingers moving, grasping at something.

"The weapons stopped them, but not for long. The tytans hit them with elemental magic."

"But they are here, they are alive!"

"Yeah. The elves retreated, the tytans apparently didn't go after them." Haplo saw the elflord cast a glance around the group assembled in the coppice, saw him draw Paithan farther into the trees, apparently for private conversation.

"Dog," Haplo said. The animal lifted its head. A gesture from its master sent the dog padding swiftly, silently after the two elves.

"Pah!" The dwarf spit on the ground at his feet.

"You don't believe them?" Haplo asked, interested. "You know what elemental magic is?"

"I know," grunted Drugar, "though we do not use it ourselves. We use"—he pointed a stubby finger at the Patryn's sigla-covered hands—"that magic."

Haplo was momentarily confounded, stared dumbly at the dwarf.

Drugar didn't appear to notice the man's discomfiture. Fumbling at his throat, the dwarf drew out an obsidian disk worn on a leather thong, and held it up for the Patryn's inspection. Haplo leaned over it, saw carved on the rare stone a single rune—a Sartan rune. It was crudely drawn; by itself it possessed little power. Yet he had only to look on his arms to see its counterpart tattooed on his own skin.

"We cannot use them as you do." The dwarf stared at Haplo's hands, his gaze hungry and yearning. "We do not know how to put them together. We are like little children: We can speak words, but we don't know how to string the words into sentences."

"Who taught you . . . the rune magic?" Haplo asked when he had recovered sufficiently from his shock to be able to speak.

Drugar lifted his eyes, stared far off, into the jungle. "Legend says . . . they did."

Haplo was confused, thought at first he meant the elves. The dwarf's black eyes were focused higher, almost to the tops of the trees, and the Patryn understood. "The tytans."

"Some of us believed they would come to us again, help us build, teach us. Instead . . . " Drugar's voice rumbled to silence, like thunder fading in the distance.

Another mystery to ponder, to consider. But not here. Not now. Alone . . . and far away. Haplo saw Paithan and the elflord returning, the dog trotting along unnoticed at their heels. Paithan's face reflected some internal struggle; an unpleasant one, to judge by his expression. The elflord walked straight to Aleatha who, after assisting Roland with Haplo, had been left standing aloof, alone, at the edge of the copse.

"You've been ignoring me," she stated.

Lord Durndrun smiled faintly. "I'm sorry, my dear. The gravity of the situation—"

"But the situation's over," said Aleatha lightly. "And here am I, in my 'warrior maid' costume, dressed to kill, so to speak. But I've missed the battle seemingly." Raising her arms, she presented herself to be admired. "Do you like it? I'll wear it after we're married, whenever we have a fight. Though I dare say your mother won't approve—"

The elflord blenched, covered his pain by averting his face. "You look charming, my dear. And now I have asked your brother to take you home."

"Well, of course. It's almost dinnertime. We're expecting you. After you've cleaned up—"

"There won't be time, I'm afraid, my dear." Taking the woman's hand, Lord Durndrun pressed it to his lips. "Good-bye, Aleatha." It seemed he meant to release her hand, but Aleatha caught hold of his, held him fast.

"What do you mean, saying 'good-bye' in that tone?" She tried to sound teasing, but fear tightened, strained her voice.

"Quindiniar." Lord Durndrun gently removed the woman's hand from his.

Paithan stepped forward, caught Aleatha by the arm. "We've got to go—"

Aleatha shook herself free. "Good-bye, My Lord," she said coldly. Turning her back, she stalked off into the jungle.

"Thea!" Paithan called, worried. She ignored him, kept going. "Damn, she shouldn't be wandering around alone—" He looked at Roland.

"Oh, all right," muttered the man, and plunged into the trees.

"Paithan, I don't understand. What's going on?" asked Rega.

"I'll tell you later. Somebody wake up the old man." Paithan gestured irritably to Zifnab, who lay comfortably beneath a tree, snoring loudly. The elf glanced back at Lord Durndrun. "I'm sorry, My Lord. I'll talk to her. I'll explain."

The elflord shook his head. "No, Quindiniar. It's best you don't. I'd rather she didn't know."

"My Lord, I think I should come—"

"Good-bye, Quindiniar," Lord Durndrun said firmly, cutting off the young man's words. "I'm counting on you." Gathering his weary troops around him with a gesture, the lord turned and led his small force back into the jungle.

Zifnab, assisted by the toe of Rega's boot, woke with a snort. "What? Hoh? I heard every word! Just resting my eyes. Lids get heavy, you know." Joints popping and creaking, he rose to his feet, sniffing the air. "Dinnertime. The cook said something about tangfruit. That's good. We can dry 'em and eat the leftovers on our journey."

Paithan gave the old man a troubled look, switched his gaze to Haplo. "Are you coming?"

"Go on. I've got to take it easy. I'd only slow you down."

"But the tytans—"

"Go on," said Haplo, in pain, beginning to lose patience.

Taking hold of Rega's hand, the elf followed after Roland and his sister, who already had a considerable head start.

"I have to go!" said Drugar and hurried to catch up with

Paithan and Rega. Once he was even with them, however, he fell about a pace behind, keeping them constantly in his sight.

"I suppose I'll be forced to walk all that way!" muttered Zifnab peevishly, tottering off. "Where's that dratted dragon? Never around when I want him, but the moment I don't, there he is, leaping up, threatening to eat people or making rude remarks about the state of my digestion." Turning, he peered around at Haplo. "Need any help?"

The Labyrinth take me if I see you again! Haplo told the old man's retreating back. Crazy old bastard.

Beckoning to the dog, the Patryn motioned the animal close and rested his hand on its head. The private conversation, held between Paithan and the elflord, overheard by the dog, came to Haplo clearly.

It wasn't much—the Patryn was disappointed. The elflord had said simply that the elves didn't have a chance. They were all going to die.

"You're a real bitch, aren't you?" said Roland.

He'd had a difficult time catching up with the elf woman. He didn't like crossing the narrow, swinging, ropevine bridges that stretched from treetop to treetop. The jungle floor was far beneath him, the bridge swayed alarmingly whenever he moved. Aleatha, accustomed to walking the bridges, moved across them with ease. She could, in fact, have escaped Roland completely, but that would have meant walking the jungle alone.

Hearing him right behind her, she turned and faced him.

"Kitkninit.[1] You are wasting your breath conversing with me. You even talk like a barbarian!" Aleatha's hair had come completely undone; it billowed around her, swept back by the speed of her movement along the bridge. A flush of exertion stained her cheeks.

"Like hell you kitkninit. You were quick enough to follow my instructions when I told you to hold onto our patient."

Aleatha ignored him. She was tall, almost as tall as Roland. Her stride—in the leather pants—was long and unencumbered.

They left the bridge, striking a trail through the moss. The path was narrow and difficult to traverse, made no easier by the

---

[1] Elven for "I don't understand."

fact that Aleatha increased Roland's difficulty whenever possible. Drawing aside branches, she let them go, snapping them in his face. Taking a sharp turn, she left him floundering in a bramble bush. But if Thea was hoping to make Roland angry, she didn't succeed. The human seemed to take a perverse pleasure in the trouble she was causing him. When they emerged onto the sweeping lawn of the Quindiniar mansion, she discovered Roland strolling along easily by her side.

"I mean," he said, picking up the conversation where he had left off, "you treated that elf pretty badly. It's obvious the guy would give his life for you. In fact, he's going to—give his life, that is—and you treat him like he's—"

Aleatha whirled, turning on him. Roland caught her wrists, her nails inches from his face. "Listen, lady! I know you'd like to tear my tongue out so you don't have to hear the truth. Didn't you see the blood on his uniform? That came from dead elves! Your people! Dead! Just like mine! Dead!"

"You're hurting me." Aleatha's voice was cool, calming Roland's fever. He flushed, and slowly released her wrists. He could see the livid marks of his hand—the marks of his fear— imprinted on the fair skin.

"I'm sorry. Forgive me. It's just—"

"Please excuse me," said Aleatha. "It's late, and I must dress for dinner."

She left him and walked over the smooth expanse of green moss, heading for the house. Horn calls rose again, sounding flat and lifeless in the still, muggy air. Roland was still standing in the same place, staring after the woman, when the others caught up with him.

"That's the signal for the city guard to turn out," said Paithan. "I'm part of it. I should go fight with them." But he didn't move. He stared down at the house, at *Dragon Wing* behind it.

"What'd the elflord tell you?" Roland asked.

"Right now, people think that our army's driven the tytans off, defeated them. Durndrun knows better. That was only a small force. According to our scouts, after the monsters attacked the dwarves, they split up—half went vars to deal with Thillia, half went est, to the Fartherness Reaches. The two armies of tytans are rejoining for an all-out assault on Equilan."

Paithan put his arm around Rega, drew her close. "We can't

survive. The lord ordered me to take Aleatha and my family and flee, to get out while we can. He meant, of course, to travel overland. He doesn't know about the ship."

"We've got to get out of here tonight!" said Roland.

"*If* that Haplo plans to take any of us. I don't trust him," said Rega.

"Which means I run away, leave my people to perish . . . " murmured Paithan.

No, said Drugar silently, his hand on his knife. No one will leave. Not this night, not ever.

"When the dog barks," announced the old man, panting, toddling up from behind. "That's the signal. When the dog barks."

CHAPTER ♦ 31

TREETOPS,

EQUILAN

♦

Haplo took a last walk around the ship, inspecting the repairs he'd made with a critical eye. The damage had not been extensive; the protective runes had, for the most part, served him well. He'd been able to heal the cracks in the planking, reestablish the rune magic. Satisfied that the ship would hold together throughout its long voyage, Haplo climbed back up on the top deck and paused to rest.

He was exhausted. The repairs to his ship and the repairs to himself after the fight with the tytan had drained his energy. He knew he was weak because he was in pain; his shoulder ached and throbbed. If he had been able to rest, to sleep, to let his body renew itself, the injury would, by now, have been nothing more than a bad memory. But he was running out of time. He could not withstand a tytan assault. His magic had to be spent on the ship, not on himself.

The dog settled itself beside him. Haplo rubbed his hand against the animal's muzzle, scratching its jowls. The dog leaned into the caress, begging for more. Haplo thumped it on the flanks.

"Ready to go back up there again?"

The dog rolled over, stood, and shook itself.

"Yeah, me too." Haplo tilted his head back, squinting against the brilliance of the sun. The smoke of the fires, burning in the elven city, kept him from seeing the stars.

Steal our eyes! Blind us to the bright and shining light!

Well, why not? It makes sense. If the Sartan . . .

The dog growled, deep in its throat. Haplo, alert, wary, glanced swiftly down at the house. They were all inside, he'd seen them go in after their return from the jungle. He'd been somewhat surprised they hadn't come to the ship. The first thing he'd done on his own return had been to strengthen the magical field surrounding it. On sending the dog to reconnoiter, however, he'd discovered them doing what he should have guessed they'd be doing—arguing vehemently among themselves.

Now that the dog had drawn his attention to it, he could hear voices, loud, strident, raised in anger and frustration.

"Mensch. All the same. They should welcome a strong ruler like My Lord—someone to enforce peace, bring order to their lives. That is, if any of them will be left in this world when My Lord arrives." Haplo shrugged, rose to his feet, heading for the bridge.

The dog began barking, a warning. Haplo's head jerked around. Beyond the house, the jungle was moving.

Calandra stormed up to her office, slammed the door shut, and locked it. Drawing out her ledger, she opened it, sat rigidly in her straight-backed chair, and began to go over the previous cycle's sales figures.

There was no reasoning with Paithan, absolutely none. He had invited strangers into her house, including the human slaves, telling them that they could take refuge inside! He had told the cook to bring her family up from the town. He'd whipped them into a state of panic with his gruesome tales. The cook was in hysterics. There'd be no dinner this night! It grieved Calandra to say it, but her brother had obviously been stricken with the same madness that plagued their poor father.

"I've put up with Papa all these years," Calandra snapped at the inkwell. "Put up with the house being nearly burned down around our ears, put up with the shame and humiliation. He is, after all, my father, and I owe him. But I owe you nothing, Paithan! You'll have your share of the inheritance and that's all. Take it and take your human trollop and the rest of your scruffy followers and try to make your way in this world! You'll be back. On your knees!"

Outside, a dog began to bark. The noise was loud and startling. Calandra let fall a drop of ink on the ledger sheet. A burst of noise, shouts and cries, came from downstairs. How did they expect her to get any work done! Angrily grabbing the blotter, Calandra pressed it over the paper, soaking up the ink. It hadn't ruined her figures, she was still able to read them—the neat, precise numbers marching in their ordered rows, figuring, calculating, summing up her life.

She replaced the pen, with care, in its holder, and walked over to the window, prepared to slam it shut. Calandra caught her breath, stared. It seemed the trees themselves were creeping up on her house.

She rubbed her eyes, squinching them shut and massaging the lids with her fingers. Sometimes, when she worked too long and too late, the numbers swam before her vision. I'm upset, that's all. Paithan has upset me. I'm seeing things. When I open my eyes, everything will be as it should be.

Calandra opened her eyes. The trees no longer appeared to be moving. What she saw was the advance of a horrible army.

Footsteps came thudding up the stairs, clattered down the hall. A fist began to pound on the door. Paithan's voice shouted, "Callie! They're coming! Callie, please! You have to leave, now!"

Leave! And go where?

Her father's wistful, eager voice came through the keyhole. "My dear! We're flying to the stars!" Shouting from below drowned him out, then, when Callie could hear, there came something about "your mother."

"Go on downstairs, Father. I'll talk to her. Calandra!" Beating on the door. "Calandra!"

She stared out the window in a kind of hypnotic fascination. The monsters seemed uncertain about venturing into the open expanse of green, smooth lawn. They hung about the fringes of the jungle. Occasionally one lifted its eyeless head— they looked like sloths, sniffing the air and not much liking whatever it was they smelled.

A thud shook the door. Paithan was trying to break it down! That would be difficult. Because Calandra often counted money in this room, the door was strong, specially designed, reinforced.

He was pleading with her to open it, to come with them, to escape.

Unaccustomed warmth stole over Calandra. Paithan cared about her. He truly cared.

"Perhaps, Mother, I haven't failed, after all," said Calandra. She pressed her cheek against the cool glass, stared down at the expanse of moss and the frightful army below.

The thudding against the door continued. Paithan would hurt his shoulder. She'd better put an end to it. Walking stiff, erect, Calandra reached up her hand and threw the bolt, locked it fast. The sound could be heard clearly on the other side, and it was met with shocked silence.

"I'm busy, Paithan," Calandra said firmly, speaking to him as she had spoken when he was a child, teasing her to come play. "I have work to do. Run along, and leave me alone."

"Calandra! Look out the window!"

What did he take her for—a fool?

"I've looked out the window, Paithan," Calandra spoke calmly. "You've caused me to make a mistake in my figures. Just take yourselves off to wherever it is you're going and leave me in peace!"

She could almost see the look on his face, the expression of hurt, bewilderment. So he'd looked the cycle they'd brought him home from that trip with his grandfather, the day of Elithenia's funeral.

Mother's not here, Paithan. She won't be here, ever again.

The shouts from below grew louder. A shuffling sound came outside the door—another one of Paithan's bad habits. She could almost see him, head bent, staring at the floor, kicking moodily at the baseboards.

"Good-bye, Callie," he said, his voice so soft she could barely hear it above the whirring of the fan blades, "I think I understand."

Probably not, but it didn't matter. Good-bye, Paithan, she told him silently, placing her ink-stained, work-calloused fingers gently on the door, as she might have placed them gently on a child's smooth cheek. Take care of Papa . . . and Thea.

She heard footsteps, running rapidly down the hall.

Calandra wiped her eyes. Marching to the window, she slammed it shut, returned to her desk, and sat down—back stiff and straight. She lifted her pen, dipped it carefully and precisely in the inkwell, and bent her head over the ledger.

◆

"They've stopped," said Haplo to the dog, watching the movements of the tytans, seeing them keep to the jungle. "I wonder why—"

The ground rumbled beneath the Patryn's feet and he had his answer. "The old man's dragon. . . . They must smell it. Come on, dog. Let's get out of here before those creatures make up their minds and realize that there are too many of them to be scared of just one dragon."

Haplo had almost reached the ladder leading to the bridge when he looked down and discovered that he was talking to himself.

"Dog? Blast it! Where—"

The Patryn glanced back over his shoulder, saw the dog leap from the deck of the ship onto the mossy lawn.

"Dog! Damn it!" Haplo ran back across the deck, peered down over the ship's rail. The animal stood directly beneath him, facing the house. Legs stiff, fur bristling, it barked and barked. "All right! You've warned them! You've warned everybody in three kingdoms! Now get back up here!"

The dog ignored him, perhaps it couldn't hear over its own barking.

Grumbling, dividing his attention between the monsters still lurking in the jungle and the house, Haplo jumped down onto the moss.

"Look, mutt, we don't want company—"

He made a grab for the animal, intending to grasp hold of it by the scruff of its neck. The dog didn't turn its head, didn't once look back at him. But the moment Haplo drew near, the animal leapt forward and went speeding over the lawn, galloping toward the house.

"Dog! Get back here! Dog! I'm leaving now! You hear me?" Haplo took a step toward the ship. "Dog, you worthless, flea-ridden— Oh, hell!" Breaking into a run, the Patryn dashed across the lawn after the animal.

"The dog's barking," shouted Zifnab. "Run! Flee! Fire! Famine! Fly!"

No one moved, except Aleatha, who cast a bored glance over her shoulder.

"Where's Callie?"

Paithan avoided his sister's eyes. "She's not coming."

"Then I'm not either. It's a stupid notion anyway. I'll wait here for My Lord."

Keeping her back to the window, Aleatha walked to the mirror and studied her hair, her dress, her adornments. She was wearing her finest gown and the jewels that had been part of her inheritance from her mother. Her hair was artfully arranged in a most becoming style. She had, the mirror assured her, never looked more beautiful.

"I can't imagine why he hasn't come. My Lord is never late."

"He hasn't come because he's dead, Thea!" Paithan told her, fear and grief shredding him, leaving him raw, burning. "Can't you understand?"

"And we're going to be next!" Roland gestured outside. "Unless we get to the ship! I don't know what's stopping the tytans, but they won't be stopped for long!"

Paithan looked around the room. Ten humans, slaves who had braved the dragon to stay on with the Quindiniars, and their families had taken refuge in the house. The cook was sobbing hysterically in a corner. Numerous adult and several half-grown elves—perhaps the cook's children, Paithan wasn't certain—were gathered around her. All of them were staring at Paithan, looking for leadership. Paithan avoided their eyes.

"Go on! Run for it!" Roland shouted, speaking in human, gesturing to the slaves.

They needed no urging. The men lifted small children, the women hitched up their skirts and raced out the door. The elves didn't understand Roland's words, but they read the look on his face. Catching hold of the sobbing cook, they hustled her out the door and ran after the humans across the lawn, up the slight rise to where the ship stood on the top of the hill.

Human slaves. The elven cook and her family. Ourselves. The best and the brightest . . .

"Paithan?" Roland urged.

The elf turned to his sister. "Thea?"

Aleatha grew paler, the hand that smoothed her hair trembled slightly. She clamped her teeth over her lower lip, and when she knew she could speak without her voice breaking, she said, "I'm staying with Callie."

"If you're staying, I'm staying."

"Paithan!"

"Let him go, Rega! He wants to commit suicide that's his—"

"They're my sisters! I can't run away!"

"If he stays, Roland, then I'm staying—" Rega began.

The dog bounded up on the porch, shot into the hallway, gave a loud, sharp, single "Whuf!"

"They're on the move!" cried Roland, from his vantage point by the window.

"When My Lord comes, tell him that I will be in the parlor," said Aleatha, calmly gathering her skirts, turning her back, and walking away.

Paithan started after her, but Roland caught hold of his arm. "You take care of Rega."

The human strode after Aleatha. Catching hold of her, Roland scooped the elfmaid up in his arms, tossed her over his shoulder and carried her—head down, kicking and screaming and pummeling him on the back—out the door.

Haplo rounded a corner of the house and skidded to a halt, staring in disbelief at the swarm of elves and humans suddenly appearing before him, all bound for his ship!

Savior.

Ha! Wait until they hit the magical barricade.

Haplo ignored them, chased after the dog, and saw the animal leap up onto the porch.

"We're coming!" shouted Paithan.

"You're not the only ones," Haplo muttered.

The tytans had begun their advance, moving with their silent, incredible speed. Haplo looked at the dog, looked at the large group of elves and the humans hastening toward his ship. The first few had already reached it, were endeavoring to get close, had discovered it was impossible. Runes on the outside hull glowed red and blue, their magic guarding against intruders. The mensch were shouting, clasping their arms around each other. Some turned, prepared to fight to the death.

Savior.

Haplo heaved an exasperated sigh. Swearing beneath his breath, he lifted his hand and swiftly traced several runes in the air. They caught fire, glowed blue. The sigla on the ship flickered in answer, their flames died. His defenses were lowered.

"You better hurry up," he shouted, giving the leaping, dancing dog a swift kick that landed nowhere near its target.

"We're going to have to run for it, Quindiniar!" shouted Zifnab, hiking up his robes, revealing a broad expanse of bony leg. "By the way, you were wonderful, Lenthan, my friend. Superb speech. I couldn't have done better myself." He laid his hand on Lenthan's arm. "Ready?"

Lenthan blinked at Zifnab in confusion. The elf's ancestors drifted back to a time beyond memory, leaving behind the wreck of a middle-aged man. "I'm ready," he said vaguely. "Where are we going?" He allowed Zifnab to propel him along.

"To the stars, my dear fellow!" cackled the wizard. "To the stars!"

Drugar ran after the others. The dwarf was strong, his endurance was great. He could have gone on running long after the humans and the elves had collapsed by the wayside. But with his short, stocky legs and heavy leather armor and boots, he was no match for them in a race. They had all soon outdistanced him in their mad dash for the ship, leaving him far behind.

The dwarf pressed on stubbornly. He could see the tytans without turning his head; they were behind him, but fanning out on either side, hoping to capture their prey by enclosing it in a huge circle. The monsters were gaining slowly on the elves and humans, more rapidly on the dwarf. Drugar increased his speed, running desperately, not out of fear of the tytans, but out of fear that he would lose his chance for revenge.

The toe of his thick boot caught on his heel. The dwarf stumbled, lost his balance, and pitched facefirst into the moss. He struggled to stand, but his boot had slipped down halfway over his foot. Drugar hopped on one foot, fighting to pull the boot on, his hands slippery with sweat. Smoke stung his nostrils. The tytans had set fire to the jungle.

"Paithan! Look!" Rega glanced behind. "Blackbeard!"

The elf skidded to a halt. He and Rega were within a few strides of the ship. The two had stayed behind the others to act as rear guard, protecting Zifnab, Haplo, and Lenthan, pounding ahead of them, and Roland and the furious Aleatha. They had, as usual, forgotten about the dwarf.

"You go on." Paithan started back down the slight slope. He saw the flames shoot up out of the trees, the black smoke swirl into the sky. It was spreading fast, toward the house. He wrenched his gaze away, kept it on the floundering dwarf, the approaching tytans.

Movement at his side caused him to glance around. "I thought I told you to go to the ship."

Rega managed a twisted smile. "Make up your mind, elf! You're stuck with me!"

Paithan smiled wearily back, shaking his head, prevented from saying anything by the fact that he had no more breath with which to say it.

The two reached the dwarf, who had, by this time, torn the boot off and was hobbling forward—one boot on and one boot off. Paithan caught hold of him by one shoulder, Rega grabbed the other.

"I don't need your help!" growled Drugar, glaring at them with startling vehemence. "Let me go!"

"Paithan, they're gaining!" Rega shouted, nodding over her shoulder at the tytans.

"Shut up and quite fighting us!" Paithan told the dwarf. "You saved our lives, after all!"

Drugar began to laugh—a deep, wild bellow. Paithan wondered again if the dwarf was going mad. The elf didn't have time to worry about it. He could see, out of the corner of his eye, the tytans getting nearer. They didn't stand a chance. He glanced at Rega, she glanced at him, shrugged slightly. Both tightened their hold on the heavy dwarf, and started running.

Haplo reached the ship ahead of the others, the runes traced on his body doing what they could to bolster his flagging strength, lent speed to his stride. Men, women, and shrieking children straggled over the deck. A few had found the hatchway and had gone down into the ship. More were standing at the rail, staring at the tytans.

"Get below!" Haplo shouted, pointing at the hatch. He pulled himself up over the railing and was starting—again—for the bridge when he heard a frantic whimper and felt a tug at his heel.

"What now?" he snarled, whirling to confront the dog, who had nearly pulled him over backward. Looking out over the lawn, peering through the gathering smoke, he saw the human, the elf, and the dwarf surrounded by tytans.

"What do you want me to do? I can't— Oh, for—!" Haplo caught hold of Zifnab, who was trying unsuccessfully to pull himself and Lenthan Quindiniar up over the railing. "Where's that dragon of yours?" The Patryn demanded, yanking the old man around to face him.

"Flagon?" Zifnab blinked at Haplo like a stunned owl. "Good idea! I could use a snort—"

"Dragon, you doddering idiot! Dragon!"

"Dragon? Where?" The old wizard looked highly alarmed. "Don't tell him you saw me, there's a good chap. I'll just go below—"

"Listen to me, you worthless old geezer, that dragon of yours is the only thing that's going to save them!" Haplo pointed at the small group struggling valiantly to reach the ship.

"My dragon? Save anybody?" Zifnab shook his head sadly. "You must have him confused with someone else—Smaug, perhaps? No? Ah, I've got it! That lizard who gave Saint George such a nasty time of it! What was his name, now *there* was a dragon!"

"And you are implying that I'm not?" The voice split the ground. The dragon's head shoved up through the moss. Shock waves rolled, rocking the ship, throwing Haplo back into a bulkhead. Lenthan clung to the railing for dear life.

Pulling himself up, Haplo saw the tytans come to a halt, their eyeless heads swiveling toward the gigantic beast.

The dragon's body slid up out of the hole it had created in the moss. It moved rapidly, green scaly skin rippling, glistening in the sunlight. "Smaug!" the dragon thundered. "That vain-glorious fop! And as for that sniveling worm who took on St. George—"

Roland reached the ship, lifted Aleatha up over the railing to

Haplo, who caught hold of the woman, dragged her on board, and turned her over to the care of her father.

"Get up here!" Haplo offered his hand.

Roland shook his head, turned, and ran back to help Paithan, disappearing in the gathering smoke. Haplo peered after him, cursing the delay. It was difficult to see now—much of the jungle was completely engulfed in flames—but Haplo had the impression that the tytans were falling back, milling about in confusion, caught between their own flame and the dragon.

"And to think I ended up with a worthless old faker like you!" the dragon was shouting. "I could have gone someplace where I would have been appreciated! Pern, for example! Instead, I—"

Coughing, tears streaming down their cheeks, the small party made its way through the smoke. It was difficult to tell who was carrying whom; they all seemed to be leaning on each other. With Haplo's help, they managed to climb up over the railing and collapsed on the deck.

"Everybody below!" the Patryn snapped. "Hurry up. It's not going to take the tytans long to figure out they're not as frightened of the dragon as they think they are!"

Wearily, they made their way forward, stumbled down the hatch to the bridge. Haplo was about to turn and follow when he saw Paithan, standing at the railing, staring through the smoke, blinking back tears. His hands clenched the wood.

"Come on, or you're riding out here!" Haplo threatened.

"The house . . . can you see it?" Paithan wiped his eyes with an impatient gesture.

"It's gone, elf, burning! Now will you—" Haplo paused. "There was someone in there. Your sister."

Paithan nodded, slowly turned away. "I guess it was better that way than . . . the other."

"We're likely to find out if we don't get out of here ourselves! Sorry, but I've got no time for condolences." Haplo grabbed hold of the elf, hustled him down below.

Inside, it was deathly quiet. The magic protected the ship from the smoke and flame, the dragon outside guarded it from the tytans. The humans and elves and the dwarf had taken refuge in whatever open spaces they could find, huddled together, their eyes fixed on Haplo. He glanced around grimly, not liking his passengers, not liking the situation. His gaze flicked over the dog, lying nose on paws on the deck.

"You happy?" he muttered.

The animal thumped its tail wearily on the boards.

Haplo put his hands on the steering stone, hoping he had strength enough left to take the ship aloft. The sigla began to glow blue and red on his skin, the runes on the stone lit in response. A violent shudder shook the vessel, the boards creaked and shivered.

"Tytans!"

This was the end. He couldn't fight them, didn't have the strength. *My Lord will know, when I fail to return, that something must have gone wrong. The Lord of the Nexus will be wary, when he comes to this world.*

Green scales covered the window, almost completely blocking the view. Haplo started, recovered. He knew now what was causing the ship to quake and creak like a rowboat in a storm—a large, scaly body, winding itself round and round.

A fiery eye glared through the window at the Patryn.

"Ready when you are, sir," the dragon announced.

"Ignition! Blast off!" said the old man, settling himself on the deck, his battered hat sliding down over one ear. "The vessel needs a new name! Something more appropriate to a starship. *Apollo? Gemini? Enterprise.* Already taken. *Millennium Falcon.* Trademarked. All rights reserved. No! Wait, I have it! *Dragon Star!* That's it! *Dragon Star!*"

"Shit," muttered Haplo, and put his hands back on the steering stone.

The ship rose slowly, steadily, into the air. The mensch stood up, stared out the small portholes that lined the hull, watched their world fall away from them.

The dragonship flew over Equilan. The elven city could not be seen for the smoke and flames devouring it and the trees in which it had been built.

The dragonship flew over the Kithni Gulf, red with human blood. It flew over Thillia—charred, blackened. Here and there, crouched alongside the broken roads, a dazed, lone survivor could be seen, wandering forlornly through a dead land.

Rising steadily, gaining altitude, the ship passed over the dwarven homeland—dark, deserted.

The ship sailed into the green-blue sky, left the ruined world behind, and headed for the stars.

CHAPTER ♦ 32

DRAGON

STAR

♦

THE FIRST PART OF THE VOYAGE TO THE STARS WAS RELATIVELY PEACE-
ful. Awed and frightened by the sight of the ground sliding
beneath them, the mensch—elven and human—huddled together, pathetically eager for each other's company and support.
They talked repeatedly of the catastrophe that had struck them.
Wrapped in the warm blanket of shared tragedy, they attempted
to draw even the dwarf into their circle of good fellowship.
Drugar ignored them. He sat morose and melancholy in a corner
of the bridge, moving from it infrequently, and then only under
the duress of dire need.

They spoke eagerly about the star to which they were sailing,
about their new world and new life. Haplo was amused to
observe that, once they were actually on their way to a star, the
old man became extremely evasive in describing it.

"What is it like? What causes the light?" asked Roland.

"It is a holy light," said Lenthan Quindiniar in mild rebuke.
"And shouldn't be questioned."

"Actually, Lenthan's right . . . sort of," said Zifnab, appearing to grow extremely uncomfortable. "The light is, one
might say, holy. And then there's night."

"Night? What's night?"

The wizard cleared his throat with a loud *harrumph* and
glanced around as if for help. Not finding any, he plunged
ahead. "Well, you remember the storms you have on your world?

Every cycle at a certain time it rains? Night's similar to that, only every cycle, at a certain time, the light . . . well . . . it disappears."

"And everything's dark!" Rega was appalled.

"Yes, but it's not frightening. It's quite comforting. That's the time when everyone sleeps:. Makes it easy to keep your eyelids shut."

"I can't sleep in the dark!" Rega shuddered, and glanced at the dwarf, sitting silently, ignoring them all. "I've tried it. I'm not sure about this star. I'm not sure I want to go."

"You'll get used to it." Paithan put his arm around her. "I'll be with you."

The two snuggled close. Haplo saw looks of disapproval on the faces of the elves, who were watching the loving couple. He saw the same expressions mirrored on the faces of the humans.

"Not in public," Roland said to his sister, jerking her away from Paithan.

There was no further conversation among the mensch about the star.

Trouble, Haplo foresaw, was coming to paradise.

The mensch found that the ship was smaller than it had first appeared. Food and water supplies disappeared at an alarming rate. Some of the humans began to remember they had been slaves, some of the elves recalled that they had been masters.

The convivial get-togethers ended. No one discussed their destination—at least as a group. The elves and humans met to talk over matters, but they met separately now and kept their voices low.

Haplo sensed the growing tension and cursed it and his passengers. He didn't mind divisiveness. He was, in fact, intent on encouraging it. But not on his ship.

Food and water weren't a problem. He had laid in stores for himself and the dog—making certain he had a variety this time—and he could easily replicate what he had. But who knew how long he would have to feed these people and put up with them? Not without a certain amount of misgiving, he had set his course based on the old man's instructions. They were flying toward the brightest star in the heavens. Who knew how long it would take them to reach it?

Certainly not Zifnab.

"What's for dinner?" asked the old wizard, peering down

into the hold, where Haplo stood, pondering these questions. The dog, standing at Haplo's side, looked up and wagged his tail. Haplo glanced at it irritably. "Sit down!" he muttered.

Noting the relatively small amount of supplies remaining, Zifnab appeared slightly crestfallen, also extremely hungry.

"Never mind, old man. I can take care of the food!" said Haplo. It would mean using his magic again, but at this point, he didn't suppose it mattered. What interested him more was their destination and how long it would be before he could rid himself of his refugees. "You know something about these stars, don't you?"

"I do?" Zifnab was wary.

"You claim you do. Talking to them about"—he jerked a thumb in the direction of the main part of the ship where the mensch generally gathered—"this 'new' world . . ."

"New? I didn't say anything about 'new,' " Zifnab protested. The old man scratched his head, knocking his hat off. It tumbled down into the hold, landed at Haplo's feet.

"New world . . . being reunited with long-dead wives." Haplo picked up the battered hat, toyed with it.

"It's possible!" cried the wizard shrilly. "Anything's possible." He reached out a tentative hand for the hat. "M—mind you don't crush the brim."

"What brim? Listen, old man, how far are we away from this star? How many days of travel to get there?"

"Well, er, I suppose." Zifnab gulped. "It all depends . . . on . . . on how fast we're traveling! That's it, how fast we're traveling." He warmed to his subject. "Say that we're moving at the speed of light. . . . Impossible, of course, if you believe physicists. Which I don't, by the way. Physicists don't believe in wizards—a fact that I, being a wizard, find highly insulting. I have taken my revenge, therefore, by refusing to believe in physicists. What was the question?"

Haplo started over again, trying to be patient. "Do you know what these stars really are?"

"Certainly," Zifnab replied in lofty tones, staring down his nose at the Patryn.

"What are they?"

"What are what?"

"The stars?"

"You want me to explain them?"

"If you wouldn't mind."

"Well, I think the best way to put this"—sweat broke out on the old man's forehead—"in layman's terms, to be concise, they're . . . er . . . stars."

"Uh huh," said Haplo grimly. "Look, old man, just how close have you actually been to a star?"

Zifnab mopped his forehead with the end of his beard, and thought hard. "I stayed in the same hotel as Clark Gable once," he offered helpfully, after an immense pause.

Haplo gave a disgusted snort, sent the hat spinning up and out of the hatchway. "All right, keep playing your game, old man."

The Patryn turned back, studying the supplies—a barrel of water, a cask of salted targ, bread and cheese, and bag of tangfruit. Sighing, scowling, Haplo stood staring moodily at the water barrel.

"Mind if I watch?" asked Zifnab politely.

"You know, old man, I could end this real quick. Jettison the 'cargo'—if you take my meaning. It's a long way down."

"Yes, you could," said Zifnab, easing himself onto the deck, letting his legs dangle over the edge of the hatch. "And you'd do it in a minute, too. Our lives mean nothing to you, do they, Haplo? The only one who has ever mattered to you is you."

"You're wrong, old man. For what it's worth, one person has my allegiance, my loyalty. I'd lay down my life to save his and feel cheated that I couldn't do more for him."

"Ah, yes," Zifnab said softly. "Your lord. The one who sent you here."

Haplo scowled. How the hell did the old fool know that? He must have inferred it from things I've let drop. It was careless, very careless. Damn! Everything's going wrong! The Patryn gave the water barrel a vicious kick, splitting the staves, sending a deluge of tepid liquid over his feet.

I'm used to being in control; all my life, every situation, I've been in control. It was how I survived the Labyrinth, how I completed my mission successfully on Arianus. Now I'm doing things I never meant to do, saying things I never meant to say! A bunch of mutants with the intelligence of your average rutabaga nearly destroy me. I'm hauling a group of mensch to a star and putting up with a crazy old man, who's crazy like a fox.

"Why?" Haplo demanded aloud, shoving aside the dog, who was eagerly lapping up the spill. "Just tell me why?"

"Curiosity," said the old man complacently. "It's killed more than a few cats in its day."

"Is that a threat?" Haplo glanced up from beneath lowered brows.

"No! Heavens, no!" Zifnab said hastily, shaking his head. "Just a warning, dear boy. *Some* people consider curiosity a very dangerous concept. Asking questions ofttimes leads to the truth. And *that* can get you into a great deal of trouble."

"Yeah, well, it depends on what truth you believe in, doesn't it, old man?"

Haplo lifted a piece of wet wood, traced a sigla on it with his finger, and tossed it back into the corner. Instantly, the other pieces of broken barrel leapt to join it. Within the space of a heartbeat, the barrel stood intact. The Patryn drew runes on both the barrel and in the empty air next to it. The barrel replicated itself, and soon numerous barrels, all filled with water, occupied the hold. Haplo traced fiery runes in the air, causing tubs of salted targ meat to join the ranks of water barrels. Wine jars sprang up, clinking together musically. Within a few short moments, the hold was loaded with food.

Haplo climbed the ladder leading up out of the hold. Zifnab moved aside to let him past.

"All in what truth you believe in, old man," the Patryn repeated.

"Yes. Loaves and fishes." Zifnab winked slyly. "Eh, Savior?"

Food and water led, somewhat indirectly, to the crisis that came near solving all of Haplo's problems for him.

"What is that stench?" demanded Aleatha. "And are you going to do something about it?"

It was about a week into their journey; time being estimated by a mechanical hour flower the elves had brought aboard. Aleatha had wandered up to the bridge, to stand and stare out at the star that was their destination.

"The bilge," stated Haplo absently, trying to devise some method of measuring the distance between themselves and their destination. "I told you, you're all going to have to take turns pumping it out."

The elves of Arianus, who had built and designed the ship, had devised an effective system of waste management, utilizing elven machinery and magic. Water is scarce and extremely valuable on the air world of Arianus. As the basis for monetary exchange, not a drop is wasted. Some of the first magicks created on Arianus dealt with the conversion of waste water back into pure liquid. Human water wizards dealt directly with nature's elements, obtaining pure water from foul. Elven wizards used machines and alchemy to achieve the same effect, many elves swearing that their chemical wizardry produced better-tasting water than the humans' elemental magic.

On taking over the ship, Haplo had removed most of the elven machinery, leaving only the bilge pump in case the ship took on rainwater. The Patryns, through their rune magic, have their own methods of dealing with bodily waste, methods that are highly secret and protected—not out of shame, but out of simple survival. An animal will bury its droppings to keep an enemy from tracking it.

Haplo had not, therefore, been overly worried about the problem of sanitation. He'd checked the pump. It worked. The humans and the elves aboard ship could take turns at it. Preoccupied with his mathematical calculations, he thought no more of his conversation with Aleatha, other than making a mental note to set everyone to work.

His figuring was interrupted by a scream, a shout, and the sounds of voices raised in anger. The dog, dozing beside him, leapt to its feet with a growl.

"Now what?" Haplo muttered, leaving the bridge, descending to the crew's quarters below.

"They're not your slaves any longer, Lady!"

The Patryn entered the cabin, found Roland—red-faced and shouting—standing in front of a pale, composed, and icily calm Aleatha. The human contingent was backing up their man. The elves were solidly behind Aleatha. Paithan and Rega, looking distraught, stood, hand in hand, in the middle. The old man, of course—when there was trouble—was nowhere to be found.

"You humans were born to be slaves! You know nothing

else!" retorted a young elf, the cook's nephew—a particularly large and strong specimen of elven manhood.

Roland surged forward, fist clenched, other humans behind.

The cook's nephew leaped to the challenge, his brothers and cousins behind him. Paithan jumped in, attempted to keep the elf off Roland, and received a smart rap on the head from a human who had been a slave of the Quindiniar family since he was a child and who had long sought an opportunity to vent his frustrations. Rega, going in to help Paithan, found herself caught in the middle.

The melee became general, the ship rocked and lurched and Haplo swore. He'd been doing that a lot lately, he noticed. Aleatha had withdrawn to one side, watching with detached interest, keeping her skirt clear of possible blood.

"Stop it!" Haplo roared. Wading into the fight, he grabbed bodies, flung them apart. The dog dashed after him, snapping and growling and nipping painfully at ankles. "You'll knock us out of the air!"

Not exactly true, the magic would hold the ship up, but it was certainly a frightening concept and one that he calculated would end the hostilities.

The fight came to a reluctant halt. Opponents wiped blood from split lips and broken noses and glowered at each other.

"Now what the hell is going on?" Haplo demanded.

Everyone started to talk at once. At the Patryn's furious gesture, everyone fell silent. Haplo fixed his gaze on Roland. "All right, you started it. What happened?"

"It's Her Ladyship's turn to pump out the bilge," said Roland, breathing heavily and rubbing bruised abdominal muscles. He pointed at Aleatha. "She refused to do it. She came in here and ordered one of us to do it for her."

"Yeah! That's right!" The humans, male and female, agreed angrily.

Haplo had a brief and extremely satisfying vision of using his magic to part the ship's staves and send all these wretched and irritating creatures plummeting down however many hundreds of thousands of miles to the world below.

Why didn't he? Curiosity, the old man had said. Yes, I'm curious, curious to see where the old man wants to take these people, curious to see why. But Haplo could foresee a time—and it was rapidly approaching—when his curiosity would begin to wane.

Something of his ire must have been visible on his face. The humans hushed and fell back a pace before him. Aleatha, seeing his gaze come to focus on her, paled, but held her ground, regarding him with cold and haughty disdain. Haplo said nothing. Reaching out, he caught hold of the elf woman's arm and hauled her from the cabin.

Aleatha gasped, screamed, and held back. Haplo jerked her forward, dragging her off her feet. Aleatha fell to the deck. The Patryn yanked her back up, and kept going.

"Where are you taking her?" Paithan cried, real fear in the elf's voice. From out of the corner of his eye, Haplo saw Roland's face drain of color. From his expression, it looked as if he thought Haplo were going to hurl the woman from the top deck.

Good, he thought grimly, and continued on.

Aleatha soon had no breath left to scream; she had to cease her struggles and concentrate on keeping on her feet or be pulled along the deck. Haplo descended a ladder, the elf woman in tow, and stood between decks in the small, smelly, dark part of the ship where the bilge pump stood. Haplo shoved Aleatha forward. She stumbled headlong into the apparatus.

"Dog," he said to the animal, who had either followed him or materialized beside him, "watch!"

The dog sat obediently, head cocked, eyes on the elf woman.

Aleatha's face was livid. She glared at Haplo through a mass of disheveled hair. "I won't!" she snarled and took a step away from the pump.

The dog growled, low in its throat.

Aleatha glanced at it, hesitated, took another step.

The dog rose to its feet, the growl grew louder.

Aleatha stared at the animal, her lips tightened. Tossing her ashen hair, she walked past Haplo, heading for the passage that led out.

The dog covered the distance between them in a jump, planted itself in front of the woman. Its growl rumbled through the ship. Its mouth parted, showing sharp, curved, yellow-white teeth. Aleatha stepped backward hastily, tripped on her skirt, and nearly fell.

"Call him off!" she screamed at Haplo. "He'll kill me!"

"No, he won't," said the Patryn coolly. He pointed to the pump. "Not so long as you work."

Casting Haplo a look that the woman obviously wished was a dagger, Aleatha swallowed her rage, turned her back on the dog and the Patryn. Head held high, she walked over to the pump. Grasping the handle in both delicate, white hands, she lifted it up, shoved it down, lifted it up, shoved it down. Haplo, peering out a porthole, saw a spew of foul-smelling water gush out over the ship's hull, spray into the atmosphere below.

"Dog, stay. Watch," he instructed, and left.

The dog settled down, alert, vigilant, never taking its eyes from Aleatha.

Emerging from below deck, Haplo found most of the mensch gathered at the top of the ladder, waiting for him. He drew himself up level with them.

"Go back about your business," he ordered, and watched them slink off. He left them, returning to the bridge and his attempts to fix their position.

Roland massaged his aching hand, injured when he'd delivered a hard right to the elf. The human tried to tell himself Aleatha got just what she deserved, it served her right, it wouldn't hurt the bitch to turn her hand to a little work. When he found himself walking the passageway, heading for the pumping room, he called himself a fool.

Pausing in the hatchway, Roland stood silently and watched.

The dog lay on the deck, nose on paws, eyes on Aleatha. The elf woman paused in her work, straightened and bent backward, trying to ease the stiffness and pain in a back unaccustomed to bending to hard labor. The proud head drooped, she wiped sweat from her forehead, looked at the palms of her hands. Roland recalled—more vividly than he'd expected—the delicate softness of the small palms. He could imagine the woman's skin, raw and bleeding. Aleatha wiped her face again, this time brushing away tears.

"Here, let me finish," offered Roland gruffly, stepping over the dog.

Aleatha whirled to face him. To his amazement, she stiff-armed him out of the way and began to work the pump with as much speed as the weariness of her aching arms and the smarting of her stinging palms would allow.

Roland glared at her. "Damn it, woman! I'm only trying to help!"

"I don't want your help!" Aleatha shook the hair out of her face, the tears out of her eyes.

Roland intended to turn on his heel, walk out, and leave her to her task. He was going to turn and go. He was leaving. He was . . . putting his arm around her slender waist and kissing her.

The kiss was salty, tasting of sweat and tears. But the woman's lips were warm and responsive, her body yielded to him; she was softness and fragrant hair and smooth skin—all tainted faintly by the foul reek of the bilge.

The dog sat up, a slightly puzzled expression in its eyes, and glanced around for its master. What was it supposed to do now?

Roland drew back, releasing Aleatha, who staggered slightly when his arms were withdrawn.

"You are the most pig-headed, selfish, irritating little snot I ever met in my life! I hope you rot down here!" said Roland coldly. Turning on his heel, he marched out.

Eyes wide in wonder, mouth parted, Aleatha stared after him.

The dog, confused, sat down to scratch an itch.

Haplo had finally almost figured it out. He had developed a crude theodolite that used the stationary position of the four suns and the bright light that was their destination as common reference points. By checking daily the positions of the other stars visible in the sky, the Patryn observed that they appeared to be changing their position in relationship to *Dragon Star*.

The motion was due to the motion of his ship, the consistency of his measurements led to a model of amazing symmetry. They were nearing the star, no doubt about it. In fact, it appeared . . .

The Patryn checked his calculations. Yes, it made sense. He was beginning to understand, beginning to understand a lot. If he was correct, his passengers were going to be in for the shock of their—

"Excuse me, Haplo?"

He glanced around, angry at being interrupted. Paithan and

Rega stood in the doorway, along with the old man. Trust it— Zifnab'd show up now that the trouble was settled.

"What do you want? And make it quick," Haplo muttered.

"We . . . uh . . . Rega and I . . . we want to be married."

"Congratulations."

"We think it will draw the people together, you see—"

"I think it'll more likely touch off a riot, but that's your problem."

Rega appeared a bit downcast, looked at Paithan uncertainly. The elf drew a deep breath, carried on.

"We want you to perform the ceremony."

Haplo couldn't believe he'd heard right. "You what?"

"We want you to perform the ceremony."

"By ancient law," struck in Zifnab, "a ship's captain can marry people when they're at sea."

"Whose ancient law? And we're not at sea."

"Why . . . uh . . . I must admit, I'm rather vague on the precise legal—"

"You've got the old man." The Patryn nodded. "Get him to do it."

"I'm not a cleric," protested Zifnab, indignant. "They wanted me to be a cleric, but I refused. Party needed a healer, they said. Hah! Fighters with all the brains of a doorknob attack something twenty times their size, with a bizillion hit points, and they expect *me* to pull their heads out of their rib cages! I'm a wizard. I've the most marvelous spell. If I could just remember how it went. Eight ball! No, that's not it. Fire something. Fire . . . extinguisher! Smoke alarm. No. But I really think I'm getting close."

"Get him off the bridge." Haplo turned back to his work.

Paithan and Rega edged in front of the old man, the elf put his hand gingerly on the Patryn's tattooed arm. "Will you do it? Will you marry us?"

"I don't know anything about elven marriage ceremonies."

"It wouldn't have to be elven. Or human, either. In fact it would be better if it weren't. That way no one would get mad."

"Surely *your* people have some kind of ceremony," suggested Rega. "We could use yours. . . ."

. . . Haplo didn't miss the woman.

Runners in the Labyrinth are a solitary lot, relying on their speed and strength, their wits and ingenuity to survive, to reach their goal. Squatters rely on numbers. Coming together to form nomadic tribes, the squatters move through the Labyrinth at a slower pace, often following the routes explored by the runners. Each respects the other, both share what they have: the runners, knowledge; the squatters, a brief moment of security, stability.

Haplo entered the squatter camp in the evening, three weeks after the woman had left him. The headman was there to greet him on his arrival; the scouts would have sent word of his coming. The headman was old, with grizzled hair and beard, the tattoos on his gnarled hands were practically indecipherable. He stood tall, though, without stooping. His stomach was taut, the muscles in the arms and legs clean cut and well defined. The headman clasped his hands together, tattooed backs facing outward, and touched his thumbs to his forehead. The circle was joined.

"Welcome, runner."

Haplo made the same gesture, forced himself to keep his gaze fixed on the squatter's leader. To do anything else would be taken for insult, perhaps would even be dangerous. It might appear that he was counting the squatter's numbers.

The Labyrinth was tricky, intelligent. It had been known to send in imposters. Only by adhering strictly to the forms would Haplo be allowed to enter the camp. But he couldn't help darting a furtive glance around the people gathered to inspect him. Particularly, he looked at the women. Not catching, right off, a glimpse of chestnut hair, Haplo wrenched his attention back to his host.

"May the gates stand open for you, headman." Hands to his forehead, Haplo bowed.

"And for you, runner." The headman bowed.

"And your people, headman." Haplo bowed again. The ceremony was over.

Haplo was now considered a member of the tribe. The people continued on about their business as if he were one of themselves, though sometimes a woman paused to stare, give him a smile, and nod toward her hut. At another time in his life, this invitation would have sent fire through his veins. A smile back and he would have been taken into the hut, fed and accorded all the privileges of a husband. But Haplo's blood seemed to run cold these days. Not seeing the smile he wanted to see, he kept his expression carefully guarded, and the woman wandered away in disappointment.

The headman had waited politely to see if Haplo accepted any of these invitations. Noting that he did not, the headman graciously offered his own dwelling place for the evening. Haplo accepted gratefully and, seeing the surprise and somewhat suspicious glint in the headman's eyes, added, "I am in a purification cycle."

The headman nodded, understanding, all suspicion gone. Many Patryns believed, rightly or wrongly, that sexual encounters weakened their magic. A runner planning on entering unknown territory often entered a purification cycle, abstaining from the company of the opposite sex several days before venturing out. A squatter going out on a hunting expedition or facing a battle would do the same thing.

Haplo, personally, didn't happen to believe in such nonsense. His magic had never failed him, no matter what pleasures he had enjoyed the night before. But it made a good excuse.

The headman led Haplo to a hut that was snug and warm and dry. A fire burned brightly in the center, smoke trailing up from the hole in the top. The headman settled himself near it. "A concession to my old bones. I can run with the youngest of them and keep pace. I can wrestle a karkan to the ground with my bare hands. But I find I like a fire at night. Be seated, runner."

Haplo chose a place near the hut entryway. The night was warm, the hut was stifling.

"You come upon us at a good time, runner," said the headman. "We celebrate a binding this night."

Haplo made the polite remark without thinking much about it. His mind was on other matters. He could have asked the question at any time now; all the proper forms had been observed. But it stuck in his throat. The headman asked about the trails, and they fell into talk about Haplo's journeying, the runner providing what information he could about the land through which he'd traveled.

When darkness fell, an unusual stir outside the hut reminded Haplo of the ceremony about to take place. A bonfire turned night to day. The tribe must feel secure, Haplo thought, following the headman out of the hut. Otherwise they would never have dared. A blind dragon could see this blaze.

He joined the throng around the fire.

The tribe was large, he saw. No wonder they felt secure. The scouts on the perimeters would warn them in case of attack. Their numbers were such that they could fend off most anything, perhaps even a dragon. Children ran about, getting in everyone's way, watched over by the group.

The Patryns of the Labyrinth share everything—food, lovers, children. Binding vows are vows of friendship, closer akin to a warrior's vows than marriage vows. A binding may take place between a man and a woman, between two men, or between two women. The ceremony was more common among squatters than runners, but occasionally runners bound themselves to a partner. Haplo's parents had been bound. He himself had considered binding. If he found her . . .

The headman raised his arms in the air, the signal for silence. The crowd, including the youngest baby, hushed immediately. Seeing all was in readiness, the headman stretched his hands out and took hold of the hands of those standing on either side of him. The Patryns all did the same, forming a gigantic circle around the fire. Haplo joined them, clasping hands with a well-formed man about his age on his left and a young woman barely into her teens (who blushed deeply when Haplo took her hand) on his right.

"The circle is complete," said the headman, looking around at his people, an expression of pride on the lined and weathered face. "Tonight we come together to witness the vows between two who would form their own circle. Step forward."

A man and a woman left the circle, that instantly closed behind them, and came to stand in front of the headman. Leaving the circle himself, the old man extended his hands. The two clasped them, one on either side, then the man and the woman took hold of each other's hands.

"Again, the circle is complete," said the old man. His gaze on the two was fond, but stern and serious. The people gathered around, watching in solemn silence.

Haplo found that he was enjoying himself. Most of the time, particularly the last few weeks, he'd felt hollow, empty, alone. Now he was warm, with a sense of being filled. The cold wind didn't howl through him so dismally anymore. He found himself smiling, smiling at everything, everyone.

"I pledge to protect and defend you." The couple was repeating the vows, one immediately after the other in an echoing circle. "My life for your life. My death for your life. My life for your death. My death for your death."

The vows spoken, the couple fell silent. The headman nodded, satisfied with the sincerity of the commitment. Taking the hands he held in his, he placed the two hands together.

"The circle is complete," he said, and stepped back into the circle, leaving the couple to form their own circle inside the larger community. The two smiled at each other. The outer circle gave a cheer and broke apart, separating to prepare for the feast.

Haplo decided he could ask the question now. He sought out the headman, standing near the roaring blaze.

"I'm looking for someone, a woman," said Haplo, and described her. "Stands so tall, chestnut hair. She's a runner. Has she been here."

The headman thought back. "Yes, she was here. Not more than a week ago."

Haplo grinned. He had not meant to follow her, not intentionally. But it seemed that they were keeping to the same trail. "How is she? Did she look well?"

The headman gave Haplo a keen, searching gaze. "Yes, she looked well. But I didn't see that much of her. You might ask Antius, over there. He spent the night with her."

The warmth vanished. The air was chill, the wind cut through him. Haplo turned, saw the well-formed young man with whom he had held hands walking across the compound.

"She left in the morning. I can show you the direction she traveled."

"That won't be necessary. Thank you, though," Haplo added, to ease the coldness of his reply. He looked around, saw the young girl. She was staring at Haplo, and blushed up to the roots of her hair when her gaze was returned.

Haplo returned to the headman's hut, began gathering up his meager belongings; runners traveled light. The headman followed, stared at him in astonishment.

"Your hospitality has saved my life," the Patryn gave the ritual farewell. "Before I leave, I will tell you what I know. Reports say to take the west trail to the fifty-first Gate. Rumor has it that the powerful One, who first solved the secret of the Labyrinth, has returned with his magic to clear certain parts and make them safe . . . at least temporarily. I can't say if this is true or not, since I have come from the south."

"You're leaving? But it is perilous to travel the Labyrinth after dark!"

"It doesn't matter," said Haplo. He put his hands together, pressed them against his forehead, made the ritual gesture of farewell. The headman returned it, and Haplo left the hut. He paused a moment in the doorway. The bonfire's glow lit all around it, but it made the darkness beyond that much darker by contrast. Haplo took a step toward that darkness when he felt a hand upon his arm.

"The Labyrinth kills what it can—if not our bodies, then our spirit," said the headman. "Grieve for your loss, my son, and never forget who is responsible. The ones who imprisoned us, the ones who are undoubtedly watching our struggle with pleasure."

It's the Sartan. . . . They put us in this hell. They're the ones responsible for this evil.

The woman looked at him, her brown eyes flecked with gold. *I wonder. Maybe it's the evil inside us.*

Haplo walked away from the squatter's camp, continued his solitary run. No, he didn't miss the woman. Didn't miss her at all. . . .

In the Labyrinth, a certain type of tree, known as the waranth, bears a particularly luscious and nourishing fruit. Those who pick the fruit, however, run the risk of being stabbed by the poisoned thorns surrounding it. Attacking the flesh left necessarily unprotected by the runes, the thorns burrow deep, seeking blood. If allowed to get into the blood stream, the poison can kill. Therefore, although the thorns are barbed and rip flesh coming out, they must be extracted immediately—at the cost of considerable pain.

Haplo had thought he'd extracted the thorn. He was surprised to find it still hurt him, its poison was still in his system.

"I don't think you'd want my people's ceremony." His voice grated, the furrowed brows shadowed his eyes. "Would you like to hear our vows? 'My life for your life. My death for your life.

My life for your death. My death for your death.' Do you really want to take those?"

Rega paled. "What—what does it mean? I don't understand."

" 'My life for your life.' That means that while we live, we share the joy of living with each other. 'My death for your life.' I would be willing to lay down my life to save yours. 'My life for your death.' I will spend my life avenging your death, if I can't prevent it. 'My death for your death.' A part of me will die, when you do."

"It's not . . . very romantic," Paithan admitted.

"Neither's the place I come from."

"I guess I'd like to think about it," said Rega, not looking at the elf.

"Yes, I suppose we better," Paithan added, more soberly.

The two left the bridge, this time they weren't holding hands. Zifnab, looking after them fondly, dabbed at his eyes with the end of his beard.

"Love makes the world go round!" he said happily.

"Not *this* world," replied Haplo with a quiet smile. "Does it, old man?"

CHAPTER ♦ 33

DRAGON

STAR

♦

"I DON'T KNOW WHAT YOU'RE TALKING ABOUT," SNORTED ZIFNAB AND started to walk off the bridge.

"Yes, you do." Haplo's hand closed over the wizard's thin, brittle arm. "You see, I know where we're going and I've got a pretty clear idea of what we're going to find when we get there. And you, old man, are in for a hell of a lot of trouble."

A fiery eye peered suddenly in the window, glaring ominously. "What have you done now?" demanded the dragon.

"Nothing. Everything's under control!" Zifnab protested.

"*Under* appears to be the operative word! I just want you to know, I'm getting extremely hungry." The dragon's eye closed and vanished. Haplo felt the ship shudder, the dragon's coils closing around it ominously.

Zifnab crumpled, the thin frame caved in on itself. He gave the dragon a nervous glance. "Did you notice—he didn't say, 'sir.' A bad sign. A very bad sign."

Haplo grunted. All he needed was an enraged dragon. Furious shouting had erupted from down below, followed by a crash, a thud, and a scream. "My guess is that they've announced the wedding plans."

"Oh, dear." Removing his hat, Zifnab began to twist it between trembling fingers and shot Haplo a pleading glance. "What am I going to do?"

"Maybe I can help you. Tell me who you are, what you are. Tell me about the 'stars.' Tell me about the Sartan."

Zifnab mulled it over, then his eyes narrowed. He lifted a bony finger, jabbed it in Haplo's chest.

"Mine to know. Yours to find out. So there!" Chin jutting, he smiled benignly at the Patryn and gave a brief, sharp chuckle. Jamming his maltreated hat back on his head, the old man patted Haplo solicitously on the arm and tottered off the bridge.

Haplo stood staring, wondering why he hadn't ripped off the old man's head—hat and all. Scowling, the Patryn rubbed the place on his chest where the wizard's finger had rested, trying to rid himself of the touch.

"Just wait, old man, until we reach the star."

"Our wedding was supposed to bring everyone together!" said Rega, wiping away tears of frustration and anger. "I can't think what's gotten into Roland!"

"Do you want to go through with it?" Paithan asked, massaging a bump on the brow.

Both stared dismally around the crew's quarters. Blood spattered the floor. Haplo had not appeared to break this one up, and numerous humans and elves had been carried feet first from the cabin. In a corner, Lenthan Quindiniar stood staring out a porthole at the brightly shining star that seemed to grow larger every cycle. The elf had never appeared to notice the altercation raging around him.

Rega thought a moment, then sighed. "If we could just get our people to join together again! Like they were after the tytans attacked!"

"I'm not sure that's possible. Hatred and mistrust has been building for thousands of years. The two of us aren't likely to have any effect on that."

"You mean you don't want to get married?" Rega's dusky skin flushed, the dark eyes glinted through her tears.

"Yes, of course, I do! But I was thinking about those vows. Maybe now's not the time—"

"And maybe what Roland said about you was right! You're a spoiled brat who's never done an honest cycle's work in your life! And on top of that you're a coward and— Oh, Paithan! I'm sorry!" Rega threw her arms around him, nestled her head on his chest.

"I know." Paithan ran his hand through the long, shimmering hair. "I said a few things to your brother I'm not exactly proud of."

"The words just came out, from some ugly part inside me! It's like you said, the hate's been there for so long!"

"We'll have to be patient with each other. And with them." Paithan glanced out the porthole. The star shone serenely, with a pure, cold light. "Maybe in this new world we'll find everyone living together in peace. Maybe then the others will see and understand. But I'm still not certain getting married's the right thing to do now. What do you think, Father?"

Paithan turned to Lenthan Quindiniar, staring raptly out the porthole at the star.

"Father?"

Eyes vacant, shining with the star's light, Lenthan glanced around vaguely at his son. "What, my boy?"

"Do you think we should be married?"

"I think . . . I think we should wait and ask your mother." Lenthan sighed happily, and gazed back out the porthole. "We'll see her, when we reach the star."

Drugar had not been involved in the fight. He was not involved in anything on board the ship. The others, immersed in their own troubles, ignored the dwarf. Huddled in his corner, terrified by the idea that they were higher than the clouds above his beloved ground, the dwarf tried to use his lust for vengeance to burn away the fear. But the fire of his hate had dwindled to coals.

They saved your life. The enemy you swore to kill saved your life at the risk of their own.

"I swore an oath, on the bodies of my people, to kill those who were responsible for their deaths." Feeling the flames die, feeling himself cold without their comforting blaze, the dwarf stoked the furnace of his rage. "These three knew the tytans were coming to destroy us! They knew! And they conspired together, took our money, and then deliberately kept their weapons from reaching my people! They wanted us to be destroyed! I should have killed them when I had the chance."

It had been a mistake, not murdering them in the tunnels. The fire had burned bright within him. But they would have died without the knowledge of their own terrible losses, they would have died peacefully. No, he shouldn't second-guess himself. It was better this way. They would arrive on this star of theirs, they would think that all was going to end happily.

Instead, it would end.

"They saved my life. So what? It only proves what fools they are! I saved their lives first. We're even now. I owe them nothing, nothing! Drakar is wise, the *god* watches over me. He has held back my hand, prevented me from striking until the time is right." The dwarf's fingers clenched over the bone handle of his knife. "When we reach the star."

"So, are you going to go through with this farce? Are you going marry the elf?"

"No," said Rega.

Roland smiled grimly. "Good. You thought over what I said. I knew you'd come to your senses!"

"We're only postponing the wedding! Until we reach the star. Maybe by then *you'll* have come to your senses!"

"We'll see," muttered Roland, trying clumsily to wrap a bandage around his split and bleeding knuckles. "We'll see."

"Here, let me do that." His sister took over. "What do you mean? I don't like the way you look."

"No, you'd prefer it if I had slanted eyes and soft little hands and skin the color of milk!" Roland snatched his hand away. "Get out of here. You stink of them! Elves! They trick you into loving them, wanting them! And all the time they're laughing at you!"

"What are you talking about?" Rega stared at her brother, amazed. "Tricking us? If anything I tricked Paithan into loving me, not the other way around! And, Thillia knows, no one's laughing on this ship—"

"Oh, yeah?" Roland kept his eyes averted from his sister. He spoke the next words below his breath, to her back. "We'll deal with the elves. Just wait until we reach the star."

Aleatha wiped her hand across her mouth, for the twentieth time. The kiss was like the stench of the bilge that seemed to cling to everything—her clothes, her hair, her skin. She couldn't get the taste and the touch of the human off her lips.

"Let me see your hands," said Paithan.

"Why should you care?" Aleatha demanded, but allowing her brother to examine her cracked, bleeding and blistered palms. "You didn't defend me. You took their part, all because of that little whore! You let that man drag me off to that hellhole!"

"I don't think I could have stopped Haplo from taking you," said Paithan quietly. "From the look on his face, I think you were lucky he didn't throw you off the ship."

"I wish he had. It would be better to be dead! Like My Lord and . . . and Callie . . ." Aleatha hung her head, tears choked her. "What kind of life is this!" She clutched at the skirt of her tattered and torn, dirty and stained dress, shook it, sobbing. "We're living in filth like humans! No wonder we're sinking to their level! Animals!"

"Thea, don't say that. You don't understand them." Paithan sought to comfort her. Aleatha shoved him away.

"What do you know? You're blinded by lust!" Aleatha wiped her hand across her lips. "Ugh! Savages! I hate them! I hate all of them! No, don't come near me. You're no better than they are now, Paithan."

"You better get used to it, Thea," said her brother, irritated. "One of them's going to be your sister."

"Hah!" Raising her head, Aleatha fixed him with a cold stare, her mouth pursed—prim and tight. Her resemblance to her older sister was suddenly frightening. "Not me! If you marry that whore, I have no brother. I will never see you or speak to you again!"

"You can't mean that, Thea. We're all each of us has left. Father. You've seen Father. He's . . . he's not well."

"He's insane. And it's going to get worse when we reach this 'star' you've dragged us off to and Mother's not there to greet him! It will kill him, most likely. And whatever happens to him will be all your fault!"

"I did what I thought was best." The elf's face was pale, his voice, in spite of himself, trembled and broke.

Aleatha gave him a remorseful look, reached up and smoothed back his hair with gentle fingers. She drew near him. "You're right. All we have now is each other, Pait. Let's keep it that way. Stay with me. Don't go back to that human. She's just toying with you. You know how human men are. I mean"—she flushed—"I mean, you know how their women are. When we reach the star, we'll start our lives all over again.

"We'll take care of Papa and we'll live happily. Maybe there'll be other elves there. Rich elves, richer than any in Equilan. And they'll have magnificent houses and they'll welcome us to their homes. And the nasty, savage humans can crawl back into their jungle." She rested her head on her brother's chest. Drying her tears, she drew her hand, once again, across her mouth.

Paithan said nothing, but let his sister dream. When we reach the star, he thought. What will happen to us when we reach the star?

The mensch took Haplo's threat about the ship falling out of the skies seriously. An uneasy peace descended on the ship—a peace differing from war only in that it was less noisy and no blood was shed. If looks and wishes had been weapons, however, hardly anyone aboard would have been left alive.

Humans and elves pointedly ignored each other's existence. Rega and Paithan kept apart, either acting wisely, out of mutual consent, or because the barriers being erected by their people were becoming too thick and too high for them to surmount. The occasional fight broke out among the more hotheaded of the youth and was halted quickly by their elders. But the promise was in the eyes, if not on the lips, that it would be only a matter of time.

"When we reach the star . . ."

There was no more talk of a wedding.

CHAPTER ♦ 34

THE

STAR

♦

A SHARP BARK, WARNING OF AN INTRUDER, BROUGHT HAPLO TO HIS feet, waking him out of a deep sleep. His body and instincts were fully awake, if his mind wasn't. Haplo slammed the visitor against the hull, pinned him across the chest with one arm, clamped his fingers on the man's jaw.

"One twist of my wrist and I break your neck!"

A gasp of breath, the body beneath Haplo's went rigid as a corpse.

Haplo blinked the sleep from his eyes, saw who his captive was. Slowly, he released his grip. "Don't try slipping up on me again, elf. It's not conducive to a long and healthy life."

"I . . . I didn't mean to!" Paithan massaged his bruised jaw, darting wary glances at Haplo and the growling, bristling dog.

"Hush." Haplo stroked the animal. "It's all right."

The dog's growls lessened, but it continued to keep an eye on the elf. Haplo stretched to ease the kinks in his muscles and walked over to look out the window. He paused, staring, and whistled softly.

"That's . . . that's what I came up here to ask you about." The shaken elf left the hull, detoured warily around the watchful dog, and cautiously approached the window.

Outside, everything had disappeared, swallowed up in what appeared to be a blanket of thick, moist wool pressed against the glass. Beads of water rolled down the panes and glistened on the scales of the dragon, whose body hugged the ship.

"What is it?" Paithan tried hard to keep his voice calm. "What's happened to the star?"

"It's still there. In fact, we're close. Very close. This is a rain cloud, that's all."

The elf exhaled in relief. "Rain clouds! Just like our old world!"

"Yeah," said Haplo. "Just like your old world."

The ship descended, the clouds flew past in wispy shreds, the rain streaked across the window in long rivulets. Then the cloud cover drifted past, *Dragon Star* plunged into sunlight once again. Land could be seen clearly below.

The runes on the hull that had been glowing, monitoring air and pressure and gravity, slowly faded out. The mensch pressed close to the portholes, their gazes fixed eagerly on the ground rolling beneath them.

The old man was nowhere to be found.

Haplo listened to the conversations being carried around him, he watched the expression on the faces of the mensch.

First—joy. The voyage was over, they had reached the star safely. Second—relief. Lush green forests, lakes, seas, similar to home.

The ship sailed nearer. A tremor of confusion passed among the mensch—brows contracted, lips parted. They leaned closer, pressing their faces flat against the panes. Eyes widened.

At last—realization, understanding.

Paithan returned to the bridge. Delicate crimson stained the elf's pale cheeks. He pointed out the window.

"What's going on? This *is* our world!"

"And there," said Haplo, "is your star."

Light welled up from out the variegated greens of moss and jungle. Brilliant, bright, white, pulsating, the light hurt the eyes—it was truly like staring into a sun. But it wasn't a sun, it wasn't a star. The light slowly began to dim and fade, even as they watched. A shadow moved across its surface and they could see, at last, when the shadow had nearly covered it, the light's source.

"A city!" Haplo murmured in astonishment, in his own language. Not only that, but there was something familiar about it!

The light winked out, the city disappeared into darkness.

"What is it?" Paithan demanded, hoarsely.

Haplo shrugged, irritated at the interruption. He needed to think, he needed to get a closer look at that city. "I'm just the pilot. Why don't you go ask the old man."

The elf shot the Patryn a suspicious glance. Haplo ignored him, concentrated on his flying. "I'll look for a clear place to land."

"Maybe we shouldn't land. Maybe there's tytans—"

A possibility. Haplo would have to deal with that when the time came. "We're landing," he stated.

Paithan sighed, stared back out the window. "Our own world!" he said bitterly. Putting his hands against the glass, he leaned against the panes and gazed out at the trees and mossy landscape that seemed to be leaping up to grab him and pull him down. "How could this have happened? We've traveled all this time! Maybe we veered off course? Flew in a circle?"

"You saw the star shining in the sky. We flew straight as an arrow, right to it. Go ask Zifnab what happened."

"Yes." The elf's face was strained, grim, resolute. "You're right. I'll go ask the old man."

Haplo saw the dragon's body, visible outside the window, contract. A shudder passed through the ship. A fiery red eye peered for a brief instant in the window, then suddenly the body uncoiled.

The frame shook, the ship listed precariously. Haplo clung to the steering stone for support. The ship righted itself, sailed gracefully downward, a heavy weight lifted. The dragon was gone.

Staring down, watching for a landing site, Haplo thought he caught a glimpse of a massive green body punging into the jungle, he was too preoccupied with his own problems at the moment to notice where. The trees were thick and tangled; the patches of moss were few. Haplo scanned the area below, trying to see through the strange darkness that appeared to emanate from the city, as if it had cast a gigantic shadow over the land.

That was impossible, however. To create night, the suns would have had to have disappeared. And the suns were right above them, their position fixed, unchanging. Light shone on *Dragon Star*, glistened off the wings, beamed in the window. Directly below the ship, all was dark.

Angry accusations, a shrill protest, and a cry of pain—the old man. Haplo smiled, shrugged again. He'd found a clear spot, large enough for the ship, close to the city, but not too close.

Haplo brought *Dragon Star* down. Tree branches reached out for them, snapped off. Leaves whipped past the window. The ship landed belly first on the moss. The impact, from the sounds of it, knocked everyone below off their feet.

The Patryn looked out into pitch darkness.

They had reached the star.

Haplo had marked the location of the city in his mind before the ship set down, determining the direction he would need to travel to reach it. Working as swiftly as possible in the darkness, not daring to risk a light, he wrapped up a bite of food and filled a skin with water. Scrip packed, Haplo gave a low whistle. The dog leapt to its feet, padded over to stand near its master.

The Patryn moved stealthily to the hatchway leading off the bridge and listened. The only sounds he heard were panicked voices coming from the mensch's quarters. No one breathing softly in the passageway, no one spying. Not that he expected it. Darkness had swallowed the ship whole, sending most of the passengers—who had never viewed such a phenomenon—from rage into terror. Right now they were venting their fear and fury by yelling at the old man. But it wouldn't be long before the mensch came traipsing up to Haplo, demanding explanations, answers, solutions.

Salvation.

Moving silently, Haplo crossed over to the ship's hull. Resting the scrip on the floor, he laid his hands upon the wooden planks. The runes on his skin began to glow red and blue, the flame running along his fingers, extending to the wood. The planks shimmered and slowly began to dissolve. A large hole, wide enough for a man, opened up.

Haplo shouldered the supplies, stepped onto the moss embankment on which he landed. The dog jumped out after him, tagging along at its master's heels. Behind them, the red-blue glow enveloping the hull faded, the wood returned to its original form.

The Patryn crossed the open mossy area swiftly, losing himself in the darkness. He heard enraged shouts in two languages, human and elven. The words were different, but their meaning was the same—death for the wizard.

Haplo grinned. The mensch seemed to have found something to unite them at last.

"Haplo, we— Haplo?" Paithan groped his way onto the bridge into the darkness, came to a dead stop. The runes' glow faded slowly; by its light, he could see the bridge was vacant.

Roland burst through the hatch, shoving the elf aside. "Haplo, we've decided to dump the old man, then leave this— Haplo? Where is he?" he demanded, glaring at Paithan accusingly.

"*I* haven't made off with him, if that's what you're thinking. He's gone . . . and the dog, too."

"I knew it! Haplo and Zifnab are in on this together! They tricked us into coming to this awful place! And you fell for it!"

"You were welcome to stay back in Equilan. I'm sure the tytans would have been pleased to entertain you."

Frustrated, angry, feeling an unaccountable guilt that somehow this *was* his fault, Paithan stared gloomily at the runes glimmering on the wooden planks. "That's how he did it, obviously. More of his magic. I wish I knew who or what he was."

"We'll get answers out of him."

Blue light flickered on Roland's clenched fists and scowling features. Paithan looked at the human, and laughed. "If we ever see him again. If we ever see *anything* again! This is worse than being down in the dwarven tunnels."

"Paithan?" Rega's voice called. "Roland?"

"Here, Sis."

Rega crept onto the bridge, clutched at her brother's outstretched hand. "Did you tell him? Are we going to leave?"

"He's not here. He's gone."

"And left us here . . . in the dark!"

"Shhh, calm down."

The light of the sigla was fading. The three could see each other only by a faint blue glow that grew dim, flickered briefly to life, dimmed again. The magical light glittered in sunken, fearful eyes and emphasized drawn, fear-strained mouths.

Paithan and Roland each avoided the other's direct gaze, darted suspicious glances when the other wasn't looking.

"The old man says this darkness will pass in half a cycle," Paithan muttered at last, defiant, defensive.

"He also said we were going to a new world!" Roland retorted. "C'mon, Rega, let me take you back—"

"Paithan!" Aleatha's frantic voice tore through the darkness. Lunging onto the bridge, she grasped at her brother just as the sigla's light failed, leaving them blind.

"Paithan! Father's gone! *And* the old man!"

The four stood outside the ship, staring into the jungle. It was light again, the strange darkness had lifted, and it was easy to see the path someone—Lenthan, Zifnab, Haplo, or maybe all three—had taken. Vines had been severed by the sharp blade of a bladewood sword, huge durnau leaves, cut from their stalks, lay limply on the mossy ground.

Aleatha wrung her hands. "It's all my fault! We landed in this horrible place and Papa began babbling about Mother being here and where was she and what was taking so long and on and on. I . . . I shouted at him, Paithan. I couldn't stand it anymore! I left him alone!"

"Don't cry, Thea. It's not your fault. I should have been with him. I should have known. I'll go after him."

"I'm going with you."

Paithan started to refuse, looked into his sister's tear-streaked, pale face and changed his mind. He nodded wearily. "All right. Don't worry, Thea. He can't have gone very far. You better fetch some water."

Aleatha hastened back onto the ship. Paithan walked over to Roland, who was carefully scrutinizing the ground near the fringes of the jungle, searching for tracks. Rega, tense and sorrowful, stood near her brother. Her eyes sought Paithan's, but the elf refused to meet her gaze.

"You find anything?"

"Not a trace."

"Haplo and Zifnab must have left together. But why take my father?"

Roland straightened, glanced around. "I don't know. But I don't like it. Something's wrong with this place. I thought the land near Thurn was wild! It was a king's garden compared to this!"

Tangled vines and tree limbs were so thickly massed and intertwined that they might have formed the thatched roof of a gigantic hut. A gray, sullen light struggled through the vegetation. The air was oppressive and humid, tainted with the smell of rot and decay. The heat was intense. And though the jungle must be teeming with life, Roland, listening closely, couldn't hear a sound. The silence might be amazement at the sight of the ship, it might be something far more ominous.

"I don't know about you, elf, but I don't want to stay around here any longer than necessary."

"I think we can all agree on that," said Paithan quietly.

Roland cast him a narrow-eyed glance. "What about the dragon?"

"It's gone.

"You hope!"

Paithan shook his head. "I don't know what we can do about it if it isn't." He was bitter, tired.

"We're coming with you." Rega's face was wet with sweat, her damp hair clung to her skin. She was shivering.

"That's not necessary."

"Yes, it is!" Roland said coldly. "For all I know you and the old man and the tattooed wonder are in this together. I don't want you flying off, leaving us stranded."

Paithan's face paled with anger, his eyes flashed. He opened his mouth, caught Rega's pleading gaze, and snapped his lips shut on the words. Shrugging, he muttered, "Suit yourself," and walked over to the ship to wait for his sister.

Aleatha emerged from the ship, lugging a waterskin. Her once gaily billowing skirts hung tattered and limp around her lithe figure. She had tied the cook's shawl around her shoulders, her arms were bare. Roland looked down at the white feet covered by thin, worn slippers.

"You can't go into the jungle dressed like that!"

He saw the woman's eyes go to the shadows thickening around the trees, to the vines that twisted like snakes over the ground. Her hands twisted over the leather handle of the waterskin. She clutched it tightly, her chin lifted.

"I don't recall asking your opinion, human."

"Fool bitch!" Roland snarled.

She had guts, he had to give her that. Drawing his blade, he charged into the undergrowth, hacking furiously at the vines and heart-shaped leaves that seemed the very embodiment of his admiration and desire for this maddening female.

"Rega, are you coming?"

Rega hesitated, looked behind her at Paithan. The elf shook his head. Can't you understand? Our love has been a mistake. All, a terrible mistake.

Shoulders slumping, Rega followed her brother.

Paithan sighed, turned to his sister.

"The human's right, you know. It could be dangerous and—"

"I'm going after Father," said Aleatha, and by the tilt of her head and the glint in her eye, her brother knew it was useless to argue. He took the waterskin from her, slung it over his shoulder. The two hurried into the jungle, moving swiftly, as if to outwalk their fear.

Drugar stood in the hatchway, whetting his knife against the wood. The heavy-footed dwarves are clumsy when it comes to stalking prey. Drugar knew it was impossible for him to sneak up on anything. He would let his victims get a long head start before he went in after them.

CHAPTER ♦ 35

SOMEWHERE ON

PRYAN

♦

"I WAS RIGHT. IT *IS* THE SAME! WHAT DOES IT MEAN? WHAT DOES IT ALL mean?"

Before him stood a city crafted of starlight. At least, that's how it appeared until Haplo drew closer. Its radiant beauty was incredible. He might not have believed in it, might have feared it was a trick of a mind gone stir-crazy from being cooped up with the mensch for lord knew how long. Except that he had seen it all before.

Only not here. In the Nexus.

But there was a difference, a difference that Haplo found grimly ironic. The city in the Nexus was dark—a star, perhaps, whose light had died. Or had never been born.

"What do you think, dog?" he said, patting the animal's head. "It's the same, isn't it? Same exactly."

The city was built up off the jungle floor, rising from behind an enormous wall, rising taller than the tallest trees. A towering, pillared, crystal spire balanced on a dome formed of marble arches stood in the city's center. The top of the spire must be one of the highest points in this world, thought Haplo, gazing up. It was from this center spire that the light beamed most brightly. The Patryn could barely look at it for the dazzling gleam. Here, in the spire, the light had been deliberately concentrated, sent beaming out into the sky.

"Like the light of a guide fire," he said to the dog. "Only who or what is it supposed to be guiding?"

The animal glanced about uneasily, not interested. The skin

of its neck twitched, causing the dog to lift its hind leg and start to scratch, only to decide that maybe the itch wasn't the problem. The dog didn't know what the problem was. It knew only that there was one. It whined, and Haplo petted it to keep it still.

The center spire was framed by four other spires, duplicates of the first, and stood on the platform holding the dome. On a level beneath that, stood eight more identical spires. Gigantic marble steppes lifted up from behind these spires. Similar to land steppes that had undoubtedly been their models, they supported buildings and dwelling places. And finally, at each end of the guard wall stood another pillar. If this city was built on the same plan as the city in the Nexus—and Haplo had no reason to think otherwise—there would be four such pillars, located at the cardinal direction points.

Haplo continued on through the jungle, the dog trotting along at his heels. Both moved easily and silently amid the tangled undergrowth, leaving no trace of their passage except the faint, swiftly fading glow of runes on the leaves.

And then the jungle ended, abruptly, as if someone had plowed it under. Ahead, drenched in bright sunlight, a path cut into jagged rock. Keeping to the shadows of the trees, Haplo leaned out, put his hand on the stone. It was real, hard, gritty, warm from the sun, not an illusion as he had first suspected.

"A mountain. They built the city on the top of a mountain." He gazed upward, saw the path snake across the rock.

The trail was smooth, clearly marked, and anyone walking it would be highly visible to eyes watching from the city walls.

Haplo took a swig of water from the skin, shared it with the dog, and gazed thoughtfully, intently, at the city. The Patryn thought back to the crude homes of the mensch, made of wood, perched in trees.

"There's no question. The Sartan built this. And they may be up there now. We may be walking into a couple of thousand of them."

He bent down, examined the path, though he knew it was a futile gesture. Wind whistling mournfully through the boulders would blow away any trace he might have found of people passing.

Haplo took out the bandages he had stuffed into a pocket and began to wind them slowly and deliberately around his hands. "Not that this disguise will do us much good," he advised the dog, who appeared disturbed at the thought. "Back on Arianus, that Sartan who called himself Albert caught onto us quickly enough. But we were careless, weren't we, boy?"

The dog didn't seem to think so, but decided not to argue.

"Here, we'll be more alert."

Haplo hefted the waterskin, stepped out of the jungle and onto the rock-strewn path that wound among boulders and a few scrubby pine trees clinging tenaciously to the sides. He blinked in the brilliant sunlight, then started forward.

"Just a couple of travelers, aren't we, boy? A couple of travelers . . . who saw their light."

"It's quite kind of you to come with me," said Lenthan Quindiniar.

"Tut, tut. Think nothing of it," answered Zifnab.

"I don't believe I could have made it alone. You have a really remarkable way of moving through the jungle. It's almost as if the trees step aside when they see you coming."

"More like they *run* when they see him coming," boomed a voice from far below the moss.

"That'll be enough from you!" growled Zifnab, glaring down, stomping at the ground with his foot.

"I'm getting extremely hungry."

"Not now. Come back in an hour."

"Humpf." Something large slithered through the undergrowth.

"Was that the dragon?" Lenthan asked, looking slightly worried. "He won't harm her, will he? If they should happen to meet?"

"No, no," said Zifnab, peering about. "He's under my control. Nothing to fear. Absolutely nothing. You didn't happen to notice which way he went? Not that it matters." The old man nodded, beard wagging. "Under my control. Yes. Absolutely." He glanced nervously over his shoulder.

The two men sat, resting, on the branches of an ancient tree, overgrown with moss, that stood in a cool, shady clearing, sheltered from the sweltering sun.

"And thank you for bringing me to this star. I truly appreciate it," continued Lenthan. He looked about him in quiet satisfaction, hands resting on his knees, gazing at the twisted trees and clinging vines and flitting shadows. "Do you think she's far from here? I'm feeling rather tired."

Zifnab observed Lenthan, smiled gently. His voice softened. "No, not far, my friend." The old man patted Lenthan's pale, wasted hand. "Not far. In fact, I don't think we need travel any farther. I think she will come to us."

"How wonderful!" A flush of color crept into the elf's pallid cheeks. He stood up, searching eagerly, but almost immediately sank back down. The color in the cheeks faded, leaving them gray and waxy. He gasped for air. Zifnab put his arm around the elf's shoulders, held him comfortingly.

Lenthan drew a shivering breath, attempted a smile. "I shouldn't have stood up so fast. Made me extremely dizzy." He paused, then added, "I do believe I'm dying."

Zifnab patted Lenthan's hand. "There, there, old chap. No need to jump to conclusions. Just one of your bad spells, that's all. It will pass . . ."

"No, please. Don't lie to me." Lenthan smiled wanly. "I'm ready. I've been lonely, you see. Very lonely."

The old man dabbed at his eyes with the tip of his beard. "You won't be lonely again, my friend. Not ever again."

Lenthan nodded, then sighed.

"It's just that I'm so weak. I'll need my strength to travel with her when she comes. Would . . . would you mind terribly if I leaned up against your shoulder? Just for a little while? Until everything stops spinning around?"

"I know just how you feel," said Zifnab. "Confounded ground won't stay put like it did when we were young. I blame a lot of it on modern technology. Nuclear reactors."

The old man settled back against the tree's broad trunk, the elf leaned his head on the wizard's shoulder. Zifnab prattled on, something about quarks. Lenthan liked the sound of the old man's voice, though he wasn't listening to the words. A smile on his lips, he watched the shadows patiently and waited for his wife.

"Now what do we do?" Roland demanded, glaring at Aleatha in anger. He gestured ahead of them, at the murky water that blocked that path. "I told you she shouldn't have come, elf. We'll have to leave her behind."

"No one's leaving me behind!" returned Aleatha, but she hung back behind the others, taking care not to get too near the dark, stagnant pool. She spoke her own tongue, but she understood the humans. The elves and humans might have spent their time on board ship fighting, but at least they'd learned to insult each other in each other's language.

"Maybe there's a way around it," said Paithan.

"If there is"—Rega wiped sweat from her face—"it'll take us days to cut through the jungle to find it! I don't know how those old men are making it through this tangle so swiftly."

"Magic," muttered Roland. "And it was probably magic got them over this filthy water. It's not going to help us, though. We'll have to wade it or swim it."

"Swim!" Aleatha recoiled, shuddering.

Roland said nothing, but he flashed her a glance—and that glance said it all. Pampered, spoiled brat . . .

Tossing her hair, Aleatha ran forward and, before Paithan could stop her, waded into the pond.

She sank to her shins. The water spread out in sullen, oily ripples—ripples suddenly parted by a sinuous shape sliding rapidly on top of the water toward the elf woman.

"Snake!" Roland cried, plunging into the water in front of Aleatha, slashing wildly with his raztar.

Paithan dragged Aleatha back onto the bank. Roland fought furiously, churning up the water. Losing sight of his prey, he stopped, staring around.

"Where did it go? Do you see it?"

"I think it went over there, into the reeds." Rega pointed.

Roland clamored out, keeping a sharp watch, his raztar ready. "You idiot!" He could barely speak for rage. "It could have been poisonous! You nearly got yourself killed!"

Aleatha stood shivering in her wet clothes, her face deathly pale, gaze defiant. "You're not . . . leaving me behind," she said, barely able to talk for her chattering teeth. "If you can cross . . . so can I!"

"We're wearing leather boots, leather clothes! We have a chance— Oh, what's the use!" Grabbing hold of Aleatha, Roland lifted her—gasping and spluttering—in his arms.

"Put me down!" Aleatha squirmed, kicked. She spoke human inadvertently, without thinking.

"Not yet. I'll wait until I reach the middle," muttered Roland, wading into the water.

Aleatha stared into the water, remembering, and shuddered. Her hands stole around his neck, clasping him closely. "You won't, will you?" she said, clinging to him.

Roland glanced at the face so near his. The purple eyes, wide with terror, were dark as wine and far more intoxicating. Her hair floated around him, tickling his skin. Her body was light in his arms, warm and trembling. Love flashed through him, surging in his blood, more painful than any poison the snake might have inflicted.

"No," he said, his voice harsh from being forced past the ache of desire constricting his throat. His grip on her tightened.

Paithan and Rega waded in after them.

"What was that?" Rega gasped and whirled around.

"Fish, I think," said Paithan, moving swiftly to her. He took her arm and Rega smiled up at him, hopeful.

The elf's face was grave, solemn, offering her protection, nothing more. Rega's smile waned. They continued the crossing in silence, both keeping their gaze fixed on the water. The pond, fortunately, wasn't deep, coming no higher than their knees at the middle point. Reaching the opposite bank, Roland climbed out, deposited Aleatha on the ground.

He had started to continue down the path, when he felt a timid touch on his arm.

"Thank you," said Aleatha.

The words were difficult for her to say. Not because they were in human, but because she found it hard to talk around this man, who roused such pleasing and such confusing emotions in her. Her gaze went to his sweetly curved lips, she recalled his kiss and the fire that swept through her body. She wondered if it would happen a second time. He was standing quite near her now. She had only to move closer, not even half a step. . . .

Then she remembered. He hated her, despised her. She heard his words: *I hope you rot here . . . fool bitch . . . little idiot.* His kiss had been an insult, mockery.

Roland looked into the pale face turned up to his, saw it freeze in disdain. His own desire changed to ice in his bowels. "Don't mention it, elf. After all, what are we humans but your slaves?"

He strode off, plunging into the jungle. Aleatha came after. Her brother and Rega walked apart, separate and alone, behind. Each one of the four was unhappy. Each was disappointed. Each had the resentful, angry idea that if only the *other* would say something— anything—then everything would be put right. Each had determined, however, that it was not his or her place to speak first.

The silence between them grew until it seemed to become a living entity, keeping company at their side. Its presence was so powerful that, when Paithan thought he heard a sound behind them—a sound as of heavy boots wading through water—he kept quiet, refusing to mention it to the others.

CHAPTER ♦ 36

SOMEWHERE,

PRYAN

♦

HAPLO AND THE DOG WALKED UP THE PATH. THE PATRYN KEPT CLOSE watch on the city walls, but saw no one. He listened carefully, and heard nothing except the sighing of the wind through the rocks, like a whispering breath. He was alone upon the sun-baked mountainside.

The path led him straight to a large metal door formed in the shape of a hexagon and inscribed with runes—the city's gate. Smooth white marble walls towered high above him. Ten of his people could have stood on each other's shoulders and the top-most person would not have been able to see over the wall's edge. He put his hand on it. The marble was slick, polished to a high finish. A spider would have difficulty climbing up the side. The city's gate was sealed shut. The magic guarding it and the walls made the sigla on Haplo's body crawl and itch. The Sartan were in absolute control. No one could enter their city without their permission and knowledge.

"Hail the guard!" shouted Haplo, craning his neck, peering up to the top of the walls.

His own words came back to him.

The dog, disturbed by the eerie sound of its master's echo, threw back its head and howled. The mournful wail reverberated from the walls, disconcerting even Haplo, who laid a quieting hand on the dog's head. He listened when the echoes died, but heard nothing.

He had little doubt now. The city was empty, abandoned.

Haplo thought about a world where the sun shone constantly and the impact of this new world on those accustomed to regular periods of day and night. He thought about the elves and humans, perched in trees like birds, and the dwarves, burrowing into the moss, desperate for a reminder of their subterranean homes. He thought about the tytans and their horrible, pathetic search.

He looked back at the slick and gleaming walls, resting his hand against the marble wall. It was oddly cool, beneath the glaring sun. Cool and hard and impenetrable, like the past to those who had been shut out of paradise. He didn't understand completely. The light, for example. It was much like the Kicksey-winsey on Arianus. What was its purpose? Why was it there? He had solved that mystery—or rather, it had been solved for him. He felt certain he would solve the mystery of the stars of Pryan. He was, after all, about to enter one.

Haplo glanced back at the hexagonal gate. He recognized the rune structure embossed on its shining silver frontage. One rune was missing. Supply that sigil, and the gate would swing open. It was a simple construct, elementary Sartan magic. They had not gone to a lot of trouble. Why should they? No one but the Sartan knew the rune-magic.

Well, almost no one.

Haplo ran his hand up and down the smooth-sided wall. He knew Sartan magic, he could open the gate. He preferred not to, however. Using their rune structures made him feel clumsy and inept, like a child tracing sigla in the dust. Besides, it would give him great satisfaction to break through these supposedly impenetrable walls using his own magic. Patryn magic. The magic of the Sartan's bitter enemies.

Lifting his hands, placing his fingers on the marble, Haplo began to draw the runes.

"Hush."

"I wasn't saying anything."

"No, I mean hold still. I think I hear something."

The four ceased all movement, freezing in place, ceasing to breathe. The jungle, too, held still. No breeze stirred the leaves, no animal slithered past, no bird called. At first they heard nothing. The silence was heavy, oppressive as the heat. The shadows of the thick trees gathered around them, more than one shivered, wiped cold sweat from their foreheads.

And then they heard a voice.

"And so I said to George, 'George,' I said, 'the third movie was a bummer. Cute little furry things. Those of us with any sense had a wild desire to have them all stuffed—' "

"Wait," came another voice, rather timid and weak. "Did you hear something?" The voice grew more excited. "Yes, I think I did. I think she's coming!"

"Father!" cried Aleatha, and dashed headlong down the path.

The others followed and burst into the clearing; the elf and the two humans with weapons drawn and ready. They came to a halt, looking and feeling rather foolish at finding nothing more dangerous than the old human and the middle-aged elf.

"Father!" Aleatha made a dart toward Lenthan, only to find her way blocked by the old man.

Zifnab had risen from his seat against the tree and stood before them, his face grave and solemn. Behind him, Lenthan Quindiniar stood with arms outstretched, his face illuminated by a radiance that was not of the flesh, but of the soul.

"My dear Elithenia!" he breathed, taking a step forward. "How lovely you look. Just as I remember!"

The four followed the line of his gaze and saw nothing but dark and shifting shadows.

"Who's he talking to?" asked Roland, in an awed undertone.

Paithan's eyes filled with tears, he bowed his head. Rega, stealing near, took the elf's hand in hers and held on fast.

"Let me past!" cried Aleatha angrily. "He needs me!"

Zifnab put out his arm, grasped her in a firm grip, startling in the seemingly frail old arms.

"No, child. Not anymore."

Aleatha stared at him, wordless, then at her father. Lenthan's arms were open wide, he reached out, as if to grasp the hands of some dear one approaching him.

"It was my rockets, Elithenia," he said with shy pride. "We traveled all this way because of my rockets. I knew you would be here, you see. I could look up into the sky and see you shining above me, pure and bright and steadfast."

"Father," whispered Aleatha.

He didn't hear her, didn't notice her. His hands closed,

grasping convulsively. Joy filled his face, tears of pleasure streamed down his cheeks.

Lenthan drew his empty arms to his chest, clasped the still air, and fell forward onto the moss.

Aleatha broke past Zifnab. Kneeling beside her father, she lifted him in her arms. "I'm sorry, Papa," she said, weeping over him. "I'm sorry!"

Lenthan smiled up at her. "My rockets."

His eyes closed, he sighed, relaxed in his daughter's arms. It seemed to those watching that he had just fallen into a restful sleep.

"Papa, please! I was lonely, too. I didn't know, Papa. I didn't know! But now we'll be together, we'll have each other!"

Paithan gently drew away from Rega, knelt down, lifted Lenthan's limp hand, pressed his fingers over the wrist. He let the hand drop to the ground. Putting his arm around his sister, he held her close.

"It's too late. He can't hear you, Thea." The elf eased the body of his father from his sister's grasp, rested the corpse gently upon the ground. "Poor man. Crazy to the end."

"Crazy?" Zifnab glowered at the elf. "What do you mean crazy? He found his wife among the stars, just as I promised him he would. That's why I brought him here."

"I don't know who's crazier," Paithan muttered.

Aleatha kept her gaze fixed upon her father. She had ceased crying with sudden abruptness, drawn a deep, quivering breath. Wiping her hands across her eyes and nose, she rose to her feet.

"It doesn't matter. Look at him. He's happy, now. He was never happy before, none of us were." Her voice grew bitter. "We should have stayed and died—"

"I am glad you feel that way," said a deep voice. "It will make the end easier."

Drugar stood on the path, his left hand grasping Rega tightly by the arm. The dwarf's right hand held his dagger to the woman's stomach.

"You bastard! Let her go—" Roland took a step forward.

The dwarf thrust the knife's point deeper, making a dark indentation in the woman's soft leather clothing.

"Have you ever seen anyone with a belly wound?" Drugar

glowered round at them. "It's a slow, painful way to die. Especially here, in the jungle, with the insects and the animals . . ."

Rega moaned, trembling in her captor's grip.

"All right." Paithan raised his hands. "What do you want?"

"Put your weapons on the ground."

Roland and the elf did as they were told, tossing the raztar and a bladewood sword onto the path at Drugar's feet. Reaching out with a thick boot, he kicked at the weapons, knocked them back behind him.

"You, old man, no magic," growled the dwarf.

"Me? I wouldn't dream of it," said Zifnab meekly. The ground shook slightly beneath his feet, a worried expression crossed the wizard's face. "Oh, dear. I . . . I don't suppose any of you . . . have seen my dragon?"

"Shut up!" Drugar snarled. Jerking Rega alongside, he entered the clearing. He kept the knife pressed against her, his eyes watching every move. "Over there." He motioned with his head to the tree. "All of you. Now!"

Roland, hands in the air, backed up until he was halted by the trunk. Aleatha found herself pressed up against the human's strong body. Roland took a step forward, moving his body between the dwarf and Aleatha. Paithan joined him, also shielding his sister.

Zifnab stared down at the ground, shaking his head, muttering, "Oh, dear. Oh, dear."

"You, too, old man!" Drugar shouted.

"What?" Zifnab raised his head and blinked. "I say, might I have a word with you?" The wizard tottered forward, head bent confidentially. "I think we're in for a bit of a problem. It's the dragon—"

The knife slashed across Rega's leather pants, slitting them open, revealing her flesh beneath. She gasped and shuddered. The dwarf pressed the dagger's blade against bare skin.

"Get back, old man!" Paithan shouted, panic cracking his voice.

Zifnab regarded Drugar sadly. "Perhaps you're right. I'll just join the others, there, by the tree . . ." The old man shuffled over. Roland grabbed him, nearly hauling him off his feet.

"Now what?" Paithan asked.

"You are all going to die," said Drugar, speaking with an impassive calm that was terrible to hear.

"But why? What did we do?"

"You killed my people."

"You can't blame us!" Rega cried desperately. "It wasn't our fault!"

"With the weapons, we could have stopped them," said Drugar. Froth formed on his lips, his eyes bulged from beneath the black brows. "We could have fought! You kept them from us! You wanted us to die!"

Drugar paused, listening. Something stirred inside, whispering to him. *They kept faith. They brought the weapons. They arrived late, but that wasn't their fault. They didn't know the dire need.*

The dwarf swallowed the saliva that seemed to be choking him. "No!" he cried wildly. "That's wrong! It was done on purpose! They must pay!"

It wouldn't have mattered. It wouldn't have made any difference. Our people were doomed, nothing could have saved them.

"Drakar!" cried the dwarf, raising his head to heaven. The knife shook in his hand. "Don't you see? Without this, I have nothing left!"

"Now!" Roland lunged forward, Paithan moved swiftly behind. Grabbing hold of Rega, the human wrenched his sister free from the dwarf's grip and tossed her across the clearing. Aleatha held the stumbling, shaken Rega in her arms.

Paithan caught hold of Drugar's knife hand, twisted the wrist. Roland snatched the dagger from the clutching fingers, turned it point first, and held the sharp edge against the vein beneath the dwarf's ear.

"I'll see you in hell—"

The ground beneath their feet heaved and shook, tossing them about like the dolls of an irate child. A gigantic head crashed up through the moss, rending trees, ripping vines. Flaring red eyes glared down, gleaming teeth parted, black tongue flicked.

"I was afraid of this!" gasped Zifnab. "The spell's broken. Run! Run for your lives!"

"We can . . . fight!" Paithan groped for his sword, but it was all he could do to try to keep his balance on the quaking moss.

"You can't fight a dragon! Besides, I'm the one he truly wants. Isn't that right?" The old man turned slowly, faced the creature.

"Yes!" hissed the dragon, hatred dripping like venom from its fanged tongue. "Yes, you, old man! Keeping me prisoner, binding me with magic. But not now, not anymore. You're weak, old man. You should never have summoned that elf woman's spirit. And all for what? To tease a dying man."

Desperately, keeping his eyes averted from the terror of the dragon, Zifnab's voice rose in song.

> *In all the times I'd wander,*
> *for rumors I grew fonder*
> *of the man who didn't squander*
> *his good ale or his good cheer.*
> *Says Earl, he is no thinker*
> *but no wisdom there be deeper,*
> *"There's nothing so great in this whole world*
> *like drinkin' addled[1] beer."*

The dragon's head inched nearer. The old wizard glanced up involuntarily, saw the fiery eyes, and faltered.

> *I've been roamin' five and . . . er . . .*
> Let's see. *I've seen war and king and . . . uh . . .*
> *Da-de-dum . . . dum*
> *who've yet to . . . er . . . do something with a girl.*
> *I get no kick from champagne . . .*

"Those aren't the words!" cried Roland. "Look at the dragon! The spell's not working! We've got to run while we've got the chance!"

"We can't leave him to fight alone," said Paithan.

He whipped around. The old man's brows bristled in anger. "I brought you people here for a reason! Don't throw your lives away, or you'll undo all that I have worked for! Find the city!" he shouted, waving his arms. "Find the city!"

---

[1] Stout beer.

He began to run. The dragon's head darted out, caught hold of the old man by the skirt of his robes, sending him crashing onto the ground. Zifnab's hands scrabbled in the dirt in a desperate effort to pull himself free.

"Fly, you fools!" he cried, and the dragon's jaws closed over him.

CHAPTER ◆ 37

SOMEWHERE,

PRYAN

◆

HAPLO EXPLORED THE DESERTED CITY AT HIS LEISURE, TAKING HIS TIME, studying it carefully to make a clear and accurate report back to his lord. Occasionally he wondered what was transpiring with the mensch outside the walls, but dismissed the matter from his mind for lack of interest. What he found—or failed to find—inside the city walls was of far more importance.

Within the walls, the city was different from its sibling located in the Nexus. The differences explained much, but left some questions still unanswered.

Just inside the city gate stood a wide, paved, circular plaza. Haplo traced a blue, glowing series of runes in the air with his hand and stood back to watch. Images, memories of the past held fast within the stone, came to a semblance of life, populating the area with ghosts. The plaza was suddenly crowded with faint reflections of people, shopping, bartering, exchanging the news of the day. Elves, humans, and dwarves jostled between the rows of stalls. Walking among them, Haplo could distinguish the occasional white-robed, saintly figure of a Sartan.

It was market day in the plaza—market *days* would be a more proper term, for Haplo witnessed the passage of time, flowing like a swift stream before his eyes. All was not peaceful and serene within the white walls. Elves and humans clashed, blood was spilled in the bazaar. Dwarves rioted, tearing down the stalls, wrecking the wares. The Sartan were too few and helpless, even with their magic, to find an antidote for the poison of racial hatred and prejudice.

And then there came moving among the people gigantic creatures—taller than most buildings, eyeless, wordless, strong, and powerful. They restored order, guarded the streets. The mensch lived in peace, but it was enforced peace—tenuous, unhappy.

As time passed, the images became less clear to Haplo. He strained his eyes, but couldn't see what was happening and he realized that it wasn't his magic failing him, but the magic of the Sartan that had held the city together. It dwindled—fading and running, like colors in a rain-soaked painting. At length, Haplo could see nothing at all in the square. It was empty, the people gone.

"And so," he said to the dog, waking it; the bored animal having dozed off during the picture show, "the Sartan destroyed our world, divided it up into its four elements. They brought the mensch to this world, traveling through Death's Gate, as they brought the mensch to Arianus. But here, as in Arianus, they ran into problems. In Arianus—the Air World—the floating continents had everything needed for the mensch to survive except water. The Sartan constructed the great Kicksey-winsey, planning to align the islands and pump water up into them from the perpetual storm that rages below.

"But something happened. The Sartan, for some mysterious reason, abandoned their project and abandoned the mensch at the same time. On this world, on Pryan, the Sartan arrived and discovered that the world was practically—from their viewpoint—uninhabitable. Overgrown with jungle life, it had no stone readily available, no metal easily forged, a sun that shone constantly. They built these cities and kindly brought the mensch to live within their protective walls, even providing them artificial, magical time cycles of day and night, to remind them of home."

The dog licked its paws, coated with the soft white dust that filled the city, letting its master ramble, sometimes cocking an ear to indicate it was paying attention.

"But the mensch didn't react with the proper gratitude."

Haplo whistled to the dog. Leaving the ghostly square, he walked the city streets. "Look, signs in elven. Buildings done in the elvish style—minarets, arches, delicate filigree. And here,

human dwellings—solid, massive, substantial. Built to lend a
false feeling of permanence to their brief lives. And somewhere,
probably below us, I would guess we would find the dwelling
places of the dwarves. All meant to live together in perfect
harmony.

"Unfortunately, the members of the trio weren't given the
same musical score. Each sang his own tune in opposition to the rest."

Haplo paused, staring around intently. "This place *is* different from the city in the Nexus. The city the Sartan left us—for
what reason they alone know—is not divided. The signs are in
the language of the Sartan. Obviously they intended to come
back and occupy the city in the Nexus. But why? And why put
another almost identical city on Pryan? Why did the Sartan
leave? Where did they go? What caused the mensch to flee the
cities? And what do the tytans have to do with anything?"

The city's central spire of glittering, reflective glass towered
above him, visible no matter where one walked. Welling out
from it was the brilliant, white light—starlight. Its brilliance increased as the strange, magical twilight slowly began to creep
over the city itself.

"The answers have to be there," Haplo said to the dog.

The animal's ears pricked, it whimpered and gazed backward, toward the gate. The dog and its master could hear the
faint sound of voices—mensch voices—and the roar of a dragon.

"C'mon," said Haplo, his gaze never leaving the spire of
light. The dog hesitated, tail wagging. The Patryn snapped his
fingers. "I said come."

Ears down, head drooping, the dog did as it was commanded.
The two continued on down the empty street, moving deeper
into the heart of the city.

Clutching the old man in its jaws, the dragon dove back
down beneath the moss. The four waited above, paralyzed with
shock and fright. From down below, came a terrible scream—as
of a person being torn apart.

And then silence, horrible, ominous.

Paithan stirred, seemed to wake from a dream. "Run! It'll
be after us, next!"

"Which way?" Roland demanded.

"There! The way the old man showed us!"

"It could be a trick . . ."

"All right," snarled the elf. "Wait here and ask the dragon for directions!" He grabbed hold of his sister.

"Father!" Aleatha cried, hanging back. She crouched near the corpse resting peacefully on the moss.

"Now's the time to think of the living, not the dead," Paithan returned. "Look! Here's a path! The old man was right."

Grabbing Aleatha, practically dragging her, Paithan plunged into the jungle. Roland started to follow when Rega demanded, "What about the dwarf?"

Roland glanced back at Drugar. The dwarf crouched defensively in the center of the glade. His eyes, shadowed by the overhanging brows, gave no hint of what he might be feeling or thinking.

"We bring him," said Roland grimly. "I don't want him sneaking around behind us and I don't have time to kill him! Grab our weapons!"

Roland caught hold of the dwarf's thick arm, jerked him to his feet and propelled him toward the path. Rega gathered up the weapons, cast a final, fearful glance down the hole into which the dragon had disappeared, then ran after the others.

The path, though overhung with vines and plants, was wide and clear and easy to follow. They could still see, as they ran along it, the stumps of giant trees that had been leveled and gashes—now covered over by bark—where huge limbs had been hacked off to form a clear, broad trail. Each thought to himself of the immense force expended to fell such mighty trees, each thought of the powerful tytans. They didn't speak their fear out loud, but all wondered if they might be running from the jaws of one dreadful death into the arms of another.

Their fear lent them unnatural strength. Whenever they grew tired, they felt the ground rumble beneath their feet and stumbled on. But soon the heat and the heavy, stagnant air sapped even adrenaline-pumped will. Aleatha tripped over a vine, fell, and did not get back up. Paithan started to try to lift her. Shaking his head, he sank down onto the ground himself.

Roland stood above the two elves, staring down at them, unable to speak for his heavy breathing. He had dragged the dwarf the entire distance. Weighted down by his thick boots and heavy leather armor, Drugar toppled over onto the ground and lay like a dead thing. Rega tottered up behind her brother. Tossing the weapons to the trail, she slumped onto a tree stump and laid her head across her arms, almost sobbing for breath.

"We have to rest," said Paithan in response to Roland's mute, accusing glare that urged them to keep on running. "If the dragon catches us . . . it catches us." He helped his sister to a sitting position. Aleatha leaned against him, eyes closed.

Roland flung himself down on the moss. "She all right?"

Paithan nodded, too weary to reply. For long moments they sat where they had fallen, sucking in air, trying to calm the pounding of their hearts. They kept glancing fearfully behind them, expecting to see the gigantic scaled head and sharp teeth diving down at them. But the dragon didn't appear and, eventually, they no longer felt the rumbling of the ground.

"I guess what it really wanted was the old man," said Rega softly, the first words any of them had spoken in a long time.

"Yeah, but when it gets hungry, it'll be looking for fresh meat," said Roland. "What did that old fool mean about a city, anyway? If there really is one, and it wasn't another of his crazy jabberings, it would mean shelter."

"This path has to lead somewhere," Paithan pointed out. He licked dry lips. "I'm thirsty! The air smells peculiar, tastes like blood." He looked back at Roland, his gaze going from the human to the dwarf who lay at his feet. "How's Blackbeard?"

Roland reached out a hand, prodded the dwarf's arm. Drugar rolled over, sat up. Hunching back against a tree, he glared at them from beneath the shaggy, shadowing brows.

"He's fine. What do we do with him?"

"Kill me now," said Drugar gruffly. "Go on. It is your right. I would have killed you."

Paithan stared at the dwarf, but the elf wasn't seeing Drugar. He was seeing humans, trapped between the river and the tytans. Elves shooting them down with arrows. His sister, locking herself in her room. His house, burning.

"I'm sick of killing! Hasn't there been death enough without us meting it out? Besides, I know how he feels. We all do. We all saw our people butchered."

"It wasn't our fault!" Rega reached out a tentative hand, touched the dwarf on the thick arm. Drugar glowered at her suspiciously, drew away from her touch. "Can't you understand, it wasn't our fault!"

"Maybe it was," said Paithan, suddenly very, very weary. "The humans let the dwarves fight alone, then turned on each other. We elves turned our arrows on the humans. Maybe, if we had all joined together, we could have defeated the tytans. We didn't, and so we were destroyed. It was our fault. And it's starting to happen all over again."

Roland flushed guiltily, and averted his eyes.

"I used to think love would be enough," continued Paithan softly, "that it was some type of magical elixir we could sprinkle over the world and end all the hatred. I know now, it's not true. Love's water is clear and pure and sweet, but it isn't magic. It won't change anything." He rose to his feet. "We better get going."

Roland came after him. One by one, the others followed, all except Drugar. He had understood the words of the conversation, but the meaning rattled around in the empty shell that had become his soul.

"You are not going to kill me?" he demanded, standing alone in the clearing.

The others paused, glanced at each other.

"No," said Paithan, shaking his head.

Drugar was baffled. How could you talk of loving someone who was not of your race? How could a dwarf love someone who was not a dwarf? He was a dwarf, they were elves and humans. And they had risked their lives to save his. That, first, was inexplicable. Next, they were not going to take his life after he had almost taken theirs. That was incomprehensible.

"Why not?" Drugar was angry, frustrated.

"I think," said Paithan slowly, considering, "we're just too tired."

"What am I going to do?" Drugar demanded.

Aleatha smoothed back her straggling hair, dragging it out of her eyes. "Come with us. You don't want to be . . . left alone."

The dwarf hesitated. He had held onto his hate for so long, his hands would feel empty without it. Perhaps it would be better to find something other than death to fill them. Perhaps that was what Drakar was trying to prove to him.

Drugar clumped along down the path after the others.

◆

Silver, arched spans, graceful and strong, stood ranged round the bottom of the spire. Atop those arches were more arches, extending upward—silver layer upon silver layer—until they came together at a sparkling point. Between the arches, white marble walls and clear crystal windows were alternately placed to provide both support and interior lighting. A silver hexagonal door, marked with the same runes as the gate, allowed entrance. As before, though he knew the rune that was the key, Haplo forged his own way, moving swiftly and silently through the marble walls. The dog crept along behind.

The Patryn entered a vast circular chamber—the base of the spire. The marble floor echoed his booted footsteps, shattering the silence that had lasted for who knew how many generations. The vast room contained nothing but a round table, surrounded by chairs.

In the center of the table hung, suspended—its magic continuing to support it—a small, round, crystal globe, lit from within by four tiny balls of fire.

Haplo drew near. His hand traced a rune, disrupting the magical field. The globe crashed to the table and rolled toward the Patryn. Haplo caught it, lifted it in his hands. The globe was a three dimensional representation of the world, similar to the one he'd seen in the home of Lenthan Quindiniar, similar to the drawing in the Nexus. But now, holding it, having traveled it, Haplo understood.

His lord had been mistaken. The mensch didn't live on the outside of the planet, as they'd lived on the old world.

They lived on the inside.

The globe was smooth on the outside—solid crystal, solid stone. It was hollow within. In the center, gleamed four suns. Within the center of the suns stood Death's Gate.

No other planets, no other stars could be visible because one didn't look up in the heavens at night. One looked up at the ground. Which meant that the other stars couldn't be stars but . . . cities. Cities like this one. Cities meant to house refugees from a shattered world.

Unfortunately their new world was a world that would have been frightening to the mensch. It was a world that was, perhaps, no less frightening to the Sartan. Life-giving light produced too much life. Trees grew to enormous heights, oceans of vegetation covered the surface. The Sartan had never figured on this. They were appalled at what they had created. They lied to the mensch, lied to themselves. Instead of submitting, trying to adapt to the new world they had created, they fought it, tried to force it to submit to them.

Carefully, Haplo replaced the globe, hanging it above the table's center. He removed his magical spell, allowing the globe's ancient support to catch hold of it again. Once more, Pryan hung suspended over the table of its vanished creators.

It was an entertaining spectacle. The Lord of the Nexus would appreciate the irony.

Haplo glanced around, there was nothing else in the chamber. He looked up, over the table. A curved ceiling vaulted high above him, sealing the chamber shut, blotting out any sight of the crystal spire that soared directly above it. While holding the globe, he'd become aware of a strange sound. He put his hands upon the table.

He had been right. The wood thrummed and vibrated. He was reminded, oddly, of the great machine on Arianus—the Kicksey-winsey. But he had seen no signs of such a machine anywhere outside.

"Come to think of it," he said to the dog, "I didn't hear this sound outside either. It must be coming from in here. Maybe someone will tell us where."

Haplo raised his hands over the table, began tracing runes in the air. The dog sighed, laid down. Placing its head between its paws, the animal kept a solemn and unhappy watch.

Vaguely seen images floated to life around the table, dimly heard voices spoke. Of necessity, since he was eavesdropping on not one meeting, but on many, the conversation that Haplo could distinguish was confused, fragmented.

"This constant warring among the races is too much for us to handle. It's sapping our strength, when we should be concentrating our magic on achieving our goal. . . ."

"We've degenerated into parents, forced to waste our time separating quarrelsome children. Our grand vision suffers for lack of attention. . . ."

"And we are not alone. Our brothers and sisters in the other citadels in Pryan face the same difficulties! I wonder, sometimes, if we did the right thing in bringing them here. . . ."

The sadness, the sense of helpless frustration was palpable. Haplo saw it etched in the dimly seen faces, saw it take shape in the gestures of hands seeking desperately to grab hold of events that were slipping through their fingers. The Patryn was put in mind of Alfred, the Sartan he had encountered on Arianus. He'd seen in Alfred the same sense of sadness, of regret, of helplessness. Haplo fed his hatred on the suffering he saw, and enjoyed the warming glow.

The images ebbed and flowed, time passed. The Sartan shrank, aged before his eyes. An odd phenomenon—for demigods.

"The council has devised a solution to our problems. As you said, we have become parents when we were meant to be mentors. We must turn the care of these 'children' over to others. It is essential that the citadels be put into operation! Arianus suffers from lack of water. They need our power to assist in the functioning of their machine. Abarrach exists in eternal darkness— something far worse than eternal light. The World of Stone needs our energy. The citadels must be made operational and soon, or we face tragic consequences!

"Therefore, the council has given us permission to take the tytans from the citadel core where they have been tending the starlight. The tytans will watch over the mensch and protect them from themselves. We endowed these giants with incredible strength, in order that they could assist us in our physical labors. We gave them the rune-magic for the same reason. They will be able to deal with the people."

"Is that wise? I protest! We gave them the magic on the understanding that they would never leave the citadel!"

"Brethren, please calm yourselves. The council has given considerable thought to the matter. The tytans will be under our constant control and supervision. They are blind—a necessity so that they could work in the starlight. And, after all, what could possibly happen to us? . . ."

Time drifted on. The Sartan seated around the table disappeared, replaced by others, young, strong, but fewer in number.

"The citadels are working, their lights fill the heavens—"

"Not heavens, quit lying to yourself."

"It was merely a figure of speech. Don't be so touchy."

"I hate waiting. Why don't we hear from Arianus? Or Abarrach? What do you suppose has happened?"

"Perhaps the same thing that is happening to us. So much to do, too few to do it. A tiny crack opens in the roof and the rain seeps through. We put a bucket beneath it and start to go out to mend the crack but then another opens. We put a bucket beneath that one. Now we have two cracks to mend and we are about to do so when a third opens up. We have now run out of buckets. We find another bucket, but by this time, the leaks have grown larger. The buckets will not hold the water. We run after larger buckets to give us time to contain the water so that we can go up to the roof to fix the leak.

"But by now," the speaker's voice softened, "the roof is on the verge of collapse."

Time swirled and eddied around the Sartan seated at the table, aging them rapidly, as it had aged their parents. Their numbers grew fewer still.

"The tytans! The tytans were the mistake!"

"It worked well in the beginning. How could anyone have foreseen?"

"It's the dragons. We should have done something about them from the start."

"The dragons did not bother us, until the tytans began to escape our control."

"We could use the tytans still, if we were stronger—"

"If there were more of us, you mean. Perhaps. I'm not certain."

"Of course, we could. Their magic is crude; no more than we teach a child—"

"But we made the mistake of endowing the child with the strength of mountains."

"I say that maybe it's the work of our ancient enemies. How do any of us know that the Patryns are still imprisoned in the Labyrinth? We've lost all contact with their jailers."

"We've lost contact with everyone! The citadels work, gathering energy, storing it, ready to transmit it through the Death's Gate. But is there anyone left to receive it? Perhaps we are the last, perhaps the others dwindled as have we . . ."

The flame of hatred burning in Haplo was no longer warm

and comforting, but a devouring fire. The casual mention of the prison into which he'd been born, the prison that had been the death of so many of his people, sent him into a fury that dimmed his sight, his hearing, his wits. It was all he could do to keep from hurling himself at the shadowy figures and throttling them with his bare hands.

The dog sat up, worried, and licked his master's hand. Haplo grew calmer. He had missed much of the conversation, seemingly. Discipline. His lord would be angered. Haplo forced his attention back to the round table.

A single form sat there, shoulders bowed beneath an unseen burden. The Sartan was looking, astonishingly, at Haplo.

"You of our brethren who may one day come into this chamber are undoubtedly lost in amazement at what you have found—or failed to find. You see a city, but no people living within its walls. You see the light"—the figure gestured to the ceiling, to the spire above them—"but its energy is wasted. Or perhaps you will not see the light. Who knows what will happen when we are no longer here to guard the citadels? Who knows but that the light will dim and fade, even as we ourselves have done.

"You have, through your magic, viewed our history. We have recorded it in the books, as well, so that you may study it at your leisure. We have added to it the histories kept by the wise ones among the mensch, written in their own languages. Unfortunately, since the citadel will be sealed, none of them will be able to return to discover their past.

"You now know the terrible mistakes we made. I will add only what has occurred in these last days. We were forced to send the mensch from the citadel. The fighting among the races had escalated to such a point that we feared they would destroy each other. We sent them into the jungle, where they will, we hope, be forced to expend their energy on survival.

"We had planned, those of the few of us who remain, to live in the citadels in peace. We hoped to find some means to regain control over the tytans, find some way to communicate with the other worlds. But that is not to be.

"We, ourselves, are being made to leave the citadels. The force that opposes us is ancient and powerful. It cannot be fought, cannot be placated. Tears do not move it, nor do all the weapons we have at our command. Too late, we have come to admit its existence. We bow before it, and take our leave."

The image faded. Haplo tried, but the rune-magic would summon no one else. The Patryn stood for a long time in the chamber, staring in silence at the crystal globe and its feebly burning suns surrounding the Death's Gate.

Seated at his feet, the dog turned its head this way and that, searching for something it couldn't identify, not quite heard, not quite seen, not quite felt.

But there.

CHAPTER ♦ 38

THE CITADEL

♦

THEY STOOD AT THE EDGE OF THE JUNGLE, ALONG THE PATH ON WHICH the old man had sent them, and stared up at the shining city on the mountain. The beauty, the immensity awed them, it seemed outlandish, other worldly. They could almost believed that they had actually traveled to a star.

A rumbling, a tremor of the moss beneath their feet recalled the dragon. Otherwise, they might never have left the jungle, never walked forward upon the mountainside, never dared approach the white-walled, crystal-spired sun.

Frightened as they were by what lurked behind them, they were almost as frightened of the unknown that stood ahead. Their thoughts ran similar to Haplo's. They imagined guards standing on the towering walls, surveying the craggy, rock-strewn paths. They wasted precious time—considering the dragon might be surging after them—arguing about whether they should advance with weapons drawn or sheathed. Should they approach meekly, as supplicants, or with pride, as equals?

They resolved at last to keep their weapons out and clearly visible. As Rega counseled, it made sense to do so, in case the dragon came upon them from behind. Cautiously, they stepped out of the shadows of the jungle, shadows that suddenly seemed friendly and sheltering, and walked out into the open.

Heads swiveled, keeping nervous watch before and behind. The ground no longer trembled and they argued over whether this was because the dragon had ceased to pursue them or because they stood on solid rock. They continued on up the path, each tensed to hear a hail or answer a challenge or perhaps fend off an attack.

Nothing. Haplo had heard the wind. The five didn't even hear that for it had ceased to blow with the coming of the twilight. At length, they reached the top and stood before the hexagonal gate with its strange, carved inscription. They straggled to a stop. From a distance, the citadel had filled them with awe. Up close, it filled them with despair. Weapons dangled from hands gone listless.

"The gods must live here," said Rega in a hushed voice.

"No," came the dry, laconic answer. "Once, you did."

A portion of the wall began to shimmer blue. Haplo, followed by the dog, stepped out. The dog appeared glad to see them safe. It wagged its tail and it would have dashed over to greet them but for a sharp reprimand from its master.

"How did you get inside there?" Paithan demanded, his hand flexing over the handle of his bladewood sword.

Haplo did not bother to answer the question, and the elf must have realized interrogating the man with the bandaged hands was futile. Paithan did not repeat it.

Aleatha, however, approached Haplo boldly. "What do you mean, once *we* lived behind those walls? That's ridiculous."

"Not you. Your ancestors. All your ancestors." Haplo's gaze took in the elves and the two humans who stood before him, regarding him with dark suspicion. The Patryn's eyes shifted to the dwarf.

Drugar ignored him, ignored them all. His trembling hands touched the stone, the bones of the world, that had been little more than memory among his people.

"*All* your ancestors," Haplo repeated.

"Then we can go back in," said Aleatha. "We would be safe in there. Nothing could harm us!"

"Except what you take in with you," said Haplo, with his quiet smile. He glanced at the weapons each held, then at the elves standing apart from the humans, the dwarf keeping apart from the rest. Rega paled and bit her lip, Roland's face darkened in anger. Paithan said nothing. Drugar leaned his head against the stone, tears coursed down his cheeks and vanished into his beard.

Whistling to the dog, Haplo turned, and began to walk back down the mountainside toward the jungle.

"Wait! You can't leave us!" Aleatha called after him. "*You* could take us inside the walls! With your magic or . . . or in your ship!"

"If you don't"—Roland began swinging the raztar, its lethal blades flashed in the twilight—"we'll—"

"You'll what?" Haplo turned to face them, traced a sigil before him, between himself and the threatening human.

Faster than the eye could see, the rune sizzled through the air and smote Roland on his chest, exploding, propelling him backward. He landed hard on the ground, his raztar flew from his hand. Aleatha knelt beside him, cradled the man's bruised and bleeding body in her arms.

"How typical!" Haplo spoke softly, not raising his voice. " 'Save me!' you cry. 'Save me or else!' Being a savior's a thankless job with you mensch. Not worth the pay, because you never want to do any of the work. Those fools"—he jerked his head in the direction of the crystal spire—"risked everything to save you from us, then tried to save you from yourselves—with results that are plainly obvious. But just wait, mensch. One day, one will come who will save you. You may not thank him for it, but you will achieve salvation." Haplo paused, smiled. "Or else."

The Patryn started off, turned again. "By the way, what happened to the old man?"

None of them answered, all avoided his eyes.

Nodding, satisfied, Haplo continued down the mountain, the dog trotting along at his heels.

The Patryn traveled safely through the jungle. Arriving at the *Dragon Star*, Haplo found the elves and humans roaming the jungle, embroiled in a bitter battle. Each side called on him to come its aid. He paid no attention to any of them and climbed aboard his empty ship. By the time the combatants realized they were being abandoned, it was too late. Haplo listened in grim amusement to the terrified, pleading wails spoken together in two different languages, reaching his ears as one voice.

The ship lifted slowly into the air. Standing at the window, he stared down at the frantic figures.

" 'He it is, who, coming after me, is preferred before me,' " Haplo tossed them the quote, watching them dwindle away to nothing as his ship carried him into the heavens. The dog crouched at his feet and howled, upset by the pitying cries.

Below, the elves and humans watched in bitter, helpless impotence. They could see the ship shining in the sky a long time after its departure; the sigla emblazoned on its hull blazing fiery red in the false darkness created by the Sartan to remind their children of home.

CHAPTER ◆ 39

THE CITADEL

◆

THE DRAGON CAME UP ON THE FIVE, CATCHING THEM MASSED IN FRONT of the gate of the citadel, trying vainly to get inside. The marble walls were slick and smooth, without a handhold or foothold in sight. They banged upon the gate with their fists and, in desperation, hurled themselves against it. The gate didn't so much as quiver.

One of the five suggested battering rams, another magic, but the talk was half-hearted and desultory. Each knew that if elven or human magic had been effective, the citadel would have been occupied.

And then the strange and terrible darkness once again began to flow from the city walls, creeping over the mountain and the jungle like slowly rising flood waters. Yet though it was dark below, it was light above, the crystal spire casting its radiant white call out into a world that had forgotten how to answer. The bright light caused every object to be either seen or unseen—illuminated brilliantly by its glow or lost in impenetrable shadow.

The darkness was terrifying, more so because they could still see the sun shining in the sky. Because of the darkness, they heard the dragon coming before they saw it. The rock shook beneath their feet, the city walls trembled under the dwarf's hand. They started to flee to the jungle, but the sight of the darkness submerging the trees was appalling. For all they knew, the dragon would come from that very direction. They clung to the city walls, unwilling to leave its shelter, though they knew it couldn't protect them.

The dragon appeared, out of the darkness, breath hissing. The starlike light glittered off the scaled head, reflected red in the gleaming eyes. The dragon's mouth parted, the teeth were stained with blood that was black in the white light. A bit of mouse-colored cloth fluttered horribly, impaled upon a sharp, glistening fang.

The five stood together; Roland protectively in front of Aleatha, Paithan and Rega beside each other, hand in hand. They held desperately onto their weapons, though they knew they were useless.

Drugar's back was to the danger. The dwarf paid no attention to the dragon. He was gazing, fascinated, at the hexagonal gate, its runes thrown into sharp relief by the starlike light.

"I recognize each one," he said, reaching out his hand, running the fingers lovingly over the strange substance that gleamed brightly, reflecting the light, reflecting the image of approaching death.

"I know each sigil," he repeated, and he named them, as a child who knows the alphabet but does not yet know how to read will name the individual letters it sees upon the sign hanging from the inn.

The others heard the dwarf muttering to himself in his own language.

"Drugar!" Roland called urgently, keeping his gaze fixed on the dragon, not daring to turn around and look behind him. "We need you!"

The dwarf did not answer. He stared, mesmerized, at the gate. In the very center of the hexagon, the surface was blank. Runes surrounded it in a circle on all sides, the strokes of the tops and bottoms of the sigla merging together, breaking apart, leaving broad gaps in an otherwise continuous flow. Drugar saw, in his mind, Haplo drawing the runes. The dwarf's hand slipped into the tunic of his blouse, chilled fingers wrapped around the obsidian medallion he wore on his chest. He drew it forth, held it up before the gate so that it was level with the blank spot, and slowly began to rotate it.

"Leave him alone," said Paithan, as Roland began to curse the dwarf. "What can he do anyway?"

"True enough, I guess," Roland muttered. Sweat mingled with the blood caked on his face. He felt Aleatha's cool fingers on his arm. Her body pressed closer to his, her hair brushed against his skin. His curses hadn't really been aimed at the dwarf at all, but hurled bitterly against fate. "Why doesn't the damn thing attack and get it over with!"

The dragon loomed in front of them, its wingless, footless body coiling upward, its head almost level with the top of the smooth city walls. It seemed to be enjoying the sight of their torment, savoring their fear, a sweet aroma, tempting to the palate.

"Why has it taken death to bring us together?" whispered Rega, holding fast to Paithan's hand.

"Because, like our 'savior' said, we never learn."

Rega glanced behind her, wistfully, at the gleaming white walls, the sealed gate. "I think we might have, this time. I think it might have been different."

The dragon's head lowered; the four facing it could see themselves reflected in the eyes. Its foul breath, smelling of blood, was warm against their chilling bodies. They braced for the attack. Roland felt a soft kiss on his shoulder, the wetness of a tear touch his skin. He glanced back over his shoulder at Aleatha, saw her smile. Roland closed his eyes, praying for that smile to be his last sight.

Drugar did not turn around. He held the medallion superimposed over the blank spot on the gate. Dimly, he began to understand. As had happened when he was a child, the letters C . . . A . . . T were no longer letters to be recited individually by rote but were transformed before his eyes into a small, furbearing animal.

Elated, transfixed by excitement, he broke the leather thong that held the medallion around his neck and lunged at the gate.

"I have it! Follow me!"

The others hardly dared hope, but they turned and ran after him.

Jumping as high as he could, barely able to reach the bottom of the large round blank in the center, Drugar slammed the medallion against the surface of the gate.

The single sigil, the crude and simple rune that had been hung around the dwarf child's neck, a charm to protect him from harm, came into contact with the tops of the runes carved upon the bottom of the gate. The medallion was small, barely larger than the dwarf's hand, the sigil carved upon it smaller still.

The dragon struck at last. Roaring, it dove upon its victims.

The sigil beneath the dwarf's hand began to glow blue, light welled up between stubby fingers. The light brightened, flared. The single rune increased in size, becoming as large as the dwarf, then as broad as a human, taller than the elf.

The sigil's fire spread across the gate, and wherever the light of the rune touched another rune, that rune burst into flame. The flames expanded, the gate blazed with magical fire. Drugar gave a mighty shout and ran straight at it, shoving with his hands.

The gates to the citadel shivered, and opened.

CHAPTER ◆ 40

SOMEWHERE,

PRYAN

◆

"I THOUGHT THEY'D NEVER FIGURE IT OUT!" STATED THE DRAGON IN exasperation. "I took my time getting up there, then they made me wait and wait. There's only so much slavering and howling one can do, you know, before it loses its effectiveness."

"Complain, complain. That's all you've done," snapped Zifnab. "You haven't said a word about my performance. 'Fly, you fools!' I thought I played that rather well."

"Gandalf said it better'?"

"Gandalf!" Zifnab cried in high dudgeon. "What do you mean, he said it 'better'?"

"He gave the phrase more depth of meaning, more emotive power."

"Well, of course he had emotive power! He had a Balrog hanging onto his skivvies! I'd emote, too!"

"A Balrog!" The dragon flicked its huge tail. "And I suppose *I'm* nothing! Chopped liver!"

"Chopped lizard, if I had my way!"

"What did you say?" the dragon demanded, glowering. "Remember, wizard, that you're only my familiar. You *can* be replaced."

"Chicken gizzard! I was discussing food. I'm extremely hungry," said Zifnab hastily. "By the way, what happened to all the rest of 'em?"

"The rest of who? Chickens?"

"Humans! Elves, you ninny."

"Don't blame me. You should be more precise with your pronouns." The dragon began to carefully inspect its glittering body. "I chased the merry little band up into the citadel where they were welcomed with open arms by their fellows. It wasn't an easy task, mind you. Blundering through the jungle. Look at this, I broke a scale."

"No one ever said it would be easy," said Zifnab, with a sigh.

"You're right there," agreed the dragon. His fiery-eyed gaze lifted, went to the citadel, shining on the horizon. "It won't be for them, either."

"Do you think there's a chance?" The old man looked anxious.

"There has to be," answered the dragon.

EPILOGUE

My lord,

My ship is currently in flight above . . . below . . . through
. . . (I hardly know how to describe it) the world of Pryan. The
flight back to the four suns is long and tedious, and I have decided
to take the time to record my thoughts and impressions of the so-
called stars while they are still fresh in my mind.

From my research gleaned in the Hall of the Sartan, I am able
to reconstruct the history of Pryan. What the Sartan may have
had in mind when they created this world (one wonders if they
had *anything* on their minds!) is unknown. It is obvious to me
that they arrived on this world expecting something other than
what they found. They did their best to compensate, by building
magnificent cities, shutting the mensch and themselves up inside, shutting the rest of the world out, and lying to themselves
about the true nature of Pryan.

All went well for a time, apparently. I would guess that the
mensch—reeling from the shock of the disintegration of their
world and the move to this one—had neither the inclination nor
the energy to cause trouble. This state of peace passed rapidly,
however. Generations of mensch came along who knew nothing
about the terrible suffering of their parents. The citadels, no
matter how big, would inevitably be too small to contain their
greed and ambition. They fell to squabbling and feuding among
themselves.

The Sartan, during this period, were interested solely in their
own wondrous projects and did their best to ignore the mensch.
Intensely curious about this project, I traveled into the heart of
the crystal spire from which beamed the "star" light. I found
there a huge machine, somewhat similar in design to the Kicksey-

winsey that I discovered on the world of Arianus. This machine was much smaller and its function, as far as I was able to determine, is extremely different.

To describe it, I first put forth a theory. Having visited two of the four worlds built by the Sartan, I have discovered that each was imperfect. I also discovered that the Sartan were apparently trying to make up for the imperfections. Arianus's floating continents need water. Abarrach's Stone World (which I plan to visit next) needs light. The Sartan planned to supply these deficiencies by using energy drawn from Pryan—which has it in abundance.

The four suns of Pryan are surrounded by stone that completely encases their energy. This energy is beamed down constantly onto the world surrounding the suns. The plants absorb the energy and transfer it down deep into the bedrock that supports them. I would estimate that the heat built up at this lower level must be incredible.

The Sartan constructed the citadels to absorb this heat. They dug deep shafts down through the vegetation into the rock. These shafts act as vents, drawing the heat off and expelling it back into the atmosphere. The energy is collected in a place known as the sanctuary, located in the center of the complex. A machine, running off the energy, transfers the power to the central spire, which in turn beams it out to the sky. The Sartan did not do this by themselves, but used their magic to create a race of powerful giants, who could work in the citadel. They called them tytans and gave them crude rune-magic, to help them in their physical labors.

I admit that I have no proof, but I submit to you, My Lord, that the other "stars" visible on Pryan are light-and-energy-gathering machines such as this one. It was the intention of the Sartan, as clearly explained in the writings left behind in the citadel, to use these machines to transmit the abundance of light and energy to the other three worlds. I read their descriptions of precisely how this feat was to be accomplished, but must confess to you, My Lord, that I can make little sense of what they propose. I brought the plans with me and I will turn them over to you so that you may study them at your leisure.

The transference of energy was, I am certain, the primary purpose of the "stars" of Pryan. However, I believe, although I was not able to test my theory, that the "stars" could be used to communicate with each other. The Sartan mentioned being in contact with their brethren on this world and, not only that, but were apparently awaiting to hear from other Sartan located on other worlds. The ability to establish interworld communication could be of inestimable value to us in our drive to reestablish ourselves as the rightful rulers of our universe.

One can see why the Sartan were eager to complete their work, but the growing turmoil among the mensch in the citadels made it difficult, if not impossible. The Sartan were constantly being called from their tasks to quell the battles. They were frustrated, desperate—for all they knew, their brethren in other worlds were dying for lack of the energy they alone could provide. The Sartan set the tytans to look after "the children."

As long as the Sartan were around to control the tytans, the giants were undoubtedly highly useful and beneficial. They were extremely effective at policing the mensch. They took over all the hard physical labor and the mundane, day-to-day chores of running a city. Free at last, the Sartan were able to concentrate all their efforts on building the "stars."

Up to this point, my account of the history of Pryan has been clear and concise. Now, it will of necessity become somewhat vague, in that I was completely unable to discover the answer to the mystery of Pryan, a mystery that is shared by the world of Arianus: What happened to the Sartan?

It was obvious to me, in my research, that the Sartan were becoming increasingly few in number and that those few were having an increasingly difficult time dealing with the rapidly deteriorating situation among the mensch. The Sartan came to realize their mistake in creating the tytans and in giving them rudimentary rune-magic. As Sartan control over the giants decreased, the tytans' ability to use the rune-magic increased.

Like the legendary golems of old, did the tytans turn on their creators?

Having fought their magic myself, I can report that it is crude but exceedingly powerful. I am not yet certain why, not having finished analyzing the attacks. The nearest analogy I can furnish at the moment is to say that they hit the complex, delicate structure of our runes with one single, simple, uncomplicated sigil that has the force of a mountain behind it.

Now the citadels stand empty, but their light still shines. The mensch lie hidden in the jungle and fight among themselves. The tytans wander the world in a hopeless, deadly quest.

Where do the dragons enter in, if at all? And what is the "force" the Sartan spoke of in his last statement to me? "The force that opposes us is ancient and powerful." The force that "cannot be fought, cannot be placated." And finally, what happened to the Sartan? Where did they go?

It is possible, of course, that they didn't go anywhere, that they are still living on the other "stars" of Pryan. But I don't believe that is the case, My Lord. Just as their grand project on Arianus failed, so their grand project on Pryan came to nothing. The "stars" shine for a decade or so, then their power supply becomes depleted and their light grows dimmer and dimmer and fades out altogether. Some, perhaps, never recover. Others, after a period of years, slowly gather more energy, and gradually the "star" is reborn, sparkling in a "heaven" that is in reality nothing but ground. Might this not, My Lord, be an analogy for the Sartan?

Of course, there exist two other worlds left for us to explore. And we know that one Sartan—at least—still lives. Alfred, too, seeks his people. I begin to wonder if our quest may be similar to that of the tytans. Perhaps we are searching for an answer that doesn't exist to a question that no one remembers.

I have just now reread what I have written. Forgive these ramblings, My Lord. The time hangs heavily on my hands. But, speaking of the tytans, I venture to add one important observation before I close.

If a way can be discovered to control these creatures—and I am certain, My Lord, that you with your vast power and skill could easily do just that—then you will have an army that is powerful, effective, and completely amoral. In other words, invincible. No force, not even one that is "ancient and powerful" could oppose you.

I see only one danger to our plans, My Lord. The possibility of this danger is so minuscule that I hesitate to mention it. I am mindful, however, of your desire to be completely informed on the situation in Pryan, and so I present the following for consideration:

If the mensch could ever find their way back inside the citadels, they might—by working together—be able to learn to operate the "stars." If you will remember, My Lord, the Gegs on Arianus were quite adept at running the Kicksey-winsey. The human child named Bane was intelligent enough to figure out the machine's true purpose.

The Sartan, in their infinite wisdom, have left lying about innumerable books written in human, dwarven, and elven. The books I saw dealt mainly with the history of the races, going clear back to the ancient world before the Sundering. There were, however, too many to peruse closely and so it may be, among the tomes, that the Sartan left information relevant to the "stars," to their true purpose, and to the fact that other worlds besides Pryan exist. It is not beyond the realm of possibility that the mensch might even find information regarding Death's Gate.

However, from what I observed, the likelihood of the mensch discovering such information and using it appears extremely remote. The gates of the citadel are closed and, unless the mensch come up with some sort of "savior" I predict that these gates will remain sealed shut to them forever.

I remain, My Lord, respectfully devoted to your service.

—Haplo [1]

PATRYN RUNES

and the

VARIABILITY OF MAGIC

◊

A Basic Overview for Patryn Aspirants

Transcription Note: *The Sartan have always found the Patryn approach to rune magic far too dry and clinical for their liking. The Patryn, on the other hand, have always sniffed at the Sartan's rather mystical and philosophical approach to what they see as a mixture of art and power. This passage on magic was certainly scribed by a Patryn. It may yet be considered abrasive to many who read it. For example, the use of the term* object, *or* objects, *in this text is not limited to inanimate things but is applied to people as easily as to a chair. The Patryns, who consider it their destiny to order all creation under their rule, make no distinction between the two.*

To manipulate an object you must understand it. This basic principle is at the heart of all Patryn rune magic. It is the key to our destiny of order.

We who see and understand an object for what it truly is—in all its aspects—have control over it. That quality and power that we use as magic is actually the manipulation of the power of existence. We are but minds that observe the full truth of the world around us. Magic is the recognition of the fire burning behind us when all else see only their own shadow on the wall. Rune magic defines in symbols the true quality of all things that might exist.

PATRYN RUNE MAGIC:
THEORY AND PRACTICE

Patryns altering any part of the world about them, first attempt to "name" an object fully. An object's *true name* is far more than a convenient description. In Patryn magic, an object's name defines precisely the state of the object relative to the underlying Wave of Possibility. Naming an object completely is critical to the level of success that the Patryn will have in later "renaming" the object into an alternate state or form.

Runes provide a set of symbols by which we can name (understand) and rename (change) any object. The student of Patryn magic is a student of the rune, for it is only through the runes that an object can be most fully named.

Theory and Concept

Runes give formal structure to our magic. Our runes generally form magic in the following ways:

1. Naming of the object. Any rune of power first identifies the object being changed to its true extent—in other words, names the original object fully.

2. Calling on the Sympathetic Name. In this, we build (1) the power runes required to alter the state of the present object and (2) state-of-being runes that define the position on the Wave of Probability where such a state would be expressed. These two combined—power and position—form the Sympathetic Name.

3. The object is renamed. By applying the Sympathetic Name to the object, the object's state changes and the object is renamed. This new name becomes the object's name for as long as the magic dictates. Powerful Sympathetic Names can be permanent, while those that are not so powerful may last only a moment.

The Laws of Rethis

While the principles of rune magic had been known many epochs before the Sundering of Worlds, abnormalities and inconsistencies still existed in the shaping of magic. One of the great thrusts in magical research was the defining of these abnormalities.

However, in our Year of Exile 1391, Sage Rethis of the Vortex[1] structured several basic laws of rune magic, which endeavored to encompass the anomalies that had been experienced since time began. Although his works were initially greeted with such skepticism as to result in his eventual death at the decree of the Lords in Exile, they were later accepted by that supreme body and are now the standard foundation of our understanding of magic.

THE BALANCE IN ALL NATURE. Rethis began with the understanding that all things must have balance to exist. The full name of an object has balance for it defines the state of harmonious existence in the Wave of Possibility. While this principle was well known among rune magicians, Rethis placed it as the foundation of his reasoning—and thus the First Law of Rethis:

An Object's Name Has Balance

EQUILIBRIUM FACTOR. One of the greatest puzzles in magic was its tendency to occasionally go awry. The precise intent of the wizard's rune structure would work to specifications on any number of similar objects only to suddenly, and for no obvious reason, behave differently on an object that was for all intents and purposes identical to those previously renamed.

This effect, noted Rethis, is similar to those seen constantly in apprentices who are first learning to master the runes and often structure runes that are not balanced. Such unbalanced runes still functioned but often with bizarre results.

---

[1]The Fifth Realm—often called Limbo or simply the Nexus by those who are unfamiliar with its structure—is divided into three concentric regions. The outermost region is called the Nexus and is the place where the Deathgates of all realms converge. Four of the Deathgates lead to the Elemental Realms while the fifth gate leads into the Labyrinth. Beyond the Labyrinth lies the Vortex. It was in this place that the Sartan originally imprisoned the Patryns. After three millennia, the Patryns managed to escape the Vortex through the Labyrinth and gain control over the Nexus and all of its Deathgates.

Rethis reasoned that such poor structures still functioned because the magic itself sought its own balance when the rune did not supply it. This became the Second Law of Rethis:

An Unbalanced Name
Will Tend to Balance Itself

RUNIC IMBALANCE. Having established his first two rules, Rethis addressed directly the problem of the master wizards who still, on rare occasion, found their spells going awry.

Since the apprentices' spells obviously had odd results due to imbalance and since the master wizards' spells showed similar failures (although far less often), Rethis reasoned that they must somehow be related. He asked himself, What could account for imbalance in a master wizard's spells?

GRAIN OF MAGIC AND VARIABILITY. As Rethis worked on these problems, he came across an obscure monograph submitted to the Lyceum where he studied. It had been written by Sendric Klausten, a Nexus runner of great reputation in the Labyrinth but little known in the Vortex itself. It had apparently been penned on a rare return through the First Gate based on the runner's experience in the Labyrinth.

Nexus runners were attempting to break through the Labyrinth to the legendary Nexus on the far side. In those early days, the effort was still in its infancy and many centuries would pass before the runners would prove successful.

There was no greater testing ground for runes than the Labyrinth because it required greater complexity and finesse than did common use in the Vortex. Klausten, in his adventures in the Labyrinth, discovered that there was an actual limit to the detail to which a rune could be constructed.

Balance in the magic and ultimate definition of the probability being woven are crucial to the user of rune magic. Unless the weave of magic is infinitely precise, the effect will be different in detail from that originally envisioned by the magician. All rune theory seeks to define the balance of the rune as a Sympathetic Name to the object that exists.

Rune structures may, as you know, contain other rune structures. This seemingly endless progression of smaller and smaller levels of detail attempts to redefine the balanced and ordered state of objects into another state. Each level of detail more intimately defines the object until—in theory—the object is fully defined and, therefore, stable.

Klausten discovered, however, that as the rune grew more and more detailed, the *presence of the rune itself affected the state of the object*. A rune could be crafted into such detail that its own detail in turn affected the object the magician intended to affect. Thus the object's name would be subtly changed. The rune—balanced for the object before the change—would then be unbalanced. Further balancing of the rune would then continue to change the object, again forcing the rune to be unbalanced. Thus, Klausten explained, there was a limit to how detailed a rune could be created toward its effect. Klausten called this the Barrier of Uncertainty.

The Barrier of Uncertainty is a level of definition beyond which the runes cannot penetrate. This limit to a rune's detail is apparently related to the ancient Empirical Constant ($6.547E^{27}$ or h)—although why this is so remains a mystery.

Beyond the Barrier of Uncertainty, rune structures fail to have their anticipated effects. No further rebalancing seems evident in magics that attempt such artful subtlety.

This bottom level of detail in rune structures (which has been proven to hold true in both Sartan and Patryn magic) is referred to as the *Grain of Runes*. It is the most detailed structure that can be constructed from runes without the presence of the runes themselves changing the magic being attempted.

THIRD LAW OF RETHIS. Rethis found in Klausten's writings the key to why even the most detailed magic occasionally fails. Rethis theorized that if the object being renamed was balanced beyond the Barrier of Uncertainty, then no rune could produce a Sympathetic Name with sufficient detail to rename the object with balance. His own Second Law would then take effect with occasionally random results for even the most advanced wizard.

So it was that Rethis penned this third—and most controversial—law:

No Rune Has Infinite Balance

When a rune structure approximates a new state, the Wave of Probability produces a phenomenon called Stasis Reflex. This, basically, is nature's way of correcting for the small imbalances in all magic rune structures that may evidence themselves through the Barrier of Uncertainty.

The Third Law of Rethis has also been occasionally rephrased as "no rune is perfect." The Barrier of Uncertainty seems to condemn rune structures to a most elemental imperfection when dealing with magic at its most delicate base.

While this may prove to be rather disturbing from a philosophical standpoint, in everyday use it is of little value. Because the Second Law of Rethis tells us that even an unbalanced object will tend to seek its own balance, rune magic continues to operate as the great force in our destiny.

It was, however, the philosophical ramifications that caught up with Rethis. The Lords in Exile successfully prosecuted him for anarchistic heresy and his life was forfeit. Today, songs are sung in his praise, although he never had the opportunity to hear them.

Dimensional Magic and Future Development

All our current rune structures are based around patterns in two dimensions. New research by the Master Cryptographers of the Vortex would suggest that stable rune structures might be assembled along three-dimensional lines as well. Such runes might be crudely thought of as boxes, spheres, multihedrons, and a variety of linking conduits for power transference and effect definition.

While such structures might introduce a revolution in rune structures and power, such structures have not yet been developed that retain stability as well as our traditional structures. Dimensional structures also appear to be subject to the same Barrier of Uncertainty as standard runes. Perhaps, in time, such runes will be a part of our society and our purpose.

A WORD ABOUT SARTAN RUNE MAGIC

From time to time, you may find yourself intrigued by the mystic and backward approach of the Sartan runes. These runes—after one cuts away all of the pseudoreligious and simple-minded claptrap—function in ways similar to our own runic structures.

There is, however, a most fundamental—and dangerous—difference between the Sartan approach to magic and our own: Our inductive reasoning as opposed to the deduction of the Sartan.

In Patryn rune magic we seek out the essence of the individual object and from it induce and effect the more general principles of the universe that surrounds us. Thus we alter the balance in an individual object and then allow that rebalancing to impact the general principles that originally supported the object.

The Sartan, on the other hand, attempt to alter the general principles of existence to achieve specific results. This dangerous thinking might be likened to altering the universal laws of genetics to obtain a better lunch for yourself on a particular day.

Our magic works from the specific case out toward the more general (induction) while Sartan magic works from the general principles of existence inward toward a specific solution (deduction). Both approaches are powerful. The War of Admigon—the last great war before the Captivity of Beybon and the Sundering of Time—was fought between the Sartan and ourselves with bitter results. The Labyrinth that surrounds us and imprisoned our people at the time of the Sundering is the prime example of both the power of the Sartan and their irresponsible and reckless use of it. All creation now seeks a state that will again bring balance and harmony to all.

The time for the New Balance—our order—has come.

For my mother, Daisy Deaver

The Lay of Thillia

Words by Kevin Stein   Music by Janet Pack

With haunting intensity

ALTO RECORDERS

VOICE

DRUM

1. From thought and love all things— once born, earth,

and sky,— and know— ing sea. From

6 dark—ness old, all light— is— shorne, and

8 rise— a—bove,— for— ev— er free.

10 2. In rev— erent voice, five bro—thers spoke

52 em– brac– ing de– mesne,– all rul– ing fair.

54 Just– ice and strength, wis– dom full lent,

56 each mouth to voice a grate– ful aire.

58 8. Yet fates cruel games their pure hearts waste,

60 and each to arms this tryst– a– bove.

62 Five men con—sumed for wo—man chaste,

64 and all lives touch'd for stri—dent love.

66 9. As gen—tle as a poem's—heart,

68 was— the beau—te—ous wo—man born.

70 As sub—tle as all na—ture's art,

82 · 11. Five ar—mies clashed,　　their　plows　to　swords,

84　far—mers from fields,—　　pas—　sion's com—mands.

86　Bro—thers once　fair　　and　lov—　ing wards,

88　sent salt　to　sea—　　and　wound—ed th'　lands.

90 12. Thil—le—　a　stood　　on　blood—ied　plain,

102 They cried a—bove,— their hearts— held whole,

104 and vowed to rise— 'neath war— rior's night.—

106 14. In faith they walked with— mo—dest stride,

108 to sleep—ing Thil—le—a be— neath. The

110 crash— ing waves their vir— tue cried,

the king– doms wept their wa– t'ry– wreath. From

thought and love all things— once– born, earth,

air,– and sky,– and know– ing sea. From

dark– ness old, all light– is– shorne, and

rise– a– bove,– for– ev– er free.

Scoring: Voice (or tin whistle) and guitar

Bonnie Earl

Words by Kevin Stein

Music by Janet Pack

1. When young I start-ed seek-ing for love and things in
dream-ing I set out with clouds a' stre-am-ing and a hat up-on my
head. I be-gan with grave in-ten-tion, hop-ing for di-vine in-ven-tion,
No-thing could pre-pare- me for the things I learned in-stead. At—
first I looked for bat-tle seek-ing mail and sword to rat-tle but they herd-ed us like
cat-tle and we ne-ver did see-a fight I-stood in fields for
hours,- a-mong the pikes and flow-ers; I de-ci-ded it was time to go and—

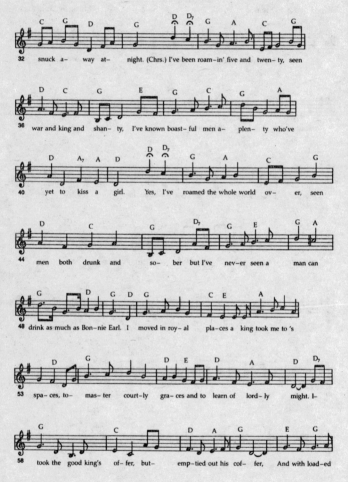

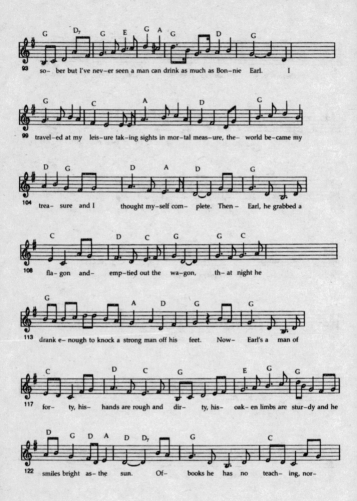

126 wise men and their preach–ing, but a hap–py man he'll al–ways be and–

130 drink–ing– is his– fun. (Chrs.) I've been roam– in' five and twen– ty, seen–

134 war and king and shan– ty, I've known boast–ful men a– plen– ty who–'ve

138 yet to kiss a girl. Yes, I've roamed the whole world ov– er, seen

142 men both drunk and so– ber but I've nev– er seen a man can

146 drink as much as Bon–nie Earl. In all the times I'd wan– der, for

150 ru– mors I'd grow fond– er of the man who did– n't squan– der his good

Words copyright 1990 by Weis and Hickman

Music copyright 1990 by Janet Pack

ABOUT THE AUTHORS

MARGARET WEIS and TRACY HICKMAN are the *New York Times* bestselling authors of the *Dragonlance®* series, *The Darksword Trilogy,* and the *Rose of the Prophet* trilogy. With over ten million copies of their novels in print around the world, they are among the bestselling fantasy writers of all time.

THE DARKSWORD TRILOGY

■

Three volumes of the exciting adventures of Joram, the one man born without magic in a land where everyone has magic. Prophecy said he would change their world forever.

Forging the Darksword, Volume I

Joram is helped—and sometimes hindered—by Simkin, an unusual man with uncommon talents even in this land.

"No, really, 'pon my honor," Simkin protested, hurt, "I truly do call it *Night of the Peacock*. But I assure you, I wouldn't dream of telling her how to copy it . . ."

Blachloch picked up his pen and returned to his work as his man drew nearer.

In a flash of color, Simkin changed back to his exotic clothes. Rising to his feet gracefully, he glanced around. "Don't touch me, lout," he said, sniffing and wiping his nose. Then, placing the silk in the sleeve of his coat, he looked down at the warlock. "By the way, Cruel and Pitiless One, would you like me to offer my services to this catalyst as guide through the wilderness? Something incredibly nasty's liable to snatch him otherwise. Waste of a good catalyst, wouldn't you say?"

Apparently absorbed in his work, Blachloch said without looking up, "So there really is a catalyst."

"In a few weeks, he'll be standing before you."

"Weeks?" The henchman snorted. "A catalyst? Let me and the boys go after him. We'll have him back here in minutes. He'll open the Corridors to us and—"

"And the *Thon-Li*, the Corridor Masters, will slam shut the gate." Simkin sneered. "Neatly trapped you'd be then. I can't think why you keep these imbeciles around, Blachloch, unless, like rats, they're cheap to feed. Personally, I prefer vermin . . ."

The henchman made a lunge at Simkin, whose coat suddenly bristled with thorns.

Blachloch moved his hand; both men froze in place. The warlock had not even looked up but continued to write in the ledger.

"A catalyst," Simkin murmured through stiff lips. "What . . . power . . . give us! Combine . . . iron and magic. . . ."

Raising his head, ceasing to write, though he kept

his pen poised, the warlock looked at Simkin. With a word, he removed the spell.

"How did you discover this? You weren't seen?"

"Of course not!" Lifting his pointed chin, Simkin stared down at Blachloch in injured dignity. "Am I not a master of disguise, as you well know? I sat in his very hovel, upon his very table—a very teapot! Not only did he *not* suspect me, he even washed and dried me and set me on his shelf quite nicely. I—"

Blachloch silenced Simkin with a glance. "Meet him in the wilderness. Use whatever tomfoolery you need to get him here." The cold blue eyes froze the young man as effectively as the magical spell. "But get him here. Alive. I want this catalyst more than I've wanted anything in my entire life. Bring him and there will be rich reward. Return without him and I will drown you in the river. Do you understand me. Simkin?"

The warlock's eyes did not waver.

Simkin smiled. "I understand you, Blachloch," he said softly. "Don't I always?"

With a sweeping bow, he started to take his leave, his mauve cape trailing the floor behind.

"Oh, and Simkin," Blachloch said, returning to his work.

Simpkin turned. "My liege?" he asked.

Blachloch ignored the sarcasm. "Have something unpleasant happen to the catalyst. Nothing serious, mind you. Just convince him that it would be unwise for him to ever think of leaving us. . . ."

"Ah . . . " remarked Simkin reflectively. "Now this *will* be a pleasure. Farewell, lout," he said, patting the guard on the cheek with his hand. "Igh . . .

Making a face, he wiped his hand on the orange cloth and swept majestically out the door.

"Say the word . . . " muttered the guard, glaring through the doorway after the young man, who was sauntering through camp like a walking rainbow.

Blachloch did not even deign to reply. He was, once more, working in the ledger.

"Why do you put up with that fool?" snarled the guard.

"The same might be asked of you," Blachloch answered in his expressionless voice. "And I might make the same reply. Because he is a useful fool and because someday I *will* drown him."

Doom of the Darksword, Volume II

Joram has many enemies, but his one true friend throughout the series is the catalyst Saryon. Only Saryon is capable of the ultimate sacrifice.

Joram stood alone upon the sand.

With a loud cry, muffled by his hood, the Executioner called for Life. Head bowed, each catalyst concentrated all his energy upon the warlock, drawing magic from the world. Opening their conduits, they sent Life flowing into the wizard's body. So powerful were the focused energies of all the catalysts that the magic was visible—blue flame swirled about the bodies and clasped hands of the priests. Flaring like blue lightning, it leaped from them into the body of the Executioner.

Suffused with power, the man pointed both hands at Joram. When he spoke next, the spell would be cast, the Turning would begin.

The Executioner drew a breath. The gray hood quivered. He uttered the first syllable of the first word and, at that moment, Saryon hurled himself forward, the catalyst's body interposing itself between the Executioner and Joram. The blue light, darting from the warlock's hand, struck Saryon. Gasping in pain, he tried to take a step, but he could not move.

His feet and ankles were white, solid stone.

"My son!" Saryon cried, his gaze never shifting from Joram, "the sword!" With his last strength, even as the terrible, cold numbness was spreading up into his knees, Saryon flung the weapon from him.

The Darksword fell at Joram's feet. Anger and grief propelled him to action. Reaching down, he drew the sword from its scabbard in one swift stroke and turned to meet his enemies.

Garald's teaching came to him. Joram swung the sword in front of him, meaning at first only to keep the *Duuk-tsarith* at bay until he could fall back and assess his position. But he had not counted upon the sword's own power.

The Darksword came forth into air that was charged with magic as Life flowed fron the catalysts into the Executioner. Thirsting for that Life, the Darksword began to suck the magic into itself. The arc of blue light jumped, flaming, from the Executioner to the sword. The catalysts cried out in fear, many trying to close the conduits. But it was too late. The Darksword gained in power every second and it kept the conduits open forcibly, draining the Life from everything and everyone around it.

Running forward to stop Joram, spells crackling at their fingertips, the warlocks saw a radiant blue light flare from within deep darkness. A ball of pure energy hit them with the force of an exploding star and the black-robed bodies disintegrated in a blinding flash.

The Darksword hummed triumphantly in Joram's hands. Blue light twined from its blade around the young man's body like a fiery vine. Dazed by the shattering explosion and the sudden disappearance of his enemies, Joram stared at the sword in disbelief and uncertainty. Then the knowledge of the tremendous power he held swept over the young man. With this, he could conquer the world! With this, he was invincible!

Shouting in exultation, Joram whirled around to face the Executioner—

—and saw Saryon.

The spell had been cast. The power of the Darksword could neither alter it, change it, nor stop it.

Saryon's feet, limbs, and lower body were white stone, solid, unmoving. The bitter-cold numbness was rising; Joram could see it freeze the catalyst's flesh as he watched, advancing upward from the groin to the waist.

"No!" Joram cried in a hollow voice, lowering the sword.

Springing forward, Joram grasped Saryon's arms. With a wrenching effort, the catalyst raised his hands in supplication.

"Run!" Saryon managed to utter the single word before his diaphragm froze, choking off his voice. "Run" pleaded the man's eyes through a shadow of pain.

Rage filled Joram. Floundering through the sand, he came to stand before the Executioner. The Darksword burned blue, continuing to suck Life from the world, and the Executioner had fallen to one knee. The casting of the spell had cost him much of his energy and the Darksword was draining even more. But he managed to lift his hooded head, staring at Joram with cool detachment.

"Reverse the spell!" Joram demanded, raising the sword, "or by the Almin I swear I will strike your head from your body!"

"Do what you like!" the warlock said weakly. "The spell, once cast, cannot be called back. Not even the power of that weapon of darkness can change that!"

Triumph of the Darksword, Volume III

In the third volume, the prophecies seem to have come true. War has come to the kingdom of Merilon and Joram has somehow gone from destroyer to savior.

EMPEROR OF MERILON

Night attempted to lull Merilon to sleep, but its soothing hand was thrust away by those preparing for war. Joram took command of the city, naming Prince Garald his military leader. He and the Prince immediately began to mobilize the population.

Joram met with his people in the Grove. Gathering around the ancient tomb of the wizard who had brought them to this world, many of the citizens of Merilon wondered if that almost forgotten spirit stirred restlessly in his centuries-old sleep. Was his dream about to end and yet another enchanted kingdom fall to ruin?

"This is a fight to the death," Joram told the people grimly. "The enemy intends to wipe out our entire race, to destroy us utterly. We have seen proof of this in the wanton attack upon innocent civilians on the Field of Glory. They have shown no mercy. We will show none." He paused. The silence that flowed through the crowd grew deeper, until they might have been drowned in it. Looking at them from where he stood on the platform above the tomb, Joram said slowly, emphasizing each word, "Every one of them must die."

Though the outside world was dark and slumbering, the city of Merilon burned with light. It might have been day beneath the dome—a terrible, fear-laced day whose sun was the fiery glow of the forge. The *Pron-alban* had hastily conjured up a workplace for the blacksmith. He and his sons and apprentices like Mosiah worked to repair weapons damaged in the previous battle or create new ones. Though many in Merilon looked with horror upon the Sorcerers, practicing their Dark Art of Technology, the citizens swallowed their fears and did what they could to assist.

The *Theldara* tended the injured, buried the dead, and hastily began working on enlarging both the Houses of Healing and the Burial Catacombs. The druids knew that, by the rising of the moon tomorrow night, they would need many more beds . . . and graves.

Joram watched over everything. Everywhere he went, people greeted him with cheers. He was their savior.

Taking the romantic half-truths Garald had woven around the true story of Joram's lineage, the people further embroidered it and decorated it until it was practically unrecognizable. Joram tried to protest, but the Prince silenced him.

"The people need a hero right now—a handsome king to lead them into battle with his bright and shining sword! Even Bishop Vanya doesn't dare denounce you. What would *you* give them?" Garald asked scornfully. "A Dead man with a weapon of the Dark Arts who is going to bring about the end of the world? Win this battle. Drive the enemy from the land. Prove the Prophecy wrong! *Then* go before the people and tell them the truth, if you must."

Joram agreed reluctantly. Surely Garald knew what was right. *I can afford honor,* the Prince had once told him. *You cannot.*

DARKSWORD ADVENTURES

———————————— ■ ————————————

Many role-playing gamers know the value of a good sourcebook, but **Darksword Adventures** *offers something for the just plain enthusiast as well. In these pages is nearly everything a reader could want to know about the world of the Darksword.*

Welcome to the magical realm of Thimhallan.

We know many of you already. You are "gamers" who have visited other worlds of sword and sorcery with us before, and we're pleased that you have decided to join us again.

There are, however, many of you interested in Thimhallan who have never participated in role-playing games. Perhaps you thought they were too difficult or complicated to learn. Perhaps you were intimidated by massive, expensive volumes of rules filled with incomprehensible numbers and strange abbreviations.

We want you to join us in the fun and excitement we experience visiting Thimhallan in our imaginations. Therefore we are pleased to present a complete role-playing game and source book in an affordable, entertaining format. Everything you need to play is included in this one volume—game rules, statistics, character and monster descriptions, suggested scenarios—presented in the form of interesting and revealing reports on Thimhallan compiled by the *Duuk-tsarith* to be given to Major James Boris. We have devised a very simple system for role-playing that you can learn easily.

There may be those of you who are not interested in role-playing but would simply like to have more information about the world and its people. You will find all that in this volume, without being distracted by a lot of rules. Included are a History of the World, a description of Thimhallan written by a young man who survived many wild adventures in the various parts of the realm, descriptions of the wondrous creatures that inhabit Thimhallan, information on the major and minor characters, and more.

Whether you journey by yourself or in the company of friends, we hope you enjoy your visit to the magical realm of Thimhallan. May your trip be an adventurous one!

Tracy Raye Hickman
Margaret Weis

THE ROSE OF THE PROPHET

---◼---

The outrageously funny trilogy (with dark secrets) about the twenty gods who ruled the universe—until one of them upset the balance of power. Now everyone is scrambling for control, not the least of which are the humans and their djinn.

The Will of the Wanderer, Volume I

The god Quar had hoped to upset the balance completely before any of the others had realized they'd been stripped of their powers, but someone always notices . . .

The scent of roses hung heavily in the air. A nightingale trilled unseen in the fragrant shadows. Cool water fell from the marble hands of a delicate maiden, spilling into a large conch shell at her feet. The multicolored tiles, laid out in fantastic mosaics, sparkled like jewels in the twilight. But Quar took pleasure in none of this beauty. The God sat upon the tiled rim of a fountain's basin, absently tearing apart a gardenia, moodily tossing the waxy, white petals into the rippling water.

The luck of Sul, that's what it was. The luck of Sul, which was no luck at all. The luck of Sul had taken those damned and blasted priests of Promenthas's into the way of a few dozen of Quar's faithful. At least he assumed they had been his faithful. The God had not realized his followers had grown quite that fanatical. Now Promenthas was angry and not only angry, suspicious as well. Quar was not prepared for this. He had intended to deal with Promenthas, of course, but further—much further—down the long and twisting road of his scheming.

And there was Akhran to consider. He would act swiftly to take advantage of the incident. The Wandering God was undoubtedly persuading Promenthas to some sort of action. Not that Promenthas could do much. His followers had all died on the swords of the righteous. Hadn't they? Quar made a mental note to check. But now that Promenthas was alerted, he would be watchful, wary. Quar would have to move faster than he'd anticipated.

Akhran the Meddler. He was the scorpion in Quar's bed sheets, the *qarakurt* in Quar's boot. Just days ago Quar had received a report that two tribes of Akhran's followers had banded together in the Pagrah desert. Relatively few in number compared to Quar's mighty armies, these nomads were more of a nuisance than a direct threat. But Quar had no time for nuisances right now.

The one factor on which Quar had counted in his design to overthrow Akhran was the constant feuding and strife among the Wandering God's followers. The old axiom: divide and conquer. Who would have imagined that this Wandering God, who seemingly cared for nothing except his horse, would have been observant enough to detect Quar's plotting and move swiftly to forestall it?

"It was my fault. I concentrated on the other Gods of Sardish Jardan. I saw them as the threat. Now Mimrim of the Ravenchai, feeling herself weakening, hides on her cloud-covered mountain. Uevin of the Bas takes refuge behind his politics and siege machines, never realizing that his foundation is being undermined and soon he will fall through the cracks. But you, Horse God. I underestimated you. In looking west and south, I turned my back upon the east. It will not happen again."

The vase, once broken, cannot be mended with tears, Quar reminded himself severely. You have realized your mistake, now you must act to remedy it. There is only one way Akhran could have united his feuding tribes—through the intervention of his immortals. There were reports of Akhran's 'efreets whipping up fearsome desert storms. Apparently the unleashing of the mighty power of the djinn was enough to frighten those thick-headed nomads—

Quar paused, absently crushing the last blossoms of the ravaged gardenia in his hand.

The djinn. Why, that was his answer.

The Paladin of the Night, Volume II

Once the gods bring their war to earth, it's only a matter of time before prisoners are taken. Among these is a young prince with no future, but even he has choices.

We do not beat the whipped dog. . . . Are you going to lie down on your master's grave and die?

Crouched in his dark cell, Achmed repeated the Amir's words to himself. It was true. Everything the Amir said was true!

"How long have I been in prison? Two weeks? Two months?" Despairing, Achmed shook his head. "Is it morning or night?" He had no idea. "Have I been fed today, or was that yesterday's meal I rememberber eating? I no longer hear the screams. I no longer smell the stench!"

Achmed clutched at his head, cowering in fear. He recalled hearing of a punishment that deprived a man of his five senses. First the hands were cut off, to take away the sense of touch. Then the eyes were gouged out, the tongue ripped from the mouth, the nose cut off, the ears torn from the head. This place was his executioner! The death he was dying was more ghastly than any torture. Misery screamed at him, but he had lost the ears to hear it. He had long ago ceased being bothered by the prison smell, and now he knew it was because the foul stench was his own. In horror, he realized he was growing to relish the guards' beatings. The pain made him feel alive. . . .

Panic-stricken, Achmed leaped to his feet and hurled himself at the wooden door, beating it with his fists and pleading to be let out. The only response was a shouted curse from another cell, the debtor having been rudely awakened from a nap. No guards came. They were used to such disturbances. Sliding down the doorway, Achmed slumped to the floor. In his half-crazed state, he fell into a stupor.

He saw himself lying on a shallow, unmarked grave, hastily dug in the sand. A terrible wind came up, blowing the sand away, threatening to expose the body. A wave of revulsion and fear swept over Achmed. He couldn't bear to see the corpse, decaying, rotting. Desperately, he shoveled the sand back over the body, scooping it up in handfuls and tossing it onto the grave. But every time he lifted a handful, the wind caught it and blew it back into his face, stinging his eyes, choking him. He kept working frantically, but the wind was relentless. Slowly, the face of the corpse emerged—a man's face, the withered flesh covered by a woman's silken veil. . . .

The scraping sound of the wooden bar being lifted from the door jolted Achmed out of his dream. The shuffling footsteps of prisoners being herded outside and the distant cries of women and children told the young man that it was visiting time.

Slowly Achmed rose to his feet, his decision made.

The Prophet of Akhran, Volume III

When the final battle comes, it is up to the most unlikely of people to set things in motion—a woman, who prefers to dress in men's clothing . . . and a man who must wear a woman's.

The following dawn the sun's first rays skimmed across the desert, crept through the holes in Majiid's tent, bringing silence with them. The arguing ceased. Zohra and Mathew glanced at each other. Her eyes were shadowed and red-rimmed from lack of sleep and the concentration she had devoted to her work. Mathew knew his must look the same or perhaps worse.

The silence of the morning was suddenly broken by the sound of feet crunching over sand. They heard the guards outside scramble to their feet, the sound of footsteps draw nearer. Both Mathew and Zohra were ready, each had been ready for over an hour now, ever since first light. Zohra was clad in the women's clothes Mathew had brought her. They were not the fine silk she was accustomed to wearing, only a simple *chador* of white cotton that had been worn by the second wife in a poor man's household. Its simplicity became her, enhancing the newfound gravity of bearing. A plain white mantle covered her head and face, shoulders and hands. Held tightly in her hands, hidden by the folds of her veil, were several pieces of carefully rolled-up goatskin.

Mathew was dressed in the black robes he had acquired in Castle Zhakrin. Since he was able to come and go freely, he had left the tent in the middle of the night and searched the camp in the moonlit darkness until he found the camels they had ridden. Their baggage had been removed from the beasts, thrown down, and left to lie in the sand as though cursed. Mathew could have wished the robes—retrieved by Auda from their campsite on the shores of the Kurdin Sea—cleaner and less worse for wear, but he hoped that even stained and wrinkled they must still look impressive to these people who had never seen sorcerer's garb before.

Stealing back to the tent once he had changed his

clothes, Mathew noted the figure of the Black Paladin sitting unmoving before Khardan's tent. The slender white hand, shining in the moonlight as if it had some kind of light of its own, beckoned to him. Mathew hesitated, casting a worried glance at the watchful guards. Auda beckoned again, more insistently, and Mathew reluctantly approached him.

"Do not worry, Blossom," the man said easily, "they will not prevent us from speaking. After all, I am a guest and you are insane."

"What do you want?" Mathew whispered, squirming beneath the scrutiny of the flat, dispassionate eyes.

Auda's hand caught hold of the hem of Mathew's black robes, rubbing the velvet between his fingers. "You are planning something."

"Yes," said Mathew uncomfortably, with another glance at the guards.

"That is good, Blossom," said Auda softly, slowly twisting the black cloth. "You are an ingenious and resourceful young man. Your life was obviously spared for a purpose. I will be watching and waiting. You may count upon me."

He released the cloth from his grasp, smiled, and settled back comfortably. Mathew left, returning to Zohra's tent, uncertain whether to feel relieved or more worried.

THE DEATH GATE CYCLE

Known for their innovation, Margaret Weis and Tracy Hickman reach an entirely new level with The Death Gate Cycle. *For this seven-book extravaganza they have developed four completely realized worlds. In the first four novels, a new adventure with both continuing and new characters will be set on each of the four worlds. In later volumes, the realms begin to interact, with the supreme battle for control of all the worlds in the final novel.*

Dragon Wing, Volume 1

Generations ago, magicians sundered the world into four distinct realms. Now, few even know of the other worlds. Haplo has been sent through the treacherous Death Gate to explore the realms and stir up dissension. The first visit is to Arianus, a world where islands float in the sky and men travel by enchanted dragonships.

Elven Star, Volume 2

Haplo's second journey takes him to the jungle world of Pryan. Here the three races of men, elves, and dwarves seem to have already completed Haplo's task of causing unrest—not even the threat of annihilation can bring these peoples together.

Fire Sea, Volume 3

The story takes a truly dark turn, as the enemies Haplo and Alfred are forced to travel together for their first visit to the world of Abarrach. Here, these powerful magicians discover that the barren Realm of Stone is also the land of the dead.

Serpent Mage, Volume 4

In the world of Chelestra, realm of water, Haplo the Patryn discovers the seas counteract all magic—and leave him nearly powerless against a new threat.

The Hand of Chaos, Volume 5

The Lord of the Nexus has ordered Haplo and the human child known as Bane to the world of

Arianus, realm of air. Now Haplo must decide whether to obey his master or betray the powerful Patryn.

Into the Labyrinth, Volume 6

Xar, Lord of the Nexus, has learned of the existence of a Seventh Gate, which grants the power to create worlds—or destroy them. Only Haplo knows its location, and so he must seek sanctuary in the Labyrinth, a prison maze whose inhabitants are condemned to death.

The Seventh Gate, Volume 7

The titanic Death Gate saga concludes as Haplo must enter the deadly Seventh Gate, with the fate of the sundered realms in the balance. This scene sets the situation.

Vasu stood on the wall above the gates of the city of Abri, stood silent and thoughtful as the gates boomed shut beneath his feet. It was dawn, which meant, in the Labyrinth, nothing more than a graying of night's black. But this dawn was different than most. It was more glorious than most . . . and more terrifying. It was brightened by hope, darkened by fear.

It was a dawn which saw the city of Abri, in the very center of the Labyrinth, still standing, victorious, after a terrible battle with its most implacable enemies.

It was a dawn smudged with the smoke of funeral pyres; a dawn in which the living could draw a tremulous breath and dare to hope life might be better.

It was a dawn lit by a lurid red glow on the far distant horizon, a red glow that was brightening, strengthening. Those Patryns who guarded the city walls turned their eyes to that strange and unnatural glow, shook their heads, spoke of it in low and ominous tones.

"It bodes nothing good," they said grimly.

Who could blame them for their dark outlook? Not Vasu. Certainly not Vasu, who knew what was transpiring. He would have to tell them soon, destroy the joy of this dawning.

"That glow is the fire of battle," he would have to say to his people. "A battle raging for control of the Final Gate. The dragon-snakes who attacked us were not defeated, as you thought. Yes, we killed four of them. But for every four that die, eight are born. Now they are attacking the Final Gate, seeking to shut it, seeking to trap us all in this dread prison.

"Our brothers, those who live in the Nexus and those near the Final Gate, are fighting this evil—so we have reason to believe. But they are few in number and the evil is vast and powerful.

"We are too far away to come to their aid. Too far. By the time we reached them—if we ever did reach them, alive—it would be too late. It may already be too late.

"And when the Final Gate is shut, the evil in the Labyrinth will grow strong. Our fear and our hatred will grow stronger to match and the evil will feed off that fear and that hatred and grow stronger still."

It is hopeless, Vasu told himself, and so he must tell the people. Logic, reason said to him it was hopeless. Yet why, standing on the wall, staring at that red glow in the sky, did he feel hopeful?

It made no sense. He sighed and shook his head.

A hand touched his arm.

"Look, Headman. They have made it safely to the river."

One of the Patryns, standing beside Vasu, had obviously mistaken his sigh, thought it indicated fear for the two who had left the city in the dark hour before the dawn. They were embarking on a dangerous and probably futile search for the green and golden dragon who had fought for them in the skies above Abri. The green and golden dragon was the Serpent Mage, who was also the bumbling Sartan with the mensch name, Alfred.

Certainly Vasu was afraid for them, but he was also hopeful for them. That same illogical, irrational hope.

Vasu was not a man of action. He was a man of thought, of imagination. He had only to look at his soft and pudgy Sartan body, tattooed with Patryn runes, to know that. He must give thought to what his people should do next. He should make plans, he should decide how they must prepare for the inevitable. He should tell them the truth, give his speech of despair.

But he didn't do any of that. He stood on the walls, watching the mensch known as Hugh the Hand and the Patryn woman Marit.

He told himself he would never see them again. They were venturing out into the Labyrinth, dangerous at any time but doubly dangerous now that their defeated enemies skulked about in anger and waited for revenge. The two were going on a foolhardy and hopeless mission. He would never see them again, nor Alfred, the Serpent Mage, the green and golden dragon, for whom they searched.

Vasu stood on the wall and waited—hopefully—for their return.

STAR OF THE GUARDIANS

■

Volume One
The Lost King
By Margaret Weis

Even before Margaret Weis teamed up with Tracy Hickman, she had several writing projects in the works. Now, more than ten years in the making, **Star of the Guardians** *is finally published. It's the page-turning tale of the man known as the Warlord and his search for the lost heir to the galactic throne.*

"Ah, Dr. Giesk. I was beginning to think you might fail me."

The deep baritone voice was emotionless, almost pleasant and conversational. But Dr. Giesk shuddered. *Failure* was a word the Warlord never spoke twice to any man. The doctor could not remove his hands from the controls of his delicate equipment, but he managed to give the Warlord a beseeching look.

"The subject proved unusually resistant," Giesk quavered. "Three days, my lord! I realize he was a Guardian, but none of the others held out that long. I can't understand—"

"Of course you can't understand." The Warlord stared down impassively at the man on the table. He laid a guantleted hand upon the quivering chest of the man with as little regard as he would have laid that same hand upon the man's coffin. Yet, when the Warlord spoke, his voice was soft, tinged with a sadness and, it seemed, regret.

"Who is there left now who understands, Stavros?"

The gloved fingers touched a jewel the man wore around his neck. Hanging from a silver chain, the jewel was extraordinarily beautiful. Carved into the shape of an eight-pointed star, the gleaming jewel was the only object worn by the naked man, and it had been left around his neck by the Warlord's expressed command.

"Who knows of the training, the discipline, Stavros? Who remembers? And you. One of my best."

The man on the table moaned. His head moved feverishly from side to side. The Warlord watched a moment in silence, then bent close to speak softly into the man's ear.

"I saved your life once, Stavros. Do you remember? It was at the Royal Academy. On a dare, you had climbed that ridiculous thirty-foot statue of the king. You were what—nine? I was thirteen and she . . ." the Warlord paused, "she would have been six. Yes, it was soon after she came to the Academy. Only six. All eyes and hair, wild and lonely as a catamount." His voice softened further, almost to a whisper. The man on the table began to shiver uncontrollably.

"Fascinating," murmured Giesk with professional interest, monitoring his instruments. "I haven't been able to elicit a response that strong in three days."

The Warlord moved his hand up to the man's head, the gauntleted fingers stroking back the graying hair almost caressingly. "Stavros," commanded the Warlord, his helmeted visage bending over the man. "Stavros, can you hear me?"

The man made a slight moaning sound. A froth of blood appeared on his ashen lips.

"Be quick, my lord!" cried Dr. Giesk, "or you will lose him!"

The Warlord brought his face so near to that of his victim that his breath touched the man's skin, displacing the bubbles of blood and saliva on the gaping mouth.

"Where is the boy?"

The man shivered, fighting with himself. But it was useless. The Warlord regarded him intently. The gauntleted hand moved to rest upon the cold white forehead.

"Stavros?"

In a wild, tortured shriek, the man screamed out words that made no sense to Giesk. He glanced at the Warlord uncertainly.

The Warlord slowly rose and straightened. "Well done, Dr. Giesk. You may now terminate."